# THE
# RESISTANCE

Also by
# PETER STEINER

*Le Crime*

*L'Assassin*

*The Terrorist*

# THE
# RESISTANCE

### A Thriller

# PETER STEINER

**MINOTAUR BOOKS**
A THOMAS DUNNE BOOK
NEW YORK

This is a work of fiction. All of the characters, organizations, and events portrayed in this novel are either products of the author's imagination or are used fictitiously.

A THOMAS DUNNE BOOK FOR MINOTAUR BOOKS.
An imprint of St. Martin's Publishing Group.

www.thomasdunnebooks.com
www.minotaurbooks.com

Design by Steven Seighman

ISBN 978-1-250-00371-3 (hardcover)
ISBN 978-1-250-01130-5 (e-book)

First Edition: August 2012

10  9  8  7  6  5  4  3  2  1

*For Jane*

# THE
# RESISTANCE

# I.

"THE SECRETARY OF STATE would like to see you."

"Thank you," said Louis Morgon.

He rose, turned, and gazed at President Nixon's photo hanging behind his desk, not out of any sense of devotion to the president, but to check his own reflection in the glass. He gave the knot of his tie a little upward tug.

"I'll be right back," he said.

"Good luck," his secretary said, thinking he had spoken to her.

Louis had recently been commended for several initiatives, and he guessed, not unreasonably, that he was about to be promoted. Instead he was led before the grim-faced secretary of state and presented with a list of charges against him, ranging from incompetence to something just short of treason.

Two uniformed guards escorted him back to his office. They watched while he gathered his belongings—personal papers, photos of Sarah and the children—and put them in a box. They walked him to the building's entrance and waited while he got into a cab.

"He always seemed like a nice guy," said one of the guards.

"It just goes to show you," said the other.

The cab swung out of the circular drive and into traffic.

———

An hour later Louis sat at his dining table with his head in his hands. "How can this be happening?"

"How could it *not* happen?" said Sarah angrily. "You're in espionage; you work with spies. Treachery is your business."

Louis did not answer.

"Say something," she said.

"Like what?" said Louis.

"It's like you've gone into hiding," she said.

Sarah was right. He *had* gone into hiding. "I don't know who you are anymore," she said. "You're a stranger. To me and to your own children." She was right about that too. He was even a stranger to himself.

Sarah took the children—Jennifer and Michael—and moved out.

Louis spent long, empty hours staring into the garden. The flowers nodded prettily in the hot breeze. But Louis saw only wreckage and desolation.

"What should I do?" he said one morning over coffee.

"You look terrible," someone answered. Louis could no longer remember who she was.

"Thank you," he said.

"You should go somewhere. Somewhere . . . far away."

"Where?" said Louis.

"France," she said. "Why don't you go to France?"

"France?" said Louis.


Louis tried teaching. He tried writing. Nothing worked. Then one day he stuffed a backpack with a few necessities and flew to Paris. He stared through the plane's small round window into the empty night sky. He was thirty-five and as lost as he had ever been. "I understood things better when I was four."

The woman seated next to him pretended not to hear.

The best part of Louis's work had always been the going away. He loved being far from home. He had always found solace—he did not know why—in being a stranger. This aspect of his personality had helped him become an effective diplomat and a superb spy. It had served him well in dangerous negotiations in North Africa and in the Middle East. Talking to an adversary was not that different from talking to a friend; it turned out that most adversaries were no less trustworthy than most friends.

In the Paris airport Louis retrieved his backpack. He tightened the laces in his boots. He swung the pack onto his back and cinched up the straps. He marched through the terminal and out into the gray morning. A small service road took him out of the airport. The soft rain cooled his skin as he walked, and the noise and bustle of the airport fell away behind him. Each step carried him further into a quiet, unfamiliar place where he felt somehow that he belonged.

Louis followed small country lanes and farm roads, stopping now and then to check where he was against the map. He gazed at the landscape, across the green fields, into the mist. He turned slowly in a circle to take everything in. He did not want to miss anything. "This is where I am right now," he said. "Nowhere else." He walked along muddy field roads, through woods and villages.

That first day of walking Louis stopped for lunch in the small village of Beaumarchais. He sat on a bench as the church bell rang noon. He gazed at the monument with its long list of those who had died in the two world wars. There were more from the First than the Second World War. But given the size of Beaumarchais, the numbers were staggering.

Louis ate a baguette, which he cut into hunks and stuffed with Gruyère cheese. The cheese was soft and oily from being in his pack. He went to the grocery across the square. "*Cerises*," he said. The grocer weighed some cherries and put them in a paper bag. Louis went back to the bench by the monument. He closed his eyes as he ate each cherry. Someone might easily have supposed he had never eaten cherries before.

Louis walked west toward the Atlantic coast for several days and then turned southwest along the Loir River (the one without an *e*), which would lead him eventually to the other larger and better known Loire River. He slept in hotels when they were convenient. But he slept just as happily in barns and churches and even haystacks.

Some nights, when the weather was fair, he simply lay back under the black sky and stared upward until he was lulled to sleep by the sight of infinity. One night he slept in a cemetery, beneath a large monument. He discovered the next morning that the cemetery was for German soldiers.

It hardly mattered to Louis if it rained, was cold, was hot, if he got blisters, was bitten by insects, if he lost his way and had to retrace his steps until he found it again. For the first time in his life, inconvenience did not matter, nor did delay. He felt neither urgency nor languor. Every step he took seemed to take him further out of himself and, at the same time, bring him closer to himself. He could not understand or explain it. He sometimes had the feeling he was walking through his own mind.

Louis stopped in ancient churches, in part because they were ancient. He stood on the worn stairs and felt the depressions worn into the stone over hundreds of years by rivers of feet. He rubbed his fingers over worn walls, touched the worn edge of the font where countless hands had dipped into holy water. The traces of passing generations, of centuries of suffering and redemption, comforted him. He regularly paused before monuments honoring the dead of the two world wars. He read the names and felt both their presence and their absence. He stood in for their loved ones.

He existed in a thousand heres and a thousand nows. Walking through thick fog one morning, he was overcome with the sense that at any moment he was going to meet himself coming toward him. Instead an old man emerged from the fog. The man was bent over. He wore a hat that resembled a helmet, and he had a gun on his shoulder. *The ghost of a soldier,* thought Louis. As he passed, the man greeted Louis with a salute and disappeared back into the fog.

Louis was taking inventory without knowing he was doing so. His own past seemed to recede into some other plane of being, where it could be organized. In the State Department and the CIA, intrigue and disingenuousness had been his undoing. Now all machination receded from his consciousness. A new reality slowly took its place. His sordid past—there really was no better word for it than *sordid*—seemed to belong to someone else, someone more foolish, but smarter too and more cynical than he. And now there was something darker, something intractable and ancient that rose up around him, that came upon him like that ghostly man, like the fog itself.

One chilly afternoon Louis ducked under the small roof over a wooden entry gate to wait out a passing downpour. Down the hill in front of him he could see the Loir River. The gate behind him passed through a high stone wall to a modest and slightly ramshackle Renaissance château. Phillipe de Bourchon, the house's owner, returned just then from walking his dogs. After a brief exchange of pleasantries, he invited Louis inside.

"There's a nice fire," said Phillipe. "Some brandy." Phillipe lived alone except for a maid who had been with the family her entire life. Phillipe's wife was dead, his children grown.

Louis and Phillipe sat with their feet stretched toward the fire. Louis revealed himself to be an interesting and engaging conversation partner, and so Phillipe invited him to stay for dinner. "A cassoulet; Janine's version; nothing fancy."

During the meal the two men talked briefly about current world politics, then abandoned that for the more agreeable subject of the joys of walking. Phillipe was interested in Louis's long walk. How did one see an entire country on foot? Didn't a country lose its continuity, its national identity, when visited in such small segments?

Louis did not think so. At least not so far. There were regional differences, of course, but there was also still France, something he could clearly identify as France.

"Is it a good place?" Phillipe wondered.

Louis did not think *good* could apply to an entire country. "It is an agreeable place."

Phillipe wondered whether walking was better with dogs or without dogs. Louis thought that it was probably better with dogs, since that way the walk became a kind of silent, yet purposeful, conversation. Phillipe countered it might be better without dogs—just for the sake of the argument—since seeing to the dogs was a distraction from the walk itself.

As Janine cleared the dishes—she was old and slow, and it took her many trips to the kitchen to do so—the tone of the conversation shifted. Louis had made an allusion to the misery he left behind as he walked, and Phillipe was struck by his words.

"Misery? But you are too young to know real misery. Besides, you are American. You have never been hungry. You have never had your country attacked or occupied. And you certainly were never tested by the moral ambiguities we French have encountered."

"Moral ambiguities?" said Louis. It was a question that was not a question.

Phillipe smiled, pleased to have gotten a reaction. "Yes, moral ambiguities." Phillipe raised his glass as though he were toasting the concept. "In June of 1940, for instance—were you alive then? Well, maybe just barely—when the Germans arrived in France, it was not at all obvious that their occupation was the worst fate that could befall us. Not obvious at all. Remember, at that time the communists were trying to establish a Soviet state in France, and they saw the war as the moment to do it. France became a battleground between fascism and communism, the two great evils of our time. We French seemed to be faced with a choice between cooperating with the Germans or becoming another Soviet satellite.

"To me and to many others it is not a choice at all. Communism was by far the greater danger. History has proved that to be true. Many Frenchmen cooperated with the occupying power. . . ."

"You mean they collaborated with the Third Reich," said Louis.

Again Phillipe smiled. He opened a box of cigars and held it toward Louis like a reward for having spoken up again. "No thank you," said Louis.

"Of course, all right, yes, 'collaborated with the Third Reich,'" said Phillipe. "And by collaborating we avoided the destruction of France, preserved her liberty and independence, and prevented a Soviet takeover."

"And the Jews?" said Louis.

Phillipe held his glass in front of his face and peered at Louis over the edge. "Ah, yes. The Jews. They always come up in these discussions, don't they? You bring them up, just as you bring up the Third Reich and collaboration, as though their part in all this clarifies things, as though the fact of their persecution—which, by the way, I do not deny—renders all moral ambiguity irrelevant.

"Are you Jewish by any chance?" Phillipe smiled but did not wait for Louis to respond. "It doesn't matter. Whether you are or aren't doesn't change anything. The occupying Germans, the *victorious* Germans, were determined that there should be no Jews left in Europe. The French government in Vichy had little choice but to cooperate in their deportation from France."

"But Vichy didn't just cooperate, did they?" said Louis. "They weren't reluctant partners. They jumped in with both feet. The Vichy government was zealous. They eagerly anticipated the Nazis' wishes. They were arduous in their pursuit of Jews and in their deportation to death camps. The French, on their own initiative, rounded up tens of thousands of Jews, including French citizens, war heroes, women, children, and sent them to their deaths."

Louis had not meant to be so vehement. "I am sorry to offend your hospitality," he said. "But did you really think at the time that your collaboration in the persecution of the Jews would preserve France's independence?"

"But you are mistaken, monsieur," said Phillipe, raising his eyebrows. He smiled at Louis again. He took time to light his cigar. "No, no, no. You misunderstand me completely. It is true, I do not like Jews.

And I liked them even less back then. But I opposed, and still oppose, their persecution. And I came to my position on collaboration—some of my friends have grown afraid of that word—only after the war was over. After weighing all the facts in my mind. After doing extensive research. After following the criminal proceedings against Vichy officials. My goodness. No, no, monsieur, you are quite wrong. I was a member of the resistance."

Louis's face did not betray his surprise, but Phillipe smiled anyway. He had a charming and handsome smile. "That was not as you might imagine it either. Nothing heroic. No, no. On the contrary. I was a young man at university in Bordeaux. I was bored with my studies and bored with my life. That is the only way I can explain it.

"One day I was eating in a well-known restaurant in the old city, and a group of German officers came in. They sat down and ordered steak, which arrived after a while. I like steak and had not eaten one for a long time. I studied the menu, but I did not see steak listed. When the waiter came to my table, I asked for a steak. He told me there was no steak available. I gestured in the direction of the German officers. 'There is no steak available,' he said again.

"Imagine. German soldiers could get steak, but a French citizen could not. I can still taste that steak I could not get, better than any steak I have ever eaten. Soon after that I joined a local group of resisters. We blew up a few train tracks and telegraph lines, that sort of thing. It seemed to me at the time that I had no choice. But of course I did have a choice, and I believe now I made the wrong one."

It had gotten late. Count Phillipe de Bourchon invited Louis to spend the night, and Louis accepted his invitation. The following morning Phillipe served Louis a generous breakfast of bread, butter, jam, cheese, and coffee. Then, with his dogs trotting before them, he accompanied Louis on his way.

The moral ambiguities they had spoken of over dinner were of course known to Louis. Phillipe was mistaken if he believed an ocean could protect you from moral ambiguity. Moral ambiguity was the lifeblood of human commerce.

In fact Louis's career had been built on moral ambiguity. His work in the State Department and then in the CIA had been to find the American advantage in various situations in the Middle East. Where was the morality in that? Louis had helped write American policy and then sought to implement it. This depended in large part on the manipulation of others—people and countries—frequently to their own detriment and even harm. Louis befriended people, in Algeria for example, and then recruited them to his purposes without telling them what those purposes were. Where was the morality in that?

Louis had convinced himself at the time that he had to lie, prevaricate, manipulate in order to assure the success of the enterprise. And in a sense it was true. But he soon found himself mired in a moral swamp from which he could not escape. His downfall came precisely *because* he was aware of the moral ambiguities.

On the sunny afternoon of June 21, Midsummer's Eve, after nearly three weeks of walking, Louis came to the village of Saint-Léon-sur-Dême. He slipped off his pack and took a seat at a table on the terrace of the Hôtel de France on the town square. The plane trees around the square had had their branches pruned back severely the previous fall, and the new leaves now emerging from the woody knobs at the ends of the branches cast the square in lovely dappled sun.

Louis sipped a beer and watched the preparations for that evening's celebration. Men on ladders hung colored lanterns from lampposts around the square, while other workmen hammered together a small stage for the musicians. First Madame then Monsieur Chalfont—they owned the hotel—engaged Louis in conversation. Louis was a reluctant partner at first. But the Chalfonts saw welcoming conversation as part of their duty as innkeepers, and before long they knew all about Louis's strange pilgrimage. They insisted that he stay the night.

"We have a charming small room available. A last-minute cancellation, monsieur. You will be our guest," said Madame Chalfont.

"And there will be excellent food, monsieur. From our kitchen of course," said Monsieur Chalfont. He leaned toward Louis as though he were sharing a great confidence. "The event is not to be missed."

"And dancing," said Madame Chalfont. "There will be dancing." Her eyes flashed happily.

Louis did not like celebrations, but that night he celebrated. He did not like to dance, but he danced. He waltzed with Madame Chalfont, of course, and with Solesme Lefourier, who would later be his neighbor and then his lover.

"You are American?" Solesme said as they were swept along with the crowd.

"Yes," said Louis.

The Gypsy musician sang in a high, lonesome voice, lyrics that Louis thought could have been written for him.

*Charles the great has come at last,*
*Come at last to stay.*
*He knows not where he's going, though*
*He thinks he knows the way.*

"Are you here for a while?" said Solesme. Her mouth was close to his ear so he would be able to hear.

"One night only," he said.

"Are you on the run then?" She laughed.

"In a manner of speaking," he said.

Dance after dance they circled around the square until the crowds went home and the music stopped.

After leaving Saint-Léon the following morning, Louis continued south. He walked for many more weeks, stopping finally in Santiago de Compostela in Spain, where Saint James, the apostle, is supposed to have first set foot in Europe, the final destination of pilgrims for many centuries.

During all his walking a new idea had slowly found its way into Louis's consciousness. It was that France, and more specifically the village of Saint-Léon-sur-Dême, were exactly where he longed to be.

Louis did not know exactly how or why. Was it the celebration, the kindness of the Chalfonts, the feeling of Solesme in his arms, moving with him around the square to the music of the *bal musette*? He did not know what had brought him to this longing, but he did not doubt that it was as true as anything else he knew. He decided he should return to the United States and bring what he needed—mostly his books— back to France, and he should live in Saint-Léon.

"France? Are you crazy?" said Sarah. Their divorce was final. "Christ, Louis. You're unbelievable. You think it's all right to just move away? Without discussing it with anyone? What about our children? *Your* children? What about Jennifer; what about Michael? You're their father."

Louis did not have an answer for Sarah, or for Jennifer or Michael. In truth he had hardly ever been there for his children. He had been tending to his career when they were little. And now that they were teenagers, he was tending to his failure.

Louis flew back to Paris and drove a rental car back to Saint-Léon. He took a room in the Hôtel de France while he looked at properties. A week later he drove south to a *notaire*'s office in Tours. And an hour after that he drove back north again. He patted the manila folder on the seat beside him to reassure himself that he had in fact done what he had just done. He had bought a house. In France. My God.

The folder was stuffed with official documents, none of which he could read and all of which he had signed. After the signing, the *notaire* had with great ceremony opened a bottle of champagne. The two men had raised their glasses to Louis's new home, which was in fact a disheveled and abandoned cottage on a hill above the village of Saint-Léon with a charming view and which had almost certainly never before had a champagne glass raised in its direction.

The only other time Louis had driven from Tours, he had missed the turn toward Saint-Léon. This time it was the way home and he did not miss it. A small milestone said it was five kilometers to Saint-Léon. The narrow road wound between pastures and fields. Louis stopped the car just before town beside a little stream, which turned out to be the Dême.

The water was swift and narrow. Louis broke the baguette he had bought earlier. Breadcrumbs exploded in every direction. He unwrapped the Gruyère and cut off a chunk. Since his long walk, whenever he ate this way—cheese and bread on an unfamiliar road—he felt happy. Louis sat on the bank of the Dême and tried to see through the murky water to the trout that were supposedly there. He tore off a crumb of bread and dropped it onto the surface. Something took it immediately.

Louis tried to picture the house he had just bought. He couldn't remember what it looked like. He was not even sure he could find the place. He sat back and let the sun shine full on his face.

Louis found the way to his house without asking. He turned left up the small lane and then left again up the driveway. The house came into view.

It had not been lived in since before the war. It had most recently served as a hay barn, and even that had been many years earlier. There were no trees around it, no bushes or flowers either. The roof was sagging badly, and there were gaping holes where slates had blown away. Windowpanes were broken and shutters were missing. The exterior walls had turned black with mold. Pieces of the carved cornice had fallen away. The door was held shut by a wooden peg on a wire stuck behind a bent nail.

Not long after the Second World War, the French regional authorities had decided to consolidate some of the police operations in the district. This meant that the small police outpost in Saint-Léon, along with several other village police stations, had been closed and relocated to the police barracks in the nearby town of Château-du-Loir.

This had remained a satisfactory arrangement for more than twenty-five years. But now it had been decided, for political as well as administrative reasons, that police operations should again be dispersed among the various villages, and that Saint-Léon should once again have its own police station. Though Jean Renard had only recently graduated from the national police academy, he seemed an excellent choice to man the new outpost.

"He's very young, sir," said the lieutenant studying Renard's file. "Inexperienced."

"He's smart," said the captain in charge. "He'll make a good policeman. Besides, he's from Saint-Léon. People there know him. They'll trust him. He'll fit in better than a stranger might."

"What about his father?" said the lieutenant.

"His father?" said the captain.

"The old gendarme, Yves Renard. You know—the war, his collaboration, prison in Russia," said the lieutenant. "That could be a problem."

"It's ancient history," said the captain. "Besides, it has nothing to do with young Renard."

"Not yet thirty years. Not ancient enough for some people," said the lieutenant. "I'm not talking for myself, Captain," he added quickly. "But for some it's not a very long time in the overall scheme of things."

The son, Jean Renard, received the appointment and showed up one sunny spring morning for his first day of work. Those having their coffee on the terrace at the Hôtel de France watched as he parked his car in front of the old police station. He turned the iron key in the office door. It was probably the same key his father had used before him. The door swung open with a groan.

Renard—even his wife, Isabelle, called him Renard—stepped inside and pulled back the heavy curtains. Dust swirled in the slanting morning sun. He carried boxes of files inside and stacked them next to the large wooden filing cabinet. He dropped the box containing current files on top of the desk with a thud, making the dust swirl again.

Renard wiped off the chair with his hand and sat down. He went through the box to remind himself of what needed to be done. There were a few bulletins and notices that needed posting on the bulletin board. There were some recent incidents that needed looking into. There was a thick dossier about a troublesome property dispute that had gone on far too long. He decided he would start with that. But even that could wait a bit. He looked around the office.

The room had been used for storage for decades. All but one of the old filing cabinets and stacks of excess furniture had been removed in anticipation of his arrival. The desk, a couple of chairs, one file cabinet, and a few other rudimentary pieces of furniture were all that remained. Along with the dust.

Renard spent the rest of the day cleaning and arranging the furniture to his liking. He took out all the desk drawers and emptied them into a garbage bin. He swept and mopped the floor. By the end of the afternoon the office was in a reasonable state. "Not bad," he said with a satisfied clap of his hands.

Renard locked the office and walked over to the Hôtel de France. He looked around. The hotel was covered with flowering vines, just as it always had been. The Hôtel Cheval Blanc had been closed at the end of the war and had remained so ever since. Cars and bicycles came and went. A moped clattered by. People shopped for supper, bought bread, vegetables, meat. They moved among the various shops, stopping on the square to visit with neighbors.

"So how was your first day?" said Claude, the waiter, as he poured Renard a glass of wine.

"As a first day should be," said Renard. "Quiet."

"Renard!" cried Madame Chalfont. She rushed up and embraced the policeman. "Congratulations. And welcome home. Claude," she instructed the waiter, pointing at the glass in front of Renard, "*that* is on the house."

"Oui, madame," said Claude.

"Merci, madame," said Renard.

"Ha," said Claude when she had gone. "Your first day on the job, and already you've been bought off."

# II.

Louis Morgon had spent his first weeks in Saint-Léon removing trash from outside and inside the house. Soon there were great mounds of broken plaster, slabs of rotting wood and crumbling cement, broken slate and glass, old tires, old clothes, rusting appliances, and other junk at the top of his driveway. He hired someone to haul it all away. He stood on a stepladder and swept down the ceilings and walls with a broom until he was covered with dust and could not stop coughing and sneezing.

He found someone to repair the roof. "It will need replacing before long," said the roofer.

"Before long?" said Louis.

"In the next few years," said the roofer. "See there? The nails are breaking. They're rusting through. We use aluminum or stainless nails these days. And the *charpente*—the wood—needs attention."

Louis put new panes in the windows where there was serviceable woodwork. He bought glazing compound, rolled it into snakes, pressed it along the panes, and smoothed it with a putty knife. He hired a carpenter to build new windows where they needed replacing. The carpenter did such a nice job that Louis hired him to make a new front door as well. Louis pronounced the door and windows "*belles.*" The carpenter shrugged. "It is what I do, monsieur," he said.

Eventually Louis's belongings arrived from the United States, a few clothes and mementos and boxes of books. "There are more books back at the post office," said the mailman. "They keep arriving."

"I know," said Louis, shrugging. "I apologize."

"He must be a professor or something," said the mailman. It was six o'clock in the afternoon, and he was having a glass of wine at the bar on the square.

"What's he like?" asked his friend.

"Nice enough, I think," said the mailman. "A gentleman. Judge for yourself. There he is."

Louis crossed the square in front of them on his way to the hardware store. He saw the mailman and his friend sitting at the bar and gave a courtly nod in their direction.

At first Louis had dinner most evenings at the Hôtel de France. Whenever he arrived, one of the Chalfonts, usually Madame, greeted him with exclamations of delight, ushering him to a table by a front window, which soon became "his" table.

"Ah, Monsieur Morgon, your table is waiting. My husband has something in the kitchen he made specially for you."


Solesme Lefourier called on him not long after he moved into his house. He was working on the windows when she came walking up his driveway. She was carrying a package. Solesme had a deformed back, which caused her to walk with a peculiar motion. The way she walked—a kind of skipping step, as though she were starting to dance—was the first thing Louis loved about her.

"I've brought an onion tart for your lunch," she said.

"Did you make it?" said Louis. She laughed. Of course she had made it. He peered under the cloth covering it. "It looks delicious. Would you like to join me for lunch? I'll make a salad."

"My husband, Pierre, is waiting for his lunch. But thank you. Another time."

"It was very kind of you to bring it."

"It is my pleasure."

Louis thanked her again and watched as she walked back down the driveway.

A week later Solesme invited Louis to dinner. "The tart was wonderful," he said.

Solesme asked Louis about life in Washington.

"Washington is, in its way, a small provincial city. It has its charms."

"What was your life like?"

"Oh, I worked in government," said Louis. "Then for a short while I wrote articles and taught political science. It was an ordinary, uninteresting life."

"I remember that you walked here. But why France?"

Louis explained as well as his French allowed that someone had suggested he should come to France. It would be the perfect antidote for his malaise.

"And was it the perfect antidote?" Solesme wondered.

"I think it was," said Louis. "Your dinner is delicious. The chicken roasted with lemons. Can I have the recipe?"

"Of course," said Solesme. "You roast a chicken with lemons."

"Anything else?"

"Lots of garlic, if you like it. I do. And cut the lemons in half."

Throughout the dinner Solesme's husband, Pierre, loomed silently like a monument, like the Sphinx, full of portent and indecipherable significance.

"He is a troubled man," said Solesme later. They were having coffee in Louis's kitchen. "He has had a difficult life."

"I am sorry to hear it," said Louis.

"Everyone of his generation had a difficult life. It doesn't matter," said Solesme, stirring the little cup.

"It doesn't matter?"

"To you, I mean. Don't trouble yourself about it."

"How has his life been difficult?" Louis said.

"It was before I knew him."

"But how?"

"I don't know. He hasn't told me," Solesme said. "He was still in Paris."

"Was he in the war?"

"Why are you asking all these questions?"

"I'm sorry," said Louis. "You're right. It's none of my business."

Louis and Solesme became lovers. She sometimes spent afternoons with him. "Do you think Pierre suspects?" Louis said. They lay on his bed. Her head was cradled in his arm. She did not answer. "Does Pierre . . . ?"

"He was in the war," she said. "I know he was wounded somehow, but I don't know where or how. After the war he . . . when I first knew him he used to make vague allusions. He liked the expression 'the dogs of war.' He said he was one of the dogs. He talked about 'doing business.' About 'customers' and 'clients,' French and German. Before he stopped talking altogether. My brother said something once that made me think Pierre was a smuggler and that he had to get out of Paris in a hurry."

"How do you live with someone who has stopped talking?"

"It's not as bad as you might think," said Solesme. She turned and smiled at Louis. "It means they stop asking questions." Louis could not stop asking questions.

Other people Louis had met in his short time in France mentioned the war sooner or later. It always seemed to come up. He had not expected that the war would still be so alive.

"But why would that surprise you?" said Solesme. "We French still have royalists six generations after the last king was guillotined. And Dreyfus is still an open wound. This war that killed many tens of thousands and tore France apart only ended thirty years ago. Less. And the recriminations and retribution went on full steam for years after that. For every score that was settled, there are still a hundred that were not."

By late summer the windows, the front door, the roof on Louis's house had been repaired. Sagging timbers under the ceiling had been shored up with a new beam and supporting posts at either end. Louis left the old plaster walls as they were, patching them where they needed it but not doing much else. They were mottled and stained, but Louis decided he would wait and see whether they really wanted painting. He liked seeing their history.

The floors were made of red clay tile. Around the edges of the living room and kitchen the tiles were in good shape, but in the center, the business part of the floor, some tiles were cracked, broken, or missing altogether. The carpenter who had done the windows and doors had found some old tiles in a barn he was working on. They were a reasonable match, and he persuaded the farmer to sell them to Louis.

As Louis was removing some of the broken tiles and their underlayment, which was also crumbling, something in the crawl space below caught his eye. He got a flashlight and shined it into the darkness. He saw what looked like a cloth package. There was no way into the crawl space, but it was shallow enough so that Louis could lie on his side and, with his arm fully extended through the hole in the floor, reach the package with his fingertips. After a few tries, he got hold of it and hauled it up. It was covered with dust and mold.

Louis undid the wire that held it together, and pulled back the rotting canvas. There was a wooden box of the kind a small machine or implement might have come in. The wooden lid was set in tracks and, after some prying and tapping, it slid aside. Inside was an oil-stained cloth, and wrapped in that were six little pistols. Each had been stamped out of a single piece of metal, which had then been folded over to form the crude weapon. Louis could tell from their heft that they were loaded.

Louis had an acquaintanceship with firearms, and he had read about these pistols. They were called Liberators, and during the war the Americans and the English had dropped them in France by the thousands for use by resistance fighters. He turned the pistols over and examined them. He laid them aside. There was a small box of .45 caliber ammunition, which he also laid aside.

Next he withdrew a stack of what looked like old handbills. The paper was dark and brittle. Only the once-oily rag over the pistols had kept it from turning to dust. Louis gingerly pulled the sheets of paper apart and saw that they were mimeographed copies of the same page. He carried one outside into the light, but he could not make out the words. The blue ink had faded almost beyond recognition.


Renard looked up from his work as Louis entered the office. He recognized Louis as the American who had recently bought the small house on the hill above where Pierre and Solesme Lefourier lived. Renard did not know much English. He waited for Louis to speak.

"Bonjour, monsieur," said Louis.

His French sounded very American, but at least it was French. "How may I help you, monsieur?" said Renard.

Louis placed a small wooden box on Renard's desk. "Monsieur Renard, I am Louis Morgon. In restoring the house I bought, which is above—"

"I know the house, monsieur," said Renard.

"In restoring the floor of the house I discovered some objects in the space underneath"—*how did you say crawl space?*—"which I think may be of interest to you." He carefully withdrew the handbills and laid them on the gendarme's desk.

"What is this, monsieur," said Renard, "and how does it concern me?"

"Madame Chalfont at the hotel suggested I show this to you since your name—your family name, that is—appears on this . . . page."

"What is this, monsieur?" said Renard.

"I am not certain, but I believe it is from the Second World War, from the period of the German occupation, and I believe the name mentioned, the Renard mentioned, might be a relative of yours. The Renard mentioned on the page"—*what was the word for handbill?*—"was also a gendarme in Saint-Léon. In any case, I thought it would interest you."

"May I see?" said Renard. Louis handed him one of the handbills.

Renard leaned close to the paper, then held it up close to his face, then stepped to the window. The blue ink was impossible to decipher. "Are they all the same? Are others any easier to read?"

"They are all more or less the same, monsieur. None of them can be read, at least not by me. But you see here?" Louis pointed. "Here is your name."

"May I borrow this, Monsieur Morgon?"

"Of course. You may keep it. I hope you will tell me what it is when you figure it out."

Renard gave Louis a quizzical look.

"It's just that I'm curious," said Louis. "History interests me."

At the end of the day Renard took the faded paper home. The house was filled with the smell of a roasting chicken. Renard laid the paper on the counter. Isabelle wiped her hands on her apron and stepped closer.

"What is it?" she said, bending over for a better look.

"I don't know," he said. "A clue maybe. To a mystery."

"A mystery or a crime?"

"For now only a mystery. It's from the war. It's got Papa's name in it."

"Where did you get it?"

Renard began to set the table. "From Louis Morgon. You know, the new American. He found it in his house."

"Really?"

"Under the floor. I'm going up there tomorrow to have a look. To see what else there is."

They sat down to eat.

"Delicious," said Renard.

"Because of your father," said Isabelle. She reached across the table and took his hand.

"His name is there."

"It's long ago," she said.

"That's what he always says."

"I'm only saying, it's not your responsibility."

When they had finished dinner and washed the dishes, Renard sat under a bright lamp and studied the faded paper with a magnifying glass. He held the paper close to his face and then at arm's length. He made notes.

"January twelfth or seventeenth, I can't tell which. 1941. Issue one," he said.

"Issue one? Of what?"

"I don't know."

"Do you think there were other issues?"

"I don't know." Renard scanned down the page until he found *Renard*. "Here it is. . . . And here it is again. Renard." Each time he saw the name, he touched it with his finger.

After an hour of looking at the paper every way he could think of, Renard started seeing words where there weren't any. He rubbed his eyes with the heels of his hands. So far he had deciphered very little. *Nazi could . . . without assistance of compl[?] . . . Judge Herr Denis Tem[po/eig?] . . . shadows. The [Du?]quesne boys . . . denounced.*

There followed six lines that had almost completely disappeared. Then there were names: *[?]ider, Chenu, Arn[?], Bertra[?], Renard . . . men[?tion].* Another interruption, then: *Renard's office and he is under . . . protectors have abandoned.*

"What do you think it is?" said Isabelle. She had brought coffee.

"It's a handbill of some sort. Look here: A French judge is called '*Herr.*' Calling a French judge '*Herr*' would probably be meant as a defamation. This could be from the resistance."

"Was there a resistance in Saint-Léon?"

"I don't even know that for sure."

"Are those names?"

"Yes. There's Renard. See?" He touched the word. "And here is . . . do you know anyone starting with *A-R-N*?"

"Arnaud," said Isabelle.

"Right. Of course. Good," said Renard and wrote it down.

The next day Renard went to Louis's house. "I'm pretty certain this is an underground newspaper," he said, when Louis opened the door. "A handbill, really, from early 1941. About six months after the German invasion. My father is named. There are other names too: Chenu, Arnaud, Duquesne."

"There is no need to stand at the door, Monsieur Renard," said Louis. "Please come in. I can offer you coffee—"

"No, no, monsieur," said Renard. "Thank you. I cannot stay. I only wanted to ask whether you have found anything else."

"Pistols," said Louis.

"Pistols? You found pistols?"

"Little pistols. Liberators, they were called. Putting two and two together, I would guess they were hidden here by the resistance."

"Two and two?"

"An expression in English. Do you not say that in French? I mean, the pages are a resistance leaflet, and they were in the same box as the Liberators. And they were hidden under the floor. It seems a safe conclusion."

"Were you a policeman in America, Monsieur Morgon?"

"No," said Louis. He could not tell whether Renard was being sarcastic.

"May I see the pistols?" said Renard.

"Of course," said Louis, and turned to get them. Renard followed him inside. The box, the circulars, and the pistols were sitting on the kitchen table. "Be careful; they are loaded. I found them that way." Louis turned on the stove. "I'll heat up the coffee," he said.

"Thank you," said Renard. He turned one of the pistols over in his hands. "How were they loaded?" he said.

"Through the barrel. They were made as cheaply as possible. You pushed the shells in one by one with a pencil," said Louis. "They hold five rounds. But the only way to unload them is to fire them. Here is the safety."

The two men sat at the table. Renard took his notes from his pocket and pointed out the words he had deciphered. Louis looked from Renard's notes to the paper and back again. "May I?" he said. He wrote Renard's words on another piece of paper and added some new words in between.

Renard peered at what Louis had written. "I don't see those words you added," he said.

"I don't either," said Louis.

"Ah," said Renard.

"But look. This most likely is a verb, isn't it, between *boys* and *denounced*. Tell me if I am wrong. But I think it has to be a verb, and it has to fit this space. And it has to make sense. So it must be: *The Duquesne boys were denounced.*"

"Or *have* denounced," said Renard. "*The Duquesne boys have denounced.*"

"Maybe," said Louis. He considered for a moment. "Except denunciation would usually be made by one person at a time, wouldn't it? By this Duquesne or that Duquesne, but not by *the Duquesne boys* together. That seems odd to me. So let's try *were.*"


"Well," said Isabelle that evening, "he sounds reasonable. And smart. Was this Morgon a policeman in America?"

"I asked him the same thing," said Renard. "He said no. But he knows about guns. And the way he thinks. . . . There's one other thing about this document. The names all seem to be accused of . . . something."

"Of what?"

"Well, probably collaboration."

"All of them?" said Isabelle.

"All of them," said Renard. "Papa too. But we don't know why they were accused or by whom. They may have been named just because they were officials. Then again . . . maybe Papa . . . Who knows? In a case like this anything is possible."

Renard gazed into the garden, trying to imagine how it must have been for his father. What if he had been ordered to round up Jews or

take hostages or hunt down resisters? There had been many collaborators among the police all over France.

The garden's high wall suddenly seemed insubstantial to Renard,
useless, incapable of affording any protection against . . . anything. The
evil in those times had been everywhere. Evil had seeped over and
around and through walls and found its way straight into your soul.

# III.

MAY 10, 1940. When the attack finally came, it did not come where the French generals had expected. The massive German army swept across the Low Countries—the Netherlands, Belgium, Luxembourg—and through the Ardennes. Onesime Josquin, a rifleman, waited with his company on the Maginot Line. He and his comrades peered across the fields, past the tank traps and barbed wire. But all they saw were crows feeding on the abandoned wheat. The main German force was already past them, deep into France and halfway to Dunkirk by the sea.

Onesime Josquin deserted his post and started west. After a day of walking he came upon trampled fields and pastures. Dead soldiers, mostly French, lay sprawled among bloated cows and horses with their stiff dead legs in the air. The stench was nearly as terrible as the sight. Onesime broke into a run and ran until he couldn't run any more.

After a few days he came upon a vast column of people going south. They were hardly moving, their way clogged by too many cars and trucks and bicycles, horse-drawn carts, hand trucks, and wheelbarrows—every manner of conveyance packed with people and belongings. In order to pass they had to move the carcasses of vehicles that had been strafed by German planes the day before. Some contained the corpses of their passengers.

Food and gasoline had all but run out. The only things in abundant supply were fear and desperation. Onesime left the road and set off cross-country. He came upon a broad, swift river; he did not know which one. He swung his rifle in a great arc and threw it far out into the water.

By June 14, German officers were relaxing in Parisian cafés and photographing one another in front of the Eiffel Tower. On June 22, France signed an armistice with Adolf Hitler. Under the agreement the seat of the French government moved from Bordeaux, where the old government had fled, to the city of Vichy. The Vichy government would administer most of the southern third of the country. The northern two-thirds, including the village of Saint-Léon-sur-Dême, where Onesime was bound, would be directly under German control.

A truck carrying fifteen people and their bundles wheezed and bucked and rattled to a stop. The driver thumped on the back window with his fist. Onesime had already slid his backpack to the edge of the truck's wooden bed. He jumped down. The truck lurched away in a cloud of dust.

Onesime blinked his eyes. Saint-Léon seemed like a splendid mirage, although the village was as plain then as it is today. But in the last few weeks, it had been transformed from a sleepy farm town into a scene of chaos and terror. The town was jammed with cars and trucks, and people milled about waiting for something good to happen.

The Hôtel de France was filled to overflowing. The refugees stayed one night, several families to a room, each paying double or triple the normal rate. The next day they would be gone and others would take their place. At the Cheval Blanc across the square, only the bar was open despite desperate appeals from those who couldn't find space in the Hôtel de France. The Cheval Blanc's upstairs windows were shuttered and covered with cobwebs and dust. "Anything will do," people begged, holding up their crying children. "Please. We'll pay whatever you want." Hubert, the barman, heard their pleas a hundred times a day. He did his best to meet their eyes, but all he could do was shrug. "I'm sorry, monsieur. I am only the barman."

Next to the Hôtel de France was a small mechanic's shop. You could hear the sound of metal being hammered coming from the shop's open doors. On the south side of the square between the two hotels, in a row of squat buildings, were the police station, a butcher with very little to sell, and an *épicerie*—a small grocery with mostly bare shelves. On the north side was a dry-goods store and a baker. At least the baker had bread, but only first thing in the morning. By nine he was sold out. The plane trees, lining the cobbled square and the *boules* pitch, had had their branches cut back to knobs the previous fall. Their leaves were only now coming into their fullness, casting dappled shade on the scene of desperation.

"Jean!" said Onesime. The man pushing the bicycle with a flat tire stopped and turned to look. Jean did not recognize his own brother. "Jean," Onesime said again. "It's me!"

Jean dropped the bicycle and ran as best he could through the tangle of cars and people to embrace the apparition with the knapsack. He held Onesime's head and kissed his cheeks. "Oni," he said as tears ran down his own cheeks. "Oni, I didn't think we'd ever see you again."

"And yet here I am," said Onesime, and Jean kissed him all over again. The two men steered each other through the crowd of refugees toward the Cheval Blanc. Two or three men stepped to the sidewalk to see who else had come back from the dead. They clapped Onesime on the back, took his knapsack, pushed him onto a stool, and stood a glass of beer in front of him. Then the questions began. "Where were you?" "What did you see?" "How did you get home?"

"It was a short war, but not short enough. We were ready; we were up to it," said Onesime. "But the generals lined us up in rows, and the Germans went around us. The generals expected the Germans to do the same thing they did in the Great War. The fucking generals." He spit toward the door. The other men were silent. "Who else made it back?" he asked.

"So far Raymond is back. Let's see; who else?"

"Léon, Henri, they're back."

"Léon got shot up pretty bad. François, Gilles, Jean Luc, they're all missing. Prisoners of war, let's hope."

"*Merde*," said Onesime. "The generals."

"Let's not forget Paris, that whole rotten bunch."

"I can't say I'm glad to see the Germans, but . . ."

"But what?"

"Well, it means the end of the damned Republic, doesn't it?"

"Maybe now they'll get serious."

"Are you crazy? They're firing one idiot and appointing another. And de Gaulle is abandoning ship."

"Who?"

"De Gaulle, a general. He went to England. He's been making grand speeches on the radio."

"Good riddance."

"Let's go home, Oni," said Jean.

Onesime drained his beer. Everyone clapped him on the back again. They patted Jean too. He had his brother back. Onesime slung his pack over one shoulder. Jean collected his bicycle, which lay where he had dropped it, and the two men walked up the hill out of town, trying to decide how best to arrive at their mother's house without giving her a fright. Of course she saw them coming up the lane. She recognized Onesime's pigeon-toed walk and raced from the garden to embrace him.

That night Onesime burned his uniform, his pack, and everything else left over from his brief war. He poked at the embers until everything was ash. He gathered up the charred metal buttons and buried them in the garden. There was no telling what they might do with deserters if they caught them.

There was plenty of work to be done around the place, and Onesime threw himself into it. The house needed attention. The barn and sheds did too. The garden needed digging. They needed to plant more tomatoes and beans and squash. There was little food for sale anywhere, and now there was one more mouth to feed.

Riding his bicycle to a cousin's house one afternoon to get more garden seed, Onesime came over a rise and saw below him the highway leading south. A stream of refugees reached as far as he could see. They moved slowly but urgently, jostling and pushing to get ahead, raising great clouds of orange dust, which hung in the hot, still air. Along the side of the road were burned-out cars and the carcasses of horses and people. Even from this distance he could smell the stench of death and hear the sounds of pandemonium.

It had been a warm spring. The fields were golden with wheat that was ready to cut. In many families there was no one to cut it. Cows grazed in the Dême Valley, and the fences were arranged, as they still are to-day, so that the cows could wander back and forth across the shallow stream to wherever the grass was sweeter. The mud stirred up by the cows did not deter the fish or the fishermen. Then, as now, the Dême and its even smaller tributaries were rich with trout.

Prosperity had visited France in the nineteenth century. And for a few years even Saint-Léon had been a lively and prosperous place, with four hotels and a number of decent restaurants, several tailors and dress shops, and a railroad station outside of town from which you could take the train all the way to Paris. By 1918, however, when the Great War had ended, so had Saint-Léon's brief flirtation with prosperity. It had slid back into being one poor farm town among countless others.

The French were among the victors of that war, but the cost of their victory was staggering. The war memorial in front of Saint-Léon's church listed more than a hundred of her sons who had been lost. There were two Josquins—Onesime and Jean's father and their uncle. All six Restaing brothers were killed, along with nine of their uncles and cousins. Entire families ceased to exist.

Nearly a whole generation of French men had disappeared into the mud. Some of the survivors were able to pull themselves from under the crush of reality. But in villages like Saint-Léon, where life was hard in the best of times, that war had inflicted an unbearable burden. And now here it came all over again. No one knew how many dead there were this time. Or how many there would yet be. And this time France had lost.

Saint-Léon braced for the onslaught. People hid their precious belongings. If they lived in town and were able, they moved out to the countryside to stay with cousins. In the country they took their animals inside. Everyone stockpiled what they could and waited for the worst.

The Germans arrived in Saint-Léon in a tidy convoy of two dozen trucks led by a sedan with a driver and a sergeant in front and a colonel in back. Except for the colonel, they all wore low helmets and buttoned-up tunics—even though the day was warm. Their blank faces were menacing and reassuring at the same time. The people of Saint-Léon watched from behind curtained windows as the small convoy passed and then stopped on the square. Soldiers spilled out of the trucks and into the side streets. They stationed themselves around the town.

The sergeant stepped from the sedan and held the rear door for the colonel. Everyone tried to catch a glimpse of him, as though he were the bridegroom in an arranged marriage. What would he be like? Would he be kind? Brutal? The sergeant followed the colonel into the Cheval Blanc. The colonel announced that the upstairs of the empty hotel would be his headquarters, billets, and mess.

By the time the mayor of Saint-Léon rushed into the hotel, guards had been posted at the door, and he had to wait to be admitted to see the colonel. The mayor, Michel Schneider, was Alsatian by birth. But any notion he might have entertained that his Germanic origins would be helpful in dealing with the occupiers was misplaced. The Hôtel de France was empty now, its last guests having fled the advancing Germans the day before. The colonel requisitioned the Hôtel de France, along with several private residences. Mayor Schneider could only stand by helplessly while all this was accomplished.

And yet the colonel—Colonel Helmut Büchner—did not seem unreasonable. The curfew he imposed was lenient. The bar on the ground floor at the Cheval Blanc was allowed to remain open until a half hour before dark, which at this time of year was well after ten. And the people who had been forced to leave their homes were compensated.

"Compensated?" The men on the *boules* pitch stood weighing the steel balls in their hands. Thierry Simonet looked about nervously and leaned into the circle. He could see a German guard in the hallway at the Cheval Blanc across the way. And for all he knew, the colonel was watching them from a window. "You call that compensation?!" Thierry said. "How do you compensate for something like that?"

"They could have just thrown them out, you know," said Arnaud Ladurielle. He and Thierry had both been in the trenches in the Great War. "After all, they won."

"They're an orderly lot," said someone else. "That's for sure."

"That's why they beat us," said Arnaud. He drew on his cigarette and exhaled a cloud of smoke. "When they do something, they're serious about it."

"This is still France," said Thierry.

"Is it?"

"So what?"

"And what a mess. What did that kid Léon lose his legs for?" There had been gangrene. The surgery was unavoidable. Léon Mettery spent his days in his parents' house looking out onto the fields he had once tended. The grain waved at him, mocking him.


Young Yves Renard had been the town policeman for exactly eight weeks when he found himself accompanying Mayor Schneider and other members of the town council up the staircase and into the presence of Colonel Büchner. The colonel had set up his office in the large meeting room just above the bar in the Cheval Blanc. He was seated at a heavy oak table. A young lieutenant was standing in the corner of the room leaning against the wall with his hands behind his back.

The colonel remained seated and gestured toward chairs that had been set up facing him across the table. The council members filed in and sat down. Behind the colonel hung a large portrait of Adolf Hitler. Hitler had rosy cheeks and soft eyes and was gazing dreamily into the distance. Faint blue mountains rose into the golden clouds behind him.

The colonel and the townsmen regarded one another in silence. The mayor cleared his voice, but the colonel raised his hand to stop him before he could speak. "Monsieur Mayor, please. I will explain why I have summoned you," said the colonel. His French was correct and lightly accented. "Then you may ask questions, and I will clarify anything that might require further explanation.

"The French defeat is complete," he said without pausing. "Let us be clear about that. Your government has been totally defeated. Your corrupt leaders have either fled or been removed. Your new government will serve you better than the old one did.

"I will be the commandant of the Saint-Léon-sur-Dême garrison. I am in charge of the town and the surrounding canton. This does not mean, however, that you have been released from your official capacities. I expect you all to continue to serve. You, Monsieur Schneider, are still the mayor, and you, gentlemen"—and here he read off their names one by one—"are still the town council, and you, Monsieur Renard, are still the policeman. The only policeman in Saint-Léon, as I understand it." Colonel Büchner paused and studied Yves for a moment. Yves dropped his gaze.

"How old are you, Monsieur Renard?"

"I am twenty-one, monsieur," said Yves.

"Twenty-one. And were you in the army?"

"No, monsieur, I was not. I was in the police academy until April. Then I was assigned to Saint-Léon."

"And Saint-Léon is your home?"

"It is, monsieur."

"And your superior is . . . ?"

"Captain Lupardennes in Tours."

"From now on, Monsieur Renard, you will report to me. At least for the moment, until the gendarmerie is reconfigured."

"Oui, monsieur," said Yves Renard without raising his eyes.

"And you, Monsieur Mayor, where are you from?"

"Wissembourg, *Herr Oberst*." The mayor spoke some German.

"Wissembourg?" said the colonel, raising his eyebrows slightly. His face seemed to soften. He leaned back in his chair and studied the mayor. "I was stationed in Alsace from 1916 . . . not far from Wissembourg. I know Wissembourg. We were . . . invited to leave." He stopped, having said more than he had meant to.

"In any case, as I was saying"—he folded his hands on the table in front of him—"you will continue as before. With a few small but perhaps significant changes. The first of which is that where you once reported to your superiors at the prefecture level, you will now report through my adjutant, Lieutenant Ludwig, to me." He gestured with his right hand toward the lieutenant, who did not move. "I hope to keep this reporting to a minimum, since I will be fully occupied with my military duties. Nothing would please me more than to have everything continue as it was before my arrival, to have Saint-Léon function as it did before.

"To that end one other change will be in effect. You understand undoubtedly that we as occupiers are bound by the rules of war and of civilization to look out for the general welfare of the citizens under our control, to see to their security and safety. And it is certainly my intention to do so. It is my duty to see that the citizens of Saint-Léon-sur-Dême and in the entire canton are safe and secure in their towns and in their homes. I don't need to point out that this is especially important in a time of war. There must be no disorder, no disruption of the peace.

"Therefore each of you is charged with assuring that the safety and security of Saint-Léon is not disturbed by disruptive or criminal elements. This is a very serious charge, and the failure to meet it will result in serious consequences for the citizens of Saint-Léon and of course for each of you." Colonel Büchner paused and gazed at the faces looking at him. "I want to make certain that what I have just said is clear. Does anyone have any questions about his responsibility in this matter?"

Jean Charles Arnaud, a member of the town council, slowly raised his hand. He glanced about and shifted uneasily in his seat. "Excuse me, Monsieur Colonel, but I do not think I understand. How are we to maintain order? I am a pharmacist, not a policeman. I am not trained—"

"I do not think I need to tell you, Monsieur Arnaud," said the colonel, "that there are those who would like nothing better than to undermine the armistice and overthrow our new regime. It should come as no surprise that certain elements—communists, revolutionists, anarchists, other terroristic elements—do not welcome us in France. They fear the order we will bring about. You all"—and here Colonel Büchner made an inclusive gesture with both hands—"may even know such people. Perhaps," he said, leaning forward slightly, "some of you even feel that way yourselves." He raised his eyebrows and smiled in what he meant to be an ironic gesture.

Just as quickly as it had come, the smile vanished. "Regardless," he said, "it will be your job to assure that there is no such trouble. And if there is, you will be held responsible. Monsieur Arnaud?"

"Excuse me, Monsieur Colonel, but . . . how can we be held responsible?"

"You are the people's representatives," said the colonel. "Who else should be held responsible? When they misbehave, it is as though you have misbehaved. We will punish them harshly for their misbehavior. And we will punish you for failing. . . ."

"But Monsieur Colonel, how are we to control—"

"We," said the colonel, "will of course assist you, if it comes to that, in exercising that control. The general safety and security are everything. . . ."

"But Monsieur Colonel," said Arnaud, unable or unwilling to accept the harsh reality. "I still do not understand."

"What is there to understand, Arnaud?" said the mayor suddenly. He leaned forward and fixed Arnaud with a fierce gaze. "We are in essence official hostages. Isn't that correct, Monsieur Colonel? Our lives depend on keeping any trouble at bay. Isn't that correct, Monsieur Colonel?"

The lieutenant pushed himself off the wall. "May I, *Herr Oberst?*" The lieutenant had a high, clear voice. His French was less fluent than the colonel's. He looked at his hands for a moment before he looked up and smiled. "Monsieur Arnaud, you should listen to your mayor. While he says it rather more bluntly than Colonel Büchner or I might, I believe he has correctly understood the situation. This is war, and we cannot be lax when it comes to suppressing uprisings and insurgencies. They must be crushed before they begin.

"You will find us patient and generous if you cooperate and fulfill your duty. But the mayor is essentially correct. By virtue of your official standing in this town, you are men of influence. You are also far more knowledgeable than we can ever be about what goes on in Saint-Léon. We must therefore depend on you. And to assure ourselves of your dependability, you become hostages, if you will. It is the only means by which we can keep the peace. If things go awry, if there is local resistance or insurrection, terrorism of any kind—which we certainly hope and expect will not happen—then you and your citizens will pay a heavy price.

"Of course," he added, almost as an afterthought, "look to Poland if you want to see the cost of insurrection. The Poles decided to resist our governance, and the entire country has answered for it. We believe you French are . . . more reasonable. That is why the Führer agreed to an amicable armistice and collaboration in the first place."

Colonel Büchner was eager to move on. "Your estimable General Pétain and his colleagues will see to your well-being," he said.

Arnaud wanted to speak, wanted to protest against the unfairness of it all. He was a simple pharmacist, after all, not a policeman, not a spy, not a soldier. His service on the town council consisted of preparing budgets and hiring the town secretary and deciding when a road should be repaved, not of discovering and subverting terror and insurrection.

Arnaud did not favor resisting the new German government. Not at all. Like many Frenchmen—maybe most—he thought that the order the Germans imposed might finally be what France needed, even if it did come from an unwelcome source and with an iron fist. After all, look how Hitler had restored Germany to order and prosperity after the Great War. Arnaud wanted to say all this. But the silence of the others in the room caused him to keep silent. The lieutenant stepped back against the wall and resumed his former posture.

Colonel Büchner cast his eyes around the room. He planted his hands palms down on the table. "Gentlemen," he said, "I believe our business is concluded for the moment. Thank you all for coming." He sat and watched as the men stood and filed silently from the room. They walked slowly with their eyes cast down, as hostages would.

# IV.

THE GERMAN GARRISON, once it was fully manned, consisted of 185 officers and men. They were billeted in the two hotels and in confiscated buildings in and around Saint-Léon. Their mission was to establish munitions, fuel and transportation depots, and to maintain security in the area.

Saint-Léon had been chosen by the Germans as a supply depot because it lay near the conjunction of several major highways from the east, and no more than four hours by convoy from the North Atlantic coast and the English Channel to the west. It was sufficiently close to the coast to make its stores readily available, and sufficiently rearward to afford protection and some room for maneuver.

There was another geographical quality that recommended the town to the Germans. All of the great châteaux—Chambord, Chenonceau, Amboise—and most of the lesser châteaux and houses of the region had been built using a particular chalklike limestone peculiar to the region. *Tuffeau,* as it was called, was soft enough to be cut into building blocks with an ordinary saw. It could easily be carved into elegant decorations with a mallet and chisel. And it was ubiquitous. As a result it had been extracted from hillsides over the centuries in such quantities that the entire area was now laced with quarry caves.

There was, for instance, a network of caves that went deep into the hillside behind the Cheval Blanc, where Colonel Büchner had his head-quarters. It had long been used by the town's hotels and restaurants to keep wine, as well as for general storage. The mushroom cooperative used another set of caves to grow the much prized *champignons de Paris,* although for now the crop of mushrooms was greatly curtailed. Above town you could see windows in the sides of hills and chimneys jutting out above, where caves had been transformed into dwellings.

The Germans saw the caves as ready-made maintenance hangars and fuel and munitions storage facilities. The humidity might be a problem over the long haul, but that disadvantage was more than offset by the security the caves afforded. They were easy to secure and impervious to attack from the air. It took the Germans a few weeks to locate and requisition the caves they wanted, and then a few more weeks to adapt those caves to their needs and to make them secure. By early August, trucks were arriving and unloading fuel and munitions into the caves.

Onesime Josquin leaned on his hoe and watched two German trucks pass the field where he was working. They were out of sight when he heard their brakes squeal. He knew they were turning up the lane toward what had once been his grandfather's house. The house had not been lived in since his grandfather's death. Onesime remembered standing with the old man at the entrance to the cave behind the house and peering into the blackness. The cool, damp air pressed against him, pushing him backward into the light. He remembered the shivers of boyish terror and how the hair on his neck had stood on end.

Most of the caves had been only dug deep enough so that the *tuffeau* could be easily extracted. But some of the oldest caves—like his grandfather's—were deeper. They had been quarries first, but in the fourteenth and fifteenth centuries, when the warring French and English armies had swept back and forth across the countryside, the caves became protective hideouts and secret passages between fortified farms.

"I followed it once," said Onesime's grandfather, pointing into the cave. Onesime remembered the weight of his grandfather's hand on his shoulder. "I followed it for a very long way and never found the end of it. I only turned around after going for more than an hour. The cave runs all the way to Tours. The oil in my lamp would have run out if I had gone any farther. Without a light, you could hold your hand like this—two centimeters from your nose—and not see it. You could get lost in there and never be found. It has happened." Grandfather had built a wall a hundred meters inside, to close off the endless cavern.

Onesime was sitting in front of the fire with his mother and Jean. Anne Marie Josquin was sewing a patch on a torn shirtsleeve. She leaned toward the lamp and squinted as she passed the needle back and forth through the heavy fabric.

"The Germans are using Grandfather's cave," said Jean. "I saw them today. I was at the barn when they passed."

Anne Marie cut the thread with her teeth. "Your grandfather would not be happy about that," she said.

"I saw them too," said Onesime. "There were two trucks. Fuel tankers, it looked like."

Later in his room, he opened his drawing pad and leafed through the drawings he had made since he had been home. There was a nice one of the house. One of some sunflowers with a little bit of color. One from memory of the stream of refugees. One from memory of a dead soldier. You could not tell from the drawing whether the dead man was French or German. His eyes were open. There was a small drawing of Marie Piano sitting on the ground looking up at him. He had not gotten her eyes just right. Her real name was Marie Livrist. But because she loved to play the piano, everyone called her Marie Piano, to distinguish her from the other Maries in town.

Onesime took a blank piece of paper from the pad. He opened his paint box and took out a pencil. He sharpened it to a fine point. He used a ruler to draw a grid on the page. Then he drew the several streets of town in the center of the page. He drew carefully, paying attention to the scale of the drawing. He drew the roads leading from town, including the road leading to his mother's house, where he and Jean lived.

He drew the lane to his grandfather's house and marked the cave where the two trucks had gone. He made a small 2 beside the cave, to signify the two trucks. He wished he had noticed the numbers on the trucks, so that he could write them on the map. He drew other roads and other caves he knew about.

"Oni," said Jean. He was standing in the doorway. Onesime quickly slid the map inside the pad. "What are you doing?" said Jean.

"I'm drawing," said Onesime. "You shouldn't sneak up on me like that."

"I didn't sneak up. Don't be so touchy."

"Yes, well. I just don't like to be surprised like that."

"What are you drawing?"

"It's not finished. I'll show you when it's finished."

"What do you think the Germans are doing in the cave?" said Jean.

"How should I know?"

"But what do you think?"

"I don't know and I don't care," said Onesime.

Jean paused. "Did you ever go all the way in?" he asked.

"Grandfather walled it up. What do you mean, 'all the way in'?"

"All the way in. Past the wall."

"Once."

"How far?"

"Not far. Did you?"

"I did. But from the other end."

"The other end? Really? Where was it, the other end?"

"You won't believe it."

"Tours?" said Onesime.

Jean laughed. "Closer," he said.

"Show me," said Onesime, and pulled his map from the drawing pad.

Jean bent over the map. "Where's the Beaumont château?" His finger wandered around on the paper.

"Wait," said Onesime, and drew a square at the edge of the village. "Here. And here's the tower." The château had a tall, narrow tower of

brick, built in the nineteenth century more as a folly than for any prac-
tical purpose.

"Then the end of the cave is right . . . Draw the wall." Onesime
drew the wall around the château, closer on one side than the other.
"It's just inside the west wall . . . here. There's a huge bush of lavender,
or there used to be."

"It's still there," said Onesime.

"And when you pulled it aside there were stairs that went down. I
used to sneak down there with Janine Girault."

"They keep their wine in that cave," said Onesime.

"I know. One day we were down there, and someone started coming, so we went inside and hid until they left. It didn't seem to end, so
I went back later with a lamp and followed it. And it ended at the wall
at the back of Grandfather's cave."

They looked at the map. "So how far was it, do you think?"

"A thousand meters, maybe. Twenty minutes, maybe. I don't know
exactly. I wish I had measured it. It was pretty easy going."

"Grandfather said—"

"Yeah, well," said Jean. "That was Grandfather."

"Does it come up anywhere else? Are there branches going off
from the main cave?"

"I don't remember. I don't think so. It was a long time ago."

Onesime drew a dotted line from the château to his grandfather's
house.


Count Guillaume de Beaumont had built the château in the fifteenth
century on land given him by King Charles VII in gratitude for his service in the war against the English. Beaumonts had lived there ever
since. The current count, Maurice de Beaumont, lived there with his
wife, Alexandre, and their two small children, along with a housekeeper,
Silvie Josquin, Onesime's cousin.

Onesime had begun working at the Beaumont estate while he was
still in school, and when he left school, the count hired him full time.

Onesime mended fences, cut firewood, plowed, cultivated, and harvested wheat. He did whatever needed doing. And when there was too much work for him, he found others to help. He worked for the count until he was called into the army, and when he returned from the war his old job was waiting for him. "If you still want it, Onesime."

"Oui, monsieur. I am glad to have it."

Onesime rode his bicycle toward town and turned up the lane that went along the west wall. He stopped and unlatched the large wooden gate, swung it aside, and pushed the bicycle inside. He could see the house and tower through the trees. All the windows were shuttered. One of the Beaumont cars was in the drive in front of the house, but that did not mean that anyone was home. The Beaumonts had other properties where they spent time, including an apartment in Paris. Onesime leaned his bicycle against the wall. He heard the sound of a cuckoo. He stood still and listened until it stopped.

He found the stone stairs behind the lavender bush. He went down and pulled on the iron gate. It was unlocked. He took two steps into the dark cold and switched on his flashlight. Its beam swept around to reveal a narrow vault. There were stacks of wine bottles lying on their sides against the left wall. They had no labels on them. Labels were useless here; they would be devoured by the damp in no time. Each stack of bottles had a roof slate stuck behind it telling in chalk letters what it was: 1929 Yquem; 1937 Tallon Noir; 1924 Pouilly-Fuissé. A thick gray blanket of mold had grown over the Pouilly so that the bottles seemed transformed into some grotesque geological formation.

The floor of the cave was level, and the ceiling was high enough so that Onesime could walk upright. He moved carefully past the wine and then quickened his pace, shining the light left and right ahead of himself. Shallow passages led off to either side. The main passage continued straight ahead. After a few minutes the floor of the cave became more uneven; the walls narrowed and the ceiling dropped until he had to walk in a half-crouch to avoid hitting his head.

Because there were no familiar points of reference—no markers, no sky, no earth—Onesime did not have an exact sense of his direction or changes in elevation. His light did not penetrate far into the darkness. And though his line of march seemed to be straight ahead, when he pointed the light farther on, he could see that the cave ahead veered gradually out of sight.

Time does not seem like a spatial concept. But, in fact, we often count off the minutes and hours of a journey by means of geographic landmarks, an intersection of roads, a building, a village, an ancient tree. Without landmarks, with only the light passing along the chalky vault above him, time disappeared for Onesime. He thought he had only been walking a short while when he found himself standing at what he took to be the back wall at his grandfather's cave. Blocks of stone had been stacked to fill the passage, and the uneven spaces around the edges had been stuffed with stone scraps and dust. There was no mortar holding it all together. It stood as it had for many years.

Onesime pressed his ear to the stone and listened. He heard only the sound of water dripping behind him. He extinguished the flashlight and stood in the utter darkness. He spread his legs slightly, to keep his balance, and stared at where he knew the wall to be. He saw only blackness.

Onesime turned on the flashlight again and examined the edge of the wall until he found a spot where a block of stone came very close to the side of the cave. He picked at the dust that had been wedged into the gap, and it came away easily. Bits of stone fell at his feet with a soft sound like falling water.

After a few minutes he could feel he was nearly through the wall. He stopped and extinguished the light. This time he saw little splinters of dim light coming through the wall where he had been digging. He leaned closer but heard nothing. Now he scraped carefully at the dust and gingerly lifted the last small stones aside. He did not want to dislodge anything that would clatter to the ground on the other side. But no sooner had he had this thought than it happened. A stone the size of his head crashed to the ground, and light flooded into the passage where he stood.

Onesime tried to lean back into the shadows. He held his breath and listened. There was still only the dripping water behind him. Carefully he leaned toward the hole he had opened and peered through. He saw an empty cave ahead of him. It was wider and taller than the cave where he stood, and it was in better repair.

The light puzzled him. If the wall behind which he stood was only a hundred meters inside the mouth of the cave, then the light should have been brighter. He recalled the mouth of the cave being broad and tall, and the wall being straight back from the mouth. Even at a hundred meters, there should have been more light. He looked again. They have built a door, he thought. Or there was something blocking the entry and the light. Trucks or crates or something.

But the cave wasn't straight. In fact, it was sufficiently curved so that the front half of the cave was out of his sight. Onesime was peering intently through the small opening when suddenly the light changed and he heard voices. He almost fell over backward trying to get away from the opening he had made. The voices came closer. He hurried away until, looking back, he could no longer see the opening. He leaned against the side wall and waited. All he could hear now was the pounding of his heart.

He no longer heard the voices. He returned to the wall and, after waiting for a while, carefully filled in the opening he had made.

When he climbed the stairs at the other end of the cave, there was the count, Maurice de Beaumont, striding in his direction. "Ah, it's you, Onesime."

"Oui, monsieur. It's me."

"I saw your bicycle, but I didn't see you."

"I didn't see you anywhere, monsieur."

"I was in the house, Onesime."

"I knocked, monsieur, and the gate here was open, so I thought you might be inside. . . ."

"You knocked?"

"Yes."

"When?"

"Before."

"Not very loudly."

"I suppose not, monsieur. I came to see about the hay."

"Yes," said Maurice. He was studying Onesime. "The hay."

"Yes," said Onesime. "It's ready, I think. I thought we could take it all at the same time this time. If we let the field out by the Dême go another few days, then the vineyard field"—he gestured beyond the château—"will be ready too. It looks like a nice stretch of good weather. Jean will help me. Others if we need them."

"Yes, that's fine," said Maurice, still looking at Onesime a little too hard. Onesime looked down at his feet. "The gate was open?"

"Oui, monsieur. Open."

"And you locked it?"

"No, monsieur. Should I?"

"Onesime, look here. When you come to cut hay or to do other work, no matter what it is, I want you to always knock at the house first. Do you understand?"

"I knocked, monsieur."

"Yes, well. I want you to always knock and to let someone know you are about."

"Oui, monsieur. I knocked."

"That's clear then, is it?"

"Oui, monsieur. Quite clear." But he was speaking to Maurice de Beaumont's back, because the count was already striding toward the house, his tall black boots crunching in the gravel. Onesime watched him all the way to the terrace. Then he turned and walked to his bicycle.


The thing about a cave is that it is no darker at night than it is by day. Once you are inside, it is all the same, so you might as well visit it at your convenience. Onesime, Jean, and their mother had finished supper. The three of them cleared the table and put things away.

"I'm going out," said Onesime. Neither Jean nor his mother said anything. Onesime had always been one to wander about at odd hours, and since he had come back from the war, his peculiar habits had only gotten more peculiar. Sometimes it seemed as though he had become a night creature. Jean would wake up in the middle of the night and look out the window to see Onesime sitting in the garden. It would be three in the morning and he would be there in the dim moonlight, his pad on his lap, drawing something.

Onesime took his cap and closed the door behind him. After a few minutes Jean got up and went upstairs. He stood in the hallway for a while listening and then went into Onesime's room. He closed the door without a sound. He found Onesime's drawing supplies. After searching for a while, he found the drawing pad. But the map was not inside. He could not find it anywhere.

Onesime found the château's west gate locked. He climbed the wall easily and dropped silently to the ground. He paused and listened. He heard a fox barking in the woods. He wondered whether the count had locked the cave. He was about to go down the stone steps when he heard the faint sound of laughter coming from the house.

Onesime approached the house through the trees and saw that there were quite a few cars parked in the driveway. He studied them from behind the thick trunk of an ancient cedar. He recognized two Beaumont cars and two other cars. Several cars were unfamiliar to him. There was also a German military sedan. He was about to try to get closer so that he could note the numbers of the German car, when a figure stepped from between the cars and drew on a cigarette, which he held cupped in his hand. A German soldier.

Onesime backed up carefully and circled back into the trees. He hesitated a moment and then went around the house to where the great room looked out on a broad stone terrace. He kept to the shadows and made his way over the balustrade to a window. The heavy curtains were drawn, but they were not quite closed. He could see between them into the room.

The count, Maurice de Beaumont, stood with his back to the window. Facing him was Colonel Büchner. Both men held champagne flutes and were leaning forward listening to a third person, whom Onesime could not see. Beyond them he could see other people. He recognized some of them. Alexandre de Beaumont, the count's wife, was there, beautiful and very elegant. She had a glass in one hand and a cigarette in the other. She stood alone with a half smile on her face. Monsieur Dupont, the owner of a small factory in town, a balding, round man with wire glasses and a little mustache, was talking to Madame Terterrain. She was taller than Dupont and leaned over him as he spoke. It was her high laughter Onesime had heard. Monsieur Terterrain must have been there somewhere, but Onesime did not see him. There was a priest he had seen before.

The count tapped on his champagne glass with his ring. He made an announcement Onesime could not hear. He put his free hand on the colonel's back and ushered him to the left and out of Onesime's sight. The others also turned and walked to the left. Onesime slipped over to the next window. But the curtains in that window were drawn completely, as they were in the next one. He looked across the terrace and around the yard, to make certain no one was there, before he moved farther to his left.

There were no curtains over the door leading into the drawing room. The bright light poured from the room and fell onto the stone terrace in golden squares. Onesime could not easily look in without revealing himself to those inside. He retraced his steps back past the windows, went back over the low balustrade and around the terrace, where he could remain in the shadows and still have a view through the doors. As he moved along, stooped down and peering between the concrete balusters, a piano began to play.

He could see the backs of the guests seated in chairs, looking to his left toward the piano, which was out of his sight. He moved to his right and watched through the balusters. It was as though he were seeing a flickering movie. Someone started to sing.

*Du bist wie eine Blume,*
*So hold und schön und rein;*
*Ich schau' dich an, und Wehmut*
*Schleicht mir ins Herz hinein.*

There was no mistaking that sweet voice. Onesime moved farther right, but he still could not see Marie Piano. When she had finished the song in German, she sang it in French. Everyone applauded enthusiastically. There was a brief pause, and then she began playing again. She did not sing this time. Onesime had heard the music before, but he did not know what it was.

Back at the mouth of the cave, Onesime hesitated before descending the stairs. He did not know how long he had been inside the château walls. He had failed to check whether the German soldier was still with the cars. He felt that he should still go into the cave, but why? What was he looking for? The count, who was friendly with the Germans, was already suspicious of him. Why was he putting himself in danger this way?

Onesime could not find answers to these questions. All he could come up with was the sound of Marie Piano singing a German song. She played and sang like an angel. So why shouldn't she sing anything and everything, and for anyone and everyone? Even the Germans?

The memory of her singing rang softly in his head. The door was not locked. He pushed it open and hurried through the cave to its walled end, counting his steps as he went. Once again he cleared a small space at the edge of the wall and looked through the hole as best he could. The cave was lit as before, but this time he could see rows of wooden boxes stacked on pallets. He had seen boxes like this before. They contained artillery shells. He could see what looked like a small table beside the far wall. He listened but did not hear any sound coming from the other side of the wall. He filled the hole he had opened and opened one on the opposite edge of the wall.

From this vantage he could see the table more clearly and the chair beside it. He could just make out the edge of the heavy door that had been installed at the mouth of the cave. Again he watched and listened and heard nothing. He studied the wall. If you were to remove one of the *tuffeau* blocks, a man could easily get into the cave through the space. But it would take two men to lift the block down from the wall and then to replace it.

An hour later Onesime lay on his back in his bed with his hands behind his head. He stared into the darkness. What was he doing, he wondered, spying on the count, spying on the Germans? The war was lost. It was over. France had been invaded, but what was that to him? What little he knew about Pétain and all the rest of them filled him with disgust. They were fighting over power. Like the Germans. People like Onesime and Jean and their mother were always the ones caught in the middle and ground into sausage.

France's brilliant leaders had sent his father and his uncle and hundreds of thousands of other fathers and brothers and uncles and sons to die in the mud in the Great War, and now they had done it again. He thought of his dead father, his dead uncle, of François, Gilles, and Luc, who were dead or in prison, of Léon with his legs cut off, of all the dead soldiers he had seen, French and German, and of those he hadn't seen. He thought of the dead refugees by the roadside. The dead, the dead, the dead. Onesime saw them in a great pile rising into the darkness above him. He rolled onto his side with his back to the window.

Onesime did not know that the words Marie Piano had sung had been written a century earlier by a Jew, Heinrich Heine. Because the poem was universally known and loved in Germany, the Nazis could not ban it. So they had declared it a folk song and declared Heine a non-person. Onesime did not know any of that. He did not know whether he had ever even met a Jew. He fell asleep to the memory of Marie Piano singing.

# V.

THE MEETING ROOM in the Saint-Léon town hall was always dark, even on the brightest days. But now with only one bulb burning, thanks to electrical shortages, most of the room lay in deep shadow. The town council sat in silence. It was not their first meeting since the Germans had come. But Jean Charles Arnaud was still afraid. "Should we be meeting? Did you clear it with Colonel Büchner?"

"It is our regular meeting," said Michel Schneider, the mayor, sitting up straight and speaking forcefully. "We are carrying on as usual." He shuffled the papers before him. "We have some town business to deal with. And, yes, Jean Charles, I told the colonel that we are meeting. I invited him to attend. He declined."

"He declined? But did you get his permission? Why did he decline?" Arnaud grasped the edge of the table with both hands, as though it might be a life raft adrift in a stormy sea.

"Perhaps we should leave the door open. That way . . ." This was Pierre Chenu. "I mean, just how can we go on with business as usual?"

"We can and we must," said the mayor. He studied the agenda before him, looking for minefields. The allotment for a new town garage door was easily dealt with. An estimate of the costs had been submitted. Mayor Schneider had sent a copy to Colonel Büchner and had heard no objection from his office. A supplemental allotment of petrol for the town to run its tractor had also been negotiated. The veterans' celebration—a toast and speech to be held in front of town hall—was another matter.

"The veterans' celebration is a bad idea," said Pierre Chenu.

"We do not want to antagonize . . . anyone," said Jean Charles Arnaud.

"We should let it drop," said Pierre. "Like we did Bastille Day. Whose idea was it, anyway?"

"Is this what it has come to?" said René Bertrand. Bertrand was the schoolmaster, a tall, ungainly man with a fringe of hair above his ears and a little spike of a beard. He enjoyed rising to his full height when he had an important point to make, as he did now. "Has it come to this?" His chair scraped across the floor, and Arnaud and Chenu looked right and left as though someone might come charging in because of the noise.

"Has it come to what?" said Mayor Schneider, rattling his papers angrily. He wanted to keep the council moving ahead in an unobtrusive and cooperative way. "If you have some objections to the cancellation of the veterans' celebration, then state them, please, in a businesslike and civil fashion. My understanding is that it will be forbidden anyway. Like July fourteenth. In the interest of tranquility."

"Businesslike and civil?!" said Bertrand. He seemed to be considering where he should begin.

But before he could speak, Yves Renard, the young policeman who sat on the town council *ex officio,* as its only unelected member, spoke up. His voice was soft, his tone was deferential. "I hope you will remember, Schoolmaster Bertrand, what exactly our situation is. We are obliged to keep . . ."

Bertrand's face grew red, and he seemed to stand even taller as he listened to the admonition of the young policeman, who had been his pupil not very many years before. "It is exactly this situation, *Monsieur Renard*"—he spoke the policeman's name with a sneer—"that I believe must not be allowed to continue."

The other members of the council froze. They stared at the schoolmaster in horror. The German colonel had laid down the rules, which, harsh though they might be, were understandable in light of the fact that Germany was at war on various fronts. Of course they would want, above all, to maintain strict order in the territory they occupied. And whether one liked it or not, they had the right and the power to do so.

Yves Renard spoke up again. "I am deeply sorry, Monsieur Schoolmaster, to be obliged to warn you to watch what you say. You are walking on dangerous ground. I am the representative of the law. And the prevailing law forbids saying . . . certain things in . . . certain ways."

Renard's awkward expression caused Bertrand to explode in derisive laughter. "The prevailing law?" he said. *"The prevailing law?"* But before he could continue along that path, his former pupil was on his feet and at the schoolmaster's side. "Come with me, Monsieur Bertrand. I am taking you to the police station."

Now the men around the table erupted in outrage and disbelief. "See here, Renard. . . ." "You can't mean it. . . ." "You can't just . . ." The din stopped only when Renard took the schoolmaster firmly by the arm and marched him from the room.

"I am astonished," said the schoolmaster, and indeed he looked truly astonished. His eyebrows were as high as he could raise them. He had removed his glasses, the better to bathe the young policeman in his angry gaze. The two men sat facing each other across the policeman's desk. "Shame on you, Yves Marie Renard," said Bertrand. The schoolmaster was the only one who had ever called Yves by all three names. And the last time he had done so, Renard had been sitting at a school desk in his class.

"I am doing my duty, Monsieur Bertrand," said Yves. He continued filling out a form without looking up. "My duty is to keep order in the town."

"I taught you better than this, Renard," said the schoolmaster. "You know better than this. You *are* better than this."

"What is your full name, monsieur? And your exact address?"

Bertrand suddenly looked old. His shoulders slumped and his head hung. Only his eyes still burned as he glared at Yves. He recited the information as though he were speaking to a functionary he had never seen before. He added, "Occupation: schoolmaster," without being asked.

Yves wrote everything down in his careful hand. Then the two sat in silence while the policeman filled in a number of boxes, completing one side of the form and turning the paper over. Bertrand spoke. "And you are charging me with . . . ?"

"You violated the law by speaking seditiously about our occupiers," said Yves, reading everything over to be certain he had filled in every blank space.

"And I suppose I am going to be punished? For doing what everyone *should* be doing? For saying what everyone should say: France is crushed and the world is in mortal peril—" he began.

Yves interrupted. "Monsieur Bertrand, I am not the one who punishes those who break the law. I only report what they have done to the judicial authorities, who then decide the punishment. Whether or how you are punished is not up to me."

"And if it were? These are things you should think about, Renard. These are things I taught you. . . ."

"Monsieur Bertrand," said Yves, and he spoke with such authority in his voice that Bertrand stopped speaking.

"Monsieur Bertrand," said Yves again. "Do you hate the occupation of our country by the Germans and the collaboration required by the armistice? Do you hate Marshal Pétain and the National Revolution?"

"I believe . . . ," began Bertrand.

"Forgive me, monsieur, but it is a question that can be answered with a simple yes or no."

Bertrand laughed derisively. "And you expect me to fall into your childish trap and incriminate myself further?"

"You are mistaken, monsieur. It is not a trap. I expect you to say, no, you do not hate the occupation of France or the armistice or the

National Revolution. I expect that of you, because I think of you as a wise and prudent man—and a thoughtful man."

Bertrand sat up straight and stared at the young policeman.

Yves Renard crossed his hands in front of him and studied them before he continued. "Perhaps you remember, monsieur," he said, looking directly into the schoolmaster's eyes, "how in the sixth grade I got into a terrible fight with Jacques Courtois because he had been teasing me. He teased me so relentlessly and continuously that one day I simply exploded and went after him in the middle of French class. He, of course, knocked me over with one punch and bloodied my nose. You punished him severely. He was caned and was required to remain after school for an entire month."

"Of course he was, because . . ."

"Excuse me, monsieur, but I am not finished. Perhaps you remember that you punished me too?" Bertrand looked at the young policeman; he did not remember the incident. "Well, you did. You punished me too.

"And do you remember *why* you punished me? Let me remind you, monsieur, because it is important. You said in front of the class and in front of Jacques Courtois that you were punishing me for taking the law into my own hands. But then, afterward, when you and I were alone in the classroom, you told me what the more-serious infraction had been. You don't remember it, but I will never forget it.

"You punished me for not being patient, for not waiting for the right moment, the right time and place, to sort things out with Jacques. 'Victory,' you said, 'always goes to the patient. Take a good and true measure of the situation and act accordingly, Renard.' Those, monsieur, were your exact words, which I never forgot. 'Victory always goes to the patient.'

"And so, with the utmost respect and admiration, monsieur, I repeat them back to you now, your own wise words: 'Victory always goes to the patient. Take a good and true measure of the situation and act accordingly.'"

Bertrand had been a strict schoolmaster. He still was. Never in his recollection had one of his students, or for that matter one of his *former* students, spoken to him in this manner. Reflexive indignation rose through his body like volcanic magma. But before he could erupt, young Yves Marie Renard, not his best student ever but a decent student all the same, raised a finger in front of Betrand and added: "Monsieur, you are in danger. And if you are in danger, then you might endanger others. You are in danger, and the best thing I can do for you is to remind you of the wisdom of your own words."

Bertrand sat with his mouth agape, staring in shock and only slowly dawning comprehension of what this boy with the wispy, blond moustache—a boy really; not even a man—was telling him. "Your speech, monsieur," Yves continued, "which was clearly going in a seditious direction, was not yet serious enough to warrant my forwarding a report. But I am issuing you this written warning, monsieur." With that Renard passed an official-looking paper across the desk.

Bertrand was having difficulty grasping what had just transpired. He studied the document that the policeman had put in front of him. "You arrested me, you humiliated me in front of the council, in order to warn me?" The schoolmaster was incredulous.

Yves Renard studied his former teacher for a moment. "Monsieur," he said, "you are free to go."


When Renard returned to the town council meeting, the room fell silent. "Where is Monsieur Bertrand?" they wanted to know. "Did you arrest him?"

"I did not arrest him," said Renard. "I issued a written warning. And I will not hesitate to issue more such warnings or to make arrests when the circumstances warrant it. We are charged with keeping order, and we must do so for the well-being of our citizens as well as for our own well-being." He sat down at the table and waited for the meeting to continue.

As it happened, the next order of business, the situation with the unauthorized use of an abandoned barn, fell under the policeman's purview. Reports had reached the mayor that a private house, which years before had been converted into a hay barn and then had eventually been abandoned, was being used at night for secret rendezvous of a mysterious nature. "Is it partisans?" Arnaud wondered immediately. "What if it's partisans?"

"It's probably Gypsies," said the mayor. "Someone filed a complaint. They saw a light. . . ."

"Who?" said Chenu.

"Someone reliable. I have the name. That is all you need to know. She saw a light. And heard something too."

"Ah," said Arnaud. "That will be Louisette Anquetille. She's always seeing things. Imagining things."

"Someone reliable, I said."

"I will investigate tonight," said Yves Renard.

"And report back," said the mayor.

"Of course," said the policeman.

The abandoned hay barn was not far from town. Yves walked there that night. He found a loose shutter and pulled it aside. He shined his flashlight through the window. The glass was dusty and covered with cobwebs. The inside was empty of furniture, and no one was there. But there was a dark stain on the center of the floor, and a large hook hung from the ceiling.

"There is nothing going on at the barn," said Yves the next morning.

"I am glad to hear it," said the mayor. "I'll look for your report."

That night, Yves returned to the barn. This time light was coming through a space where the shutters didn't quite meet. Yves stopped and listened. He heard low voices inside. He knocked on the door, and everything fell silent. After a long pause the door opened a crack. "What do you want," said Jacques Courtois.

"Someone saw a light up here. This building is private property and is not authorized for your use, as far as I know."

"As far as you know," said Jacques. Yves could see several men behind Jacques.

"Well," said Yves, "I have to check. Let me in."

Jacques had no choice. He opened the door. But he did not step aside. Yves had to squeeze past him. The other men—there were three of them, and Yves knew all three—muttered a greeting.

The room was dimly lit by a kerosene lantern. A half-butchered pig hung from the hook, its black blood dripping into a tub. Two of the men held knives, and there were packages of meat wrapped in greasy paper stacked beside the door. "What you are doing is illegal," said Yves. "Whose pig is it?"

"Mine," said one of the men.

"You can check," said Jacques.

"You still need special permission to slaughter animals, except chickens and rabbits. You know that."

"We have to eat," said Jacques. "We've got families."

"You need permission," said Yves, "and you don't have it. I will have to file a report."

"Do what you have to do," said Jacques.

"And we'll do what we have to do," said one of the other men.

"I will file my report tomorrow," said Yves.

The men remained silent while he walked to the door. Jacques stood in front of the door for a long moment and then stepped aside so that Yves could leave.

As he passed her house, Louisette Anquetille opened the door and peered into the darkness until she could make out Yves walking past.

"So, who was it?" she shouted. "What's going on up there?"

"Go back to bed, Madame Anquetille. Everything is all right."

"And what about the light?" she said. "Who's up there?"

"Gypsies," said Yves.

"Gypsies?" she said. *"Mon dieu."*

"Just children, madame. Gypsy kids. Kids being kids. I sent them home."

"You're just a kid yourself," said Madame Anquetille with a snort, and closed her door.

"Oui, madame," said Yves.

The next day he filled out his report and took it to the mayor. "It was just as you said, Monsieur Mayor. It was Gypsies. I chased them away. Here's your copy." He handed the mayor a description of his encounter with the children, how he had admonished them and chased them back to their encampment on the edge of town.

"So," said the mayor, studying Yves. "Gypsies."

# VI.

ONESIME KNOCKED LOUDLY on the heavy door, and Maurice de Beaumont appeared. "Monsieur," said Onesime, "I think today is a good day to cut hay." Maurice stepped outside. The two men stood in front of the château on the terrace. It was made of flagstones with moss growing between them and, like the back terrace, it was surrounded by a low stone balustrade.

"Yes," said Maurice, squinting into the bright September sky. Tiny clouds drifted here and there. "Where will you start?"

"I'll start out back, if that is convenient with you, and then get the outlying fields tomorrow. It looks like a very sweet crop. What with all the rain we've had."

"That's fine, Onesime."

"I just wanted to be sure to tell you, monsieur. Before I get the horses."

"Thank you, Onesime. Only use the tractor. I'll unlock the barn."

"The tractor, monsieur? You have petrol?"

"For now I do. Use the tractor."

Maurice went inside and returned with a ring of keys. The two men walked around the house to the barn. Onesime avoided looking at the terrace where he had listened to Marie Piano play.

They approached a great stone building with enormous wooden doors suspended from rollers on metal tracks. The count unlocked the padlock and slid the doors aside. The tractor was parked just inside, covered with a tarpaulin. The two men pulled the tarpaulin aside. Onesime climbed onto the seat of the tractor, pulled out the choke, and pressed the ignition switch. After several tries, the engine started with a roar. Gray smoke belched from the exhaust stack.

Outside, the count pulled a cover from the mower bar while Onesime drove the tractor from the barn. The two men maneuvered the bar into place and secured the hitch. "Off you go, Onesime," said the count.

"Oui, monsieur," said Onesime, and saluted. The tractor sputtered and bucked a bit, and he closed the choke. He put the tractor in gear and drove away as the count stood and watched. Onesime drove through the trees and past a small pond. A heron stood peering into the water. It took flight as the tractor approached.

When Onesime broke from the trees, the sun nearly blinded him. The hay lay before him, a sea of various greens with bits of color where wildflowers were in bloom. Onesime drove to the edge of the field. He pulled the lever that lowered the mower bar until it hung close above the ground. He pushed another lever, and the mower blade started slicing back and forth. He put the tractor in gear and began cutting.

The grass collapsed in apparent ecstasy as the mower touched it, as though it had been waiting for this moment. The sweet aroma of the hay filled Onesime's nostrils. He closed his eyes briefly and smiled to himself. He did not breathe too deeply or the dust would make him sneeze. The seat of the tractor was heavily sprung, and Onesime bounced up and down easily as he mowed up one side of the field, around the edges, and down the other side. He went around the field, moving in toward the center after each circuit.

It was a large undulating field, and it took him the rest of the day to cut it all. Mowing with the horses would have taken longer. The new hay lay on the ground like a great, fragrant blanket. Birds came from everywhere to feast on the insects he had stirred up. He drove back to the barn and dropped the mower bar where he had picked it up. He left the tractor inside the barn. He found his bicycle where he had left it and rode home.

The next day he was back early to get the tractor and mow the other fields. He stopped at the château, and Maurice again accompanied him to the barn. He filled the tank with petrol from a great, black storage tank at the back of the barn. Again the count helped Onesime mount the mower bar. Then he rode with him to the front gate.

Maurice stood lightly on one foot on the tractor step and held on to the handle at the top of the engine cover. When they reached the gate, he hopped down and unlocked the gate. He swung one side of it open and waved Onesime through. "I will leave it unlocked until you get back," he said. Onesime touched his hand to his cap and drove off down the road.

The day was as beautiful as the day before had been, and Onesime was happy to be out on the tractor. The fields he would cut today lay two kilometers west of town, just below the Beaumont vineyards. This was a parcel of smaller fields. They adjoined one another but were separated by fences or by the Dême, which wound its way through and between them. Mowing here was more complicated but also more amusing. And Onesime could take his lunch beside the small river or in the shade beside one of the *maisons des vignes,* the small huts scattered here and there in the vineyards overlooking the fields.

The cutting went well. Onesime maneuvered the tractor along the bank of the river by the poplars. He mowed around the periphery of the field. Then he went back and forth across the field inside the border he had cut. The delicious smell of the cut grass almost made him giddy.

He decided to have his lunch at the hut just above where he had been cutting. He pulled the tractor up beside it and opened the hamper, where his mother had put half a baguette, a small round of goat cheese from old Monsieur Courbeau, and a jar of tea. There were radishes from the garden too and a peach.

Onesime spread his jacket on the ground in the shade in front of the little house. He could see the entire valley spread out before him. There was Saint-Léon in the distance, up against the ridge that formed the other side of the valley. Off to the north was the village of L'Homme and its network of farm roads. Someone was cutting hay by L'Homme. Onesime could not tell who it was, but the air was so dry and still that he could hear the *clack-clack* of the sickle bar and the clucking of the driver as he urged his horse along. In another direction two men were cutting a small field with scythes. It looked like the Livrists, Marie Piano's brothers, even though they too were too far away for him to be sure.

Maurice de Beaumont had been the first farmer in the valley to have a tractor, and there were still only a few of them around. Everyone else mowed behind horses or by hand. It still made sense to cut hay that way. The fields were small, and you could get more of the hay than you could with a tractor. With a tractor there was more waste. And now there was the problem getting petrol.

Some had already managed to rake their hay into windrows, and in one field—he thought it must be Bandot; they always managed to be early—they had already mounded the hay into long coils ready to be loaded onto wagons and taken into the barn.

A truck lumbered along the main road that passed through L'Homme in the direction of Le Mans. Onesime heard the bells on the church in L'Homme and then a minute later those in Saint-Léon. It was noon. He sat with his legs drawn up and his arms around his knees.

A small convoy of dark green trucks came slowly down the highway. They turned up a narrow road in his direction. Onesime did not know why he did it exactly, but he slid farther back into the shade to be out of sight. As the trucks reached the Bandot place, they turned south. Each truck had to stop and back up several times to negotiate the narrow turn between the house and barn. They proceeded slowly and then stopped maybe four or five hundred meters from where he sat. The drivers turned off their engines and stepped out of the cabs. He could hear their voices as they hollered to one another.

"I could have understood their words if I had known German," he said to Jean that evening as they were clearing the supper table. "They unloaded something."

"Bandot's cave?" said Jean.

"Either his or the one next to it. I think that one belongs to the count, but I'm not sure."

"The count has lots of caves," said Jean. "I doubt that he even knows where they all are."

"Do you?" said Onesime.

Jean laughed.

"I had my binocs," said Onesime. "I got the truck numbers."

"What are you boys going on about?" said Anne Marie Josquin from the next room.

"Oni needs me to help him with Beaumont's hay," said Jean.


The next day the beautiful weather continued and so did the hay making all over the valley. Onesime and Jean went out to turn the hay Onesime had cut.

"Shall we do it by hand?" Onesime asked.

"Take the tractor," said the count.

They attached the rake behind the tractor and drove out to the fields. They took turns driving the tractor. The rake had many long legs, like a row of grasshoppers. The legs contracted and rotated on springs that released them so that they tossed the hay in the air. Whoever was walking behind caught the hay on a large wooden fork and shook and turned it and spread it on the ground so that it would dry more quickly and more evenly. It was important to have the hay completely dry. Two years before, a farmer in the next valley by Bueil-en-Touraine had taken his hay in too soon. As it settled in the barn, the moisture still in the hay caused it to begin decomposing, which caused it to heat up. A week after he had taken it in, the smoldering hay burst into flame, and an hour later the barn was in ruins.

After a few hours Onesime and Jean sat in front of the hut and ate their lunch. The convoy Onesime had seen arrive the day before was gone. He trained the binoculars on where the Bandot cave must be, but the angle from here was bad, and there was nothing to be seen.

"Let me look," said Jean. He peered through the binoculars. "There are quite a few caves down there," he said. "Including Bandot's, which is pretty shallow, and some Beaumont caves. I don't know how deep they are."

"Have you been in them?"

"Bandot's, once," said Jean. "To taste his wine. That whole lane there—you see where the willow is?—has caves all along it."

"Look at that," said Onesime. Jean lowered the binoculars and looked in the direction Onesime was pointing. "It's Beaumont's car, isn't it?"

Jean lifted the binoculars. "It is."

"Is he alone?"

"He's alone." They watched the car approach and then turn where the trucks had turned.

"He's stopping right by Bandot's cave. Right where the Germans were."

"What's he up to?" said Jean. "He's getting out. He's by himself. He's carrying something."

"Can you see what it is?"

"No. It looks like something long, something rolled up. Like a carpet or something."

"Let's go see," said Onesime.

Jean lowered the glasses. "You mean sneak up on him?"

"No. We don't have to sneak. He knows we're here. We can just go down. It's perfectly normal."

They stopped the tractor behind the gray sedan. There were tire marks in the dust where the German trucks had stopped the day before. The count was nowhere in sight. The heavy wooden door to one of the caves was open, and they could see that an electric light was on. Onesime walked to the door of the cave. "Monsieur," he called. "Are you there? Monsieur?"

There was no answer, so Onesime stepped inside. He called again.

"Who is it?" said Beaumont, coming from farther inside. "What do you want?" Onesime and Jean were silhouettes against the open door.

"It's me, Onesime Josquin, monsieur. Jean is here too. Is everything all right? Do you need any help?"

"Ah, Onesime," he said. "It's you. No. No, thank you, I don't need any help. Thank you." He stepped into the light. His pants were dusty, and he brushed them off. "What are you doing here? Hello, Jean."

"Hello, monsieur," said Jean, and removed his cap as though they were in the count's home.

"We were having lunch at one of the huts. We saw you drive up and wondered if you needed a hand," said Onesime.

"And we wanted to tell you," said Jean, looking at Onesime. "We're only about a third done, so we're not going to finish."

"That's right, monsieur. It's thick, and it's taking more time to rake and turn than the earlier crop. There's more hay than last year. It's a good year, isn't it, Jean? So I don't know how long it will take, and once it's ready I don't know whether it will fit in the second barn. You should probably open the third barn, just in case. And we might need some help to get it in. I can get two others to help, and we can get it done faster."

"We already talked about that, Onesime," said the count.

"I know," said Onesime, "but not about the extra barn. I wanted to ask you about that specifically."

"It's empty," said Beaumont. "I'll open it and clean it out."

"I know the roof is fixed," said Onesime. "Do you want any help cleaning it out?"

"The roof is fixed," said the count. "It's mostly cleaned out already."

"All right then; thank you, monsieur," said Onesime. "If you need any help with it, let us know. We'll get back to raking then, right, Jean? The weather is perfect, so we better get back to it."

They were about to leave when Onesime stopped and turned. "By the way, monsieur, there were some Germans here yesterday. A convoy. I thought you should know, monsieur."

The count stood silently for a moment before he spoke. "A convoy, you say? Here?"

"Oui, monsieur. They seemed to unload something into one of the caves. I couldn't tell which one. But since your cave is here, I thought you should know."

The count paused again before he said, "Well, that doesn't concern me, does it? And don't let it concern you." Another pause. "But thank you for telling me."

"Very well, monsieur. Well, Jean, let's go. We have some hay to cut."

The count watched the two men turn to leave. Then he said, "Wait a minute. Before you go, there is something you can help me with. Come with me. Both of you. There are some timbers I've got stored here that I wanted to move eventually. And since you're here, I can't do it by myself, and since you're here . . . follow me." He turned and walked into the cave.

An electric line looped along the ceiling, and every fifteen meters or so a bare bulb was attached to the top of the rough stone vault. The light they put out was dim, and so the three men moved mainly in darkness between islands of twilight. They walked on for two hundred meters and then turned abruptly to the left. A locked door blocked their way. The count took a large key from his pocket, unlocked the door, and pushed it open. They stepped inside.

They found themselves in an enormous rectangular room lit by one bare bulb suspended from the center of the ceiling. There was a large fireplace in one wall. The floor was partly covered with huge stone tiles. There was a pile of timbers in the center of the room. A large wooden tablet was leaning against the wall opposite the fireplace. There were a table and some chairs beside the tablet. What looked like a rolled-up carpet lay across the table.

"I want to move these timbers to the side of the room," said the count.

"Where do you want us to take them, monsieur?" asked Jean.

"Just over there and against the wall," said the count. "Out of the way."

"And what about all this," said Onesime, pointing to the tablet and the furniture.

"That stays where it is," said the count.

The men carried the timbers to the side of the cave.

"Did someone live here once?" said Onesime, looking at the carved fireplace and the high ceiling.

"During the revolution. Some of the Beaumonts hid here."

"You could almost live here now," said Jean.

"I doubt it," said Beaumont. "And why would you want to?"

"Who locks a cave inside a cave?" said Onesime as they drove the tractor back up the hill. "And what was on that big wooden tablet?"

"A map," said Jean.

"You saw it?"

"One corner was pulled away from the board. It looked like a map."

"Of what?"

"I don't know. But it was a map. It was white with green and red roads."

"Was it a military map?" Onesime had seen military maps that used those colors.

"I couldn't tell," said Jean.

"And what about his reaction to the Germans?" said Onesime.

"Seemed normal to me," said Jean.

"Maybe. But was it that he didn't care or already knew? I have to think, if the Germans were doing something next door to *my* cave, I'd be interested."

"Maybe he already knew. Would your reaction be any different if someone told you the Germans were in Grandfather's cave? I mean, you don't know how to react, do you? If you're too interested, they might think . . . one thing; if you're not interested enough, they'll think something else. Since the Germans arrived, words have lots of meanings they didn't have before."

"It was like he wanted us to see the room, to know it was there," said Onesime.

When they had turned all the hay, Onesime climbed down from the tractor. He took a rake and joined Jean raking the hay into windrows. Insects rose everywhere, and birds darted to and fro. Swallows swooped close to the two men as they worked their way up the field and then back down again. Some years you had to wait days before you could take in the hay. But it had not rained for two weeks, and the weather was hot and dry. The hay would be dry enough in one more day to put in the barn.

The next morning when Onesime and Jean arrived, Jacques Courtois and August Pappe were already waiting. Their bicycles were leaning against a post. They stood with their rakes under their arms. They put out their cigarettes in the dust, pulled their caps down low over their eyes, and the four men began working, turning and collecting the windrows and shaping them into stacks two meters high and two meters wide. When one stack was finished they moved down the row and began the next. Most people in this part of the country put their hay in coils, but the count liked his hay stacked just in case rain came before they got it all in, even though no rain was expected. They worked quickly, and by the end of the morning they had finished stacking two-thirds of the hay.

Onesime looked across the rest of the field. "We can get some into the barn yet today," he said. "But tomorrow looks good too."

The men sat in the shade by the wine hut. They would have avoided the climb if they could have, but it was hot and there was no deep shade anywhere else. They looked out over the fields. Someone was cutting a small field. You could see three men swinging scythes. It looked like Bandot and his sons. In the clear air you could hear them whet their blades every few minutes, first one then another. It sounded like birds calling back and forth.

Nothing was going on at the caves. The four men ate their lunch, tearing chunks off loaves of bread, cutting pieces of cheese, and pulling at a bottle of wine they shared. Except for Onesime, who drank tea from a jar. "What's that you're drinking?" said Jacques, even though he knew Onesime drank tea. "You might as well be a goddamn Englishman." Onesime did not answer.

"And what," said Jacques, making what he took to be a fancy gesture, "is with the napkin?" Onesime had tucked his handkerchief under his chin. Wearing a napkin when he ate was a habit he had carried over from childhood, and because it was slightly eccentric, it pleased him and he continued to do it. Again Onesime did not answer and Jacques let it rest.

"What do you make of Renard?" said August, looking for something to talk about. Jacques's teasing had made him uncomfortable.

"Renard?" said Onesime.

"Yves. The cop," said August.

"He caught us butchering a hog the other night up in the old Tricon place. Old lady Anquetille reported us," said Jacques, and laughed.

"It's not so funny," said August. "The Germans don't show much mercy with that kind of thing."

"The Germans," said Jacques. "Do the Germans give a shit about a pig?"

"Renard's all right," said Jean.

"All right? He was there to report us," said Jacques. "We gave some pork to the mayor to put the lid on it, but Renard still showed up."

"Did he file the report?" said Onesime.

"Schneider said he did," said August. "But Schneider's sitting on it."

"Or so he says," said Jacques. "But Yves Renard was always a jerk."

"Maybe," said Jean. "But I don't think he'd work with the Germans."

"Sure he would," said Jacques. "He's a cop. Who else is he going to work for? The cops work with whoever's in charge. And even if it weren't his job, he's the type. He's afraid of them."

———

In his room that night Onesime worked on his map. He drew Bandot's farm, his cave, the Beaumont vineyards and caves. He drew the big room they had visited as best as he could locate it, and then on a transparent overlay on onionskin he added the numbers of the four trucks and the date. He knew they belonged to an artillery battalion. The map was now full of information about trucks, numbers of men, movements of *matériel* from one cave to another. He now knew most of the caves the Germans had appropriated. When Jean knocked on the door, Onesime said, "Come in," without putting the map away.

Onesime expected to be scolded by his older brother. Instead Jean said, "You've been paying attention." He studied the map. "I'm impressed," he said. "What do you plan to do with it?"

"Nothing," said Onesime. "It just interests me." Then: "Who knows? It might be useful someday."

"Do you think so?" said Jean. He considered Onesime's map for a moment. "I'll be right back," he said, and left the room. When he returned he was carrying a large black ledger under his arm. He put it on Onesime's table beside the map and opened it to the first page. It appeared to be a sort of logbook or calendar. Each page had a date at the top followed by columns of entries. Jean wrote in large round letters like a schoolboy. Everything was clearly legible, although the meaning of things was not readily apparent.

"What is it? What's this?" said Onesime, pointing to the first entry.

"Nine-forty, that's the time—9:40; *CB* means Cheval Blanc, and the name followed by *in* means that person went in, and *out* means that person came out. The notes say anything else I noticed at the time. Like here, at 9:40 Schneider went in and came out here, at 10:04. He was carrying a briefcase."

"How did you see all this?"

"I work at Melun's, remember? And I get our rations. I don't see everything, and I'm not there all the time. But the lines are long, and when I'm waiting I watch. I mean bread, groceries, it's all right by the hotel. Look: Here's the German colonel leaving with his driver and going east out of town. And here . . ."—he turned a few pages—"here they are again the next day leaving in the same direction at the same time."

"Where are they going, I wonder," said Onesime.

"I don't know. Toward Villedieu, but once they leave the square I don't know."

"Let me see something," said Onesime, turning a few pages ahead, then back. He found an entry that had the colonel leaving with his driver. It was the evening he had seen them at the count's. "They went to a party at the château here," he said. "I saw them."

"You were there?" said Jean. "So that's where you went."

"I was. I went to explore Beaumont's cave. I followed it to Grand-father's. But there was a party, and I looked through the windows."

"I'll write it down," he said. "Who else did you see?" He paused in his writing.

Onesime tried to remember. "The count. His wife. The colonel. Maybe another German in plain clothes. Monsieur Dupont. Madame Terterrain. The priest—what's his name? Father something. Some others I don't know. A German in uniform was outside with the cars. Probably the driver. I have the numbers of some of the other cars on the map. And Marie Piano."

"Marie Piano was there? Really?"

"She sang. In German."

Onesime suddenly felt slightly dizzy. He was struck by the momentousness of what he and Jean were doing, by how dangerous it was. "We're spying, Jean. Aren't we?" He spoke softly.

"I guess you could say we are spying," said Jean, "although I don't think of it that way. I mean, we're not working for anyone."

"Still. They'd kill us for this if they caught us."

"So why are you doing it?"

"I don't really know," said Onesime. "Isn't that amazing when you think about it? It just somehow seems right to do it. But I don't really know why. I'm not spying for anybody. Are you?"

"No," said Jean. "Like who?"

"I don't know. The English maybe."

"Me? No," said Jean. "Are you against the Germans?" Jean was whispering now.

"Yes. I was in the war against them. Although I can't say I feel anything much about them. I didn't have to shoot them. But I would have. Still, I don't like having them running things, no matter how bad our own government was. I just don't like it. This is France, not Germany."

"Me either," said Jean. "I hate that they killed Papa and Uncle in the Great War. And just seeing them in their trucks and uniforms makes me angry. I mean, it's like we're prisoners in our own town. In our own house. I just go out, and sooner or later I run into them and feel like I'm in prison and they're the guards. That makes it feel almost natural to work against them."

"I guess so," said Onesime. He paused. "I have the feeling that things are going to get worse too. They'll crack down at some point, come down hard on somebody for something. And when they do, then I *will* be against them. Automatically. Definitely. I'll have to be against them. There won't be a choice. I might as well get ready for that day. Then all this—my map and your diary—might be important. Do you think we're the only ones?"

"The only ones?" said Jean.

"The only ones watching them, keeping track."

"I don't know. But I don't see how we could be."

"Who else do you think could be . . . involved? The way we are, I mean?"

"Involved?" said Jean. "Are we involved in anything?"

"It's not whether we think we're involved in anything. It's what the Germans would think, or the mayor would think, or the police would think. They would all say we're seriously involved, so I guess we are. And you know? I don't think there's any turning back." They sat silently and thought about that for a minute.

"So who else is involved?" said Jean finally. "Do you think the mayor is, or Renard?"

"No," said Onesime. "They can't be. Although they must both know a lot about what's going on. More than we do."

"Do you think they're against the Germans or with them?" said Jean.

"I don't know," said Onesime.

"What about Jacques?"

"Courtois? No, Jacques is mainly a big mouth. If he's up to anything, it's to show off. He'll be the first one to get in trouble. The thing with the pig almost got him in serious trouble. And Renard stopped it."

"What about Monsieur Bertrand? He almost got arrested for speaking out. That's what I heard, anyway."

"What about the count? He's a bit of a puzzle," said Onesime.

"He's been in and out of the Cheval Blanc on a regular basis. And he had that party. And he's got petrol, which makes me wonder how he gets it."

"Yes, but there's the room in the cave and the map turned to the wall. What's he doing with a secret map? Maybe we could get a look at the map. That might tell us something."

"That won't be so easy."

"Nothing's going to be easy from here on out. And the Germans are only going to get tougher as time passes. Someone'll get in trouble, and then they'll crack down hard. Sooner or later it'll happen. It has to. We've got to be careful from now on. Where do you keep your ledger? No, don't tell me. But hide it really well."

"But we should share information."

"Some of it. But not all of it. What we're doing changes things. Even being brothers."

# VII.

THE GERMAN OCCUPATION had changed everything in Saint-Léon-sur-Dême. And it had changed nothing. The people went about their business as usual. They tended their gardens, their chickens, their goats. They picked the count's grapes and the grapes in the other vineyards. They crushed them in the big wooden hoppers. The sweet liquid drizzled into barrels, which were rolled into the caves to ferment and age. They made cheese, they gathered eggs, milked their cows, and traded with one another—cheese for eggs, milk for cigarettes, lettuce for peas or potatoes. They fished in the Dême. The days shortened, the weather cooled, the shadows grew longer.

The severe shortages and deprivation that people in the cities and larger towns suffered as rationing tightened did not come to the French countryside. Some things were in short supply of course. But no one was going hungry, as they were in Paris or Tours or Le Mans. Everyone in Saint-Léon had potatoes and squashes and pumpkins spread on the floors in their cellars and caves. They had stores of wine and brandy and honey and cheese. They learned to make coffee from barley, and tea from mint and chamomile. They went to the forests and woodlots to cut firewood for their stoves, as they always had.

The last hay had been cut and put away. The winter wheat was planted. Hunting season came, and the count invited Colonel Büchner to hunt with him. The colonel accepted his invitation. The hunting party shot pheasant and rabbit and boar.

It seems astonishing now, but Pétain and his colleagues in Vichy, the mayors and other officials of Tours and Le Mans and Nantes, even most officials of the small towns and villages behaved as though the German occupiers were their partners. They truly seemed to expect that the spirit of collaboration and cooperation would continue and would hold the wrath of the Nazi regime at bay indefinitely. And their citizens by and large believed it too.

In July the Free French radio had reported from London that there had been a plot against Hitler by some of his own generals. There had been arrests in Germany and in Paris, and more arrests were expected.

*"Even the Führer's own generals know him to be an insatiable monster. They know he is driving his own country—and all of Europe—to ruin. Do not be fooled, Frenchmen, Frenchwomen. Do not be seduced by the smooth face of collaboration. Collaboration is wicked at its very heart. General Pétain is a traitor to France."*

"They are wearing gold stars in Tours," said Claude Melun one rainy morning. He had just come back from the city where he had gone to get bicycle parts.

"Gold stars?" said Jean. "Who is wearing gold stars?"

"Jews are. To show that they're Jews," said Claude. "I saw them. And shops have had signs painted on them saying they belong to Jews."

Jean said nothing.

"I'm just saying . . . ," said Claude, but he did not know how he should finish the sentence. He determined that he would return to Tours again for a better look.

"Let me know when you go," said Jean.

The shortage of petrol meant steady work for Jean and Claude at Claude's shop. A lot of bicycles were being pulled out of barns and sheds and were in need of rehabilitation. Claude had also figured out how to retrofit gasoline engines—on motorcycles in particular, but also in cars—so they would run on kerosene. He was trying to figure out how to make a car run on wood.

Most nights Jean and Onesime compared notes and exchanged information. Onesime had a series of maps covering all of the months of occupation. He went around the valley, buying cheese from Courbeau, trading bread his mother baked, milk from the cow, butter and eggs for what he could get, and gathering information.

The more Jean and Onesime discovered, the more complete the picture of the occupation of Saint-Léon emerged. By laying maps and logs side by side, they could track the expansion of the German network of caves, the patterns of importation of *matériel* by truck and by train, as well as which caves were being used for the storage of which *matériel*. There were artillery shells in some, stores of petrol and kerosene in others. Some appeared to be emergency bunkers, and two had been outfitted to become field hospitals, if the need arose. There were also stockpiles of automatic weapons, of uniforms, and of small canisters, which Onesime speculated might contain poison gas.

"We had a general here last week," said Louisette Anquetille. "He passed right by here in a big sedan."

"A general?" said Onesime. He sounded doubtful. He looked at his feet and shuffled them through the leaves that had blown into a pile by her doorstep. "Here are the eggs you wanted. Four, you said. Is that right?"

"I know a German general when I see one," she said. "He went up to Ageneau's farm, turned around, and came back. I saw him twice."

Jean kept the door of the mechanic's shop open so he could see what was going on. "Close the door," said Claude. "Jesus. It's freezing out there."

"Well, it's too hot in here," Jean said.

Claude put another log in the stove.

Colonel Büchner's weekly departures toward Villedieu eventually took him to Tours to meet with his superior, General Otto von

Wuthenow, the general Madame Anquetille had seen. "There he goes," said a customer, nodding in the direction of the hotel. The colonel's car was pulling away. Jean was working on the man's bicycle. He focused on the chain wheel he was repairing. "Hold this," he said to the man, as he strained to loosen the rusty connection. Jean leaned on the large wrench, and the wheel broke free.

"You know where he goes?" said the man. He wanted to talk.

"Who?" said Jean.

"Your colonel."

"No, where?" said Jean, trying to sound indifferent.

"He goes to Tours," said the man.

"That's not the way to Tours," said Jean.

"He goes by way of Troppard."

"Troppard? Where's that?"

"The widow Troppard. Her husband was killed at Verdun."

"Do you know Madame Troppard?" Jean asked his mother that evening. They were eating the last of a bread pudding Madame Josquin had made the day before.

"In Villedieu? I do," she said. "Edith Troppard. Her husband died at Verdun the same day your father did."

The two sons sat silently for a long time.

Finally Jean spoke. "Someone was talking about her today. At the shop."

"You mean about the German colonel?" said their mother.

Jean and Onesime did not conceal their astonishment.

"Why are you looking at me that way?" she asked.

"How did you know that?" said Jean.

"I know a lot of things you don't know," said Anne Marie. "Why should that surprise you?"

"What things?" Both Jean and Onesime spoke.

"For one thing," she said, "I know loneliness." She rose from the table to clear dishes. Her sons watched her.

"How did you know about the German colonel?" Onesime said.

"I go to town too," she said. "I talk to friends. Now don't you interrogate me. And until you lose your spouse and have lived with that loss for half a lifetime, don't you dare judge anyone who has."

"The German . . . ," began Jean.

"His name is Helmut Büchner," she said. "He is a widower."

"You know him?" said Jean.

"I know about him," said Anne Marie.

Back in his room Onesime looked at the maps and overlays he had drawn. He turned them over one by one. Jean knocked and came in.

"What are we doing?" said Onesime. "What is all this?" He waved his hand at the stack of maps.

"I know," said Jean. "That was a surprise to me."

"Do you think she knows what we've been doing?" said Onesime.

"I didn't think so before. Now I don't know."

"Do you think she would be . . . against it?" said Onesime. "Against our doing it?"

"I don't know," said Jean.

"Should we tell her?" said Onesime.

"No," said Jean.

"Aren't we placing her in danger?"

Jean did not answer. Finally he said, "Yes, I think we are. Either way, we're placing her in danger. Whether we tell her or not."

"Still," said Onesime, "we should talk to her. We have to talk to her. We can't just leave it like this." The two men went down the narrow, sloping stairs. Their mother's room was behind the kitchen. Her door was closed. Jean raised his hand to knock and then stopped. He put his finger in front of his lips. "Listen," he whispered.

Onesime inclined his head toward the door. His mother had the radio on. The signal was very poor and there was a lot of static, so she had turned up the volume as loud as she dared. Onesime pressed his ear to the door. He heard someone speaking English, which he could not understand. Then someone began in French.

*"My fellow citizens, Frenchmen, Frenchwomen, I send you greetings, during this, France's darkest hour. I am speaking to you from*

*London, where thousands of French heroes, brave men and women, have assembled with the sole purpose of rescuing our imperiled country from the invaders. We may accomplish this with the aid of our English allies. But nothing can be accomplished without you. You are now the guardians of our great and noble civilization. The Nazi occupiers will do everything they can to break your spirit. They will try to divide you, Frenchman against Frenchman, but it is up to you to resist. . . ."*

Onesime turned toward Jean and motioned urgently with his hands to leave. "It's de Gaulle!" he whispered once they were back upstairs. "She's listening to General de Gaulle!"

All over France people were listening to Charles de Gaulle speaking from England. They leaned toward their radios and listened as though their very own fate were addressing them, finding its way faintly though clearly through the static and the jamming directly into their souls.

The next morning Saint-Léon-sur-Dême awoke to discover that during the night someone had painted red *V*'s and Lorraine crosses— symbols of resistance—all over town. They were on lampposts and road signs and walls, even on the front walls of the Cheval Blanc and the police station. Some of the graffiti had already been scrubbed away by villagers worried about making the Germans angry. German soldiers were working furiously on the rest. Before ten o'clock the marks were gone, and only faint *V*- and cross-shaped scrub marks remained.

"Who did it?" Jean asked, when he arrived at the shop.

"There's a lot of speculation," said Claude Melun, "but nobody knows."

By the next morning the villains had been caught, and everybody knew. Stephane and Antoine Duquesne, seventeen- and fifteen-year-old brothers, had been denounced by someone in the village. They were escorted into the Hôtel de France by German soldiers. Antoine was crying. After a short time a black Citroën left the hotel's courtyard and sped away with the two boys inside.

Yves Renard and Michel Schneider were summoned to the Cheval Blanc. "I am pleased to learn," said Schneider, before he was seated, "that you have the culprits in custody. As you can see, *Herr Oberst*, our citizens are true to the armistice and loyal to the collaboration. They have taken it upon themselves to see that the wrongdoers were immediately turned over to you."

Colonel Büchner studied the mayor's face for a long moment. "I am afraid, Monsieur Mayor, that the situation is far more serious than that. It has already gone beyond that. This is exactly the kind of civil disobedience I had hoped to avoid. I have military duties, and I had hoped that I could entrust the orderly governance of Saint-Léon to you and your council."

"But, with due respect, *Herr Oberst*—"

The colonel raised his hand and cut the mayor short. "I already said, it is too late for that, Mayor. These things always have a way of escalating. What may seem a harmless prank—"

"Harmless? By no means, Herr . . ."

"What you may consider a harmless prank, Monsieur Mayor, is precisely the sort of thing that will escalate into terrorism unless it is stopped cold. We have stopped it cold, and I consider the matter closed. The perpetrators are on their way to Tours to be tried. They will be dealt with harshly, as a deterrent to others who might want to follow suit."

"But, *Herr Oberst*," said the mayor, "they are boys. It was a prank, nothing more. Surely we can deal with it. . . ."

"And you, Renard, what do you have to say about this business?" The colonel leaned toward the policeman. He seemed genuinely curious to hear the young gendarme's response.

"Nothing, Monsieur Colonel."

Both the mayor and colonel studied the young policeman. He sat looking straight ahead.

"Nothing," said the colonel. "I see."

"Nothing?!" said the mayor, after he and Yves were back in the policeman's office. "That was all you could think of?! That is what happens when they send a boy to do a man's work. You should have offered reassurances, measures you would take."

"Which measures might those be, Monsieur Schneider? I am alone in this office, the only gendarme in town. Without assistance. Without power. Which measures can I take to assure that things that I don't know about do not happen? If the boys had been reported to me instead of denounced to the Germans, I could have taken measures. But they were not reported to me."

Stephane and Antoine Duquesne were quickly brought to trial. Their appointed attorney argued that their youth was to blame. They had been incited by the broadcasts being beamed from England. What they had done surely must be considered mischief and not a crime.

The judge was not persuaded. He found them guilty of seditious and terroristic acts. Because of their youth, they were sentenced to only five years at the nearby detention camp at Saint-Pierre-des-Corps. Their parents were summoned to the Cheval Blanc, where they were taken to a small, windowless room in the upper stories of the building and seated on straight-backed chairs under a bright lamp. They were interrogated by Lieutenant Ludwig and three Germans in plain clothes: Had the Duquesne parents been listening to the prohibited radio broadcasts? Did the parents know whether their children had? Did any of them entertain anti-German sympathies? Did they know anyone who did?

The questioning was difficult and lasted several hours. It ended with stern warnings that even the slightest infraction by their other three children or by themselves would lead to harsh punishment for everyone in the household. If any information of subversive activity came to their attention and they did not report it, that would also lead to harsh punishment for them all. Monsieur and Madame Duquesne left the hotel with their heads bowed. People on the square looked away as they passed.

That same afternoon three Germans in dark suits and ties appeared at Yves Renard's office. The man in charge was short and portly. He introduced himself as Lieutenant Essart and explained that because Yves was in the impossible situation of policing the entire town by himself, they were there to assist him. "You will of course still be the principal law-enforcement entity in town.

"As you might imagine"—Lieutenant Essart smiled—"we have had experience in matters like these. We will support your enforcement efforts in every way we can. You will have our authority behind you when it is required. Colonel Büchner is concerned that we maintain a discreet presence, and of course we would like to oblige him."

"I understand," said Yves. "It is reassuring to know that I will have your help."

"I am gratified," said Essart, "that you see things that way."

The lieutenant sat down in the chair facing Yves Renard's desk, carefully crossing one leg over the other. "Please." He motioned for Yves to take a seat. "Tell me what you can about suspicious activity in your town, any seditious or otherwise illegal activity, any people who bear watching. That sort of thing." He smiled again. His tone was friendly and confiding.

Yves considered the question for a long moment. "There is no one who comes to mind," he said. "You already have the two young malefactors in custody. Other than that . . . that is the first disobedience I am aware of. This is a quiet and peaceful town, as you can see. Of course, if I learn of anything, I will notify you immediately."

Lieutenant Essart studied the young gendarme. "So," he said finally. "Quiet and peaceful. If you say so. Before we leave, however, we would like to have a look at your files. Going back to the beginning of the year." Without waiting for Yves to respond, the men opened his file drawers and leafed through them, pulling out several folders and setting them aside. When they had finished, they slid the files they had removed into an envelope and closed the drawers.

"So," said Essart with a narrow smile, "it is, as you say, a quiet and peaceful village where nothing goes on. No Jews, no Gypsies, no communists, no sedition, no crime. That must be very gratifying. You must be an excellent policeman, Monsieur Renard. You have my congratulations." Lieutenant Essart signaled his two colleagues with his eyes. All three rose and left.

No Jews. No Gypsies. Yves sat at his desk for a long time and thought back to a moment just before the Germans had arrived. Had it only been weeks, or had it been a lifetime?

He had been in line to buy bread, when the two women behind him began talking in stage whispers. "Did you see the Jews staying at the hotel? There were two families of them." The women kept glancing at Yves to make certain he was listening.

"Jews? Really?" said the other woman. "What did they look like?"

"They wore all black. Even the children. And they were dark. With large noses. You know. The men had broad hats and strange hair, and the women were covered with shawls. They were from Poland. At least that is what Monsieur Dufresne said—from Poland. He said they had been driven out of their homes, and their houses were burned. But who knows. . . ."

"The Jews, they make that stuff up."

"Monsieur Dufresne said they are going south. They must be ten altogether. They had a car."

"How did Jews from Poland manage to get a car?"

"Exactly. Do you know, Yves,"—the women turned to him—"how they managed to get a car?"

"I suppose they bought it," said Yves.

"They did have to register with you, didn't they? As foreigners, I mean?"

"They filled out registration cards at the hotel. As everyone must," said Yves. "We have their cards on file if we need them." He was relieved when his turn came to buy bread. He had his ration card stamped, paid quickly, and tucked the half baguette under his arm. "Good evening," he said, and left the shop.

Now the Gestapo—for that was who Essart and his companions

were—had taken the Jews' registrations forms. They had also taken Yves's false report about the Gypsy children.

That was how things worked. You blamed Jews or Gypsies because everybody thought of them that way. They bore the mark of Cain, his father used to say. Blaming Gypsy children had allowed Yves to avoid pressing charges against Jacques Courtois. Not that he liked Courtois and his friends. But they were Frenchmen.

Michel Schneider, the mayor, had known of course that it had been Courtois and not Gypsy children in the house. But as far as the mayor was concerned, Gypsies were thieves and wastrels and deserved whatever they got. The mayor had not forwarded the young policeman's report about the Gypsies, but only because he had found it convenient for the moment that Courtois and the others believed the policeman had reported them and that he, the mayor, was their protector.

Colonel Büchner stood at his window and watched the Gestapo men get in their car and drive off. "Damn," he said. He was alone in his office, but still he spoke the word again. "Damn." He did not trust the Gestapo, and he did not relish the idea of Essart looking over his shoulder.

The colonel found himself in a complicated situation. As far as he could tell, the mayor was only out for himself. And Renard, the young policeman, was barely cooperative. And smarter than he gave on. They could both be trouble. The town was calm now. But with the Gestapo messing about, who knew how long it would stay that way? The colonel was trying to put together an arms and fuel depot, and Essart and his thugs were obsessed with finding Jews and malefactors behind every door.

Helmut Büchner could not sleep that night. He could not even close his eyes. He peered into the darkness, as though the solution to his Gestapo problem might be lurking there somewhere. Edith Troppard breathed deeply beside him, her breath issuing from her lips in soft puffs.

Edith wasn't sleeping either. She was pondering instead how her passion and, yes, love, which had died with André at Verdun more than twenty years earlier, had been brought to life again by Helmut Büchner's embrace. Helmut was a German, and though he had not killed André, some German had. And yet Helmut was kind and tender and considerate. Kinder than André had ever been, if she was honest.

The next morning red *V*'s and Lorraine crosses had again been painted on walls and doors. Once again anxious citizens scrubbed and scraped to remove the graffiti, and again German soldiers came behind them with wire brushes and bleach to remove the last remnants.

The pamphlet was another matter. This time someone had also posted a mimeographed sheet all over town. It was tacked to walls and blew about in the streets. German soldiers hurried around picking up the papers wherever they found them. But most of the pages had already disappeared into people's pockets and purses and grocery bags to be read and reread once they were safely home.

The citizens of Saint-Léon were anything but seditious. But like citizens of small towns everywhere, they were hungry for news—good or bad—about their neighbors, about France, about the war. Gossip is the currency of all small towns; malicious or harmless, it makes no difference. It all has the same high value. It fuels the social fires, the alliances and rivalries. It fires people's passions and imaginations. And that is precisely what makes news so dangerous. Or gossip, for they come down to one and the same thing. The homemade pamphlet was like gasoline on a fire. And its author had the audacity and grandiosity to designate the paper, though it was but one side of one page, Issue 1. There would be more, he promised.

Colonel Büchner knew there would be more, probably many more before all was said and done. The secret police, the Gestapo, would be back in short order with their menu of reprisals against the citizens of Saint-Léon, and he, Colonel Büchner, would be helpless to stop them. Then the resolve of the people of Saint-Léon to resist the occupation would materialize where there had been little or no resistance before.

And with each measure taken in reprisal their resolve would stiffen. And there would be nothing anyone could do to stop it. Colonel Büchner laid the sheet on his desk, leaned his head on his hands, and read:

*Liberation* . . . . . . . . . . . . . . . . . . *January 12, 1941. Issue 1*

*The German occupiers are not satisfied to have invaded and violated our country. It is not enough that they have killed more than a hundred thousand of our sons and brothers and fathers on the fields of battle and gravely wounded or imprisoned the rest of them. It is not enough that they have attacked our cities with bombs and artillery. It is not enough for them that they have named the traitor Pétain to lead a government of treasonous collaboration made up of officials who are French but who act more like Germans than the Germans themselves.*

*Now they have begun to take our children from us. The boys Antoine and Stephane Duquesne were taken from their parents, given a phony trial, and put in the Nazi prison near Saint-Pierre-des-Corps. You should know, citizens, this is a prison where the prisoners are abused and starved and otherwise mistreated. The fact that they are only boys, and not men, who committed a foolish but insignificant prank does not seem to matter to their persecutors.*

*Yes, they are persecutors, not prosecutors, for this has nothing to do with the law. The boys were assigned a lawyer, but he was not allowed to make his case or to call witnesses. The judge was French, but in name only. In his judgment he represented the fascist enemy. This trial and sentence does not have to do with keeping order or maintaining the law or justice. It has to do with the complete suppression of our liberty.*

*The Nazis could never commit these atrocities without the assistance of compliant and cowardly Frenchmen and -women. Some have already begun to show their cowardly faces, like the Judge Herr Denis Temoine. Other traitors remain hidden in the shadows. The*

*Duquesne boys were denounced by someone. We will find out who denounced them, and they will be punished. We will name everyone and seek justice for anyone who gives aid and comfort to the Nazi Vichy enemy.*

*Herr Schneider, Chenu, Arnaud, Bertrand, Renard already deserve mention. They are our representatives and our leaders, and yet they did nothing to stop the arrest and persecution of the Duquesne boys. The Gestapo has already set up shop in Herr Renard's office, and he is under their thumb. The people who are supposed to be our protectors have abandoned us. They should be on notice that we will hold them responsible for all abuses the citizens of Saint-Léon-sur-Dême are forced to endure.*

**Vive la France and Vive la Libération!!!!!!!!!!!!!!!**

No one came forward to denounce either the most recent sign painters or the author of the pamphlet, although in the case of the latter, suspicion immediately fell on René Bertrand, the schoolmaster.

Monsieur Bertrand had given long and serious thought to Yves Renard's admonitions of the previous summer and had since then restrained himself from criticizing either the occupation or the collaboration. In fact, he had gone silent. He taught his classes as he was obliged to. He greeted people when he was spoken to, and he conducted his business in the shops, at the bank, at the post office in a courteous manner. But his previous expressive and voluble self had disappeared.

René Bertrand no longer had opinions about anything, when he previously had had them about everything. He avoided political discussions, and when it became impossible to avoid them, he clamped his lips together so firmly, it looked as though his mouth were sewn shut from the inside. He did not smile or frown; his eyebrows remained firmly in place; his eyes did not widen or contract; he did not grimace.

To many it seemed suspicious that someone previously so opinionated and outspoken should suddenly go silent. Add to that the fact that the pamphlet could only have been written by someone especially adept

at lofty language and with a superior mastery of grammar and punc-
tuation, then who else could have done it?

Yves Renard arrived at his office to discover that René Bertrand
was already there and already under interrogation at the expert and
unrelenting hands of Lieutenant Essart and his two Gestapo colleagues.
They had not been at it very long, and yet they had already extracted
incriminating opinions from the terrified schoolmaster. He had been
able to restrain himself among his fellow citizens, but he was no match
for the alternately seductive and brutal Gestapo.

"Ah, Monsieur Renard. Where have you been? No matter. I believe
we have our man—the author of the seditious handbill," said Essart,
without taking his eyes from the cowering schoolmaster.

Yves Renard expressed astonishment at Essart's conclusion. He
was particularly amazed at the fact that the interrogation had proceeded at all without him. "After all, as I recall, Monsieur Lieutenant,
you said that I would still be in charge of—"

"And you would be, Monsieur Renard, if you had not failed to
maintain order as we agreed you would. In fact, you have not main-
tained order by any stretch of the imagination, have you? And things
have gotten out of hand. We are in a critical phase of things, Monsieur
Renard, and your inability, or unwillingness, to control the situation
has been all too evident."

"But Monsieur Lieutenant, that—"

Essart continued to stare at the schoolmaster as he cut off the policeman. "I would guess, Renard, that your skills as a policeman may
be adequate for simple times and ordinary circumstances. But these
are, you must have noticed, not ordinary times. Your schoolmaster has
confessed to harboring terroristic, anticollaboration, and anti-German
opinions and feelings, and we are placing him under arrest."

Yves Renard gazed at the schoolmaster. "And yet," said Renard
after a pause, "Monsieur Bertrand did not write or publish the leaflet."

Essart raised his head and faced Renard for the first time since the
policeman had entered the office. "Really?" he said. Bertrand dared to

raise his face just enough to look into Renard's face. His lip was swollen and purple, and a drop of blood hung from his ear.

"Then who did publish this seditious document, what you call the 'leaflet'?" said Essart.

Yves was relieved to see that he had become the object of Essart's interest. "That is something I am working at finding out," he said.

"I see," said Essart. "You do not actually *know* who published this filth, and yet you are certain it was not the schoolmaster?" Essart's eyes widened and he looked around the room and chuckled. His colleagues smiled back at him.

Yves Renard seemed undeterred. "That is correct, monsieur."

"The only way you could be certain it was not the schoolmaster is if you know who it was," said one of Essart's men. "Do you know who it was?"

"Or," Essart added, "if you did it yourself. Did you write this yourself?"

Yves Renard actually seemed to consider both possibilities for a moment. Then he smiled slightly and said, "There is another possibility, Monsieur Lieutenant."

Essart raised his eyebrows in astonishment. He took a step toward Yves and folded his hands in front of him. At that moment Essart himself looked like an impatient schoolmaster. "Please tell me," he said, "about this other possibility."

"I have been watching the schoolmaster for weeks," said Yves. "He has been teaching his pupils, and that is all he has been doing. He has been teaching them as he is required to. Whatever opinions or statements you might have extracted from him cannot be taken seriously. He was frightened, and he said what he thought you wanted to hear."

"You also know this to be true? That he said what he thought we wanted to hear? You seem to know a great deal more than I could have imagined it was possible for you to know. How do you know so many things? You seem to be a very smart young policeman."

"I only mean to say," said Yves, "that Monsieur Bertrand is brilliant in some things, but not in others. He could never publish such a document. I am certain that, when you do a thorough search of his house, you will not find the machine that was used to print this or any other incriminating evidence. You will not find the paper used or ink-stained rags. Nor was it printed on the mimeograph machine at the school. I have already checked. That machine is always kept under lock and key. There is nothing to connect the schoolmaster to this seditious paper. You have the wrong person."

Bertrand's mouth was opening and closing like a fish gasping for oxygen.

"You seem to have made a thorough study of the matter and of Schoolmaster Bertrand," said Lieutenant Essart. "I wonder why."

"I have investigated many of the goings-on about town. Like you, I am trying to root out any rebellion before it happens. . . ."

"Like us," said Essart. "I see."

"That is my obligation under the terms of the armistice."

"Indeed it is," said Essart. He studied the policeman for a long moment before he spoke again. "Find the author of this . . . trash." He held up the mimeographed sheet. "It is up to you, policeman. If another such provocation occurs, you will answer for it."

"I understand," said Renard. "And what about the schoolmaster?" He regretted the words as soon as they had left his mouth.

"The schoolmaster is under arrest," said Essart. "Was that ever in doubt?" With that, Essart motioned with the fingers of both hands for Bertrand to stand up. Bertrand stood slowly and turned toward the door. His legs started to give way under him, but he caught himself. His back was to Yves, but the policeman could see that his former teacher struggled to compose himself. The three Gestapo surrounded him and escorted him from the office. They put him in the back of the black Citroën.

Essart's Gestapo colleagues also got in the backseat on either side of the schoolmaster. Once they were in the car and the doors were closed, Essart turned and entered Yves Renard's office once again. "Listen to me, my little gendarme," he said before the policeman could say anything. He stepped up to Yves, so that their faces were centimeters apart. "I do not have time to waste on you; I will say it as plainly as I can." Yves could feel the German's breath on his face. He could see the veins in the yellowish whites of his eyes.

"We are not partners. We are not equals. We won this war, and you lost it. Our victory was complete, and so was your defeat. Do not be confused by the armistice. You are entirely under our jurisdiction; it is our law and authority you as a policeman must enforce, not some fanciful version of justice you entertain in your head. You French no longer have any laws that belong to you, except by our sufferance; you have no authority of your own. None. Whatever law and authority seem to remain to you will cease the moment we decide to end them. They will cease the moment you are no longer useful to our purposes.

"Looking at you now"—Essart made a show of actually looking Renard up and down—"I can see why you French lost the war. You are reckless and frivolous and not as smart as you think you are. You are willing to take risks whose consequences you do not understand, to play games whose rules you do not understand.

"The only reason I do not arrest you this very moment, Gendarme Renard, is that you might still be of some use. But be advised: I see through all your maneuvering and obfuscation. I did so from the beginning. And it does not amuse me.

"Do not ever, *ever* try to play clever with me again. Do not ever, *ever* try to lead me astray again." Lieutenant Essart reached inside his jacket and withdrew a black Luger pistol. He held the pistol under Yves's nose, not pointed at him, but so that Yves could smell its oily smell, see the gleam and weight of it, and feel the cold metal next to his skin. "If you ever again attempt what you just attempted with me, I will shoot you dead. And your relatives and your charming village will all come to regret your folly."

Essart slid the gun back inside his jacket, looked into Yves's eyes for another moment, then turned and walked out the door. He got behind the wheel of the Citroën and drove it away.

The schoolmaster was not heard from again.

# VIII.

Young Yves Renard stared through the glass front of his office long after there was anything to look at. Then he turned back to his desk and sat down on the wooden chair where the schoolmaster had sat. Yves reached across the desk and took a cigarette from the blue package lying there. He had difficulty lighting it because his hands were shaking. And even when it was finally lit, the cigarette trembled so terribly that he crushed it out.

Essart was right about him, right about everything, about the game he had been playing, about his feeble attempts at deception. What had he been thinking? He had tried to outsmart and outmaneuver Essart, as though they were playing a chess game and the cleverest player would win. But it was not a chess game. And Yves was not the cleverest player. The schoolmaster would pay for Yves's carelessness.

Yves lit another cigarette. His hands had stopped shaking enough that he could smoke it, but the smoke felt like ashes in his mouth. He thought he might vomit. He smoked anyway. When the cigarette was finished, he used it to light another.

Yves lived on the top floor of a small house on the eastern edge of town. His rented rooms—a bedroom and a small kitchen—were no more than a five-minute walk from his office and only a ten-minute walk from the farmhouse where he had grown up as the youngest of ten children.

His parents were dead. Two brothers and two sisters were dead. His remaining brothers and sisters were much older than he. They lived nearby with their husbands and wives and children, but he rarely saw them. Saint-Léon was his world. And yet in some sense he was—had always been—a stranger here.

Yves had always liked it that way, had liked belonging and not belonging at the same time. He felt safest when he kept his distance. If he had not become a policeman, he might have been a writer. He could imagine sitting at the corner table at the Cheval Blanc and making notations in a small notebook. Being an outsider was his natural state.

Yves was engaged to Stephanie Letellier. He imagined that they might somehow always remain engaged. He regarded engagement as the perfect state. He liked the promise it held out, he liked the commitment without the intimacy of daily life. He could not imagine marriage, the sharing of happiness and boredom and anguish, the living in constant proximity to each other, eating, sleeping together, constantly taking account of each other.

When he and Stephanie made love, the ecstasy of it frightened him. He loved it and yet could not bear loving it. Afterward he could not fall asleep until Stephanie was asleep, in case some reason to flee should arise. None ever did, and her soft, round breathing soon lulled him to sleep.

When Yves's parents had died only a few days apart, when two sisters and two brothers died one after the other, he felt with each death a simultaneous sadness and liberation. He knew it was shameful to feel that way, but he could not help it. The less sadness remained to be lived through in the future, the freer and surer of himself he felt. He imagined he would be at his freest and surest when everyone he cared about was gone.

Yves sat motionless in his office until dark. Then he stood, went out into the cold air, locked the office door, and started walking home. It was later than usual and the streets were empty. Slivers of light showed here and there through shuttered windows. He imagined that the light was trapped inside, wanting to get out. Bits of it managed to escape but then fell in small pieces on the sidewalk like something badly broken.

Yves did not know why exactly, but he did not stop at his house or even so much as glance at it as he passed. Instead he walked out into the country, following the road toward Villedieu until, after nearly two hours of walking, he arrived at the house where Stephanie lived with her mother. It was very late by now, and the house was dark. Yves knocked at the door and then knocked again. A light came on, and after a few moments Stephanie opened the door. "The schoolmaster," said Yves. "Schoolmaster Bertrand is gone. Arrested. It is my fault."

Stephanie brought Yves inside. Her mother got up and made tea. The two women listened while Yves told them what had happened, how it had all eluded him until too late, how it was beyond him now, how he had miscalculated, underestimated, and made every other mistake it was possible to make.

"You cannot outwit them," he said. "You cannot bargain with them. They are different from us. Essart taught me that. The German lieutenant. They want something; I don't know how to describe it. It is massive and bright. A blinding light. I don't know what it is, but it is terrible to look at." The women listened. "Can I sleep here?"

"Of course you can," said Stephanie's mother.

By the end of the next day, everyone in town knew of the schoolmaster's arrest. And the day after that, it was announced that Colonel Büchner was being transferred. "He is needed back in Germany," said Colonel Ernst Wilhelm Hollinger. "I am taking over." He sat where Büchner had sat only two days earlier. Colonel Hollinger spoke a little French, but he chose to speak German.

Lieutenant Ludwig stood at his side and translated his words. The colonel faced the lieutenant and not the town council. He looked as though he might be dictating a letter. The mayor, the council members, the policeman sat before him and gazed at Lieutenant Ludwig as Colonel Hollinger spoke. "Tell them that things are really quite simple," said Hollinger.

"The colonel says that things are very simple," said Ludwig.

"Tell them that things have reached a dangerous state in Saint-Léon-sur-Dême." He pronounced the entire name of the town, as strangers often do. "And I intend to see that things are brought under control. Disruptions of the order will not be tolerated. The next sign of insurrection will result in the harshest punishment. This will include the selection of hostages from the people of this town—from your friends and neighbors—who will then be executed. A lesson must be taught. A harsh lesson." He waited until Ludwig had finished translating. Then he rose and, without looking in the direction of the town council, he left the room.

"That will be all for now," said Ludwig. The members of the town council rose and left.

On the square in front of the Cheval Blanc, the mayor pulled Yves aside. "Come with me, Renard," he said. "Come to my office. We have to talk." When they were seated at the mayor's desk, Schneider opened a drawer. He took out a bottle of cognac and two glasses. He raised his eyebrows in Yves's direction.

"Yes, thank you," said Yves, and the mayor poured two drinks.

"*À la votre,* your health," said the mayor. He drank down the cognac. "We're in a tough spot, Renard."

Yves nodded in agreement. "We are." He lowered his eyes. He took a sip from his glass.

The mayor decided to try another tack. "You seemed to be on to Bertrand from the start."

Yves did not answer.

"The schoolmaster," said the mayor. "He really went after you, didn't he?" He held up a copy of the pamphlet. "He said you were one of them. 'Under their thumb,' he said. He all but called you a Nazi. Of course he went after all of us, the whole town council. He even included himself, just to throw everyone off the scent. What a shit!"

The mayor looked at Yves, but Yves kept his gaze down and sipped from his glass. "I can't figure you out, Renard. I have to admit, I didn't like you. And I still don't know what to think. But now we're in a hard place, you and I especially, and, to some extent, the others of course. But you and I especially. The pamphlet thing's finished now with Bertrand out of the picture, but some other crap is going to happen sooner or later, more communist graffiti, another newspaper—something. And Hollinger is serious. They're going to start killing people."

The mayor paused and thought. The two men sat in silence for several minutes. Finally the mayor said, "You know about that meeting of mayors and police chiefs in Tours on the afternoon of the twentieth, right? Okay, it will mostly be about the latest changes in Vichy and at the Vichy border. They're replacing the army with customs people and motorcycles and dogs. Which should stop a lot of the easy back and forth. But it won't make a big difference. It's supposed to make it harder for the communists to get up to their shit, but who knows. And for the Jews to cross. There may be some other useful information at the meeting. It doesn't have much to do with us, but we still ought to go. You should go. We should drive down together and talk about our strategy. Mainly how we keep from getting shot. From getting our people shot."

It was raining hard the afternoon of February 20, when the mayor stopped his car outside Yves's office. The policeman sprinted out and jumped in the car. "Whew!" shouted the mayor with a laugh. He put the car in gear and they drove away. Jean Josquin stood in the mechanic's shop door and watched them go.

The mayor leaned forward, peering hard through the windshield. The rain was coming down hard. Yves stared at the fields and houses through the downpour. The first jonquils were sticking up through the gray earth. Their buds were bright yellow and only a day or two away from opening, and yet he hadn't noticed them before. It was the first rain in some time. Maybe they had just come up. Yves wondered that such a thing as spring could even be possible in a world like this.

The meeting at the provisional Hôtel de Ville—the old building had been damaged in the bombardment—was presided over by French functionaries. They read legalistic proclamations and explained why this law or that provision was crucial to the future of France and to the success of the collaboration. They announced new regulations and requirements for movement between occupied and Vichy France. They opened the floor to questions, and several mayors, mainly from towns along the Vichy border, asked about the implementation of the new stricter controls. What about the free movement of their citizens? they wondered. They would be given passes if at all possible, said one of the speakers, but some concession had to be made to the security of the country. The German officers seated around the back edge of the meeting room remained silent throughout the meeting. They left the room as soon as the meeting was over.

"Do you see anyone you recognize?" said Schneider. He knew a few of the other mayors. "Come on, let's go over," he said. He and Yves joined a small knot of mayors and policemen.

"Hey, it's Michel. You had to come all the way down for this?"

"Oh, it seemed like a good idea to keep up with things. How are you, Eduard? How are things in Saint-Pierre?"

"Okay. You know. And Saint-Léon?"

"Fine," said Michel. "Have you met my gendarme? Yves Renard."

"Did you run into that rainstorm on the way in?"

"It was unbelievable. I had to pull over, it was coming down so hard."

"It should be easier going home. It's mostly stopped."

"There were jonquils," said Yves.

"What?" said the mayor of Saint-Pierre.

"Jonquils are out. It's almost spring."

"My gendarme likes flowers," said Michel, and everybody laughed.

The rain had stopped and it was clearing. The sun had just set and the sky turned golden. Michel Schneider and Yves drove across the Loire on the battered stone bridge. There were still piles of rubble at either end from the battles the previous June. At the top of the hill, the mayor turned the car toward the east.

"Where are we going?" said Yves.

"I want to show you something," said Michel. He did not speak again for several minutes. There were not many cars on the road.

"We're in the same boat, Renard, you and I. I said it earlier. So we better start trusting each other, don't you think?" He looked over at Yves again. Yves turned and looked into the mayor's eyes with such intensity that the mayor was startled. "Jesus, Renard, you're a strange one."

More time passed. "Okay, I'm taking a big chance here," said Michel. "But I don't have much choice, do I?" It sounded as though he were talking to himself. "We're going to Château-Renault. Another meeting. Different this time. No functionaries or bureaucrats. Just French patriots. You should meet them."

They passed through the small city of Château-Renault. People standing in line at a bakery watched their car pass. They left the city in the direction of Beaumont-la-Ronce and then turned north on a narrow dirt track. They drove between thick hedgerows and after a kilometer or so came to a heavy gate hung between stone pillars. A man stepped from the shadows and, bending to look, shined his flashlight into the car. "Ah, Michel," he said.

"Yves Renard," said Michel, nodding in Yves's direction. "My gendarme." The man shined his light in Yves's face. Then he swung the gate open, and Michel drove through. After a few hundred meters the trees ended and they found themselves in front of a small Renaissance château, a graceful building of white *tuffeau*. It was dark except for a dim light in the entryway.

They were shown into the great hall, which was also dimly lit and shabbily furnished. Twenty-five men sat around the room on threadbare chairs and cracked and worn leather sofas. A fire sputtered in the enormous fireplace. "Ah, Michel," said one of the men, rising and shaking his hand. "Michel Schneider is the mayor of Saint-Léon-sur-Dême," he announced. "And this is?"

"My gendarme, Yves Renard," said Michel.

"Bravo."

Yves was given a small tumbler of wine and shown to a spot on a sofa between a white-haired man in clerical robes and a gendarme in uniform. Both introduced themselves to Yves.

"I want to welcome you all and thank you for coming," said the man who had first greeted them. "I want to especially thank the Marquis d'Estaing for inviting us into his home. The marquis wants to say a few words of welcome."

Everyone applauded. The marquis was elderly. He rose slowly. He had a cloud of white hair sitting atop his head and a clipped white mustache. He wore a nondescript gray suit over a gray sweater and white shirt buttoned to the top.

The marquis wove about unsteadily. He collected himself for a moment. "My friends," he said with a wheeze, "our beloved France is in the gravest danger, and only you can save her." He wheezed with every intake of breath. "The German assault and invasion were terrible, but we face other even graver dangers. I speak of course of the communist menace. The communists and their alien ideology have threatened the French way of life for many years, and now they sense an opportunity. They would like nothing more than to overthrow our culture, our way of life, and to bring us under the yoke of a malignant Soviet regime.

"But we also have a unique opportunity. We can sweep them out and defeat communism once and for all. To accomplish this we have to make common cause with our German occupiers. Some may find this distasteful. But the world of politics is rarely tidy. I am gratified to see so many Frenchmen here tonight willing to do what is necessary to rid our beloved France of the alien communist menace. I am happy to welcome you here in my home."

The marquis lowered himself into his chair while the others applauded. Once he was seated, he gave a little wave of his hand.

The man who had spoken before rose again. "Thank you, Monsieur le Marquis. Your welcome is appreciated. Your words are stirring to everyone who loves France. For those who don't know me, I am Jacques Richard. I am the chief of police at Château-Renault, and I must say it makes me happy to see so many of my police colleagues here tonight. Would you stand, please, and be recognized?"

Ten men, including Renard, stood. The others applauded.

"And I am happy to see so many clergymen here too. Would you also please stand?" Six men did, and the rest applauded.

"I am grateful you are all here. When I asked the marquis if we could meet here, frankly, I didn't know whether anyone would come. Being here is risky, I realize that, especially for those of you in official positions. But, like you, I believe matters are rapidly reaching a state where we have no choice but to act. The communists and their cohorts are wasting no time."

"Tell us what you suggest," said a small red-faced man. He drew impatiently on his cigarette and blew a cloud of smoke into the room.

"Vigilance, of course," said Jacques Richard. "And strict enforcement of the law."

"The communists will be vigilant," said the red-faced man. "And forget about the law. We have to fight fire with fire."

"And we will," said Richard. "We will meet provocation with an iron fist. You all know who the communists are in your communities. Stop their provocations and stop their organizing. Keep one another informed of developments, of provocative activity, of any alien presence." The meeting went on in that manner for another half hour. Everyone agreed that the communists should be watched, along with Freemasons.

"And let's not forget the Jews," someone said.

"Yes, the Jews," said the marquis, lifting his head, his eyes wide, as though he had just woken from a nap.

The priest sitting beside Yves pursed his lips and cast his eyes toward the ceiling, as though he wished he were elsewhere.

"The Germans will take care of the Jews," said the red-faced man.

As Michel Schneider and Yves drove home, Yves gazed silently through the windshield. The mayor looked over from time to time but he could not read the policeman's face. The moon had risen in front of them.

"Do we have communists?" said Yves suddenly.

"Hemon is a communist." Jules Hemon had once been mayor of Saint-Léon. He was nearly eighty years old. He had been to Moscow not long after the revolution and had returned home an enthusiast. "We know who he associates with. I don't know for sure, but I suspect the schoolmaster, Bertrand, is a communist. *Was* a communist." The mayor grinned. "And there are others. Of course we have communists. We'll smoke them out."

"Smoke them out?"

"We'll have to figure out how."

"And Jews?" Yves wondered.

"What are you getting at, Renard?"

"I'm just asking."


Jean Josquin took his ledger to Onesime's room, as he did nearly every evening now. He opened the book and read out the day's entries. "René Bertrand is at the prison at Saint-Pierre."

"Is he alive?"

"He was when he got there."

"Annette?" said Onesime.

Jean nodded. Annette Roboutin was the part-time secretary at town hall. "Bertrand was interrogated at Gestapo headquarters. He was beaten up pretty bad. Then they took him to prison."

"How does she know?"

"From her sister, Madame Duquesne. The Duquesnes tried to visit their boys in prison."

"Did they get to see them?"

"No, but they talked to the guards. And one seems sympathetic. A gendarme named Fernand. He may be able to let them see Stephane and . . . what's the other one's name?"

"Antoine. Stephane and Antoine."

"Right, Stephane and Antoine. They're not doing too well, so the Duquesnes stayed a few days with cousins by Saint-Pierre. The guard, Fernand, still couldn't arrange a visit, but they asked him about Bertrand and he remembered them bringing him in. The Duquesnes are going back to Saint-Pierre at the end of the week."

Onesime made a note at the bottom of his map about Fernand, the Saint-Pierre guard. "What else have you got?"

"Thirteen forty, Schneider, Renard drive to Tours."

"Tours? How do you know Tours?"

"There was a meeting of mayors and police chiefs," said Jean. "Annette again." He smiled. "They weren't back when I left the shop. And what about you?"

"Annette's sweet on you," said Onesime.

"Maybe," said Jean. "And what have you got."

"I saw Beaumont's map," said Onesime.

"What map?"

"The one in the cave," said Onesime. "You know, the one we saw last summer. And that's not all."

"The cave?"

"You remember. Last July. We were cutting hay. We said you could live in the cave, and the count said no, why would you, or something like that. Well, someone is."

"Who?"

"I don't know. I didn't see them. But I was pruning grapevines. I had tied the cuttings up in bundles for kindling and carried them to the cave, like the count said to, and he was there, and he told me to bring them inside. That's where he's keeping them, in the second cave, the one that locks."

"He's keeping kindling in a locked cave? Why?"

"I'll tell you. Anyway the cave was wide open, and he told me to bring them in. There was a rug on the floor and some chairs and an old table. And ashes in the fireplace."

"So he's burning the old vines in the fireplace?"

"Just wait. And the map was there, and when he went out to get some more bundles, I looked at it. It's a military map that goes south to the Cher. And there are places marked on it. Towns and villages with circles and some words I couldn't make out. It looked like names."

"Did he see you looking at it?"

"No. But it was like he wanted me to look. Like he wanted me to know what he was up to. Except I can't figure it out."

"You'll just have to ask him," said Jean.

"Or go for another look."

Later that night Jean watched from his window as Onesime hung his bicycle on his shoulder and tiptoed down the dirt lane. Once he reached the pavement, he swung his leg over the seat and set off down the road. The rising full moon lit his way perfectly. Onesime rode happily, feeling the chilly air on his face. He could smell the earth coming alive. The ground was too wet to work, but the count had already spoken of getting the plow out and turning a new field. "It won't be long now, Onesime." He had sounded wistful.

"I'm ready, monsieur," Onesime had said.

Maurice, the count, had smiled at him. "I know you are."

It was after midnight. Onesime did not know what he expected to find at the count's cave. It would be closed up and locked. If anyone was living there, they would be shut up inside and sleeping. Still he rode on.

He approached Le Pêcheur, the tavern at the edge of town. The ramshackle building sat so close to the Dême that a rear porch sagged out over the water. The road curved in front of the tavern and crossed a narrow bridge on its way past Saint-Léon and out toward the vineyards and fields across the valley. The tavern was lit up. Drunken laughter came from inside, mixed with the sound of German songs.

Despite its bucolic name, Le Pêcheur had been a disreputable roadhouse as long as anyone could remember. It had always been frequented by rowdies and drunks, until this year when the German soldiers had made it theirs. Over the years, so many drunks had staggered or ridden their bicycles, motorcycles, and even a car or two into the Dême, that some local wag had rechristened the place La Truite Enchantée—The Enchanted Trout. The name was charming, the irony was exquisite, and, regardless of what the sign out front said, the tavern quickly became known as The Enchanted Trout, or simply The Trout.

Onesime rode past the place, keeping to the far side of the road, crossed the bridge, and continued out to the cave. He leaned his bicycle against the hill beside the cave door and tried it, but of course the door was locked. He walked past the other caves. They were all locked. He climbed the hill above the caves and found their chimneys, but they were all cold. It did not matter. He was glad to be out and about. It was the time of day when he felt free.

The Enchanted Trout was dark as he approached it on the way home. The reflection of the moon danced on the surface of the Dême. The songs were finished; the soldiers had all gone home. Except for one, that is, who lay sprawled in the shadows beside the tavern. Onesime did not want to have a run-in with a drunken German, so he rode by as quickly and as quietly as he could. But something about the man made him look again.

Onesime left his bicycle by the road and tiptoed back for a closer look. He had seen men who looked like that before. He knew right away that the man was dead. The soldier had been shot through the back of the head. He lay in a puddle of his own gore.

# IX.

"Are you sure he was dead?" said Jean.

"He was dead," said Onesime. "His face was gone."

"Jesus," said Jean. He had never seen anyone who had been shot. "What should we do?"

"Let them find him," said Onesime.

"The Germans? Nobody saw you? Because if they did . . . if you don't report it . . ."

"No one saw me," said Onesime. But how could he be certain?

"If the Germans find him first . . . ," said Jean. "There will be reprisals. Hostages. They'll shoot someone. They've already said as much."

"There will be reprisals no matter who finds him. What do you think we should do?"

"I don't know," said Jean. "Jesus."

"We should tell the police, tell Yves Renard before the Germans find out."

"Do you think Yves can be trusted? Look what he did to Bertrand."

"I think he was trying to save Bertrand. That's why the Gestapo showed up."

"And what about the meeting he went to with Schneider?"

"I don't know," said Onesime. He stood up.

"Where are you going?" said Jean.

"To tell the count," said Onesime.

"What?! The count? But why? It's three in the morning."

"He was friends with the first colonel. He's got this map, people living in his cave. It's a chance to find out where he stands and what's going on."

A half hour later the two men stood in front of the Beaumont château gate. "Are you sure?" said Jean. Onesime pulled at the chain. Immediately dogs started barking. And a minute later the gate swung open. The count stood there with a large mastiff on a lead. He shined his flashlight on the two men. "Come inside," he said. No questions, no exclamations. It was almost as though he had been expecting them. Just "Come inside."

Beaumont closed the gate behind them and led the way back to the dark house. When they hesitated he turned. "Come on," he said, motioning with his head.

Maurice led them into a small study. "Sit down," he commanded, and brought out a bottle of brandy from a small cabinet. He poured three small glasses. He sat down, raised his glass in a silent toast, sipped from it, and only then did he say, "What is it? What has happened?"

"We are sorry to bother you, monsieur . . ."

"I know. Never mind with that. Just tell me what has happened."

"A German has been killed. Shot. I found him at The Trout, in front of it, actually."

"Tell me everything."

Something in the count's tone made Onesime think that he *could* tell him everything. Anyway, they wanted to find out where he stood, didn't they? What better moment than this? They were in trouble anyway. "I was on my bicycle on my way out to your caves, monsieur."

The count set down his glass and raised his eyebrows. "I know someone lives there," Onesime continued, before the count could say anything, "and I wanted to find out who. I know I shouldn't have. . . ."

"Leave the apologies, Onesime. Tell me about the dead German."

"Oui, monsieur. On my way out, I passed The Trout, and it was full of Germans. They were drinking and singing. It's like that most every night, monsieur. Anyway, when I came back, the place was closed and dark, and I saw this guy lying by the front door. I almost rode past, but something about him—he made me think of the battlefield—made me go back. He was dead."

"How?"

"Shot. Through the back of the head."

"With?"

"Large caliber, I think."

"Did you tell the police yet?"

"No, monsieur. We didn't know what to do. That is why we came to you."

"You were right to do so," said the count. "Come with me."

"Where to?"

"To the telephone. To call Renard. He's got to get there before the Germans do. They will use it for their purposes."

"But, monsieur—"

"He doesn't need to know it was you who found him, Onesime."

Lieutenant Essart and his two colleagues arrived at The Trout at around eight o'clock. They had another man, a forensics expert, with them. The sun was just rising, but it was only a faint disk gleaming through the fog. Yves Renard stood by the body, stepping from one foot to the other to stay warm. He held his coat closed around his neck.

First he had visited and secured the scene, then he had telephoned Colonel Hollinger's quarters to report the crime. Then he had called his superior, Captain Lupardennes in Tours, who called the Gestapo. Yves had hoped they might send someone besides Essart.

Yves had been at The Trout on and off for the last four hours. He had had plenty of time to look around and put two and two together. He knew from Maurice de Beaumont, who knew from Onesime, when the shooting must have occurred. You could tell just from smelling him that the soldier, Private Johannes Beckermann, had been drinking. He was shot from behind.

Essart stepped from his car. He stooped down and looked at the body. His forensics man stepped forward to have a look. Essart stood up, spun on his heels, and strode toward Yves. "Your little village is trying my patience," he said. "I know just the way to put a stop to it."

"I found this," said Renard. He held up a shell casing.

"So," said Essart, "find the gun that fired this bullet and you will have your murderer. Your friends and neighbors apparently have guns, although they should have been confiscated. A German hero was viciously executed from behind. If you were properly enforcing the laws, this could not have happened.

"You have twenty-four hours to find the villain and turn him over to me. I will notify Colonel Hollinger to begin the selection of hostages in the event you do not succeed. I do not know how many hostages my superiors will want, but I think that it should be an impressive number to atone for the murder of one of ours. Fifty sounds right to me."

Twenty-four hours came and went, and of course Yves did not have the murderer. How could he? You had to find and interview witnesses, but he was not allowed to interview any of the German soldiers who had been at The Trout when it happened. The barman thought he remembered Private Beckermann. But he could not remember when he had left or whether he had left alone.

Colonel Hollinger convened the town council. "Tell the council," he said to Lieutenant Ludwig, "that they have until tomorrow to select fifty hostages to be executed in punishment for the murder of Private Beckermann."

"But _Herr Oberst_," said the mayor, "twenty-four hours is not enough time. Renard is an inexperienced policeman, and he is entirely alone in trying to solve this heinous crime. He has neither the means nor the experience to solve a complicated case like this. At least give us more time. I beg you, sir."

For the first time since he had arrived, Colonel Hollinger looked Mayor Schneider in the eye. "Tell the mayor," he said, turning back to Lieutenant Ludwig, "that I want the fifty names on my desk in the morning. However, I will give him and his gendarme one week—seven days—to arrest and deliver the perpetrator to our criminal justice system. After that, we will shoot five hostages in the town square every week until the culprit is apprehended or all fifty hostages are dead." After Ludwig had translated his words, the colonel turned to the mayor and said in French, "Do you understand?"

Besides Pierre Chenu, Jean Charles Arnaud, Yves Renard, and Paul-Marie Fissier, who had been appointed to fill the vacant seat resulting from René Bertrand's arrest, the mayor had asked others of the town's leading citizens to assist in the selecting of hostages. Most refused immediately. A few accepted, thinking that if they were making the selections, they might better protect their loved ones from being selected. As soon as the mayor saw their strategy, he withdrew those invitations.

A few others—the priest, Father Jean; the new schoolmaster, Leroi Bennehard; the count, Maurice de Beaumont—volunteered to help, out of a sense of obligation. It was a terrible thing the citizens of Saint-Léon were being asked to do. But no one could see a way out. The mayor had also asked the prefect from Tours to be present; he had sent an observer. The group of men sat around the large table in the town hall meeting room.

"I believe," said the schoolmaster, "that we should refuse to make the selection, that the Germans should decide whom to kill."

"They will certainly do so," said the mayor, "and they will probably start with us."

"And why not? We are none of us any more innocent or guilty than anyone we might choose," said Father Jean.

The mayor regretted having invited the priest. "It does not have anything to do with innocence or guilt, *mon père*, it has to do with political expediency. We are, unfortunately, not the first French town to have faced this dilemma. It has happened in Saumur and Nantes."

"Those are big cities. So far it has happened mostly in big cities." This was the prefect's representative speaking. He tugged at his chin and peered from man to man through thick glasses. "In those places, they had the benefit of anonymity. That is, the people they ultimately selected had no connection to those doing the selecting. They also had the benefit of the availability of, for lack of a better word, certain undesirables. They had prisons they could use, which they did; they had known communists and . . . others."

"Others?" said the schoolmaster.

"Freemasons, Gypsies, Jews," said the representative. There was silence in the room.

"I believe," said the schoolmaster finally, "that we *must* refuse to make this selection."

*Him too?* thought the mayor. *He's Bertrand all over again. What is it with these schoolmasters?*

It was true, Leroi Bennehard admired René Bertrand. He had been his pupil not too many years earlier. He admired his erudition and learning. He admired his upright morality. He admired his outspokenness and had decided that he himself would not shrink, if called upon to do so, from following in his mentor's footsteps. He was a rotund, moon-faced man, with thinning light brown hair combed across his brow, but he sat tall and defiant in his chair. "If we start naming others to die, then I wish for my name to be first on the list."

Again there was silence in the room. Finally the mayor broke the silence. "We do not have a prison, but Saint-Léon has prisoners in Saint-Pierre. Can we put them on the list? I don't see why not. And we have communists. Hemon and others we can name. And there are Gypsies."

"The Gypsies are gone," said the count.

"Freemasons," said the mayor. He took a piece of paper and prepared to begin the list.

"Freemasons?" said Jean Charles Arnaud. "We have Freemasons?"


After many hours, the mayor tallied up the list and announced that they had fifty hostages. "Read through the names," someone said. The mayor hesitated.

"Give it to me," said Leroi Bennehard. His name was first on the list, his mentor René Bertrand was second, although it was doubtful that the Germans would accept him as a hostage. He was probably already dead.

Stephane and Antoine, the Duquesne boys, were already in prison and doomed. It was because of their stupid prank that the citizens of Saint-Léon were having to draw up a list of hostages. Jules Hemon and some of his communist friends. Edith Troppard had been sleeping with the German colonel. Jacques Courtois was always in trouble. The mayor had added Jacques and some of his troublemaking friends.

Father Jean was on the list because the making of the list had driven him nearly insane. Father Jean had seen each name as a drop of the blood of Christ falling on the table in front of him. He even heard the sound the drops made as they hit the tabletop. The small red puddle slowly spread in front of him. He knew it was his imagination, but the vision was so convincing that he finally cried out, "Put me on the list!" He was relieved to be done with it and began laughing wildly and could not stop for a long time. The mayor wrote Father Jean's name at number thirty-two.

Onesime Josquin, who had deserted the army, was on the list.

"Maurice Christophe Germain de Beaumont, Comte de Beaumont," the count had said. "Add my name to the list." Jean Luc Sassonier and Léon Mettery had come back from the war crippled and depressed. They had been added to the list. There were fifty. "No one must be told he is on the list. They might flee." Everyone swore no one would be told. By morning everyone in town knew there were hostages and who they were. None fled. Where could they go?

Thierry Simonet was waiting in front of Yves's office door when Yves arrived just after eight o'clock. Thierry stood at attention like the soldier he had been many years earlier. Yves unlocked the door. The two men stepped inside the office. Thierry stood at attention once again and said, "I killed the German. My brother and my son were killed in the big war," he said. "My grandson was killed in this one. I've had enough. I decided to take revenge."

"In the middle of the night at The Trout?"

"Why not?" said Thierry.

"How did you get there, Monsieur Simonet?"

"I walked."

"You live three kilometers away."

Thierry sprang from his chair. "I'm not decrepit, monsieur!"

"How did you kill him?" said Yves.

"I shot him in the back of the head when he came out of The Trout."

"You shot him with what?"

"A rifle."

"Where is the rifle?"

"In the river. What does it matter? Arrest me."

"I can't," said Yves.

"Why not?" Thierry was angry. "You know the details. You can make it stick. The *Boche* just want to execute somebody. Why does it have to be fifty? It is true when I say I've had enough. Let them put me on trial and kill me."

"They don't work that way," said Yves. "It won't work. I can't do it."

"Then put me on the list. Take someone off—one of the women. Or Jean Charles, Dominic, . . ." He named more people he knew who were on the list.

"The list is in the mayor's hands. You have to talk to him about that. But I don't think it works like that, monsieur. I'm sorry."

Yves went to the Cheval Blanc to get permission from Colonel Hollinger to interview the men who might have been at the bar that night. He could not get past the sergeant at the door. He asked his superior, Captain Lupardennes, to intercede with Hollinger or even with Lieutenant Essart. "I'm sorry, Renard. There's nothing I can do. They are adamant. A German soldier has been murdered. Someone must pay. Interview the troublemakers in town. One of them will know who did it."

Yves interviewed Jacques Courtois. Courtois laughed in his face. "Why don't you just put on a little swastika and just go to work for them?"

"I'm trying to solve a murder," said Yves.

"A *Boche*."

"It's still a murder."

"I don't know anything. Now go fuck yourself."

Yves went to The Trout again, and again combed the grounds for clues. He stared into the water looking for the shimmer of a hastily discarded weapon, something, anything, that might open up the case, something undeniable, irrefutable, compelling. But all he saw was the water swirling under the bridge.

He interviewed the barman again. "I told you all I know, Renard. I sort of remember the German, but I don't remember when he left or whether he left with anyone. Whoever did it, killing him was a stupid thing to do. Have you talked to neighbors?" There were no close neighbors. He had talked to those in nearby houses. None had seen or heard anything; none had the slightest idea who might have killed the German. He interviewed people who used to drink at The Trout before the Germans came. He interviewed everyone he could think of.

In desperation he went back to the Cheval Blanc to beg Colonel Hollinger to at least let the German soldiers talk to him about the murder. "I will only ask questions the colonel approves. I will work with Lieutenant Essart; he can conduct the interviews. If I can only hear from those who were there that night, some clue might present itself; someone will have heard the shot; someone will know when the victim left and whether he left alone; someone . . ."

Lieutenant Ludwig had been sent out to meet with Renard on the colonel's behalf. He listened to Yves's arguments. "We cannot allow those interviews. A German soldier has been shot down in cold blood. The true witnesses, those who know what happened, are your friends and neighbors. Interview them again. The answer lies with them."

Early on the morning of the eighth day, detachments of German soldiers wearing full battle gear and carrying loaded weapons appeared at the doors of the first five hostages on the list. They arrested Leroi Bennehard, the new schoolmaster, at his parents' house just off the main square. He was permitted to finish dressing before he was marched off. Another detachment went to the farmhouse where the Duquesne family lived. The parents were taken away as substitutes for their imprisoned sons. The former communist mayor, Jules Hemon; and old Thierry Simonet, who had tried to confess to the crime, lived near each other, and a detachment of soldiers first got Hemon and then Simonet. When Simonet joined Hemon the two old men embraced.

One after another, the detachments marched onto the town square with their prisoners. Otherwise the square was empty. Windows and doors were shut, curtains were drawn. Only Colonel Hollinger stood at the window of his office, flanked by Lieutenants Ludwig and Essart, and watched the proceedings. The prisoners stood with their backs against a section of wall beside the *boules* courts. They stared in front of them. Thierry Simonet tried to sing "La Marseillaise," which was forbidden, but what did it matter now? But to his shame and distress he could not remember the words, and so his voice trailed off into silence. Hemon began to sing "The Internationale," the Communist hymn, but he could not finish, either.

Yves Renard had spent the night in his office. He had sat all night at his desk. He had slept fitfully now and then, but he didn't quite know whether he was asleep or awake, since it was as though he were living a terrible dream. He knew what was going on outside his office, but he could not believe that it could actually come to pass. He stared at some papers that happened to be in front of him, as though work or even the *appearance* of work could forestall the inevitable.

The shots rang out with such ferocity that the walls shook and the windows rattled. The terrible noise seemed to go on forever. After a moment Yves realized that the horrible sound he was hearing was a scream coming from his own mouth.

The five hostages lay dead on the square. The wall where they had stood was pockmarked and spattered with blood and gore. The soldiers who had executed the five shouldered their weapons, faced right, and marched off to their quarters.

After a short while, doors opened around the square. People looked out from the bakery, the mechanic's shop, the hotel. They stepped forward gingerly, as though they were walking onto a frozen lake that had been open water the day before. They held on to their doors in case the ground should give way under them.

Suddenly the door of the Hôtel de France flew open, and Jacky, the waiter, came running out. He was small, balding, and narrow shouldered. He wore a black vest and bowtie and a long white apron that flapped about his legs. He took great leaping strides across the square. It had been years since he had last had to run, and it appeared as though he had almost forgotten how to do it.

Jacky carried a stack of folded white tablecloths on his outstretched arms. When he reached the dead bodies, he went down on his knees and began spreading the tablecloths over the corpses. He did it quickly, deliberately, with a practiced hand, for he had flung tablecloths over many a table. He covered the dead one by one, protecting them from the eyes of the living. Blood seeped up through the white cloth.

Claude Melun and Jean Josquin from the mechanic's shop were the next to arrive, and pretty soon there was a small crowd of people doing what they could to help with their dead. Renard looked up toward Colonel Hollinger's window, but the curtains were drawn.

# X.

COLONEL HOLLINGER WAS SATISFIED that he had narrowly averted disaster. The murder of a German soldier was exactly the sort of thing that emboldened those who wanted to get into mischief. Such a blatant and terrible crime could never be allowed to stand. The colonel believed that the measures he had taken had put any thoughts of further misbehavior by the citizens of Saint-Léon to rest, at least for the moment.

It was always tricky to find the correct measure of suppression. The punishment had to be sufficient to teach people the lesson that needed learning, but not so extreme as to foment open rebellion. Lieutenant Essart would have killed all fifty hostages at once. But Essart was Gestapo; they always thought that way. The colonel had prevailed upon the high command in Tours and had been allowed to implement the more moderate punishment.

"I am certain," the colonel told Lieutenant Ludwig, "we'll have the perpetrator before the week is out. The threat of five more executions, and five after that, will be too much for them to bear. Someone out there knows who did it. Someone will crack and turn the culprit in." And that is exactly what happened, although not exactly as Colonel Hollinger might have wished.

It was the day after the execution. The colonel was having lunch at his desk so that he could sort through all the business he had had to put aside in order to deal with this matter. The orderly had removed a stack of files to a side table and placed the lunch tray in front of the colonel. He had just lifted the cover from the tray when the sergeant arrived from downstairs and said that Captain Ernst Hartenstein requested to speak to the colonel most urgently.

"Did he say what it is about, Sergeant? As you can see . . ." He waved his hand toward the stacks of files. "I have a shipment arriving today which we are unprepared to—"

"He said it is about the murder, *Herr Oberst.*"

"Is it? Send him up then." The colonel had an uneasy feeling. "And send in Lieutenant Ludwig."

Lieutenant Ludwig arrived from the office next door, and a moment later Captain Hartenstein stepped into the room. He was a large bulky man with a thick, creased neck and a small bullet head. His tiny, dark eyes were set deep in a doughy face.

Like the colonel, Hartenstein had served in the Great War. But he had begun his service as an enlisted man. He had been in the trenches for two years and had, at one point, single-handedly fought off a ferocious English attack. For this he had been awarded the Iron Cross, first and second class. Shortly thereafter he had received a battlefield commission as a lieutenant.

For Captain Hartenstein, however, courage in battle had not translated into rapid career advancement. He lacked discretion and tact, which were far more important for a soldier's career than courage ever was. Captain Hartenstein carried out whatever assignment he was given in exemplary fashion. But he could not resist speaking his mind, especially at particularly inopportune times. Hartenstein came to be known as a malcontent and a troublemaker, which was why he had never advanced beyond captain.

Hartenstein gave a salute. "*Herr Oberst,*" he said.

"What is it, Captain?"

Hartenstein tried to tug his tunic into place. "It's about Beckermann, *Herr Oberst.* The dead man. He was in my company. A driver."

"I know that, Hartenstein."

"Private Wolfgang Treffel, another driver in my company, killed him."

Colonel Hollinger felt as though he was going to vomit. Lieutenant Ludwig watched the colonel turn pale. He stepped forward and spoke. "We just executed five hostages for the crime, Captain. How long have you known this?"

Hartenstein glared at the lieutenant and then addressed himself to the colonel. "Another guy in the company, Corporal Kahlenberg, knew them both. They were seeing the same girl, some little French whore, according to Kahlenberg. He heard them arguing about her, heard Treffel threaten to kill Beckermann.

"You know how the men are, *Herr Oberst*. They're always afraid to tell on one another. But when Kahlenberg heard about the executions, well, he told his sergeant, who then told me. I've got Kahlenberg and Treffel under arrest in quarters. Treffel has admitted to waiting outside the bar, Le Pêcheur, and shooting Beckermann when he came out. Both men were drunk, *Herr Oberst*."

Lieutenant Ludwig raised his eyebrows. "How were you able to . . . persuade him?" he said.

"I slapped him around a little," said the captain. "I got the truth out of him."

Colonel Hollinger looked from Ludwig to Hartenstein and back again, but he did not see anything reassuring in either face. "Have you found the murder weapon, Captain?"

"I have the murder weapon, *Herr Oberst*. It's Treffel's rifle. It's recently been fired. It's my understanding that a shell casing was found at the site of the murder. I am certain, if the casing is compared with the rifle, they'll match. You have executed five Frenchmen for nothing, *Herr Oberst*."

Hollinger stared into Hartenstein's tiny eyes, and Hartenstein stared back. *So this is the face of justice,* thought the colonel. This is what the truth looks like. "Continue to hold the two men under arrest, Captain Hartenstein. Someone will come from brigade to take them off your hands. That will be all." Hollinger could not bring himself to say thank you.

Hartenstein said, *"Jawohl, Herr Oberst."* He did not salute. He turned and walked out the door.

Hollinger stood up and walked to the window. It was a bright sunny day. The window was open, and the curtains drifted about in the warm breeze. People stood in line in front of the bakery. The mechanic's shop door was open, and he could see a man working inside. Tables and umbrellas were set up on the terrace at the Hôtel de France. The wall against which the hostages had been shot had been scrubbed clean. At the foot of the wall someone had left a bunch of daffodils with a black ribbon around them. Colonel Hollinger leaned on the windowsill and closed his eyes.

"There was some activity at German headquarters today. A captain went in about lunchtime; he had his sergeant with him. He left after fifteen minutes. The colonel stood at the window and looked around. He didn't look happy. Lieutenant Ludwig went out. Then Yves Renard went to German headquarters this afternoon at about fourteen fifteen, Schneider at about fourteen twenty. They both seemed in a hurry." Jean read from his log while Onesime sat at his table looking toward the dark window.

"They went their separate ways when they left at about fifteen hundred," Jean went on. "Then shortly after that, the colonel's car pulled up and they headed off toward Tours, both the colonel and the lieutenant. Ludwig. What do you think is going on?"

"Something. I wish I knew. Maybe nothing. Maybe we should ask."

*"Ask?* Ask *who?"*

"The count. Renard."

"I'm not sure I trust either one of them."

"I'm not either. But the count handled things just right the other night. And Renard seemed . . . correct too."

"Yeah, but what would the count know?" said Jean. "And asking Yves is a big risk."

"Well, the count's a hostage."

"So are you," said Jean.

"Well, so what's the risk? Maybe that would be an excuse to talk to him."

The count did not seem surprised to see Onesime standing at his gate once again later that night. "Come in, Onesime," he said.

Onesime began to apologize for the late hour, but the count repeated himself impatiently. "Come in, Onesime. I want to talk to you." The count led him to the small study, took out the bottle of brandy, and poured two glasses. He drank in silence.

Finally he spoke. "I'm going to plant sugar beets this year." He set his glass on the desk as though he had just made a grave announcement.

"Monsieur?" said Onesime.

"Beets. We'll be planting sugar beets."

"Excuse me, monsieur. But I do not understand. I did not come here to speak of planting. I do not mean any disrespect, monsieur."

"Well, Onesime, I am a farmer, and these are the things a farmer talks about."

"Perhaps so, monsieur. But not in the middle of the night and not in secret. One doesn't talk about sugar beets in the middle of the night. Not these days." The count looked as though he wanted to speak, but Onesime continued without pausing. "Two days ago, five of our own were shot dead on the square, monsieur, because someone killed one of the Germans. I knew them all, monsieur."

"So did I, Onesime."

"And the Germans will kill five more of us every week until they find out who did it. Forgive me, monsieur, but I am one of the hostages they will kill, and so are you. I do not think it matters much right now whether you want to plant wheat or peas or beets or anything else."

"What are you saying, Onesime?"

"I'm saying . . . I'm asking really, monsieur. How do we live in days like these? Nearly a year has come and gone since the Germans arrived. And we have continued to live our lives as though nothing has happened.

But something *has* happened. What do we do now, monsieur, now that we're on a list of hostages and are likely to be killed before we can plant beets or anything else? Should we go into hiding, do we surrender ourselves without a struggle, do we resist them somehow? Tell me, what should we do?"

"What do you have in mind, Onesime? What do you think we should do?" And so the two men circled around each other in that manner for some time, neither knowing how to ask the other what he wanted to ask or to say what he wanted to say. Finally the count reached for the telephone.

"Who are you calling, monsieur?"

"Yves Renard," said the count.

"Why him, monsieur?" said Onesime.

"Maybe he can help," said the court. "What do you think?" Onesime did not have time to answer; Yves answered the telephone on the second ring. He did not sound as though he had been asleep. "Monsieur Renard, it is Maurice de Beaumont. Could you come see me?"

"When, monsieur?"

"Now."

"Now, at this hour? It is two o'clock in the morning, monsieur."

"If possible, now, yes," said the count.

"What does it have to do with, monsieur?" said Yves.

The count looked at Onesime and thought for a moment. "It is about whether I should be thinking about planting beets this spring, monsieur."

"I will be there in half an hour," said Yves. He arrived as he had said he would. Yves and Onesime shook hands. The three men each looked into the others' eyes, trying to divine the spirit of the other, to see whether each was trustworthy or treacherous, whether they stood for anything, and what it might be, what their limits were, the limits of their resolve, of their patience, in short, all the things one has to know in such a moment but can never know about someone else.

Onesime spoke up. "Today," he said, "you and the mayor spent part of the afternoon in the Cheval Blanc. Shortly after you left, the colonel and his lieutenant departed for Tours. They went to command headquarters. What has happened?"

Yves did not seem surprised by how much Onesime seemed to know or by the directness of his question. Nonetheless he took a deep breath. It seemed as though he were embarking on a journey from which he would not be returning. His response would be a first tentative step. "Why are you asking me that?"

"Because I may be shot for the murder of a German soldier, the count also. Neither of us killed him, and we have a right to know."

"They have the murderer," said Yves.

"Did they tell you who it is?" said Onesime.

"No," said Yves. "All they said was that they have him."

"Do you know who it is?" said the count.

"They are keeping it secret," said Yves.

"Why are they keeping it secret?" said Onesime.

"I can't be sure, but I can think of only one reason," said Yves.

"The murderer is a German," said the count.

"That's what I think," said Yves. "Why else keep it secret? I found the shell casing at the scene. It might be from a military rifle. And I haven't heard of anyone of us who's gone missing or been arrested. That doesn't mean much of course. But I think it's a German. The colonel went to Tours to meet with his superiors and the Gestapo to deal with the case. As far as I can tell, Ludwig, the lieutenant, thinks they can keep it secret; the colonel doesn't. Tomorrow they will announce that they have the culprit."

"He told you this?" said the count.

"A lot of it I'm guessing. But I think we'll know more tomorrow."

"What should we do?" said Onesime.

"Wait until tomorrow," said Yves. "Then we'll see."

The next morning Colonel Hollinger called Yves Renard and Mayor Schneider back to his office. He gave them copies of an official communiqué stating that, thanks to the harsh but necessary measures of the hostage execution on Monday, the Gestapo had discovered and arrested the murderer of Private Johannes Beckermann. The culprit, who for security reasons could not be named at this time, would be tried before a criminal court in Tours and, if found guilty, as the evidence strongly suggested he would be, would be executed.

The remaining forty-five hostages were released from their summary death sentence but would remain official hostages. The German high command fervently hoped that the citizens of Saint-Léon-sur-Dême had learned a valuable lesson. Terroristic assaults on German soldiers and other officials of the Third Reich would not be tolerated and would be met with swift and severe punishment. Anyone shielding or otherwise aiding those who had committed crimes against the Third Reich would be dealt with swiftly and harshly, as if they themselves had committed the crimes.

This stern notice was posted on the front doors of the Cheval Blanc, the Hôtel de France, the post office, the town hall, and various other sites around town where people routinely read official notices.

The next morning a mimeographed sheet appeared all over town. It too was tacked up, often beside the official notice. It was also tacked to trees and fence posts, stuck on benches, café tables, windowsills, slid into mailboxes, under doors—in short, left anywhere and everywhere its author could manage to leave it without being caught.

The mimeographed sheet even found its way to Tours that same morning, and a day later it showed up in Paris and Vichy. It was of course not distributed in those places in great numbers, but its mere presence attracted notice. In Paris it was tacked to the great plane trees by the street in front of Gestapo headquarters.

*Liberation* . . . . . . . . . . . . . . . . . . . . . . . . . . . *May 10, 1941. Issue 2*

*Citizens of France. Terrible atrocities are afoot in our country. Every citizen should know about them.*

*After a soldier of the Third Reich was killed on the streets of*

Saint-Léon-sur-Dême in the department of the Sarthe, fifty citizens of the town were taken hostage and sentenced to die unless the culprit was found within a week. Five of the hostages have already been killed—Saint-Léon's schoolmaster, two veterans of the Great War, and a helpless farmer and his wife—all five shot to death on the town square for everyone to see. The town's children are left without a teacher; the service of France's brave veterans has been severely dishonored; the farmer's children are now orphans.

The killer of the soldier has been caught, we are told, and will be tried secretly and executed. Why secretly? We have not been told why, but it is obvious. It is because the killer was not French at all, as the officers and policemen in charge have pretended. Rather he was a German soldier, a minion of the Third Reich. He had argued with the dead soldier and shot him dead in a drunken fury.

Think of it, Frenchmen and -women: Five decent and innocent citizens of France have been brutally executed for crimes committed by a soldier of the Third Reich. Remember: The perpetrators of this atrocity include not only officers and soldiers of the Third Reich, but also the local and regional French police, the mayor and gendarme of Saint-Léon, and all the other cowering French civil servants who go along with such despicable business.

Citizens: Such atrocities and miscarriages of justice are happening all over France. In Tours not long ago seventy hostages were machine-gunned to death after a brutal and abusive captain of the army of the Third Reich was assassinated. He had raped French women and brutalized many others with impunity.

This is what the Third Reich does not want you to know; this is what their collaborators do not want you to know. But citizens of France, you **must** know what is being done to France in the name of the armistice, in the name of collaboration, in the name of Vichy, and in the name of the Third Reich.

Here are the names of the dead. Here are the names of the guilty soldiers and their guilty officers. Here are the names of the collaborators in Tours and in Saint-Léon-sur-Dême.

There followed a long list of names in boldface type, including Colonel Ernst Hollinger, Lieutenant Walter Ludwig, Mayor Michel Schneider, and Inspector Yves Renard. The tract ended:

> *Citizens: Know who your enemies are. The traitors in Vichy are your enemies; the soldiers of the Third Reich are your enemies; the collaborationists in Saint-Léon and elsewhere are your enemies.*
> **Vive la France! Vive la Libération!**

The author of the mimeographed tract had not gotten everything right, but the main facts of the case were sufficiently correct to have a devastating effect. Colonel Hollinger stared at the sheet and shook his head. He did not even have time to finish studying it and think of the consequences before his telephone rang and he was summoned back to Tours. "Only you, *Herr Oberst*. Leave Lieutenant Ludwig in charge. The general wants to see you." This second meeting went even worse than the first one had gone.

General Paul Wallenstein was waiting in his office, which had been the mayor's ceremonial office before the war. Several other officers, including Lieutenant Essart, were seated there with him when Colonel Hollinger arrived. During the drive to Tours Colonel Hollinger had given thought to what the response to the mimeographed tract should be. He proposed an approach that was unconventional and, as far as Lieutenant Essart was concerned, utterly appalling.

Colonel Hollinger wanted to demonstrate the superiority of German justice by not only publicly announcing that a mistake had been made, but also by having the murderer, Private Treffel, executed on the town square exactly where the five hostages had been shot. He even suggested that the Third Reich should consider paying the town reparations. "It has already been done once before, in Saumur, I believe, where French citizens were wrongly executed, and it helped to quell an incipient uprising. I understand the objections to such a proposal," he said, watching Essart out of the corner of his eye. "Even before you raise them. But let us remember that the top priority must be given to keeping whatever rebellion is brewing from erupting."

General Wallenstein said that he saw virtue in Hollinger's proposal. Still, he did not find his arguments persuasive. The thought of executing a German soldier publicly and the implicit admission of guilt made that strategy untenable. "It would certainly defuse the immediate resentment of the citizens. But might it not at the same time pour fuel on the fire of future rebellion? We have to see to it that we come out of this with the least damage to our standing and the least distraction from our overall mission."

"We need to defuse the situation as quickly and effectively as we can," said Colonel Hollinger. "Admitting to a mistake and making amends is not a confession of wrongdoing, so much as—"

Lieutenant Essart was on his feet. "Herr General, the fact that the murderer was a soldier of the Reich changes nothing. The people of Saint-Léon-sur-Dême were uncooperative to the point of resistance well before this incident. Our interest is not to be fair or just. It is to rule with an iron hand, so that insurrection does not break out, in Saint-Léon or anywhere else.

"The paper has found its way to Paris, Tours, Vichy, and who knows where else. Insurrectionists will have their eyes on Saint-Léon. They are organizing themselves as we speak and looking for chinks in our armor. We must be strong and absolutely resolute.

"Allow me to remind the Herr Colonel that this tract, _Liberation_, is an extreme provocation. It is a direct challenge to our resolve. Any admission of wrongdoing on our part, tacit or otherwise, would be a show of weakness and would be recognized as such. It would embolden the enemy and encourage them to greater and greater provocations. Or perhaps you do not believe that the French are still our enemy? In my opinion executing the remaining forty-five hostages would be an effective way of demonstrating our unyielding strength and resolve.

"In addition, Herr Colonel, I must add that someone in your

command appears to be giving information to the enemy. They must be found out immediately."

"That is ridiculous," said the colonel. "And I must strenuously protest your insinuations. There was no way to keep this secret, Lieutenant, and you are naïve to think that it is possible. My goodness. Think of it: If you arrest and execute someone in secret, after having been very public about it previously, others can only surmise that you have something to hide. And the only thing in this case worth hiding is that we have made a colossal and stupid mistake by jumping to the wrong conclusions and executing five people for no reason. The citizens of Saint-Léon will know it whether anyone tells them or not."

Lieutenant Essart felt implicated by the colonel's assessment of the situation. "Herr General," he said, "I believe this matter falls under the purview of the Gestapo, and the decision how to proceed from this point on should be the Gestapo's to make." The general did not like Essart any more than Colonel Hollinger did, but the Gestapo had extraordinary power in such matters. In addition, Essart seemed to have powerful sponsors in Paris and Berlin. The general had to tread lightly.

"It is a police decision, Lieutenant Essart, as you correctly point out, but it is mine to make. I think it would be unwise to execute any more hostages. But it would also be catastrophic to admit to any mistakes. And it would most certainly be catastrophic to publicly execute Private Treffel. If he is determined in court-martial proceedings to have committed the murder, he will be executed, but certainly not in public. And no public notice will be given."

Private Treffel was tried in a summary military trial. He was found to have murdered Private Beckermann. He was taken back to his cell and, later that same day, to the prison courtyard. His rank and insignia were removed from his uniform, and he was executed by a firing squad of six men.

As Colonel Hollinger predicted, two days later everyone in Saint-Léon knew what had happened. It was as if someone of them had been present during the deliberations in military headquarters, in the prison, at the execution, in fact, every step of the way.

*Liberation* ........................... *May 19, 1941. Issue 3*

*Citizens of Saint-Léon, citizens of France, on the night of April 29, Private Johannes Beckermann was shot and killed at the bar Le Pêcheur in Saint-Léon-sur-Dême by Private Wolfgang Treffel. Private Treffel was executed by firing squad on the morning of May 16 in the military prison at Saint-Pierre-des-Corps. The boys Stephan and Antoine Duquesne may even have heard the gunfire, since they are imprisoned there for having committed no crime whatsoever.*

*Their mother and father were two of the five hostages gunned down on the town square of Saint-Léon because the minions of the Third Reich decided, without any examination of the evidence, that Beckermann was killed by a Frenchman. Forty-five hostages under sentence of death still await an unknown fate at the hands of the evil perpetrators of this abomination of justice, should they decide to arbitrarily execute some more French citizens for their own whimsical reasons.*

*Do our German persecutors have the courage, or the decency, to admit that they fomented a terrible miscarriage and killed innocents? They do not. And what about their French collaborators, our so-called "French" officials, the police particularly, who stood by and did nothing while innocents were shot dead? They are as culpable and as cowardly as their German masters.*

*Citizens, the collaboration is a mockery. France has surrendered its liberty and self-determination and gotten nothing but misery and abuse in return. How long will we put up with the abusive occupation by the unjust and barbaric Third Reich? How long must we put up with their lackeys, the police and the officials who call themselves French?*

*Not much longer, fellow citizens. Their demise is being organized in London. The English have been under terrible and unrelenting attack by the Third Reich. But they have succeeded in courageously repelling the Nazi assault on their country. And they have destroyed thousands of Nazi planes in the process. The Third*

Reich is not invincible. The day of reckoning for Hitler's Third Reich is coming. We must organize and be ready when that day comes. Collect yourselves and be patient. If we are vigilant and brave, then victory will be ours.

**Vive la Libération! Vive la France!**

# XI.

It was a warm June evening. The moon was three-quarters full, a bright, white lozenge in the western sky. The air was filled with the sound of frogs and the smell of the warm, freshly turned earth. It was the happiest night of Onesime's life.

Dancing was not against the law, but congregating in one place was. Jacques Courtois had organized a secret dance in that abandoned house where he and his friends had been caught butchering a hog. They had carefully sealed the windows this time. No light and little sound escaped. They had arrived silently in twos and threes. Madame Anquetille, down the hill, had no idea they were there, even though there was a crowd of them and they had a gramophone and a stack of jazz records.

Onesime was the last to arrive. The music stopped when he knocked. The lights went off before the door opened. A wave of heat swept over him as he stepped inside. The door closed, the lights came up, the room was full of happy people, and there, not two meters from him, stood Marie Piano. She looked at him with a smile and mouthed a hello in his direction.

When the music started again, Jacques Courtois seized Marie's hand and spun her about. The two jumped and hopped in time to the music; her skirt swung about her knees. Beads of sweat gleamed on her lip. Her brown hair bounced to the music. Jacques turned and twirled her in a manner Onesime could only envy and admire.

The next song was slower. Onesime invited Marie to dance. He rested his hand on the small of her back. She smiled up at him. There was a slight gap between her front teeth. He could hear her humming bits of the song they were dancing to. Then the music sped up again, and he returned her to Jacques. But Jacques could see that she was still looking at Onesime. And anyway, there were plenty of other girls he wanted to dance with.

It was sweltering in the little house. At the next pause in the music, Onesime stepped outside. Before he could close the door, Marie Piano came out too. The door closed and the night enveloped them. The music started up again but it was faint and indistinct, as though it came from another, happier time. The night was bright; the moon cast sharp shadows. The sky drew their attention upward. It felt as though the sheer magnificence of it might lift them both and carry them away. *If only*, thought Marie, *it* could *take me away, take us both away.*

"You're a good dancer," said Onesime. "So is Jacques."

"Remember that drawing you did of me?" said Marie. "You promised to let me see it. But you never did."

"I will," said Onesime. "Someday. I'm not happy with it." He went silent. He had never really spoken to her very much. "I heard you sing last summer."

"You did?" she said. "Where?"

"I can't remember where it was," said Onesime.

"I don't sing that much anymore," she said. Then she suddenly sounded serious. "Where was it?"

"I shouldn't have brought it up," he said. "It doesn't matter."

"Yes, it does matter," she said.

"It's just that it was so beautiful." He could hear the melody. It had stayed anchored in his memory, so that even now, a year later, it rose to the surface. "It was . . ." He tried to hum a little bit.

"Schubert," said Marie. "I sang that at the Count de Beaumont's. I learned it in German. But you weren't there."

"It must have been somewhere else," said Onesime.

"You *were* there, weren't you?"

"No . . . yes."

"Outside."

"Yes." They were silent for a while. "I've wondered," said Onesime, "what was it like to sing for Germans?"

"Most of the guests were French," said Marie.

"But what was it like?"

"There was only the colonel," said Marie.

"But what was it like?"

"It was like singing," said Marie. "It was music."

"It was beautiful," said Onesime again, and looked away. Marie took his head in her hands and kissed him.

"What was the war like?" she wanted to know.

"I don't know," he said. How could he explain it? It was terrifying and exhilarating and stupid and sad and every other feeling rolled together. "In a way, it was like being in love," he said finally. "It was completely confusing. I still don't know what it did to me; what it took away from me and what it left behind; what part of me is gone and what is still here. I didn't lose any physical part of myself, not my legs or anything, like Léon. But I left something big there."

"And now you're trying to get it back," she said.

"What do you mean?"

"I've seen you," she said.

"You've seen me?"

"Making your rounds at night."

"No you haven't," said Onesime. He turned angrily to face her. He had done everything to make sure no one ever saw him. "When? Where did you see me?"

Marie smiled and took his hands in hers. "What were you doing at the Count de Beaumont's that night? What were you looking for?"

The only believable explanation Onesime could come up with was truth. But how could he explain it? Before he could say anything, Marie Piano said, "I have a pistol."

"What?"

"I have a pistol. A German pistol."

"Let's walk," said Onesime. He walked so quickly, she almost had to run to keep up. He led her down the long driveway and past Madame Anquetille's house and most of the way to the main road before he spoke again.

"How do you . . . *why* do you have a pistol?"

"I stole it. From a German." She laughed lightly as though she were talking about taking a cookie from her mother's kitchen. "From the colonel actually. The first colonel, when he was transferred back to Germany. I was in the bar at the Cheval Blanc when he was leaving. His things were being carried out and loaded into a truck. There was a lot of confusion. The pistol was on a side table with some other things. I slipped it under my jacket. I didn't even think about it. I just did it."

"Jesus," said Onesime. "Do you know how dangerous that is? Why did you do it?"

Marie laughed again. "Why? In case I have to kill someone," she said.

"I was at the count's that night. But I didn't know about the party ahead of time. I went there to go into his cave. You go into the cave beside the back gate."

"Why?"

"To see where it goes."

"Where does it go?"

"It goes to my grandfather's cave. The Germans are using it."

"Really? What for?"

"Storage. Ammunition. Artillery shells."

"Will you show me?"

Onesime spread his jacket on the ground, and he and Marie sat down on it. She hugged her knees to her chest and looked at the sky long and hard. "Which direction is England?" she wondered.

"There," said Onesime, and pointed in the direction of the moon. That very moment they heard a rumbling sound, as though his gesture had caused something, had summoned something. It got louder by the second. Then it was straight overhead. Airplanes. Lots of them. You could only glimpse shadows momentarily blotting out stars as they passed like ghosts.

"Bombers!" he said.

"English?"

"I don't know. They must be," he said. They were not the first bombers he had heard passing over in the night. But suddenly he felt such elation that he wanted to cry. He took Marie Piano in his arms and kissed her as hard as he could. And she kissed him back the same way, full of hope and elation and despair, all at the same time.

The Ninth Squadron out of Waddington had just attacked port facilities at Le Havre. They had damaged docks and shipyards and had managed a direct hit on some fuel storage tanks, which had erupted in a great ball of orange flame. There had been secondary explosions that leveled several buildings around the port, killing civilians. There had been surprisingly little antiaircraft fire during this particular attack. In fact, the bombing had gone so well that the commander had decided they should proceed to their secondary targets, which were the rail yards in Tours and nearby Saint-Pierre-des-Corps.

The rail yards in Tours were heavily damaged, as were those in Saint-Pierre, along with the nearby prison. There were a hundred dead in Tours and Saint-Pierre, including a few soldiers. Some inmates at the prison were also killed, including the brothers Antoine and Stephane Duquesne.

At first there was almost no antiaircraft fire, but then the world erupted. Three bombers were shot down. No one saw any of the crews bail out as the planes plunged to earth. The surviving bombers arrived back at Waddington just as the first pink of dawn was showing behind them.

After the most-recent issue of *Liberation*, everyone in Saint-Léon braced for the German response. But there was no response. Instead, the pressure seemed to abate. The change was palpable and, given the circumstances, ominous. Colonel Hollinger canceled his regular meetings with Mayor Schneider and all but disappeared from view. Lieutenant Ludwig as well. Lieutenant Essart and his Gestapo operation remained in Tours, apparently occupied with other matters. At the same time, military truck traffic in and out of Saint-Léon increased. Troops were seen being transported through Saint-Léon.

"Something is up," said Jean.

"They're going to hit us hard this time," said Claude Melun. "That damn *Liberation*." But nothing happened.

Operation Barbarossa—the invasion of Russia—had begun. Issue number 4 of *Liberation* informed the citizens of Saint-Léon that vast German armies were moving to the east. The Germans had secretly amassed more than a hundred divisions, over three million men, on the border with Russia, and on June 22 had launched a surprise attack. It was as though a volcano had rumbled to life just over the horizon. Nothing was different, and yet everything was different.

The German high command calculated that the occupation forces were more than sufficient to stabilize and secure France. Churchill was incapable of mounting an invasion any time soon. Moscow must be taken before the Russian winter set in. And so, over objections from Paris, the strength and utility of all military units were reassessed, and the redeployment of some forces began.

Colonel Hollinger was called to Tours. It had been decided, after careful assessment, that a reduction in force of 10 percent would not in any way impede his capacity to fulfill his mission. He argued vigorously. "I am already operating in a hostile environment," he said. "Security is a big concern."

"Have you had any clandestine or partisan activity?"

"We have a seditious pamphlet that regularly incites—"

General Wallenstein picked up a stack of papers from the table behind him and dropped it heavily in front of Hollinger. "Colonel," he said, waving at the papers, "*everyone* has seditious leaflets to contend with. You will just have to adjust."

As far as Colonel Hollinger was concerned, the only good thing to come out of the reduction in force was that Captain Hartenstein was gone. He had volunteered for the eastern front and was gone within a week.


Yves Renard had two strange visits that summer. The first came one sultry day in August. He was working at his desk. The overhead fan moved the air around but did little to cool him. The door to his office opened and a woman entered. Yves stood up. He did not recognize her immediately. She wore a light cotton dress, and the breeze from the fan caught her hair and tossed it about. "Monsieur Renard, I hope you are not too busy at the moment?"

"Not at all, madame." He saw that it was Edith Troppard, the widow from Villedieu. He had not remembered that she was so pretty. "Please sit down, madame." He motioned toward the chair. "What can I do for you."

"I am sorry to bother you, monsieur. It is not exactly a police matter, but then again perhaps it is. You know I live not far from Stephanie and her mother. I spoke with them both. Stephanie said that I should talk to you."

"Stephanie? I see," said Yves. "Well then. I will help if I can, madame."

"It is not something I need done, monsieur. It is . . . information that I have."

Yves held up his hand in protest. "If it is information you have, Madame Troppard, perhaps you should talk to the German officers. Or to the Gestapo."

She looked sharply at Yves before she spoke again. "I see," she said finally. "You think that . . . you know about my friendship with Helmut Büchner."

"Madame, I really do not think this is a matter that I should . . . a matter of concern to me. If you—"

"He's dead, you know. Helmut Büchner. He's dead."

Yves did not speak. What could he say? Should she be comforted for the loss of her German lover? "Madame," he said, and then nothing. He tried again. "Madame, perhaps the German officers—"

"He was executed. In Berlin. *Ein Genickschuss.* Do you know what that means, monsieur? A shot in the back of the neck. For conspiring to assassinate Hitler. He was guilty of course, if there is any guilt in that. They said he was being transferred when he left Saint-Léon, but it was only to be arrested. He was taken to Berlin, where he was tried—along with many others—and shot. They were all shot. That is what I came to tell you—that he was taken away and executed."

"Madame, why are you telling me this? It is not a police matter." Why did he keep saying this? Why couldn't he think of anything else to say?

"No, of course. I know. It is not a police matter. But people should know it, *you* should know it, everyone should know what they did, what they *do*."

Yves looked at Madame Troppard. "What can I do for you, madame? I do not see how I . . ." He could not make himself finish the sentence. "I am very sorry, madame," said Yves.

"I want it known," she said. "How he died. They are monsters, these people. But then again they are not all monsters. Still, it should be known. We should all know. That is all I wanted to say, monsieur. Thank you." She stood and held out her hand. Yves stood up so quickly that he nearly knocked over his chair. He took her hand. She smiled, thanked him once more, and left.

"Why did you tell her to see me, of all people?" Yves asked Stephanie that evening.

"She is heartbroken," said Stephanie. "And she is angry. She wants everyone to know. I think she would like to do something. To have her revenge. Of course she didn't say so, but I think that is what she would like. She has loved two men, and the Germans have killed them both."

*Liberation* . . . . . . . . . . . . . . . . . . . . . . *August 28, 1941. Issue 7*

*Frenchmen, Frenchwomen, when things start going badly for the Third Reich, they find scapegoats to punish for the evil they have brought upon themselves. They point their fingers at the Jews and the communists and the Gypsies and the Freemasons and have now set about organizing their annihilation. Mass executions of Jews using poison gas have begun in Germany and Poland. Hitler intends the extermination of all Jews. He is constructing concentration camps to accomplish this. He has begun his evil work elsewhere, but do not doubt for a moment that preparations are under way to do the same thing in France to French citizens.*

*It does not seem possible that such a thing could happen in France. And yet the vicious "Jewish Statute" of June 2, 1941 has excluded all Jews from French public service and public life. In Tours and Le Mans, Jewish businesses have been damaged or closed. On July 10 in Tours an old man wearing the required yellow badge was set upon and kicked and beaten, not by Germans, but by a group of Frenchmen and -women. On the night of August 5 the Patisserie Blumenfeld was firebombed by Frenchmen doing the business of Nazis. The French police did nothing to investigate the crime or to arrest the perpetrators. If the French police stand by while such crimes are committed against French citizens, who will protect us?*

*Camille Aron, a farmer, vintner, and benefactor to his community, has been the mayor and* conseiller-général *of Le Boulay since 1913. That constitutes twenty-eight years of loyal public service. Many of you know Camille. Now he has been forced to resign, for no other reason than that he is Jewish. Robespierre Hénault, the mayor of Saint-Pierre-des-Corps, was removed from office two years ago and replaced by a Nazi stooge. Now Monsieur Hénault has been imprisoned. The reason? He is a member of the Communist Party.*

*This cruel and inhuman persecution could not happen if the Germans had to act on their own. But unfortunately there are men* and women who call themselves Frenchmen and Frenchwomen who are more than happy to do the Germans' bidding. These attack dogs should beware of their masters. The German appetite for cruelty and brutality is insatiable, and someday they will turn on their French accomplices and collaborators. They have already begun devouring their own.

Colonel Helmut Büchner was once in charge of the German occupation in Saint-Léon. He put in place the oppression of all our citizens and oversaw the arrest of our citizens, including our schoolmaster and two children who have since disappeared into prison. We must not honor or celebrate this man, Büchner, and we do not mourn his death. But still it is worth noting that he has himself been killed by the brutal Nazi regime he served. He was executed by the Third Reich for doing one honorable thing and joining a plot to kill the abominable Adolf Hitler.

Citizens of Saint-Léon, citizens of France, the Third Reich seems indomitable. They have conquered most of Europe, and now they are marching through Russia. They seem unstoppable. But they can be stopped if we choose to stop them. THEY MUST BE STOPPED. THEY WILL BE STOPPED.

**Vive la Libération! Vive la France!**

# XII.

THE GESTAPO LIEUTENANT STOOD with his hands clasped behind his back. From the window all he could see was red-white-and-black flags everywhere. Berlin was awash with them. He turned around. "Your hands," said the Gestapo lieutenant. "Look at them."

Franzl Weinmann did as he was told. He turned his hands over, trying to see what the lieutenant saw.

"They're soft," said the lieutenant. "You see? They're smooth. Those aren't the hands of a carpenter."

"But I . . ." said Franzl. "I never said—"

"You did not have to say anything," said the lieutenant. "Your hands spoke for you." Did he actually believe that Franzl's hands showed that he was someone he wasn't? The lieutenant stood up and walked back around the desk. He walked slowly, measuring each step. He looked down at Franzl and shook his head like a disappointed uncle.

"I don't know what you want with me," said Franzl. He tried to keep his voice firm, but it wavered.

"Well, we must be mistaken then, isn't that right? Yes, the Berlin police must be mistaken, the Third Reich must be mistaken, Herr . . ."—the lieutenant looked at the dossier—"Herr Weinmann. A mistake. Just as you say: You are not Franz Weinmann, the Berlin University philosophy student and communist organizer. You are Franz Weinmann, an innocent carpenter, isn't that correct?

"Except for the hands, Herr Weinmann. You see? That is my only problem. The hands. They do not lie." The lieutenant seemed to consider things for a moment. "But, it must be, as you say, a case of mistaken identity. I'm sure it can be sorted out."

The lieutenant walked back around the desk and sat down. He looked at Franzl again; he looked at Franzl's identification card on the desk in front of him. He stood up again slowly, as though he had all the time in the world. "I think I can clear this up, and then you can be on your way. How does that sound?" He smiled at Franzl, picked up the identity card, slid it into his pocket, and left the office. Franzl heard the lock turn in the door.

What was it exactly that made Franzl certain this would end badly? It was everything, actually: that business about a carpenter's hands; then the lieutenant's exaggerated politeness and accommodation; then that smile and the locked door. Franzl wasn't the Franz Weinmann they were looking for. But he was still *a* Franz Weinmann and still a Jew. Even if they let him go today, even if they weren't looking for him today, they would be tomorrow.

Before he quite knew what he was doing, Franzl leapt from the chair and jammed it against the door. He kicked out the window and was out onto the roof in an instant. He ran along the edge of the roof, watching for a way down. He dropped onto a balcony on the floor below, and from the balcony into the courtyard. He sprinted across the concrete and scrambled over the wall and jumped down onto Wartburgstrasse. He breathlessly excused himself to the woman he almost landed on. She stared at him as though he were an apparition. "*Um Gottes Willen!*" she exclaimed, clutching both hands to her breast. Franzl made for a passing trolley, no longer an apparition, but once again just another Berliner hurrying home from work.

Franzl Weinmann had just turned eighteen the week before. He had never been political. And of course he had never been a fugitive.

But in the few seconds it had taken him to escape the Gestapo, he had become both. And in those brief seconds he discovered that his greatest ability, a precious gift really, in these times, lay not in carpentry but in being a fugitive.

Franzl no longer had an identity card. His home, Berlin, was no longer his home. The red-white-and-black flags everywhere, which had meant nothing to him before the summons earlier that week, suddenly meant danger. He had never kicked out a window before, never scampered along a roof, never vaulted a wall, and yet he had just done all these things as though they were second nature.

Franzl felt not fear, but rather an extreme form of liberty, like evaporation or death. He felt the elation one might feel on discovering he could disappear at will. Franzl could not have explained it to anyone, not even to himself, but he felt happy.

Now five years had passed since that afternoon, and during those five years Franzl had moved through a dozen countries and a hundred identities. He really had evaporated. He lived nowhere and everywhere. He had no name, he knew no one, he loved no one.

His father, mother, sister, aunts had all been taken to camps and killed in the meantime, and he was wanted by the Germans for a long list of crimes. And yet here he sat, at a table in the low October sun in front of the Hôtel de France, drinking a beer and watching the comings and goings on the square in Saint-Léon-sur-Dême, a village he had never heard of before yesterday.

He was thinner now. He had a wispy beard. He had a cap pulled low over his eyes. He was called Simon, although that name was on none of the identification cards he carried. His hands were no longer smooth.

Simon smoked a cigarette and drank and watched. He did not pretend to read a newspaper. He looked about openly, taking it all in, almost as though he wanted to be noticed. He watched the German colonel arrive on foot: very proper and erect, not young, a veteran of the Great War, undoubtedly. His career had probably been a satisfactory one, judging by his confident step. Then came the lieutenant. He looked like SS to Simon. Something about his carriage. A lieutenant with a secret. Then a sergeant left the building carrying files. Another sergeant arrived.

Yves Renard, the village gendarme, arrived and unlocked his office. Unimpressive. Not in uniform. My God, he looked young. Across the way, some women waited in line by the bakery. A man passed in front of him. The man tried to look at Simon without looking, before going into the mechanic's shop.

Yves had his back to the door when he heard it open. By the time he turned around, the man was already seated on the chair facing Yves's desk. The man sat casually and yet lightly, like a cat that could scamper away in an instant. He kept his cap on.

"Bonjour, monsieur," said Yves, "how may I help you?"

Simon smiled slightly. He did not rise or offer his hand or even speak right away. Yves began to repeat himself. "Monsieur . . ."

"Are you the gendarme, Yves Renard?" said Simon. He had a strong German accent.

"I am, monsieur," said Yves. "How may I help you?"

"I have come about this," said Simon, and unfolded a copy of *Liberation* on the policeman's desk.

Yves looked at the paper. "That is from May, monsieur. This is October. I'm afraid there have been more of these . . . tracts since then. We have tried unsuccessfully to discover . . ." Yves stopped speaking and watched the stranger watching him. "May I ask, monsieur, why this is of interest to you?"

"Let's just say, Monsieur Renard, that I am a Paris subscriber. I have come from Paris because . . . let's just say the paper interests me."

"Are you here in an official capacity, monsieur?"

"I suppose I am, Monsieur Renard. Let's just say that I am."

The stranger was not in uniform. But these days more and more Nazi officials traveled incognito.

"May I ask you for some identification, monsieur?" said Yves. He wanted to know whether he should be prepared to arrest the man or to be arrested himself. Simon reached inside his jacket and withdrew an identification card. Yves studied the card. The picture was of the man sitting across from him. He was identified on the card as Major Gerhard Hohenwald of the Waffen-SS. Yves passed the card back across the table.

"So, monsieur," said Yves yet again, "please tell me how I can help you."

"This 'tract,' as you call it—I gather you have no idea who is producing it?"

"As I said, monsieur, I have been trying since the day it first appeared to discover who is producing it. The Gestapo in Tours has tried as well. Lieutenant Essart's efforts—the Gestapo man in Tours, as you surely know—he has turned up no one. He arrested one man for publishing it. The man was not the culprit. We have had no success."

"And yet, Monsieur Renard, this is a small town, is it not? Someone must know something. You must be well connected in town. I am astonished you are unable to discover the author. Unless you are ineffectual, monsieur. I suppose incompetence is always a possibility, is it not?"

"Yes, monsieur," Yves said without hesitation and without irony, "incompetence is certainly a possibility. In fact, that must be it. Incompetence. What other reason could there be?"

Simon reached into his pocket and withdrew a different identification card.

He looked at it and then slid it across the table to Yves. The policeman looked puzzled. "Look at it, Monsieur Renard."

Yves picked it up. This card was French and identified the man in front of him as Jacques Duclos. Yves studied the identification card more carefully than he had the first. The paper felt right, the stamps seemed correct, the photo was properly embossed.

"Monsieur," he said finally, "you are carrying false identification. One or the other. If the first one is false, then you have committed a crime that carries the death penalty. . . ."

"Both," said Simon.

"What?" said Yves.

"I said both. Both identifications are false."

"May I please see—"

"I do not have a legitimate identification card, Monsieur Renard. I am a Jew from Berlin, and I left my card behind when I fled."

"Traveling without any identification, monsieur, is also a crime."

The stranger said nothing.

"What do you want from me?" said Yves.

"You still do not know, Monsieur Renard?"

"What I know, monsieur . . ."

"Simon."

"What I know, Monsieur Simon, I may not know. You leave me little choice, monsieur. It is my duty to place you under arrest."

"Let me try to dissuade you from that course of action, Renard. And let me be so explicit that your ridiculous pretend-ignorance will no longer be possible. First of all, as to identification . . ." Simon stood up and unbuckled his belt. Before Yves could protest, he had opened his pants and presented his circumcised penis. "Identification," he said. "Irrefutable." He buckled his pants and sat back down.

"Now: I want you to present me to someone local, someone you trust who is resisting the Germans in some serious fashion. It doesn't matter who it is."

It was finally impossible for Yves to contain his astonishment. "What makes you think—"

"This," said Simon, and laid a gigantic silver pistol on the desk in front of him. "Do not be coy with me, Renard. I am the real thing. And I have been directed to you, because someone believes that you are the real thing too."

"Who . . . ?"

"It doesn't matter. I will give you a while to think about it. Then I will see you again." Simon rose, stuck the pistol in his belt, and left the office. Yves watched in astonishment as Simon paused outside the door. He looked around the square, buttoned his jacket, looked around again as though he had all day, and finally sauntered off in the direction of the Hôtel de France.

"You know the guy you saw drinking beer at the hotel?" said Onesime.

"Yes?" said Jean.

"I wonder if this thing with the count has anything to do with him?"

"Exactly what did the count say?" Jean wanted to know.

"He said to go to the cave after midnight."

"He said you're going to meet someone?"

"Not exactly. But something he said made me think someone else is involved."

Midnight came. A thin drizzle was falling. Onesime carried his bicycle away from the house. He rode down the center of the road. He passed through town. The Trout was closed and dark. At L'Homme he turned toward the vineyards.

The entry door to the count's cave was shut. No cars were in sight. Onesime pulled at the door. It was open. Inside it was pitch black.

"Bring your bicycle inside." That was the count's voice. Onesime did as he was told. Once he had closed the door, a light came on. But it was not like before, where a string of bulbs had led through the darkness into the depth of the cave. Now there was one weak bulb dimly illuminating the front of the cave. Everything else was in darkness.

"Thank you for coming."

"Of course, monsieur. Has something happened?"

"Nothing has happened, Onesime."

"Monsieur?"

"When something happens, it will be because we cause it to happen."

"What might that be, monsieur?"

"That depends on you." This voice came from the darkness. Simon stepped forward into the dim light.

"Who is this, monsieur?" said Onesime. He turned to the man. "Were you in town? Are you the one who visited Renard?"

"I am Simon," said the man. "I am from Paris. Now, make up a name for yourself, and whisper it in my ear so he cannot hear."

"A name?" Onesime thought for a moment. "Van Gogh," he whispered.

"Are you an artist?" said Simon. Onesime nodded yes. "Then think up a different name, not an artist."

"Da Gama," said Onesime. It was the first thing that came to mind. He did not know why. Maybe because he was thinking of maps. Onesime wished he had thought of something more clever. "Don't tell that name to anyone who knows your real name," said Simon. "Even if you trust them. And don't tell your real name to anyone who knows you by your new name. It's for your protection and theirs. That's the first thing. And now," said Simon, "it is time to prepare to attack."

Jean had been waiting at the window for the last three hours. He woke up when he heard his bedroom door creak open. He showered Onesime with questions. "Attack? What attack? Why you? Who is he?"

"He is called Simon. It's not his real name. And it's not just me or us he's working with. He's working with others."

"Who?"

"He wouldn't say. The less we know about each other the better."

"What kind of attack?"

"We're to come up with sabotage ideas and then report back."

"How?"

"He said he will be in touch."

"Who is he?"

"He's German."

"German? How do we know it's not a trap? Drawing maps and keeping records is one thing, but blowing something up is a different story."

"He says he's a Jew. I don't know how we know it's not a trap. I guess we just have to trust him. The count seems to trust him. Are you thinking we should blow something up?"

"That just came to mind. I mean, we know where there's lots of ammunition and fuel. So . . ."

Jean and Onesime pored over their notes and came up with three ideas:

1. Blow up Grandfather's cave.
2. Blow up police department or Cheval Blanc.
3. Blow up railroad bridge south of town (Tours).

Walking home from work the next day, Jean was overtaken by a man on a bicycle. Jean recognized him as the man he had seen drinking beer on the hotel terrace. Jean called after him: "Bonjour, Simon."

The man stopped and dismounted from his bicycle. He studied Jean for a long moment. He had a puzzled look on his face. "Do we know each other, monsieur?"

"I saw you in town. I think you met my brother the other night," said Jean. "With the count. We have our—"

"You must have me mixed up with someone else, monsieur. I'm afraid I don't know what you're talking about. Good evening, monsieur." The man touched the brim of his cap, swung his leg over his bicycle, and rode off.

When Jean turned up the lane to his house, Simon was there waiting, leaning against a fence post. He was smoking a cigarette. Simon crushed out the cigarette and motioned with his head for Jean to follow. They left the lane. Simon carried his bicycle up the hill into the field. The sun was setting. The sky was overcast with low clouds, which turned orange then purple then gray. As it got dark, you could see the moon behind the clouds like a dim lamp behind a curtain.

Simon did not speak. He did not turn around until they reached a tall hedge that concealed them from the road and the lane. "Don't ever speak to me like that," said Simon. "We are not friends. We are not companions. We do not know each other. I do not *want* to know you. I do not want you to know me. Do you understand?"

"Yes." Jean looked shocked.

"And do you understand why?"

"No."

"You will," said Simon. He added, "We are doing important work; remaining unknown is a necessary and important precaution. And," he said, sensing what Jean was about to do, "do not tell me your name. Make up a name for yourself by which I and others will know you."

"A name?"

"Any name."

"Franz," said Jean. He laughed. He liked the idea of having a German name.

"Why Franz?" said Simon.

"Why not? I like the name. Is there anything wrong with it?"

"No," said Simon smiling slightly. "It's perfect."

"We have three ideas," said Jean. He was like an eager schoolboy.

"Tell me."

Jean told Simon the three ideas—one, two, three.

"And why blow up these things?" Simon wondered. "And how?"

"There are live shells stored in my grandfather's caves, and we could get to them."

"I will ask you to show me," said Simon. "But why?"

Beyond the spectacle of it, Jean could not think of a reason.

"There will be a time to do it, but blowing up the cave now will bring the wrath of the Germans down on this village, and they will easily discover it was you. It is, after all, your grandfather's cave, and you live next to it. If you can steal some arms from the cave without detection, well, that is another matter. We will need arms in the near future. Can that be done?"

Simon continued without waiting for an answer. "Blowing up the police station or the German headquarters is also too much of an extravaganza. The railroad bridge makes a bit more sense, since it disrupts their transportation, although they mainly depend on trucks, from what I can tell.

"We will want to do all these things at the proper moment, but for now they are far too extreme for our purposes. In fact, I have something else for you to do."

# XIII.

EVERY NIGHT JEAN AND ONESIME huddled over the radio and listened to the messages coming from England. Endless, odd, cryptic messages, spoken twice, in monotone, never repeated after that. They felt like their own pulse, like the murmuring undercurrent of history itself.

> *Hope does not go on feathered wings; hope does not go on feathered wings.*
>
> *The peaks and valleys of anticipation; the peaks and valleys of anticipation.*
>
> *Tiger, tiger, burning bright; tiger, tiger, burning bright.*
>
> *And yet, Jean François must mount the scaffold; and yet, Jean François must mount the scaffold.*
>
> *The soup is hot and the bread is black; the soup is hot and the bread is black.*
>
> *Slings and arrows of outrageous fortune; slings and arrows of outrageous fortune.*

Everyone listening—whether they were waiting for the phrase that would set them into motion or were trying to glean some piece of useful intelligence or were just listening with no other purpose in mind—was transported by the odd words. It was, in a very real sense, the greatest epic poem ever written, because everyone wrote it and everyone lived it.

Onesime and Jean sat by the radio night after night. Then one rainy night they heard: *Why do the bees not eat honey; why do the bees not eat honey.*

They had almost forgotten why they were listening. "That's us," said Jean. They tiptoed downstairs. There was no light under their mother's door.

"She's asleep," whispered Jean.

"Good," said Onesime. They laced on their boots and slipped into their coats and hats. Onesime took great care closing the door so the latch would not click in the lock. Anne Marie lay in the dark and listened to them go.

The rain had fallen hard all afternoon. It had stopped earlier, but there were still rivulets running down to the lane. Their gurgling was the only sound to be heard. The two men set out quickly toward the south. They followed field roads to avoid encountering anyone or being seen. It was an unnecessary precaution. No one was out at this hour.

A few leftover clouds rushed past the moon, casting the earth from brightness to darkness and back again. The temperature fell. After more than an hour of walking, they reached a broad, high pasture surrounded by tall hedges. They went to the easternmost corner and waited. They stepped from one foot to the other, patting their arms and breathing into their cupped hands to stay warm. They cocked their ears to the sky but heard nothing.

"Are you seeing Marie Piano?" said Jean.

"Yes."

"Are you in love with her?"

"Yes."

"Are you going to marry her?"

"Why are you asking all this stuff?"

"You're my little brother, Oni. I worry about you."

"Yes. I'm going to marry her. But not until the war is over and the Germans are gone."

"Have you asked her?"

"Not yet."

After a while they heard the growl of a small airplane. Onesime pointed his flashlight into the sky and turned it on, then off, then on, then off.

The plane turned and went back the way it had come. Everything was silent. Jean and Onesime stared up into the darkness.

"There!"

"Where?"

"There."

A pale form appeared above them drifting downward, then a second one just above it, then a third. Onesime flashed his light once more. They ran toward the center of the field where the first parachute had already landed with a dull thud. It was attached to a wooden crate. Onesime and Jean rushed to gather up the billowing white silk and its ropes.

Two parachutists landed nearby and pulled in their parachutes, like pulling in fishing nets. When Onesime and Jean reached them, the men were stepping out of the harnesses. Onesime and Jean had never seen such marvelous creatures, with their leather boots, heavy overcoats, and stocking caps. One of the men stepped forward, grinned, and stuck out his hand. "Here we are then," he said in English. Then: "Bonjour." Jean gave the man his hand. "Speak English?" said the other man. "No, I s'pose not."

Jean shrugged. The four men slapped one another on the arms and shoulders and laughed. One of the Englishmen pried open the lid of the crate. Onesime shined his light inside. It contained small arms and ammunition and several two-way radios. "All right, mate?" said the Englishman with a grin.

"Lead on, Macduff," said the other one, with a dramatic gesture, and the four men laughed again.

They stuffed the parachutes into their knapsacks. After two hours they arrived at the Josquin house. They put the crate in the back of the chicken coop and then went into the house. They removed their shoes and moved as silently as they could.

Madame Josquin came out of her room. "Mother," said Onesime. He had known this moment would come, but he had not thought about how he would explain himself. "These men are passing through," he said. "They'll sleep here today. In our rooms. Tonight they leave."

"Give them something to eat," she said, cinching her robe around her. "Are they English?"

"Yes," said Onesime, "they're English."

Onesime made eating motions in their direction. The two men held up their hands in protest. "No, no, don't worry about us."

"You must be hungry. Are you hungry?" said Anne Marie in English.

The two men grinned at her. "Well. Maybe just a cup of tea?" said the taller of the two. He had red hair and freckles. "Some tea would be lovely."

"But only if it's no trouble, ma'am," said the other.

"It is no trouble," said Madame Josquin. Onesime stared at his mother. Where had she learned to speak English? And when?

"If it's no trouble, ma'am, tea would be lovely."

"My Oni is a tea drinker," she said, looking toward Onesime.

"Is he now?" said the tall redhead with a grin and wink at Onesime. "Then he's half English, isn't he?"

They all sat around the kitchen table while Anne Marie poured tea for the Englishmen and for her sons. Even Jean had a cup. She brought out a loaf of dark bread and crocks of jam and honey. "Wait a sec," said the tall redhead. He went into his pack and brought out some coffee and chocolate. "*Pour vous, madame*," he said, and grinned again.

Onesime and Jean took the men upstairs. They fell deeply asleep as soon as they lay down.

"You speak English?" said Jean to his mother.

"Ah," she said, with a smile of fond recollection. But she did not say anything more.

It was eight o'clock. Onesime put on his coat and his boots. He got his bicycle from the shed and rode off to cut firewood for the count. Jean left for Melun's shop. By the time they got home that evening, the Englishmen were gone.


It was early December. The mornings were dark and frosty. When the sun finally rose around eight, it hung low and pale in the southern sky. It had rained a lot in November, and the fields of wheat and barley were vivid green. Smoke curled up from the chimneys and hung in the chilly air. Eighteen months had passed since the Germans had arrived.

Though few had imagined that it ever could, life in Saint-Léon had resumed a kind of normalcy. Even the execution of the hostages had receded into memory, hastened in that direction by everyone's fervent desire to think about other things. Besides, the necessities of life required their fullest attention. Everyone, even the families of the dead, had to struggle to keep food on the table. The surviving three Duquesne children were being cared for by uncles and aunts, who had already found life difficult enough without the extra mouths to feed.

Several local shops had cut back their hours, while others struggled just to stay open at all. Even the grocery had closed briefly—unable to put anything on the shelves, overwhelmed by all the shortages—and then reopened under new ownership. The bakery had a new owner. The old baker had committed suicide. The rumor was that he was a Jew. Was he? No one knew. The new baker was doing very well supplying everyone—French and German—with bread and baked goods. He seemed to have no trouble getting whatever supplies he needed.

Le Pêcheur—The Trout—was busy, as was the bar at the Cheval Blanc. The Hôtel de France had become a residential hotel, putting up visiting strangers—mostly Germans, but also French vendors and suppliers—while they conducted their business in town. Their bar was always busy too.

Claude Melun had taken on another employee in his mechanic's shop, a man named Piet Chabrille. Piet had an inclination to recite

Bible verses from time to time, but Claude didn't care what he recited. Piet Chabrille was a good mechanic and a hard worker. Claude had figured out how to retrofit automobiles and tractors to run on other fuels besides petrol, and people from all over the region who could afford it were lining up to get the conversions done.

The town council had not missed a meeting since the Germans had come. There was plenty of town business to deal with, war or no war. Mayor Schneider always worked through the agenda quickly and efficiently. Yves Renard attended the meetings as he was required to, although he rarely spoke.

Colonel Hollinger held occasional meetings with the mayor. But neither the colonel nor the lieutenant nor any other German official attended town meetings unless it was absolutely necessary. Once when the colonel was present, road repair was being discussed and the town's woodlots in the Forêt de Bercé came under discussion. Jean Charles Arnaud remarked that a recently cut lot was an exceptional resource for wild mushrooms.

After the meeting Colonel Hollinger approached Jean Charles. "Monsieur Arnaud, may I have a word with you?" Jean Charles had almost forgotten his old terror. "There is no cause for alarm, monsieur," said the colonel. "I was only hoping that you might tell me where you hunt for mushrooms. I myself am a mushroom enthusiast."

"Of course, Monsieur Colonel," said Jean Charles. "As you wish."

The citizens of Saint-Léon may not have liked having the Germans there, but they had come to terms with their presence, as one comes to terms with inclement weather or a sick cow or a poor crop. Soldiers crossing the square no longer caused people to stop and stare. Convoys passing on the roads, construction work at the German storage and depot facilities, the improvement of rail facilities—all of these things proceeded as a matter of course.

In fact, the German presence had its good aspects. German construction projects employed French workers who might otherwise have been without work. Improvements to the railroad station had been in the works for ten years and more, but there had never been enough money. Now there was.

*Liberation* still appeared from time to time. It still had the same alarmist tone. It still called the Germans and the Third Reich and the collaborators vile names. But the citizens of Saint-Léon read it mainly for those morsels of news that were of use to them, and they ignored the rest.

No one knew who put out the paper. There was a lot of speculation about it. But by now no one seemed to care. Not even the Germans. It was as General Wallenstein had said: Rebellious tracts were the least of their problems. In the cities there was a growing resistance to German rule, including the occasional sabotage of German facilities and the assassination of German soldiers.

Assassinations especially were met with reprisals, including the execution of hostages. But these executions did nothing to stop the assassinations. In fact, it was often the resisters' purpose to provoke harsh reprisals. The communists especially reckoned that the executions would cause the population to rise up against the Germans.

*Liberation* . . . . . . . . . . . . . . . . . . . . . . . *January 1, 1942. Issue 12*

*"The Americans do not have the will, they do not have the stomach, and they do not have the means." So says Adolf Hitler, that military genius. And of course when the Führer speaks, all his generals goose-step into formation right behind him. Now we shall see. The Americans have entered the war, which can only mean that the days of the Third Reich and Vichy France are numbered.*

*We can see how well the Führer's military genius has already served him in Russia. He decided it wise to delay his attack until June. He chose to penetrate swiftly and deeply into the Russian countryside. Now the mighty German army—millions of men, thousands of tanks—are frozen solid. Their supply lines are too long to sustain. The few generals who have the courage to advise a strategic retreat are branded traitors and shot. The Führer has commanded his soldiers to die where they stand. And that is what they are doing. German soldiers are starving. They are freezing to death. They are dying by the thousands. Stalin and the brave Russian army have mounted a resistance Hitler could never imagine. The German army will fare even worse against the Americans.*

*Colonel Hollinger recently announced that hostages will no longer be taken. Is this not good news? No, not if you know the rest of the order that comes from Germany and that Hollinger has concealed. The policy of holding and executing hostages when there are actions against the Third Reich has been replaced by a policy the Führer calls* Nacht und Nebel—*"Night and Fog." Those arrested by the Third Reich will no longer be imprisoned or tried. Now they will be transported directly to German concentration camps to be tortured for whatever information they may reveal and then to disappear forever. Night and Fog. That is what the Third Reich and its French minions have in store for you.*

**Vive la France! Vive la Libération!**

The effect of reading that last paragraph was devastating for the citizens of Saint-Léon. Those few who still entertained hope of fair treatment at the hands of the Germans could no longer do so. The last vestige of the face of the reasonable collaborator, a partner with whom one could compromise, had been peeled away once and for all.

"But how do we even know it's true?" said Guy Pettier. He leaned against the wall in Melun's shop waiting for his bicycle to be fixed. The front wheel needed straightening.

"That paper is just trying to stir things up," said Melun. "They just want to make trouble."

Jean looked up from the wheel he was working on. "They want to make trouble," he said. "But I think it's true, the Night and Fog thing."

Piet Chabrille said, "The English radio says it's true." Everyone looked at Piet. He never joined in conversations. And it was dangerous to listen to the English radio and more dangerous to admit it. But Piet's assertion made the men incautious, and they began to ply him with questions. Just then the mayor crossed the square to the Cheval Blanc.

"Look," said Jean. Everyone fell silent. A moment later they saw a German sergeant emerge from the gendarme's office with Yves Renard. They too went into the Cheval Blanc. Piet Chabrille repeated his assertion about what the English radio had said, but this time no one was listening.

Colonel Hollinger slapped the latest *Liberation* on the table in front of him. "This really cannot continue," said the colonel. "It must be stopped. It is an affront and an embarrassment."

"I quite agree, *Herr Oberst*," said Schneider. "I cannot understand, Renard, why we can't find out who is publishing these scandals and just stop them, shut them down. Why?"

Renard thought for a moment before he replied. "How am I to investigate this matter when my hands are tied? I am one man, Monsieur Mayor, Monsieur Colonel. I am expected to maintain order in the town and in the surrounding canton by myself. If I had the resources, then perhaps."

The next morning a sedan stopped in front of Renard's office, and four men got out. They strode into Renard's office. "Hello, Renard," said Jacques Courtois. We've been assigned to find the guy publishing this subversive kike-communist shit"—he produced a copy of *Liberation*— "and shut them down." He presented an identification card and watched as Renard read it.

"Gestapo?" said Yves.

Jacques smiled. "Lieutenant Essart sends his greetings," he said.

Yves went to his file drawers and withdrew a thick stack of papers, which he handed to Jacques Courtois.

"What's this?" said Jacques.

"A good place to begin your investigation," said Yves. "Some leads.

Denunciations." Yves had been receiving denunciations—mostly anonymous—for all manner of crimes since the Germans had arrived.

> *Monsieur Yves Renard: If you visit Menasse's barn, you will discover the place where this communist newspaper is being produced. Menasse is a known communist. We are all in danger, thanks to Menasse's crimes. Check out his brother too. Long live Maréchal Pétain.*
>
> *Monsieur: Madame Oser has been trading in black market goods, cigarettes, silk stockings, and other items precious to the war effort. She is also selling her daughter's body for sinful purposes. I believe they are Jews.*
>
> *Monsieur Renard: I have seen Onesime Josquin, who is an army deserter, wandering about late at night. I know for a fact that he sheltered English soldiers at his house. He could well be the author of this leaflet, since I do not put anything past him.*

One letter even accused Jacques Courtois.

> *Courtois pretends to be a patriot, but I think you will find he is the one writing the* Liberation. *He spends a lot of time away in Tours and elsewhere, where he is spying on the Germans and then printing it in Tours or in a secret location. He is also involved in the black market in meat, alcohol, and petrol.*

The group at the Marquis d'Estaing's château was three times as large as it had been at the first meeting. The room was full of men, leaning against the wall, sitting on the arms of chairs, smoking cigarettes and talking. The marquis beamed at everyone, shaking hands with those he recognized and giving a friendly wave to those he didn't.

Dr. Serge Touranot rose to call the meeting to order. He was tall and thin. He wore a dark business suit. He had a narrow black mustache, and his dark hair was combed straight back against his head.

"Gentlemen," he said. His Adam's apple moved up and down in his long neck.

"Gentlemen!" He spoke more loudly, and the room went silent. "I presume you're here because you want to put a stop to the disorder and corruption being spread through our beloved country by the communists and the Jews. They, not the Third Reich, are the real threat to our beloved France. They, not the Germans, represent an alien culture that will destroy our country if we do not take action." He spoke rapidly and assuredly, as though he had made this speech before.

"We must organize ourselves to stop them. This is a serious struggle against deadly opponents. The Third Reich is preoccupied with the war against the Bolsheviks and with building defenses against the invasion Stalin's English and American friends are planning. Meanwhile our police are powerless—I see your heads nodding, those of you who are police—powerless to do anything to help.

"I and my associates have divided the region north of Tours into sectors. You all"—he swept his arm around the room—"represent the northwestern sector. And tonight you will organize yourselves into platoons to begin the work of cleansing your sector of communists and other alien influences.

"Each platoon will have a man in charge and will cover one part of the northwestern sector. Your primary mission will be to root out subversive activity in your part of the sector and to stop it however you can. I emphasize *however you can*. This is war. The communists mean to destroy us, make no mistake, and it is up to us to destroy them first. It's really as simple as that. Our secondary mission, of course, is to alert other patriots to our cause. . . ."

Dr. Touranot instructed everyone to form into groups: "Neuillé-Pont-Pierre—over there; Tours-Nord—there; Château-la-Vallière—here by the fireplace . . ." and so on. Yves and the mayor found themselves standing with nine other men from their region, which had been designated Saint-Léon, since Saint-Léon-sur-Dême was the largest town in that part of the country.

Yves did not know any of the other men except for Piet Chabrille from Melun's shop. Some of the others looked familiar. The mayor seemed to know most of them. He shook hands with everyone.

Yves turned when he felt a hand on his shoulder. Dr. Touranot was taller than he had seemed. "You must be Yves Renard," he said, and smiled. "Lieutenant Essart has spoken of you."

"Has he?" said Yves. "I'm surprised he remembers me."

"Oh, yes," said Touranot. "I hear good things."

"Do you?" said Yves. "Well. I do what I can."

"I'm sure you do," said Touranot, and smiled again.

# XIV.

"ARE YOU READY for something else, Franz?" Jean had just left the mechanic's shop and was walking home. He had not seen Simon or heard him approach. The man came and went like a ghost. "I have something for you," said Simon. "Something important." They walked together.

"What?"

"You will be the third person in an assassination."

"What?"

"An assassination."

"An assassination? But . . . no. I don't think I could. I can't. I've never killed anyone."

"It isn't that difficult. Besides, you won't be killing anyone. You, Shakespeare, and his partner, whose name you don't need to know, will work as a team. The target is an important official responsible for the deaths of many Frenchmen and -women."

"A German?"

"A Frenchman. A traitor. His name doesn't matter."

"Who is he?" Jean wondered. "Am I allowed to know?"

"He is from Chinon. A doctor. A pediatrician. He was instrumental in organizing the resistance in Chinon in order to betray them. He sent them on a false mission. They were all killed or captured and tortured.

Those who were tortured gave up others who were then killed. This man continues as an agent and a provocateur.

"He likes to dine in the first-class buffet at the Tours railroad station. It's a public place. There are lots of police about. Many German officers dine there, so he apparently feels safe. And the food is excellent.

"Listen to the radio. Your message will come the evening before the event. The next evening after the message, you will take the train to Tours and make contact with a man—Shakespeare—outside the station. You will wait until the target has finished eating. When he comes out, Shakespeare will create a distraction. His partner will shoot the man and pass you the gun. All you have to do is leave quickly and dispose of the weapon. Do you understand?"

"Yes, I do. But I don't know. . . ."

"It isn't that difficult. You'll see. It will be over quickly. You'll go to Saint-Pierre, dispose of the gun along the way, and take the next train from Saint-Pierre back to Saint-Léon."

Two nights later Jean heard the message. *Destiny arrives on a cat's paws; destiny arrives on a cat's paws.*

"Where are you going?" Onesime said.

"Tell Maman I'll be back late," said Jean. "Don't say why."

"I don't *know* why," said Onesime. "Is Simon back?"

Jean did not answer. Onesime looked at Jean and then embraced him. "Good luck," he said.

Shakespeare was a surprise, a short man who looked to be thirty-five, with a trim black mustache and a fastidious way of dressing. His huge eyes swam behind thick lenses. A bowler hat sat squarely on his round head. Jean offered his hand, and Shakespeare took it limply in his, then let it drop. "You're new," said Shakespeare.

"Yes," said Jean.

"You get used to it."

"You've done it often?" said Jean.

"It's what I do. I'm something of a specialist. The main thing for you to remember is to move away quickly but without appearing to be hasty. Cigarette?" Shakespeare held up a package of English cigarettes, and Jean took one. Shakespeare struck his lighter, lit Jean's cigarette and then his own. Shakespeare drew deeply on the cigarette, holding it in the middle of his mouth as though it were his first ever. He blew the smoke out without inhaling.

"You see," said Shakespeare, "creating a diversion is an art. First there is the costume. For instance, if you saw me tomorrow you would not recognize me. Then when the job is done I have to stay in the crowd. To see what happens; to learn anything I can that might be useful.

"At first that frightened me, staying in the crowd. I'm not ashamed to admit it. I feared there might be some identifying thing about me, something that would give me away to the Gestapo when they looked around or questioned people. So when they looked around and their eyes met mine, I had to look back at them, but as an innocent, not as someone who knew something.

"When they questioned me, as they often have, I had to be able to mislead them subtly, just as an unobservant witness might with slightly wrong information. That also became part of the art: to mix innocently with the onlookers, to be curious about the dead man but not too curious. . . ."

Shakespeare could not stop talking. He elaborated on the various distractions he had used. He explained how he had to divert attention enough so that the assassin could do his work unseen and yet not so much that he would implicate himself as an accomplice. He was pleased to imagine that he might already have become a legend among the Gestapo, so that they yearned to get their hands on him.

Jean stopped listening. Imagine: a tedious assassin. Jean needed to focus his attention on what was about to happen. "Don't even try to plan an escape route," said Shakespeare, as though he had read Jean's mind. "There will always be someone or something in the way, and if you rely on a plan, you will be paralyzed when the plan is thwarted. The police show up in the wrong place, you see someone you recognize, an exit is blocked. Improvise and you will be safe."

Shakespeare straightened slightly. "That's him," he said. "Don't look. I'll be off." The station was so noisy that Jean didn't immediately recognize the sound of the pistol shot. He turned and saw a tall man with a pencil mustache and slicked back hair with his mouth wide open. He was looking straight in Jean's direction. Then his eyes rolled upward and his head lolled back.

Shakespeare grasped the man by the arm and gently lowered him onto a crate so that the man looked as though he might merely be ill, when in fact he was already dead. "Are you all right, monsieur?"

"Is he all right?" someone said.

"Monsieur!? Monsieur!"

"Look! There's blood!"

The dead man was surrounded by people now. Shakespeare had stepped back out of the way and let others take over. A young woman walked toward Jean. Her lips were bright red. She wore a long wool coat with a fur collar, and a magenta pillbox hat. There was a bejeweled bird bobbing on the side of the hat. She passed close by Jean, and as she did, she pressed a small pistol into his hand. It was one of those stamped-metal, disposable pistols the British had been dropping. The Liberator, it was called. The barrel burned Jean's hand, and he nearly cried out. It wouldn't have mattered if he had; everyone was shouting at once and staring at the dead man, who was now being lowered to the floor.

"Call the police."

"They're coming."

"There they are!"

Jean let the gun slide into his coat pocket. He looked toward the woman again, but she walked out of the station without looking back. The little bird on her hat bobbed. He had no idea what she looked like. Neither would anyone else.

A pair of policemen arrived through the same door. Jean turned and walked toward the dead man. He had a surprised look on his face. His eyes were wide open, his mouth too. There was a trickle of blood coming from his nose. Jean walked into the first-class buffet and out the other side. He found the streetcar to Saint-Pierre. In Saint-Pierre he bought a ticket for Saint-Léon. The woman who sold him the ticket, a pretty woman, smiled at him.

In the train Jean studied his reflection in the window. It looked back at him from outside: pale, washed out like a ghost. Jean opened his eyes wide and then his mouth and saw in the window the face of the man he had helped kill.

Simon was wrong. It wasn't easy. Shakespeare had said you get used to it. Maybe that was so. Jean hoped it wasn't.

"Ticket, please." The conductor stood beside him. "Are you all right, monsieur?"

Jean sat up straight. "Yes, yes. Thank you. I'm fine."

Jean arrived home after midnight. The lights were still on. Onesime and his mother were waiting in the kitchen. Both looked up expectantly as Jean came in. He faced the door and took off his boots. He didn't want to turn around, afraid of what might show in his face. "Are you all right, *mon petit*?" said Anne Marie. She hadn't called him that for years. "Are you hungry?"

"I'm very hungry," he said. He came to the table.

His mother stepped to the stove and opened a burner. She slid a pot over the flames. "I made soup," she said. His place at the table was set. She poured him a tumbler of wine. She cut a large slab of bread and put a crock of pork *rillettes* by his place.

"It went all right?" said Onesime.

Jean looked at Onesime.

"It went all right, *mon petit*?" said Madame Josquin.

"Oui, Maman," he said. He took a gulp of wine. He ate silently. His mother sat down opposite him and studied his face. He lowered his head as he ate, so that she could not watch him. For a long time the only sound was metal scraping against pottery while Jean ate, and occasional slurping as he sucked the broth from his spoon. He mopped his bowl with a crust of bread. "I'm going to bed," he said.

"Jean," said his mother. He did not answer. "Jean," she said again, "I have something to say to you." He did not look up. "I don't know what you had to do," she said, "and I don't want to know. It is none of my business. This goes for you and for you." She looked over at Onesime, who was staring back at her. She continued: "These days we all have to do things no one should have to do."

Now Jean looked up at her. "Yes," she said, nodding her head. "But I know you both. I trust you. I don't believe you would ever do anything to be ashamed of. It's the times," she said, "it's these times we should be ashamed of. Not what we have to do to make them better." She rose from the table and reached across and touched Jean's head.

An urgent meeting of the Saint-Léon militia was held in a room behind Aseline's plumbing shop on the outskirts of Villedieu. Mayor Michel Schneider could not attend. "You go," he had instructed Yves. "I have to be careful about where I'm seen."

Besides the plumber, Robert Aseline, there were six in attendance, including Yves Renard and Piet Chabrille from Melun's mechanic's shop.

The assassination of Dr. Touranot meant not only that one of the militia commanders and organizers was dead, which was a great loss. It also meant that there was a spy and a traitor somewhere in their organization.

"Well, that's Tours," said one man. "It happened in Tours; he was from Tours. So how does that affect us?"

"It doesn't," said someone named Joel. "Does it?" He had gone to the Château-Renault meeting full of enthusiasm. But now he was having second thoughts.

There was silence. Aseline's eyes darted nervously about the room. He was not used to being in charge. "Well," he said. "It doesn't affect us directly. But . . . it means. We should. We need a plan. We need to put together a plan. Make a list of suspects in our towns. For instance, you, Joel, make a list for Villedieu, where you live, see? Of people you think are communists or sympathizers. Then when we have a list, we'll decide who to watch and how to watch them. I mean we don't have to watch them all the time, like spy on them or anything, you see? But kind of keep an eye on them."

"What about guns?" This was Piet. All heads swiveled in his direction.

"The private ownership of guns is outlawed," said Yves.

"Let's deal with first things first, shall we?" said Aseline. He did not want the meeting to get away from him. "First we need a list of who's who, you see? We know who the communists are in our community, see? Then we can track them, see what they're up to. . . ."

"With six people?" said Joel.

"Seven," said Aseline. "Anyway, there will be more of us next time. And we'll get information. That's the main thing right now, see? Information. When we have information, we can go after them. So for now we have two jobs: First, make a list of known communists and, two, get more members."

"And how do we get more members?" said Joel.

"Well, one way is for everybody to bring somebody new to the next meeting."

"Bring somebody?"

"Tell them what we're about. Stopping the spread of communism. Saving France for the French. It won't be hard. It's what real Frenchmen believe in."

"The next meeting, which is when?" said Yves.

"Let's say . . . two weeks from tonight. Same time," said Aseline.

"Here?" said Yves.

"For now. Why not?" said Aseline. "So for next meeting, new members and a list of communists. And other troublemakers."

"And then we go after them?" said Piet Chabrille.

"And then we go after them," said Aseline.

"With guns," said Piet.

"If necessary," said Aseline. "If there's no other way."

Yves Renard did not say anything.

At the meeting two weeks later they were twenty, and they filled the small room. Yves Renard was there. Piet Chabrille. Joel was not. Still Aseline was right: It wasn't hard to get people interested. Word had gotten around that some citizens were organizing to root out communists and Jews, and people signed on eagerly. Some women wanted to come, but the men said no. For now at least. Aseline looked around the room smiling. He had compiled a list of known and suspected communists, which he read aloud.

"Robert," said a new man, "what do we do with this information?"

"Well," said Aseline, "we mount a surveillance operation. . . ."

"For what purpose," said the man. "Are we going to watch, or are we going to do something?"

"I'm getting to that," said Aseline. "I've been talking to Jacques Courtois. He's in Tours now with the German police. He says they can supply us with weapons and ammunition. . . ."

"Wait a minute, Robert," said the new man. "Should we be discussing that kind of thing in front of the cops? I mean, what we're talking about here isn't strictly—"

"Kosher?" said someone. Everybody laughed.

The new man laughed too. But then he continued. "I mean this is serious and, let's face it, technically illegal. So we should at least know where Renard stands."

Everyone looked at Yves. Yves looked around the room. "You don't know?" he said.

"How should we know?" said the man.

"You know about me the same way we know about you," said Renard. "After all, how do we know about you?"

"Wait a minute, Renard . . . ," said the man.

"Or Aseline here, or anybody? I mean, I can tell you I want to get rid of communists and Jews, if that's what you need to hear. And Gypsies and homosexuals and Freemasons, if you need more proof. Except it's not proof. It's only words. I can swear it's true. But what does *that* mean? People swear to all sorts of things these days. It comes down to this: Either you believe me or you don't. There's no way you can know for sure where I stand."

"Until the shooting starts," said Piet. Piet Chabrille's face hardly ever changed, but just now there was a broad, toothy smile spread across it, and his eyes danced. "When the shooting starts, then we'll know."

# XV.

IT WAS A WARM SPRING day. Anne Marie Josquin walked her bicycle down the lane. On reaching the road she stepped on the bottom pedal, lifted herself onto the saddle, and rode off toward town. She passed Gerard Penoit pruning his fruit trees. His wife, Roberte, was hoeing the garden. They ignored Anne Marie and she ignored them. They were not enemies, but these days it seemed better not to talk, for fear of what you might say or what you might not say.

Anne Marie felt the sun on her neck as she rode toward town. *It is time to put in lettuce and onions,* she thought. She stopped at Courbeau's, left some eggs, and collected several rounds of goat cheese. Next she stopped at Angeline's house. Angeline was her youngest, but unlike the boys, Angeline was married and already had a baby daughter. Anne Marie and Angeline embraced.

"How is Henri?" said Anne Marie. "And you, my sweet? And how is my *petite-petite?*" she cooed, leaning down so that her face was close to the baby's. "Oh, you're so big, such a big girl already." The baby smiled.

"It's unbelievable how she grows," said Angeline. "And how she eats."

"Here, my sweet," said Anne Marie, reaching into her basket. "Eggs. Only four this week. The hens aren't laying. And cheese from Courbeau."

"Come in, Maman, for some tea."

"Not this time, Angeline. Maybe tomorrow. I have my rounds today. Henri is well?"

"He's all right. He's working at least."

"Be glad of that," said Anne Marie.

"He's working for the Germans."

"Ah, well, at least it's work."

"Who knows whether it will last."

"Who knows whether anything will last these days," said Anne Marie. "The news from England—"

"Please, maman. I wish you didn't listen to that. It's dangerous. And besides, it's not true."

"The Americans—"

"Maman, stop talking about it. It's not just dangerous for you. It's dangerous for us, for me and the baby. And for Oni and Jean. The Germans shoot people for listening."

"Oni and Jean can take care of themselves, Angeline."

"Are they involved in anything, Maman?"

"Involved in anything?"

"You know. Anything . . . subversive. Henri thinks they might be."

"No," said Anne Marie. "Don't be silly. Don't worry."

"Well, stop talking about things, and stop listening to the radio, and I'll stop worrying. We all have to survive."

"You're right of course. Anyway, I have my rounds."

In town Anne Marie looked in at the mechanic's shop.

"Bonjour, madame," said Claude Melun.

"Bonjour, Claude; bonjour, Piet," said Anne Marie. "Jean? Could you look at my bicycle. The back wheel is rubbing." The two walked outside. Jean bent over to look.

"Have you seen your sister lately, Jean?" she said.

"The wheel's all right, Maman."

"I know. Do you ever see your sister?"

"No," said Jean.

"Well, maybe you should. Henri's been filling her head about you and Oni."

"Henri?"

"She says he thinks you're up to something."

"Up to something? Up to what?"

"You might want to find out what she means."

"I'll stop and see them."

Anne Marie touched his cheek and then reached up and kissed him.

"Maman, don't."

"Even a mother's kiss is suspicious?" she said. "The times are bad when a kiss is suspicious."

Anne Marie went into the bakery and bought three small custard tarts. She put the package in her basket and rode out of town. On the road to Villedieu she passed a column of men being marched under German guard. They walked with their heads down. Halfway past the column, she said in a low voice, "Hello!" in English. Several of the men looked her way. One mouthed the word *hello* back at her.

In Villedieu, opposite the church, she turned up the narrow street that went to the château ruins. She stopped in front of a small stone house with a garden out front and leaned her bicycle against the stone fence. Edith Troppard came out of the house. "You already have lettuce," said Anne Marie.

"I took a chance and planted early," said Edith, "and this year luck was on my side." The two women embraced, then stopped to admire the row of tender greens just showing above the soil.

"That settles it," said Anne Marie. "I'll plant tomorrow."

Edith laughed. "Come inside," she said. Anne Marie lifted the package from her basket. "Aah!" said Edith. She could see the butter soaking through the paper wrap.

The house was sparsely furnished. Edith Troppard was not one for fancy decorations. Downstairs was one large room that served as a living room, dining room, and kitchen. A long oak table sat at the center of the room, an iron stove against one wall with a stone sink beside it. Straight-backed chairs were lined up against the opposite wall. There were a few pictures on the walls, mostly framed landscape photos that Edith had cut from magazines.

A man was seated on one of the chairs beside the table. "Bonjour," he said, and stood up. He took a step forward and extended his hand. "Please, madame," he said, before Anne Marie could speak, "don't tell me your name. Make one up instead and whisper it to me.

Anne Marie had always liked the name *Florence*. "Florence," she whispered.

"It is a pleasure to meet you," he said. "I am Simon. Our friend"—he smiled toward Edith—"tells me great things about you."

"Well, Simon, she tells me great things about you too."

That evening at dinner Anne Marie told her sons about her day. "The chickens aren't laying. They're old. It's hard to get chicks these days. The Germans are building something in the fields just above The Trout. Did you see it?"

"I did," said Jean. "I couldn't tell anything about it. But it's got a high double fence."

"It looks like a chicken house," said Anne Marie, "but I suppose it's a barracks of some kind. Yveline at the bakery said she saw some workers up there. But they weren't from here."

"Maybe it's a prison camp," said Onesime.

"Oh, and I saw some prisoners today. Germans were guarding them. They were on the road to Villedieu. Where could they have been going?"

"Really?" said Onesime. He tried not to seem too interested.

"They were English," she said.

"How do you know they were English?" said Jean.

"Some had foreign-looking uniforms," she said.

"That doesn't mean they're English."

"I talked to them in English, and they understood me."

"You spoke to them?"

"Yes."

"With guards there?"

"The guards were far away. It was a long column, and the guards were at both ends. They didn't hear me."

"How do you know?" Jean and Onesime had dropped every pretense of being disinterested, but this time she did not answer. "How do you know?" Jean said again.

"Stop interrogating me," she said. "Both of you."

"It's just that—"

"I am not stupid," she said. "And I don't interrogate you, so you stop it."

Onesime and Jean looked at their hands in silence.

"I met Simon today," she said.

Onesime and Jean continued looking at their hands.

"You know, we can't protect one another by pretending not to know anything," said Anne Marie. "I hear you talking together. I hear you listening to the radio. I hear you go out late at night. I am not an idiot.

"In peacetime you have the luxury of thinking others are stupid or ignorant or blind. But not now. Not your enemies, not your friends, and not your mother." She paused and thought for a moment before she continued. "It is certainly not my intention to know what you are doing, and it should not be your intention to know what I am doing. But we have to all trust that we are competent. You better learn to trust me as I trust you."

There was a long silence before Jean spoke. "I saw Angeline on my way home. I stopped by their house. She said Henri is suspicious, like you said. I think he's dangerous. He seems to know something about our—Onesime's and my—activities. I don't know exactly what or how he knows it. But I don't trust him. Or Angeline." Jean put his face in his hands.

"Listen, Jean," said Anne Marie, "you can mistrust him, as I think you must. You can mistrust your sister, as I think you should, without despising either of them or even loving them less. They are arranging things as best they can for themselves. They have a certain way they believe is right. The best thing we can do for them is to not let them know anything. We must try to persuade them that we are not a danger to them."

Later that night Anne Marie lay on her bed and stared into the darkness. "Where did I find this hardness in myself? How will I ever do the things I might have to do?"

When such a sudden and enormous upheaval occurs, as there had been in France, it can only result in chaos. Once order is obliterated and the law itself becomes lawless, all anyone has left is his own moral compass. And the personal moral compass is an extremely unreliable instrument. Convenience, opportunism, greed, malice—all these things and more exert a stronger magnetic force than virtue ever could.

Simon recognized that the struggle he was engaged in was all but futile. Few were even tempted to resist the Germans. And few of those resisting would survive. The chances for success in the spring of 1942 seemed small beyond reckoning. And yet, what choice did he have but to continue building a network, training resisters, and preparing for the moment, should it come, when the Germans could be beaten?

In Paris, Savanne, his contact, scoffed at the notion. "I am sorry," she said. She drew deeply on her cigarette and studied him over the top of her glasses. "But you are mistaken. You are too sentimental. You have allowed yourself to become attached to those people. Your job is not to keep them alive. They are necessary but dispensable, soldiers in the struggle against fascism. That is what they are.

"Like you and me," she added. They were sitting at a table by the door to the kitchen in La Coupole. "Make use of them," she said. "You have those ammunition dumps down there that you talk about. Blow them up. You have German officers that need killing. Kill them. And collaborators. The train line to the coast. You say you have good people there."

"Yes," said Simon.

"Then make use of them. If there are reprisals, so much the better. The more the fascists clamp down, the worse they behave, the better for us. Stop being sentimental. Why wait? For what?" Simon had slept with her once. She had told him what to do every step of the way. Her advice was like her lovemaking. *Do this, do that, now do that.*

"Do we want fireworks?" said Simon. "Or do we want to defeat the Germans?" It was nine o'clock, and the restaurant was full. Many of the tables were occupied by uniformed German officers. For some reason their proximity comforted Simon.

"Of course we want to win," said Savanne. "But we also want to bring about a Soviet France. That is the overriding necessity." After a late start—they had been busy in Spain—the Stalinists had now maneuvered themselves into positions of control in the resistance. It had been easy. They were experienced in secret organization, and they were ruthless. Savanne noticed that Simon was silent. "The objective is not liberation. It is the overthrow of a fascist regime, whether it is German or French," she said.

"I agree," said Simon. "That is the goal. Absolutely." He wished he had not said "absolutely." He drank the last swallow of wine from his glass. "There is a train in fifteen minutes," he said. "It is time I get back."


Jean found Henri at the bar in the Cheval Blanc. It was eight o'clock, and the colonel and his staff were gone. The door leading to their upstairs offices was locked. That let the patrons talk more freely and gave the informers among them something to hope for. The bar was full. The air was smoky. "Hey, Jean," said Henri, waving. "A late night?"

"*Salut*, Henri," said Jean. "Yes, a little late. A glass of red," he said to the bartender. Jean touched Henri's glass with his own. "*Santé.*"

"So you're busy at Melun's?" said Henri.

"Pretty busy," said Jean. "What about you? I hear you got a job. That's good luck."

"Yeah, finally," said Henri. "Me and Lucien both." He leaned back a bit so Jean could see Lucien next to him. Lucien touched his hat in greeting.

"*Salut*, Lucien," said Jean. Lucien took out a package of cigarettes and offered them around. Jean took a cigarette and leaned in to light it on the match Lucien held. "So is it good work?" said Jean. "Something that will last?"

"It's all right. With the *Boche*," said Lucien. "Nothing special, but it pays."

"Let's sit down," said Jean. They moved away from the crowded bar to a small table beside the door. They sipped their wine. People came and went, greeting their neighbors. Suspicion and misgivings hung in the air like the smoke.

"What are you up to? Otherwise?" said Henri.

"Nothing much," said Jean.

"Really?" said Henri. "That's not what I hear."

"What do mean?" said Jean. "What do you hear?"

"That you're with the resistance, the *maquis*," said Henri.

"You're kidding," said Jean. "The *maquis*?"

"That's what I hear," said Henri.

"From who?" said Jean.

"Let's just say that's what I hear."

"Well whoever it is doesn't know what he's talking about. That kind of talk can get people in trouble. Me? I'm staying out of things."

"What do you mean 'get people in trouble'?" said Henri.

"I'm just saying," said Jean. "People ought to mind their own business and be sure of their facts before they open their mouths."

"You know, you can't stay out of things," said Lucien. He drew deeply on his cigarette and snuffed out the tiny stub in the ashtray. "How are you going to stay out of things? It's like saying you're going swimming and not getting wet."

"That's right," said Henri, studying Jean. "I mean there are sides; there's no middle. These days you're on one side or the other."

"Yeah?" said Jean. "Well, I don't see it that way. I'm keeping my head down, like I said."

"You should come to Aseline's on Friday," said Lucien. "It might interest you."

"Yeah?" said Jean. "What's going on at Aseline's?" It was his turn to extinguish his cigarette, and he did it as though it were a delicate operation, mashing it this way and that in the ashtray until not a spark or a wisp of smoke was left.

"Well?" said Henri, looking at Lucien. "You brought it up. So tell him."

"Well," said Lucien, "we've only been once, so I can't tell you too much. But it's a bunch of people who . . . well, we don't particularly like the Germans but . . . well, we think Pétain is doing his best to save France, and the communists are trying their best to destroy what he's building and, well, they're—the communists—behind the *maquis*, and they're the ones passing out that pamphlet, which is openly communist, and they're doing other things. . . ."

"The thing is," said Henri, "if you really think you can sit on the fence, then you need to come and see how wrong you are. Things are further along than you can imagine. The meeting is behind Aseline's shop, Friday at ten."

By the time Jean arrived, there must have been thirty men and a few women crowded into the room behind Aseline's shop and spilling out into the shop itself. He knew half of the people there.

Aseline made a little speech welcoming everyone, especially the new-comers, and most especially the women. There was talk about the local *maquis*, who they were, how they might be organized, how they might be infiltrated, and who might do it.

The most likely candidate turned out to be Jean. "After all," said someone whom Jean didn't recognize, "I hear he's one of them. That's the perfect cover. He shouldn't have any trouble getting in with them."

Jean shrugged his shoulders and turned red. Everyone was looking at him. They all seemed to agree that he should try to join the *maquis*. "Then what?" he wondered.

"What do you think?" said Piet Chabrille. "We kill them." Jean hadn't even noticed that Piet was there.

"I'll work with you," said Henri.

But within days Piet Chabrille announced triumphantly that he and Aseline, and not Jean, had flushed out a cell of resisters. The normally reticent Chabrille could not stop talking about it.

Aseline's father-in-law, himself a veteran of the Great War, had joined in a late-night card game with a group of veterans. After several hours of drinking and playing cards, the father-in-law enticed some of the men into making treasonous remarks about the Germans and Pétain. One old veteran wished aloud for the defeat of the Germans and the overthrow of Pétain. Another called Pierre Laval, the Vichy head of government, a fascist pig.

Aseline and his associates streamed into the room, herded the men together, and marched them off at gunpoint. They were driven to an abandoned warehouse behind the Dupont factory. The six arrested men were turned over one by one to a team whose job it was to extract confessions and information from them.

Piet Chabrille, the leader of the team, was an enthusiastic and enterprising interrogator. He had never been trained in that art, but he seemed to know instinctively how long you could hold a man's head in the toilet without drowning him. He knew how to use a small knife blade under a man's fingernails. He invented other methods, some so ferocious that his team members had to stop him.

To his great misfortune, Jean Charles Arnaud, the terrified pharmacist and town councilman, was among the card players. Though he had said nothing remotely treasonous—in fact he had admonished the others to be careful about what they were saying—he was tortured like everyone else. Very soon he had confessed to wishing Pétain ill, to having a variety of other treasonous inclinations, and, most damningly, to being involved in a conspiracy to commit sabotage. It was his intention, he sobbed, to blow up both the tracks and the electric lines along the Paris rail line. The men he named as partners in the conspiracy—each time his head was pulled gasping and crying from the toilet, he mentioned someone else—were obviously names that had come to mind because Jean Charles simply wanted the drowning to stop. In fact the conspiracy itself was a figment of his desperate imagination.

A number of men from the card-playing group were sent to prison to await trial at Saint-Pierre, as were several from the group named by Jean Charles. As for Jean Charles himself, whether it was the gravity of the crimes to which he had confessed or the disgust his craven fear aroused in his interrogators, he was left to the untender ministrations of Piet Chabrille, who continued working on him long after Jean Charles had anything more to say or, for that matter, *could* say anything. Eventually Jean Charles was dead, and Piet Chabrille emerged panting from the makeshift interrogation room.

# XVI.

*Liberation* . . . . . . . . . . . . . . . . . . . . . *February 18, 1943. Issue 16*

*The past year has been a dark and bitter one for France. We are living under a murderous regime governed by treachery and deceit. Our own government has made it shameful to call oneself French.*

*The persecution and deportation of Jews has begun in earnest. Last June and July tens of thousands of Jews—French and foreign— were rounded up all over France. This is part of what Hitler has called "the final solution," meaning the murder of every Jew in Europe. Our government, Pétain, and Laval have gone along enthusiastically.*

*Our civil servants and police not only aided in this cruel business, but in many cases they initiated it. All over France you could see French police forcing their way into the homes of innocent people and taking them off, never to be seen again. At first the roundup of Jews was supposed to include only those between 16 and 40 years of age, but the reprehensible Pierre Laval insisted that children under 16 should be included. Our police were not deterred. They executed the entire operation in impeccable fashion. The Nazis could not have done a more-thorough job.*

*On November 8 British and American troops landed for the first time in Morocco and Algeria. To our everlasting shame, what remains of our own French army did all it could to drive them out. General Pétain broke off relations with the United States and declared them our enemy. Meanwhile our dear friend Adolf Hitler's Third Reich army of marauders marched across the border into Vichy in complete violation of the armistice. All of France is now occupied by the German army. This is how all our French groveling has come to naught.*

*Could things get worse? They could and they have. Laval and Pétain and their minions are now enslaving Frenchmen. German soldiers are dying like flies on the vast frozen wastes of Russia. Therefore there are no longer sufficient German men in the Reich to do the devil's work. But fear not! Laval and Pétain have come to Hitler's rescue. Under their new OWS Act—the Obligatory Work Service Act; it could better be called the Slave Labor Act—they have begun to snatch Frenchmen from their homes and families and ship them off to do forced labor in the Reich's foundries and armament and munitions factories. Are they not needed at home? Do their farms and families and businesses not need them?*

*This OWS enslavement has begun in big cities and is spreading across the country. It is only a matter of time before the young men of Saint-Léon are rounded up and torn away from their loved ones. They will be packed into trains as the Jews have been. And their ultimate fate will be no different.* **WE ARE ALL JEWS NOW!!!**
**Vive la France!!! Vive la Libération!!!**

On March 8, a gray and chilly Monday, groups of young men stood huddled on the platform at Saint-Léon's station. Each had been checked against a master list of those notified to report. Each had a suitcase or a rucksack containing the provisions he was entitled to bring with him. The train of carriages waited on the track beside them, steam rising from beneath the black locomotive in great hissing bursts. Henri looked around. Onesime Josquin was there. He stood looking at the ground. Henri's friend Lucien was there. Aseline was there. No one was there to see them off. Henri searched the crowd and found others he knew.

There were already men inside the train, but you could hardly see their faces. The train had taken on men in Angers and Château-la-Vallière. It would proceed up the line to Blois, where it would be attached to another train. The windows would be blacked out, and they would continue through Paris to Germany to who knows where. Armed German Gestapo in plain clothes stood on the other side of the station house, in case of trouble. But there was no trouble.

At exactly nine o'clock the doors of the train cars opened, and a German soldier stepped from each door. Each was carrying a machine pistol. The soldiers signaled that the waiting men should board. In a few minutes they were all inside, crowded onto the wooden seats with their suitcases and bags on their laps. No bags were allowed in the aisle or on the racks above them. Onesime found a seat at the rear of the car. He clutched his small tattered suitcase to his chest. The German guards stationed themselves at both ends of the car. The train lurched into motion.

No one spoke as they rolled along the track. No one had said that they couldn't. They just didn't. What was there to say? It was sad and desperate and humiliating all at the same time. Onesime was seated not far from Henri. He kept his eyes downcast.

Henri gazed out at the landscape and watched it pass. From a train the countryside looked completely unfamiliar. The car swayed gently; the wheels clicked rhythmically on the rails. He felt as though he were dreaming.

They crossed the Dême, and the bridge made a hollow sound. Henri took a package of cigarettes from his pocket and looked toward the German guard, as though to ask whether he could smoke. The guard looked past him without expression. Henri put a cigarette between his lips. He was reaching for his matches, when the train lurched so violently that he was thrown from his seat.

The train's steel wheels locked and squealed against the tracks as the car tipped sideways. The first shot came from behind Henri, and, when he turned, he saw Onesime seizing the fallen guard's gun with one hand and putting his own pistol away with the other. A second shot rang out. The guard at the other end of the car, who was no more than a boy, really, stood with a bewildered look on his face as though he didn't yet know that he was dead. A man Henri had never seen before grabbed the boy's gun.

The train sat listing crazily halfway down the embankment. It was making strange groaning and hissing noises, like a mortally injured animal. Onesime was the first to get a door open. Outside armed men ran toward the train. Guards fired from inside the other cars, but their guns soon went silent.

Onesime turned to Henri. "Are you going, or are you going to wait here? You think the Gestapo is going to reward you for being a good boy?"

"Let's go," said Lucien. "What are you waiting for?"

Henri didn't say anything. *My life has just changed forever,* he thought. *There's nothing I can do about it. If I sit here, I'm done for; if I go, I'm done for.* He followed Lucien and Aseline out the door.

All along the train, doors opened and men stumbled out, still clutching their suitcases and packs. During the night the spikes holding the rails had been removed. The train had headed off the rail bed before sinking into the mud. The engineer stood beside his engine with his hands high in the air. "Shoot him," someone said, and someone else did.

The men fled in all directions, some inexplicably running toward town, where the Gestapo would certainly be waiting for them. Others wandered off in twos and threes, staying with those they knew, hoping to make their way back to Angers or wherever they had come from. Others attached themselves to the armed men. One consequence of the OWS Act of February 16, 1943, was that many young Frenchmen who had nowhere else to go found their way to the resistance.

Onesime joined with other armed men as they moved quickly across the fields. An hour later as they approached the Le Mans highway, Onesime broke off from the group and took a small field road that led above a quarry. He went along a vineyard, cut across another vineyard, and came down the hillside just above the Count de Beaumont's cave, near where he had cut hay what seemed like an eternity ago.

He slid down the steep hillside and knocked on the cave door. The door opened immediately. Jean pulled Onesime inside the cave and closed the door. The cave was still lit by a single small bulb. "Take my hand," said Jean. He led Onesime into the darkness. When they came to the door that had been locked the last time they were there, Jean knocked. There was silence for a few seconds before the door opened.

Alexandre de Beaumont, the count's wife, stood before him. The kerosene lanterns and candles flickering around the room bathed her in orange light. Onesime imagined that he had been killed at the train and now found himself in heaven. "Come in," she said.

There were cots around the edge of the cave, divided from one another by makeshift partitions. The large table at the center was now surrounded by chairs. The board with the map leaned against the wall.

There were people sitting together on two of the beds. They regarded Jean with curiosity. They looked like a family, except the parents were dark, the three children blond. "They're not related," said Alexandre, as though she knew what Onesime was thinking. Alexandre had a low, husky voice. Onesime had never heard her speak before. "The Shapiras have no children of their own. But they were rounded up at the same time as the Herzog children next door. The Herzog parents had been taken away the night before and the children were alone in their apartment.

"That was in Chartres. The Shapiras managed to slip under a baggage cart. They pulled the children under with them. They weren't missed and the train left without them."

"Are they French, madame?" said Onesime.

"Yes," said Alexandre.

"Where are they going?"

"We'll have to see what we can do," she said.

"Oui, madame," said Onesime.

"I have to go home," said Jean. "You're staying here for now." Onesime still had the machine gun slung over his shoulder. Jean took it. "I'll put it with the others."

Onesime lay down on a cot with his hands behind his back and gazed at the orange light dancing on the ceiling. The next thing he knew Maurice de Beaumont was shaking his shoulder. Onesime sat up. "Excuse me, monsieur."

"It's all right, Onesime. You must be exhausted. I'm glad to see that you are all right."

"I am fine, monsieur."

"More then two hundred men escaped from that train, Onesime, thanks to you and the others. By the time the Germans heard of it, the men were gone. Most will head back to their towns and the territory they know."

"What about me, monsieur?"

"For now you have to stay out of sight. But look, the Germans don't have the time or the means to look for those that evade this draft. The French police may be another story. But their hands are pretty full too. And they're short of men for this kind of thing. And frankly I don't think they have the stomach for it.

"The resistance is growing. Finally. After nearly three years, the OWS was the last straw. Lots of those men will join us. They have no choice now."

"My brother-in-law was there. He was with Aseline's militia. Aseline was there too. If they join the resistance, how can you can trust them?"

"We don't have to trust them in order to make use of them."

"Is there a 'we,' monsieur?"

"There is, Onesime. You've seen that yourself."

"What about these people?" said Onesime. "What about the Jews over there? What's to become of them?"

The count looked at Onesime for a long moment before he spoke. "That depends in part on you, Onesime. Come look at the map.

"We are here," said the count, pointing at the map. "We have to get our Jews to . . . here."

"That is not far, monsieur."

"A night's walk, Onesime. And then a night to get back."

"And why there, monsieur?"

"There is someone with whom they will be safe. And he will pass them on to someone else. That is how they got here from Chartres, and how they will get to Spain."

Onesime studied the map. "You know, monsieur, the Germans are here, right here"—he pointed. "And here too. It's a bit longer to go this way, by the marsh and then along the river, but it's wide open. No Germans anywhere."

"How do you know this?"

"I have been . . . watching, monsieur. And making maps since the Germans arrived."

"Watching?"

"Oui, monsieur. I know which caves they're in and what they have in the caves. I know where they have billets, where they have storage dumps and depots. I know how they come and go. I know, for instance, that your wine cave runs to my grandfather's cave, and that the Germans have artillery shells stored in that cave along with small arms. I know there is always a guard outside, but not inside. I know which caves meet which caves. . . . I'm sorry, monsieur. Forgive me. It was not my business, I know. And I don't know all of the caves. Not all of them, of course. But many."

"Do you indeed?" The count rarely smiled, but he did so now. "I am not surprised, Onesime. I always knew you were resourceful and smart. I knew you would find out what went on here. . . ."

"But I didn't, monsieur. I swear it. . . ."

"But I knew you *would* find out when it became necessary."

And that is how Onesime found himself leading the Shapiras and the Herzog children over field roads to the next stop on their way to Spain. They left the next evening after dark and walked all night. As the early morning sky was brightening behind them, they arrived at the small church on the edge of the village of Coulangé.

It seemed even colder inside the church than it did outside. A few votive candles were flickering up front, where someone had been saying early morning prayers. The priest was in the small room behind the church having his breakfast of bread and warm milk. He was old, and he stood up from the rickety table with great difficulty as they entered the room. He embraced Onesime, whom he had never seen before, and then pinched his cheek as though he were a boy.

One after the other he took the Shapiras' faces and the Herzog children's faces between his rough, gnarled hands and gazed at them with watery eyes in a kind of silent benediction. "Come with me, my children," he said finally, and led them into a small courtyard. He lifted a wooden trapdoor. They all followed him down a steep wooden stairway that disappeared into the darkness.

At the bottom he lit a lantern. Skulls sat stacked on crude shelves reaching all the way to the ceiling. Some of the skulls had crosses or dates painted above their empty eyes. "This is the church crypt," said the old priest. "And these are my dead parishioners." He said it as though he had known them all personally. He caressed one of the skulls. "Their spirits will all watch over and protect you." He made the sign of the cross.

The priest had arranged a table, three chairs, and two beds in the narrow space. The beds were covered with ragged sheets and blankets, and there was a threadbare cloth on the table. A jar of water held a single daffodil. A wooden crucifix hung high on the wall.

"I'm afraid it is not too commodious," said the priest, "but you will be safe here. Someone will come for you tomorrow. There are small openings up there and there." Everyone looked up to where he pointed, as though they were on a guided tour. "They let in air and a little light. I will bring you food a little later. You will be safe here. Safe. Safe." He patted each cheek as he said the word. "Safe."

Onesime had gone to church as a boy, had been confirmed, and then had stopped going. None of it had made sense to him any longer. Now, walking back to Saint-Léon alone, a pistol in his belt, a light rain falling on his head, it all seemed different than he remembered it. He thought about the skulls with the crosses on them, the Jews, the old priest with the watery eyes, and the courage that infused them all—and, yes, him too.

Other Jews and other refugees came and went at the count's cave. They arrived early in the morning and left when it was dark, led by Onesime or by others, in various directions. Other resisters showed up, including someone named Max, who was said to be very high up in the resistance and was on his way to London to meet with de Gaulle.

Onesime and two others escorted Max to a field not far from where the train had been derailed. A small plane arrived and landed in the mud. Two Englishmen hopped out, and Max and another man, who had appeared from the other end of the field with another team of three, hopped aboard while the plane was still moving. In a minute they were gone. Onesime's three and the other three saluted each other silently, and then they were gone too.

The next time Simon materialized, he wanted to see Onesime's maps. Onesime went home to get them.

"Where is Maman?" he said.

"I don't know," said Jean. "She wouldn't say. She just said it wasn't anything dangerous."

"That's what she'd say."

"Yes," said Jean. "I hope it's true."

"Me too," said Onesime. "But what's safe these days? What isn't dangerous?"

They were all part of an odd army, a phantom army. No one knew what anyone else was doing. No one knew how, or even why, it operated. Who were its officers, who were its commanders and strategists? Did the sabotage and assassinations and secret rendezvous even add up to anything?

Onesime sat at the great table in the center of the count's cave, turning over page after page and explaining his markings while Simon looked over his shoulder. Jean had brought his logbooks. There were several thick volumes by now. Each page was filled with rows and columns of careful annotations about the minutiae of the occupation of Saint-Léon.

Simon closed the last volume. "Do you know what this is?" he said. "It's a plan of attack. That's what this is. How we fight the Germans and collaborators here in Saint-Léon. It's not spelled out. But it is all here. Where they're weak, where they're strong, what we need to do, and how we do it."

# XVII.

JACQUES COURTOIS NOW LIVED in a house in Tours that had belonged to a family of Jews. They had been deported, and Jacques and the French Gestapo had moved in. From there they raided suspected resistance hideouts. They terrorized anyone they deemed suspicious. Jacques enjoyed the work. He drank heavily and bragged about their exploits to anyone who would listen.

Jacques's brutality caused some in the resistance to call for his assassination. But Simon felt otherwise. "By all means keep him alive. He's a loud mouth and a braggart. All you need to do is sit next to him in a bar. It's better than having a spy inside. We couldn't do better if he were one of our own."

Jacques Courtois could hardly believe his good fortune. He would find himself sitting at a bar, and an attractive woman would sit down next to him. Invariably she smiled at him. Or she nodded and raised her glass.

"Cigarette?" he offered. She accepted. He lit a match. She cupped his hand in hers to steady the flame.

"Thank you," she said, looking into his eyes, and exhaled. "I am Marianne."

Jacques still came to Saint-Léon from time to time. He seemed to have regular business with the mayor. And he could be counted on to stop by Yves Renard's office, usually with a couple of friends in tow.

"We're wondering what the hell you've been doing, Renard?" Jacques threw a sheaf of *Liberation*s on the desk in front of him. "Why can't you catch this son of a bitch?" Or: "Jesus Christ, Renard, if I thought you had the guts, you could almost be part of the *maquis*. I mean, I've never seen a cop as slow and incompetent as you are." Yves would be suitably cowed, and Jacques and his friends would snicker. "No wonder Essart wants your ass."

Whether this was even true or was a figment of Jacques's vindictive imagination, Yves could not tell. It didn't matter. What was important was that Lieutenant Essart had been absent from Yves's life for the better part of a year. With the dissolution of the Vichy border, Essart's area of responsibility had doubled in size.

Add to that the roundup of the Jews and then the draft of OWS workers, and Essart and his men were stretched fifty different ways. Given everything else on his plate, Saint-Léon seemed the picture of tranquility, and the little gendarme Yves Renard seemed like nothing more than an annoying memory.

That changed, of course, with the derailing of the OWS train, the escape of more than two hundred OWS draftees, and the murder of a dozen German guards. Essart arrived in Saint-Léon with detachments of German and French Gestapo.

Jacques Courtois had spent the previous evening telling the latest Marianne how he and his friends were about to teach that little piss-ant village of Saint-Léon a lesson they would not soon forget. But even without Jacques's "warning," everyone in Saint-Léon knew what was coming. Onesime and Jean, who had been staying at their mother's home, disappeared again, and so did many others.

"Where are they, Madame Josquin?" said Jacques. Anne Marie stood in the door. "We need to ask them some questions. About the OWS train."

Anne Marie looked at Jacques and then at the other men. "And who is 'we,' Jacques?"

"The police," said Jacques.

"The *German* police?"

"Just tell me where we can find them," said Jacques.

"I do not know," said Anne Marie. Jacques narrowed his eyes. "I said, I do not know," she said again.

"Listen . . . ," said Jacques. He stepped forward, forcing her to step back into the house. "We know Onesime was on that train, and now he's gone. Likewise Henri, likewise . . ." He named others.

"*You* listen, Jacques Courtois," said Anne Marie. She pronounced his full name as though he were still a boy. "You have no right to force your way in here and interrogate me this way. You simply do not have that right. Shame on you."

"It is my job to find and question your sons, madame. We believe they were involved. . . ."

"If you believe they are here, you are mistaken, whatever else you might believe."

"Let's search the place," said one of the men with Jacques. He pushed his way between Jacques and Anne Marie and into the house.

"Is that what you do now, Jacques Courtois? You invade the homes of French citizens? Push them about? I said they're not here. And they're not here."

"Let's go," said Jacques to the men.

"What?!" said the other man, who already had one foot on the bottom stair ready to go upstairs.

"I said, let's go." The man hesitated. "You heard me," said Jacques. "They're not here. If she says they're not here, then they're not here. I know her. If they were here, she'd say so. She'd rather give up her sons than tell a lie. Let's go." He turned back to Anne Marie. "When they show up, tell them we're looking for them. And we'll find them."

"Shame on you, Jacques," she said.

"Let's take her in," said the man who still had one foot on the stairs. "Maybe she's hiding something. Maybe she knows something about the train."

"Let's go," said Jacques. "We'll be back, madame."

The other man finally turned. "We'll be back," he said as he left the house.

When Maurice de Beaumont opened his front door, Lieutenant Essart and a small contingent of French and German Gestapo were waiting. "Good afternoon, Lieutenant," he said, and offered his hand. Essart took it.

"I'm sorry to bother you, Monsieur de Beaumont, but as a result of the recent terroristic activities in Saint-Léon, we are questioning everyone to discover what they know and who was involved."

"Do you suspect me?" said Maurice, raising his eyebrows.

A slight smile crept across Essart's face. "We suspect no one and everyone, Monsieur de Beaumont. In any case, we have an order allowing us to search your house and premises."

"You do not need an order, Lieutenant," said Maurice de Beaumont. "You know I have always been more than cooperative with your officers and men, and nothing is any different now."

"I am glad to hear it," said Essart. He had been an invited guest at the Beaumont home. He had found the count amusing and his wife enchanting. "Some of my men will go through your outbuildings and barns. I and my sergeant and these two associates"—he indicated two French Gestapo—"will go through the house. Is your wife at home, monsieur?"

"She is not," said Maurice.

"That is good. We do not wish to disturb her."

"Thank you for your consideration," said the count.

"May I inquire about her whereabouts?"

"She is visiting her sister in Tours."

"In Tours?"

"Yes, in Tours. May I accompany your men on their search?"

Essart studied Maurice.

"So as to avoid any misunderstandings," said the count. "To reassure myself."

"Yes, I see," said Essart. "Misunderstandings." There had been occasional "misunderstandings" on other searches. French Gestapo in particular had helped themselves to jewelry and other valuables. "Of course you may accompany the men on their search."

"And what is it you are looking for, Lieutenant?"

"I do not know exactly, Monsieur Count. We will know what we are looking for when we find it. And when is your wife returning? From Tours?"

"Later this afternoon, I would expect. She did not say exactly."

The château had many rooms, but the search did not take long and nothing was taken. The men walked from room to room. They looked inside dressers and armoires without disturbing anything. When they had finished their search, they all stood for a moment in the entryway. "Thank you," said Lieutenant Essart, "for your cooperation."

"I trust you did not find anything incriminating," said Maurice. He regretted the words as soon as he said them.

Essart smiled at him slightly. "No, we did not find anything incriminating." He turned, as if to leave, and then turned back again. "You own a great many caves, don't you, monsieur?"

"I do own a great many caves, Lieutenant. Why do you ask?"

"Oh, I was just wondering what goes on in your caves."

"What goes on in them?"

"What you use them for."

"I use them for different things, Lieutenant. For instance, some are used for wine storage, some are used for the storage of other things. I would be happy to show them to you."

"Would you? That would be very kind of you. I am of course interested in the ones where you store your wine. I am certain you have an excellent collection. But I am particularly interested in those where you store your Jews."

Maurice de Beaumont stared at Essart. Essart stared back. Essart repeated himself as though the count had not understood his words. "You know, Herr Count. Your Jews, your resisters, your other . . . problematic freight, shall we say?"

Maurice de Beaumont was silent.

"Do you have nothing to say, Herr Count? You have been so coop-erative until now, I am surprised that you are at a loss for words. Let us go have a look, shall we? Who knows whom we shall find there, at one particular cave. Maybe the lovely Madame de Beaumont will meet us there. I have the feeling she will have returned from visiting her sister."

When Lieutenant Essart and his contingent of men arrived at the entrance to the cave in question with the count in tow, Alexandre was standing there surrounded by French Gestapo. Jacques Courtois was holding her by the arm.

"Alexandre," said Maurice. "Are you back already? How was your sister?"

"You may stop playing your drama, monsieur," said Essart. "Please open the door." Maurice de Beaumont withdrew the large iron key from his pocket. He stepped forward and unlocked the door. He swung the door open and stepped aside.

"Turn on the light," said Essart.

The count stepped inside and turned the switch that ignited the one dim bulb. He came back outside.

"Sergeant, Courtois, take some others. Bring everyone inside out. Alive, do you hear me?"

"Yes, sir, Lieutenant," said Jacques. "What if they resist?"

"Alive," said Lieutenant Essart.

Jacques eagerly led the way inside. He and the others took out their guns and lit their flashlights. The beams of light danced here and there but revealed nothing other than the chalky gray walls and floor. There were a few pieces of old furniture beside the door and some timbers lay stacked farther inside. Otherwise the cave appeared to be empty.

"There's nothing here," said Jacques.

"Let's keep going," said the sergeant, and pointed ahead with his flashlight. The men walked deep into the cave, but they found nothing except a few side passages that had been walled up and a collection of ancient furniture stacked against the wall. A bed, a mattress, a dresser, an armoire, some chairs stacked on top of one another. Jacques Courtois shined his flashlight behind the huge armoire that was against the wall. "Nothing here," he said.

"There's no one in there, sir," said the sergeant, once they were back outside. "No one and nothing."

"What do you mean, nothing?" said Lieutenant Essart. He looked at Maurice de Beaumont. Maurice did not speak.

"Shall I make the bastard talk?" said Jacques Courtois.

The lieutenant ignored him. He turned to Alexandre de Beaumont. "Where were you this afternoon, madame?"

"When?" she said.

"Please, madame," he said, "don't be coy."

"I was with my sister in Tours, monsieur."

"Madame. You will excuse me for contradicting you. But you were seen this afternoon leaving this cave. You were not alone when you came out. Now, we are not in Tours. And I do not believe that your sister lives in this cave. I ask you once more, as politely and respectfully as I can, whether you were here in this cave this afternoon, whether you were with others, and who they were?"

Alexandre looked desperately at her husband. She began to speak but then could not. Finally she lowered her eyes. She muttered something inaudible.

"What did you say, madame?" said Essart.

"I said I was here, monsieur."

"What are you saying, Alexandre?" said Maurice. He tried to take a step forward, but Essart put his arm out to stop him.

"Please, monsieur," said the lieutenant. "We are about to get to the truth."

"I'm sorry, Maurice," said Alexandre.

"Do not talk to your husband, madame. Address yourself to me. Who were you with this afternoon, here at this cave, *in* this cave, madame?"

"I . . . I cannot say, monsieur," said Alexandre. Tears were running down her cheeks. "Please, monsieur, do not make me say."

Essart studied her intently before he stepped up to her and took her chin firmly in his hand. He raised her head until she could no longer avoid looking into his eyes.

"You do not seem to understand the gravity of the situation, Madame de Beaumont. Aiding the resistance, abetting *any* resistance to the legitimate rule of the law of the Third Reich is a capital offense. Now, there has been a murderous attack that has cost the lives of a dozen soldiers of the Reich, an attack to which you were at least an accomplice, if not a participant. Your life is over, madame. And your esteemed husband's may be as well. You have been consorting with enemies of the Reich and—"

"What are you saying, monsieur?!" said Alexandre. "That is not true. My God! No!" A look of such horror and revulsion had crossed her face that Essart was momentarily taken aback.

"No? What do you mean, no?" he said. "What then? *Who* then?"

"You are wrong, monsieur."

"Enlighten me," said Essart.

"Please, monsieur, I cannot."

"You have no choice."

"I was . . ." She could hardly bring herself to say the words. "I was with . . . a lover," said Alexandre. She buried her face in her hands and collapsed into sobs.

"What are you saying, Alexandre?" said Maurice.

Essart let his hand drop from her chin, and she let her own hands drop, surrendering to her anguish. Her eyes were closed, and tears streamed down her cheeks. Essart was astonished at this embarrassing turn, but he quickly regained his composure. "Then, madame, you had better tell me the name of your lover. And perhaps you can explain, madame, how it was that you were seen here this afternoon with several men."

"Please, Lieutenant, . . . don't ask me. . . ."

"Do not try my patience. How am I to believe you, madame, without—"

"He is German, monsieur. . . . He is . . . a . . . colonel. There were two men, not several. The other man you saw . . . someone saw . . . was his driver."

"You whore!" said Jacques. He jerked her roughly by the arm and raised his hand to punch her.

"Stop it!" said Essart. "Stop immediately." Jacques stood with his face contorted in hatred, his fist waving aimlessly in the air.

Essart looked from Alexandre to Maurice and back again as the drama he had inadvertently set in motion played itself out. In the end he was forced to take Maurice and Alexandre back to their château. He watched from his car as Maurice bounded up the steps and strode across the terrace. Alexandre ran after him. But by the time she reached the door Maurice had closed and locked it. Alexandre stood at the door. She pounded on the door with her fists, and called, "Maurice."

The door did not open.

# XVIII.

Lieutenant Essart had allowed himself to be diverted by the little drama the count and his wife had concocted. On reflection he did not find their story persuasive. But then again, what if it turned out to be true? What if the lovely Alexandre *did* have a German colonel as her lover? It would not be Hollinger. If there was a lover, it had to be someone from Tours. Most likely it would be someone whom Lieutenant Essart could ill afford to have as an enemy. In any case, Lieutenant Essart would have to be extremely careful. *Discretion now, above all,* he said to himself.

Essart decided to seek information from the foolish and ineffectual Yves Renard. You could easily question him without giving anything away. Talking to Renard would help to restore his equilibrium, and it might even yield useful information.

Yves jumped to attention—something he had never done before—as Essart entered the office. It made Essart think Yves had something to hide. "Sit down, Renard," he said. He studied the policeman's face until Yves began to fidget uncomfortably on his chair. "I do not suppose," said Essart finally, "that you have any useful intelligence about the attack on the OWS train."

"The men who were involved have disappeared, monsieur," said Yves. "And so have most of the draftees. I'm sure your own investigation has determined as much. The town of Saint-Léon is devoid of young men."

"Disappeared. Into thin air, I suppose."

"They could be living in any of a thousand caves around here, or—"

"Caves? I do not suppose you know which caves."

"Which caves? No, I do not know which caves. If any . . . I was only speculating about where the young men might be."

"Tell me, does the Count de Beaumont's wife have a sister in Tours?"

"A sister? I do not know, monsieur. It could be. Why do you ask?"

"Does she have a lover?"

"I could not say, monsieur." Renard cast his eyes down.

*So she does have a lover,* thought Essart. "Do you know who her lover might be?"

"I do not know anything about that, monsieur."

"What about young women, Renard?" said Essart. "Are there young women who might have been involved in the attack on the OWS train?"

Renard lowered his eyes again. "I cannot imagine that women would do such a thing, monsieur. I believe we are looking for men, monsieur. I assure you, I am. . . ."

"Yes, Renard, I'm sure you are."

The idea that there might have been women involved suddenly seemed compelling to Essart. Why had he not thought of it before? Alexandre de Beaumont had spun her tale with tears and foiled his inquiry in a way a man never could. Anne Marie Josquin had done the same with Courtois. "The way to the truth is through a woman," he said to his men. "Find me a woman we can break."


Among the letters of denunciation in the police files, there were more than one about Marie Livrist, also called Marie Piano. Essart's sergeant searched her room and found the stolen pistol. Essart had Courtois bring her in. She sat in Renard's office across the desk from the lieutenant and Jacques Courtois and admitted to stealing the gun. She sat with her shoulders back and her chin stuck out. "It was lying there," she said, "and I took it. It turned out he didn't need it where he was going."

"And why did you take it?"

"It seemed like I might have to kill someone someday."

"Kill someone?"

"A German," she said. "Someone like you."

Essart had a lazy way about him. He did not seem given to quick movements. His body looked soft and round and incapable of physical force. But when he hit Marie Piano, it came so quickly and so violently that everyone in the room jumped. There was a loud crack, and suddenly Marie's head was lying on the desk, and a small puddle of blood was forming in front of her. She lifted her head slowly. She tried to see in front of herself, but she could not focus.

Essart was behind her now, holding her head back by the hair. "A young thing like you doesn't go around killing Germans by herself, does she?"

"Why not?" she said groggily. "It's not that hard." He hit her again. Blood sprayed across the room. Yves and Jacques Courtois had backed up against opposite walls.

"I know all about you, you little French whore," said Essart. "You have a boyfriend, and I'll bet he dreams about killing Germans too, doesn't he?"

"My boyfriend? I thought you were my boyfriend," said Marie Piano. Essart hit her once more. This time she lost consciousness. "Get some water and wake her up," said Essart.

"I know her boyfriend," said Jacques. "He was on the train. It was his mother we—"

*"Get some goddamn water and wake her up!"* Essart had jumped at Jacques and was screaming.

Renard got a pan of cold water. Essart threw it in Marie's face. She spluttered but did not wake up.

"We're done here," said Essart. "Pick her up. Let's go. Put her in the car."

Jacques drove; Renard sat beside him. They watched each other out of the corners of their eyes. Essart was in the back with Marie Piano. In the mirror it looked almost as though Essart were stroking her hair.

"Someplace secluded," Essart said. Jacques drove to the stone quarry above the vineyards, not far from Maurice de Beaumont's cave. They parked above the quarry, and Yves and Jacques lifted Marie's unconscious body from the car. She seemed to weigh nothing.

"Put her down here," said Essart, pointing to a spot on the grass just beside where the wall of the quarry fell away. "You, Courtois,"—Essart pointed at Yves—"get him away from here. I'll find out what we fucking need to know."

"Lieutenant, I know her boyfriend, we can find—"

Essart jumped up and put his face in front of Jacques's face. His face was purple and his eyes were red. "You do what I tell you, damn it. And if he makes a move, shoot him."

Jacques turned toward Yves and smiled at him. "Really? I can shoot this little piss-ant cop?" Essart didn't even hear him. He was back on the ground, kneeling beside Marie Piano. He held his hands in the air in front of him, palms inward, like a surgeon deciding on the first incision.

Yves turned away. Just as he did, the shot rang out. He spun around to see Essart still kneeling. But he now wore an astonished look on his face and a purple hole in his forehead. Jacques kept the pistol—the one Marie Piano had stolen—pointed at the lieutenant until he had slowly toppled sideways onto the grass.

Jacques turned toward Yves. "See if she's all right," he said. "Come on, piss ant. Move. See if she's all right. We've got to get out of here." He started to put the pistol in his belt but decided then to leave it beside the body, at least for now. "We don't want to be driving around with a stolen pistol that killed an SS man."

"I think she'll be all right," said Yves. "But we've got to get her someplace safe."

"After that we should get *him* somewhere safe," said Jacques. "Somewhere far away."

Yves regarded Jacques Courtois for a moment. "I know just the place," he said. "But we'll have to wait until dark."

They left the dead lieutenant in the grass. They put Marie Piano in the lieutenant's car and drove to Anne Marie Josquin's house. "Do not stare at me in that way, madame," said Jacques when Anne Marie opened the door, "like you don't know who I am."

"I *don't* know who you are, Jacques Courtois," said Anne Marie. After a pause she said, "Put her in there, in my room."

"We will leave her to you, madame; we have other things to do," said Jacques.

"Thank you for taking care of her, Madame Josquin," said Yves.

The two men went outside. "It's a long time until dark," said Yves.

"I'm going to The Trout," said Jacques. "I don't suppose you want to come."

"I'll take the car. Meet me back at the quarry around sundown," said Yves.

"Don't start giving me fucking orders, Renard. In fact, don't get any ideas at all."

Yves waited alone beside Essart's stiff body. Jacques Courtois showed up well after the sun had set. He wobbled up on a bicycle he had stolen. He was drunk. Yves did not say anything.

The two men loaded Essart's body into the backseat of the car. Yves got behind the wheel. "I'm not that drunk," Jacques said, but Yves ignored him. Yves drove toward Château-Renault, while Jacques slept in the seat beside him. After an hour they reached the road to the Marquis d'Estaing's château. Jacques woke up as the car bumped along the road. "Where are we?" he said.

"Château-Renault. There's a *milice* group that meets here."

"So this is the place," said Jacques. "Schneider talked about this place. You come here too, I hear. You're full of surprises, piss ant."

"So are you," said Yves. They left the body beside the gate.

The boredom of war is the worst boredom of all. It is relentless and deep. Time stops. Maybe it even goes backward. Who knows for sure? There were days, weeks, months in this war when anything that happened seemed to happen far away, at great remove: on the ocean, in Italy, in Russia. Or nothing happened at all. The news from England was not reassuring. The invasion that everyone was sure was coming did not come.

When nothing happened it was not like when nothing happens in peacetime. You knew, *everyone* knew, that a sudden, terrible cataclysm was inevitable. It might be unexpected but no less catastrophic for being unexpected. And when nothing happened in war, *even* when nothing happened in war, people continued to die everywhere and in great numbers—from hunger and disease, from murderous attacks, from sabotage, from torture. Jews continued to be discovered and deported to extermination camps. Everyone knew by now that was where they went.

And yet life went on. That was the amazing thing. Life went on. The living had to eat, so gardens were planted and farm crops were grown. People shopped for what they could get. They visited, they sat at the Hôtel de France and had a cup of barley coffee. They gossiped. They pruned the grapevines, they picked the grapes, they made wine. There were weddings and christenings and funerals. But it only resembled in a pale and unsatisfactory way the life they really wanted. Everything was distorted as though the earth were living through a devastating and endless storm.

The murder of Lieutenant Essart was traced back to Saint-Léon, and Aseline, the plumber, was arrested for it. A neighbor had denounced him. Whoever it was—that was never revealed—claimed they had heard Aseline arguing with Essart. The accuser fabricated acrimonious dealings between Essart and Aseline, an overheard argument in which Aseline threatened Essart.

Aseline had escaped from the OWS train and was in hiding. But when he showed up to visit his wife, a neighbor called the Gestapo. They picked him up, tortured a confession out of him, and shot him.

No witnesses came forward. There was no real evidence against him. All of this bore only a passing resemblance to justice, and yet now it was called justice.


In the years that had passed since Colonel Büchner's death, Edith Troppard had never stopped grieving. She was a creature of love. And two men she had loved had been taken from her. Their deaths, as well as the terrible world around her, had distorted her grief in such a way that she saw revenge as the only course open to her. It seemed like the means by which she could begin to live again.

In March of 1943 Edith began making regular excursions to Tours. She took the train and carried a small leather valise. She spent a night, sometimes two, at a small hotel on the edge of the city. She registered under a made-up name. The city was dark and grim, and people stayed inside as much as possible to avoid trouble. When they had to venture out, they kept their eyes cast down so they would not see something they should not see. Edith walked, barely seen and entirely unrecognized, through the empty streets to the center of town.

Edith dined alone in restaurants frequented by German officers. She wore silk stockings that Colonel Büchner had given her, a black silk skirt and jacket, and a white blouse, open at the throat. She was a beautiful woman, and SS Colonel Holger Penck was not the first officer to ask permission to join her for dinner. Those who preceded him flattered her and plied her with questions. She looked into their eyes but discretely evaded their questions. "I am Suzanne La France," she said. "That is all you need to know. Isn't it?" She smiled. They ordered champagne. She inquired about them with a beguiling directness. But she did not accept their invitations to go back to their quarters.

Holger Penck was different. For one thing, there was the little death's-head on his uniform cap. Edith could see that other officers accorded him an extra measure of respect. Edith wondered what the symbol meant and what it felt like to wear something that intimidating. Colonel Penck said he was in France on special assignment. He

admitted to her, in a quite disarming way, that it was almost as intimidating to wear the death's-head as it was to encounter it.

"But why," she wondered, "would such a symbol be . . . used if it
intimidates even the wearer?"

"Ah," said Colonel Penck. "I will tell you a secret. Intimidation
may be the Führer's greatest innovation. Intimidation is the secret of
our success. In France. Everywhere, in fact. Look how it has disabled
the French government, how it bends Pétain to our will. It disarms our
opponents and impresses our friends. It is our most effective weapon."

Edith considered his words. "But how can you ever be sure of
your . . . success," she wondered, "if you have achieved that success by
means of intimidation?"

"That is the beauty of it, don't you see?" said Holger. "If one has
achieved success, one never has to wonder about *how* one has achieved
it."

"And have you achieved success?" Edith said. She crossed her hands
under her chin. Colonel Penck could not help but notice the pulse
flickering at her throat.

He lifted the bottle from the ice bucket and, holding it with his
thumb in the indented bottom, filled first her glass, then his. He lifted
his glass, closed one eye, and peered at her through the bubbles. He
lowered the glass and smiled. "I think we have achieved success," he
said. "Don't you?"

Holger Penck was a year or two younger than Edith. He was thin
and handsome and intelligent. He loved fine food and wine and opera
and ballet. He liked to think that he was introducing Edith to culture and fine living, and Edith allowed him these notions. He had
studied medicine in Heidelberg before he decided on becoming a
military officer in Hitler's new Reich. His special assignment—
overseeing the roundup and deportation of Jews and other political
prisoners from France—was, he said, the highpoint of his career. "It
should not be the highpoint, perhaps. I confess it. Not only is it not a
usual military endeavor. But I am trafficking in human unhappiness.
Except the work is purposeful and meaningful and changing the world,

I believe for the better. And one has to ask the hard question when speaking of human unhappiness: Who deserves happiness and what exactly *is* a human . . . ?"

Edith and Holger saw each other regularly through 1943 and into 1944. He took her dancing and gave her gifts of fine clothes and caviar and champagne. Oddly enough, it was the gifts that persuaded her that she would be justified in killing him.

"People in Tours are hungry while the Germans sit there eating caviar and drinking champagne. How can that be right?"

"It is not right," said Anne Marie Josquin. They were sitting in Edith's kitchen in Villedieu drinking tea. "It is not right, but it is how things are. Are you in love with him?"

"No," said Edith. "How could I be?"

"Is he in love with you?"

"How should I know? What does it matter? He traffics in human misery and finds it fulfilling. He has a wife in Heidelberg. And two children. I've seen their pictures. They are beautiful. And betrayed. What does love mean to a man like that?"

"You know, Edith, that is not how love works. It is not a rational process. I envy everyone who has love in their life."

"Don't envy me," said Edith.

Early one Sunday morning, after a sumptuous dinner, an evening at the ballet, and a night of tender lovemaking, Edith cut SS Colonel Holger Penck's throat with his own razor. Afterward, she washed, packed her small leather valise, and walked to the train station.

They found Penck's body Monday morning naked on his bed bathed in his own blood. The Gestapo launched a furious search for Suzanne La France. But no one knew who she was or where she lived. Despite widespread inquiries and intense investigation, she seemed to have disappeared from the earth.

# XIX.

MOST NIGHTS ONESIME CAME HOME to his mother's house to sit with Marie Piano. Some nights it was almost morning before he finally arrived. He fed her when she was awake. He watched while she slept. He drew her again and again, filling sheets of paper with her battered likeness, sleeping or gazing out the window as the sun rose. One morning, when he thought she had recovered sufficiently, he asked her to sing for him.

"A German song?" she said.

"Anything," he said.

Marie's nose and cheekbone healed well enough, so that you could hardly tell they had been broken. But she never saw out of her right eye again.

Maurice and Alexandre de Beaumont now moved their rescue operation from place to place, always staying a step or two ahead of the Gestapo. Maurice seemed to know, whether from Jacques Courtois's gossip or by other means, when they were closing in. The Gestapo would arrive at the cave or barn or wherever it happened to be. But there was no furniture or other evidence that anyone had ever stayed there. Jacques Courtois would threaten and rail against Maurice and his fancy-pants ways, but finally he and his Gestapo friends would have to leave empty-handed.

Onesime continued to escort refugees from Saint-Léon to Coulangé and also to other places. Le Lude was a two-day walk, but it was that much closer to safety for the refugees. Colombier en Brive was even farther.

The river route to Coulangé was no longer safe. One night as he was leading a family of Jews, Onesime came upon a column of militia walking single file along the opposite bank of the small river, not fifteen meters from where he and the family were huddled in the tall grass. He had to clap his hand over the one-year-old's mouth for fear that she would give them away. She somehow knew to stop crying.

Walking to Coulangé, he always worried whether the old priest would still be there. Onesime wondered why he worried so about someone he barely knew.

"Onesime!" called the count from the back terrace.

"Oui, monsieur," said Onesime. His knees were stiff and he stood up slowly. He had been replacing a hinge on a sagging barn door.

"Go to the back barn and fetch a harness, would you please?"

It had been more than a year since Onesime had seen Simon. Simon had changed a great deal. He was thinner, and there was an angry red scar from his forehead across his eye to his cheek. He had a tenuousness about him now that he had never shown before. His reckless confidence was gone.

"I'm glad to see you, Da Gama." Simon held on to Onesime's hand a moment too long.

Simon saw that Onesime was looking at the scar. "I was almost caught," he said. "We are thoroughly infiltrated, Da Gama. We are compromised by some of our own. As the war comes to an end, everyone is maneuvering for position. Do not trust anyone. And do not let anyone trust you. That can be just as dangerous.

"Now, do you know what these are?" Simon stooped down and opened a small canvas sack lying at his feet. Onesime leaned down and peered into the sack.

"No," he said.

"They're called pencil fuses," said Simon. He picked up one of the small copper tubes. "They're used to set off explosives."

Onesime hesitated to take the tube. "It's safe," said Simon. "There's a little glass vial inside the tube right here." He pointed. "The vial is filled with acid. When you crush the copper tube—you just step on it—the glass breaks and the acid starts eating through a wire that's holding back a striker. After you crush it, pull out this—right here, that's the safety—and then stick the whole fuse into the explosive. After a certain time, the wire releases the striker, which ignites a small charge, which sets off the main explosion. Use two fuses for every explosive charge. Just in case one doesn't work."

"And then . . . ?"

"The black fuses give you ten minutes to get as far away as you can; the red ones give you thirty minutes. You decide, depending on the situation."

"Thirty minutes in order to have enough time."

"Why not? That's up to you. You'll have extra fuses. It's an important target. We want to be certain. You decide."

"And where . . . ?"

"Your grandfather's cave."

"Ah," said Onesime.

"Will that be a problem for you?"

"It shouldn't be. There's time to get out," said Onesime.

"*All the way out*," said Simon. "And away from the door. Even at Beaumont's end of the cave, the concussion will do serious harm if you're still inside."

"And all his wine?" said Onesime.

Simon smiled. "He's already moving it. But he doesn't know why. Here are the explosives." He pulled a flat package from the canvas sack. "You've got five packages like this. Use all five. Put them in different places where you think they'll do the most damage. Put them under cases of high explosives or artillery shells. Put them where there's gasoline. Or a ceiling support. We want nothing left."

"And when?" said Onesime.

"Do you know Verlaine's 'Chansons d'Autun'?"

"What?" said Onesime.

"Poetry. 'Songs of Autumn,' by Paul Verlaine." Simon stood up straight as he must have done when he recited as a schoolboy in Berlin. "*Les sanglots longs des violons de l'automne blessent mon coeur d'une langueur monotone*" The long sobs of the violins of autumn wound my heart with a monotonous languor. "Say it back."

Onesime repeated the phrase, and Simon corrected him until he got it right.

"What does it mean?"

"The first phrase is a warning. When you hear the first phrase— 'the long sobs of the violins of autumn'—it means that you will blow up your target within the next forty-eight hours. When you hear the second phrase, which will come a day or two after—'wound my heart with a monotonous languor'—then you detonate the explosions at the first light of the next day and blow the cave to kingdom come."

"I will need help to remove stones. . . ."

"Don't tell me about it, Da Gama. It's not something I should know."

"Are you in here?" The count stood at the door with his hand shielding his eyes. He peered into the darkness.

"We're over here," said Simon. "*Not anyone,*" he whispered to Onesime.

Onesime tried to imagine what it must feel like not to trust anyone.


The grounds of the Marquis d'Estaing's château by the town of Château Renault were patrolled by armed guards. The militia group was now permanently installed there with several men in residence acting as administrators and organizers of militia activities. The members of the group believed fervently in the Vichy regime and in keeping the kind of order Vichy and the Germans represented. Of course they had all also made contingency plans just in case things should go the other way.

On a rainy night in early June, Yves rose to speak to a crowded meeting at the château headquarters. "I have an informant," he said. The others looked puzzled; they all had informants. "My informant is particularly well placed," said Yves. "According to my informant, a serious attack is planned on nearby facilities in the next few days. He's sure it's soon, and he'll let me know the night before.

"And listen to this." Yves rarely got excited, but he was excited now. "There could be as many as a hundred *maquis* involved. *A hundred*. At different sites. I have a list of the attack target sites—ten of them. Police stations, prisons, ammunition dumps. This is a big attack they're planning, and this time we'll be there waiting for them."

Most of the information that came the militia's way consisted of false tip-offs about hideouts or the supposed whereabouts of some resister. But this was an opportunity to strike at the heart of the resistance. To capture or kill a hundred *maquis*—or even a fraction of that number—would be a crippling blow to their organization. This was what the militia had been waiting for: a chance to engage the enemy in battle and to destroy them. The room erupted.

"How do you know?" "Is this reliable information?" "Who's your source?" Even the old marquis came alive and spluttered excitedly.

Yves raised his hands to be allowed to continue. "This is as reliable as such information can be. We have to be ready." He took a paper from his pocket and unfolded it on the table. "Here is where they plan to attack." Everyone crowded around to look at the small hand-drawn map.

The police chief of Château-Renault took charge. He assigned men to each site. "We will have the advantage," he said. "We will be better armed. Surprise is on our side. Time is short, but that is to our advantage as well."

*The long sobs of the violins of autumn. The long sobs of the violins of autumn.* Jean and Onesime looked at each other to assure themselves that they had heard correctly. They listened to other messages that might have meant a great deal to others but meant nothing to them.

*John has a long mustache. John has a long mustache.*
*The die has been cast. The die has been cast.*

Finally they got up from their chairs. "I can't tell you anything," said Jean, without being asked.

"I can't either," said Onesime.


Onesime found Marie Piano in the shop where she worked. He had never been inside. "You're selling clothes?"

"I'm helping out," said Marie. "And it's underwear, not clothes."

Onesime looked around to make certain no one could hear. "Are you still interested in seeing Beaumont's cave? Because I need your help."

Marie Piano's eyes lit up. "Just tell me when," she said.

"Just listen to the radio," said Onesime. "When you hear—"

"'Wound my heart . . .'?" she said.

"How do you know that?"

"Selling underwear doesn't take *all* my time."

"Maybe . . . I don't know," said Onesime.

"What don't you know?"

Onesime thought of Simon's warning. But he loved Marie; he *had* to trust her. "All right. Once you hear the wounded-heart message, meet me at three thirty the next morning at Beaumont's back gate."

"What are you two going on about?" said Madame Berger. She was the proprietor of the shop. Onesime had not heard her approach.

"I'm sorry, madame. Onesime is my fiancé," said Marie.

"Well, that's nice for you," said Madame Berger. "But not on my time he's not. There's a customer up front."

"I apologize, madame," said Onesime, and left the shop.

A few nights later Onesime and Jean heard the second part of Verlaine's verse: *Wound my heart with a monotonous languor. Wound my heart with a monotonous languor.*

Onesime tried to joke. "Marie has already wounded my heart with monotonous languor."

"Be careful," said Jean.

"You be careful too," said Onesime. "I'll see you soon."

"Me too," said Jean.

Both men felt that Verlaine's verses were the harbinger of something important. Both had big assignments, and they felt certain that others did as well. But neither man knew or could even have imagined the extent of it. Verlaine had announced Operation Neptune. At that moment an armada greater than any the world had ever seen was steaming toward the beaches of Normandy.


In Saint-Léon the night was cool. A light breeze was blowing. The moon was nearly full. Broken clouds moved across the sky. The back gate to the Beaumont château was concealed in deep shadow.

Onesime moved close to the wall to wait for Marie Piano and nearly knocked her over. She clutched his arms to keep from falling.

"Are you all right?" he whispered.

"Yes," she said.

"Am I really your fiancé?" he said, just as urgently.

Her muffled laughter sounded like some kind of night bird or a distant bell. "Yes," she said.

The gate was unlocked. He held it open while Marie stepped through. Marie took his hand as he led the way down the steps to the cave. Once inside he switched on his flashlight. The wine was gone. They walked to the far end as quickly as they could.

"The cave is on the other side of this wall," said Onesime, speaking softly. "We've got to slide this stone out so I can get inside." He shined the flashlight on the stone. "Then I've got to go through and set five charges. There'll be a guard but he'll be outside. It will be toward the end of his watch. Sometimes the guards sleep."

Onesime and Marie slid the stone toward them. When it began to tip, he counted to three, and they let it slide all the way out and to the ground in one motion. Light streamed in on them. They ducked down behind the wall and waited. Everything was silent. After a minute Onesime stood up. He stuck his head through the opening and looked around. The door to the cave was closed. Everything was as it needed to be.

"Here I go," he said, and wriggled through the opening.

Marie started to climb through too. "No," he said. "You wait here, just in case. Hand me the sack." She did as she was told.

Onesime hung the canvas sack on his shoulder. The cave was larger than he remembered, wider, deeper, and with a higher ceiling. There were no supporting pillars. And things had been shifted around since he had last looked. The heavy wooden door was closed.

Onesime moved quickly and as quietly as he could. He placed the first charge under a pallet stacked high with crates of artillery shells and shaped charges. Before he could place the second charge, he heard a truck drive up. Its lights shone under the door as it turned and came to a stop. The guards were changing early. He listened to them banter and laugh as one got out of the truck and the other got in. The truck backed up, shifted gears, and drove off.

Onesime was about to place the second charge when he heard the key turn in the lock and the door slide open. He dropped behind a stack of crates just in front of the opening he and Marie had made. He peered between crates. The guard came into view, walking along the front wall. He had his rifle slung over his shoulder. He was humming softly as he walked. When he reached the far corner of the cave, he leaned his rifle against the wall. He bent and opened a small cabinet. He took out a bottle and a glass. He poured out a portion, held it to his nose, then threw his head back and drank it.

He let out a satisfied sigh. He wiped his mouth with the back of his hand. He put the bottle and the glass back in their hiding place. He slung his rifle onto his shoulder and turned. He stopped and stared at the back wall. He had caught sight of the opening where Onesime and Marie had removed the stone. He took a step toward the back wall. Then he stopped again.

He removed his rifle from his shoulder. Onesime leaned back as far as he could so that he would be out of sight until the last possible moment. He heard the safety click on the guard's rifle. He heard the guard's footsteps as he advanced slowly.

Suddenly the German guard was standing beside him. But he was looking straight ahead, peering as hard as he could into the opening, into the cave on the other side. For a moment it seemed possible that he might not even notice Onesime, that he might turn to his right, away from Onesime, and just walk back to the front of the cave and out the door. But he didn't. He turned toward Onesime. His eyebrows rose in surprise. *"Hey, you! What . . . ?"*

Flame exploded from the opening. The shot lifted the soldier off his feet and deposited him in a heap two meters from where he had stood. The sound was colossal and echoed on and on as though it would never die. Onesime jumped up, his hands over his ears, opening and closing his mouth to relieve the pain in his ears. Marie stood on the other side of the wall holding the gun she had stolen from Colonel Büchner.

"Jesus!" said Onesime, still working his jaw to relieve the pressure.

"Jacques Courtois gave it back to me," said Marie.

"Give me one more minute and we'll get out of here."

"Use the ten-minute fuses," said Marie.

"I will. In case anyone heard that." He placed the remaining four explosives by cases of shells and mines. He stepped on ten fuses all at once and jammed two in each packet. He clambered back through the opening. Marie helped him. And the two of them ran.

At the far end they closed the door and leapt up the stairs. As they were opening the back gate, the ground beneath their feet heaved, then there was a volcanic rumble that grew into an infernal roar. Just over the hill the sky flashed orange and blue. Then there were more explosions. It sounded as if the world were exploding. The door at the bottom of the stairs blew open, and smoke billowed out into the cool night air.

As Onesime closed the back gate, lights came on in the château. He and Marie Piano ran as hard as they could. Germans would be everywhere in minutes. They heard another explosion farther off, and when they looked toward town, they saw what looked like a fire. Maybe that was Jean's doing. Or someone else's.

That night there were attacks all over France, but none were at any of the ten sites Yves Renard's source had reported. The militia men waited for the police stations to be attacked, for the prison to be assaulted, for particular ammunition dumps to be bombed. But they weren't. Nothing happened at those places. The militia men heard explosions, but they were too far away to have anything to do with them. They waited until the sun was up before they finally dispersed. "So much for your source," said Michel Schneider. He removed the clip from his machine pistol. "I'm going home."

Yves regarded the mayor with a long stare. "My source was reliable," he said. "Someone on our side gave the plan away. Some traitor." He stared at Michel Schneider as though the mayor himself might be the culprit.

Colonel Hollinger was awakened by the sound of Onesime's charges going off and then the secondary explosions as the ammunition was ignited. Hollinger sat up in bed and listened. Lieutenant Ludwig rushed into the colonel's quarters. "We're under attack, Ludwig."

"Yes, sir."

"It sounds like an air assault. Get my staff together and get a damage report." Hollinger was concerned but not alarmed. Most of his depots were situated in caves and well protected from the air. They were under guard against a ground assault. And lately there had been a heavy Gestapo and militia presence in the area. It was impossible that the local *maquis* could do any serious damage.

The damage report said otherwise. Two fuel dumps and one ammunition depot had been completely destroyed, and a number of soldiers—mostly guards—had been killed. In addition, a significant section of rail bed and a large number of rail carriages and baggage cars had been destroyed. The only good news was that the cars and carriages were mostly empty. A barracks had been attacked. "How the hell is all this possible, Ludwig?"

"That is what we are trying to find out, sir."

Then the colonel's telephone began ringing. It was Tours and then Paris calling.

# XX.

Liberation . . . . . . . . . . . . . . . . . . . . . . .*June 14, 1944. Issue 17*

*You have already heard, citizens: The English, the Canadians, the Americans, and our Free French Forces are now in France. A week ago they landed in Normandy. First they came by air—by glider and parachute—and landed behind German lines. Then they came ashore on the beaches by Cherbourg, Saint-Lô, and Caen. They came in great numbers and at an enormous cost in lives. They have suffered thousands of dead and wounded. But they killed many thousands of the Germans as well.*

*The Germans were completely taken by surprise. Our liberation is inevitable. Yes, the Allies' advance will be difficult. Yes, they have met with stiff resistance. But they are gaining momentum as the armies of the "invincible" Third Reich fall before them.*

*There is wonderful news from the village of Sainte-Mère-Église: The French flag flies over the town hall once again. The citizens of Sainte-Mère-Église are free. The Tricolor flies in Carentan also, where the citizens have met the liberating troops with choruses of "La Marseillaise."*

*The city of Caen is surrounded by Allied forces, and it too will soon be free, and other cities and towns will follow. The entire Nazi army along with their French lapdog collaborators can do nothing to stop the Allies' relentless advance. The thousand-year Reich is finished.*

*A great deal of fighting remains to be done, a lot of blood remains to be shed. How slowly or how quickly the enemy is defeated, how soon our own Saint-Léon is free—that is up to us. You can hide in your kitchens and wait for the end. Or you can join the effort to finally defeat Nazi tyranny and oppression. Help our liberators. Feed them, take them in, hide them, give them what help you can. Defeat and resist the Germans at every turn, in every way. And defeat the French collaborators when and where you meet them. They have brought suffering upon us. Whatever humiliation they may suffer, they have brought upon themselves. Resist, resist, resist!*

**Vive la Libération!!!! Vive la France!!!!**

Colonel Hollinger received urgent requests from the front in Normandy for ammunition and supplies. But the recent attacks had severely reduced his stockpiles and crippled his ability to move them forward. Many railroads and highways had been attacked and were now impassable. Military convoys were now being routinely attacked by armed partisans. Not that that mattered, as far as Colonel Hollinger was concerned. His motor pool had been sabotaged, and most of his vehicles were now useless. Worse than useless, since they could easily be attacked and destroyed.

"Useless?" said General von Wuthenow on the telephone from Tours. "Please, Colonel . . ."

"I do not exaggerate, *Herr General.* The sabotage was complete."

"But, Colonel," said the general, "tell me. How is that even possible?"

"It is not possible, *Herr General.* And yet it happened."

There had been a heavy guard, and yet saboteurs had managed to damage every single vehicle. In fact, the colonel could not be certain that his own soldiers were not involved. After all, if there were no trucks, there would be no dangerous convoys. In any case, it looked now as though it would be some time before any supplies would be leaving Saint-Léon. Colonel Hollinger did not have enough mechanics to even begin making all the necessary repairs.

"Then draft local mechanics," said the general. "Do you have local mechanics? You must have local mechanics." Claude Melun was enlisted to oversee the repair effort. Claude spoke a little German. And Colonel Hollinger had used him in some limited capacity before.

When the colonel showed up at the motor pool to see how the work was progressing, Claude Melun asked to speak with him. "You have a bigger problem than you think, Colonel," said Claude, wiping grease from his hands. "Let me show you." He climbed onto the bumper of a truck and pointed into the engine compartment.

"I am not a mechanic," said the colonel.

"It doesn't matter," said Claude. "Look." The colonel was obliged to climb up beside Claude. "Look there. See? This vehicle was sabotaged by plugging the gas line to the carburetor. That's a crude trick, and a quick and easy repair to make."

"So what's the problem?"

"The problem is down here," said Claude, pointing lower in the engine compartment.

"I don't see anything," said the colonel.

"I almost didn't either. But you see that cable? See, right there, where it's shiny? It's been cut. Not all the way through. But just enough so that somewhere out on the road it will break and the brakes will fail."

"And the vehicle will be useless and, worse, helpless," said the colonel, finishing Claude's thought.

"Exactly," said Claude. "Now, the vehicle next to it doesn't have *that* particular problem. But after looking it over for a while, I found it has a pinhole in the gas line. That one will give out somewhere out on the road too, just like the first one, also with possibly disastrous consequences. A snapped brake line could lead to an accident; a punctured gas line could too."

"How many are there like this?" said Colonel Hollinger.

"There's no way to know without doing a thorough inspection of every truck. How many do you have?"

"A hundred and ten," said Colonel Hollinger.

"You're talking about many days. At least," said Claude. "Probably weeks. And even then we might not catch everything."

Colonel Hollinger stepped down from the bumper. He turned in a slow circle, regarding the entire fleet of useless trucks. "This is sophisticated work," he said finally. "Who around here could do such a thing?"

"Who?" said Claude. "Well, Colonel, pardon me for saying so, but your men could."

"Who else?" said the colonel.

"Well, Colonel, we're forty kilometers from Le Mans. The twenty-four-hour races used to happen there. Plus there's the Renault factory. There are hundreds of men who could do such a thing. Maybe thousands."

"Well, Melun, you had better get started."

Colonel Hollinger returned to his office to consider his options. They were not many and not good. He summoned Lieutenant Ludwig and the captain in charge of the motor pool. "I can do the inspections and repairs on every vehicle and delay the resupply until the trucks are safe. . . ."

"That is unacceptable, Colonel," said Ludwig. "That would cost lives in Normandy. Why not send the trucks out with mechanics in each convoy?"

"And where will all these mechanics come from?" said the motor pool captain.

"From the French. The same men who are doing the inspections," said Ludwig.

"And the same men who did the sabotage," said Hollinger.

"If that is the case, then they are as dangerous here as they are on the road," said Ludwig.

"No, they're not," said the captain. "Here we can keep our eyes on them."

"Like you did the other night?"

Hollinger called Tours. "Make the repairs," said the general. "We've got other sources for now. But hurry."

"Yes, sir," said Hollinger. And he had every intention of hurrying. If only his French mechanics had been faster. As it turned out, though, the first day they could only complete four trucks.

"Four?!" said Hollinger. "That is unacceptable, Melun. Impossible."

"Colonel, you have to understand," said Claude. "First of all, the possibilities for sabotage on a large, complicated vehicle are endless. We have to check every centimeter, and we don't even know what we're looking for. So far we've found a brake cable cut, a brake cylinder leaking, a gas line leak, and a damaged steering column. So far."

Claude did not name what was "second of all," which was the fact that it was Claude Melun himself who had damaged the vehicles in the first place. Claude was not part of Simon's network, nor of any other network, for that matter. Claude had finally just had enough. He had gotten sick and tired of Germans. Germans here, Germans there. Four years of Germans was enough.

Claude already knew his way around the motor pool. He knew when there were more guards on duty and when there were fewer, where they patrolled, and when certain corners of the yard went unobserved. He had come under the fence one afternoon, while the guards were all at the front gate to change shifts, and had hidden in a truck until nightfall. Then he had gone from one truck to the other—the trucks were high enough off the ground so that he could work from underneath—doing quick and simple damage to as many of them as he could. He started in the middle of the yard, where there were no guards, and worked outward. It took a minute or two to plug a gas line or cut a tire.

He had only done the subtler damage—the pinhole and the partially cut cable—to two trucks, and he had only done it after the colonel had summoned him and brought him to the motor pool. Now he had all the time in the world to damage all the rest, even as he worked on repairing the damage he had just done.

A mixed force of British and Canadian parachutists was to make a landing fifteen kilometers north of Saint-Léon. It was to happen within the week. The signal would be the phrase *The carrots are cooked*. "Who dreams up these signals?" said Anne Marie.

Simon laughed. "I don't know," he said. "Someone who does not like cooking, if I had to guess. But listen: This is an important operation," he said. "And a big one." Anne Marie—Florence, as he called her—and her colleagues would meet at midnight at the designated field. They would signal the planes and guide a full company of parachutists down with light signals. The parachutists would divide themselves into smaller units. Anne Marie and the others—two for each small group—would escort them to designated hiding places. "In your case and your partner's, it's Chêne Boppe, the giant oak in the Bercé Forest. Someone else will take them from there."

"That's a full night's walk," she said.

"That far?" said Simon. "I didn't realize. Are you up to it?"

"Of course," she said.

"Do you need a weapon?" he said. "Or ammunition?"

"I have them," she said.

"Do you need anything else?" said Simon.

"Don't we all?" she said.

Anne Marie had two radios at home. She listened to the one in her room, and the boys listened upstairs. She tried to keep them from knowing how involved she was. She was not so much worried about security as she was about Jean and Onesime. She knew they would be worried about her. And these days she also had to worry about Marie Livrist—called Marie Piano by the boys—who was in love with Onesime. And then there was Angeline's Henri, although she didn't know exactly how she ought to be worried about him. Since the day he had fled the OWS train, she did not know which side he was on.

Four nights after Simon had made his rounds in Saint-Léon, the message came.

*The carrots are cooked. The carrots are cooked.*

All over Saint-Léon, people turned off their radios at the same time. They ate supper or drank a glass of wine or played checkers or did crosswords. They oiled and polished their weapons, they checked and rechecked their ammunition, the batteries in their flashlights. They smoked. No one would be leaving for a while yet, and they had to have something to do. They were like a professional army, except no one knew who would be standing next to him.

Yves Renard took note of the carrot message. "Ah, there it is." But he sat with his ear close to the radio and continued to listen. He listened night after night with a pencil in his hand, whether he expected a message or not. Once in a while, for some reason known only to himself, he would write down one of the phrases. By now he had a notebook whose pages were filled with the phrases he had written. They were in chronological order, and the date he heard them was noted in a column on the side of the page.

*The enchanted trout still eats her young. The enchanted trout still eats her young.*

Yves sat up straight in his chair. "Did you hear that?" he said.

"What?" said Stephanie.

"The enchanted trout still eats her young," said Yves.

"The enchanted trout?" she said.

". . . still eats her young."

"Does it mean something?" said Stephanie.

"I don't know," said Yves. "But it's strange, don't you think?"

"You mean because it's about something here in Saint-Léon? The German bar?"

"The messages don't usually mean anything in that way. They don't usually refer to anything like that. For instance, if it were a real message, and not just a decoy, then it could compromise security, give something away."

"What?"

"I don't know. A meeting place, or . . ."

"Maybe it's a coincidence," said Stephanie.

"Maybe." Yves wrote the message in his notebook. He turned off the radio.

Yves went into the bedroom and put on his boots. He and his partner, whoever that might be, would be walking all the way to the

Chêne Boppe in the Bercé Forest. "I won't be back until tomorrow," he said, and leaned over to kiss Stephanie on the forehead.

Stephanie looked at Yves. He was almost twenty-five now, but he still looked more like a boy than a policeman. His mustache was blond and wispy. And his eyes still had that look of eternal wonder that she had always loved. He started to turn, but she stood up quickly and wrapped him in her arms.

Because Yves was frightened of expressions of affection—things could change so easily; love could disappear in an instant—Stephanie usually avoided declaring her feelings for him. And he did the same with her, as though their happiness were too, too fragile. In fact Yves had once made her promise *not* to declare her love for him. "I know that . . . how you feel about me, and you know how I feel," he said. He was afraid saying it would jinx the whole thing. "Just tell me," he said, "when you *don't* love me anymore."

Now Stephanie clung to Yves. She did not know why. Perhaps it was the odd message about the enchanted trout.

"Maybe there is another Enchanted Trout somewhere else in France," she said.

"Like you said," said Yves. "It's just a coincidence. It isn't any stranger than cooked carrots. Or John has a long mustache. That was a message the other night. It means nothing." But then suddenly Yves took Stephanie's head between his hands and pulled her to him. He held here there so that his mouth was right beside her ear. Stephanie hugged him to her even tighter. Then he said in a voice that was so tiny that she almost missed it, "Yves loves Stephanie. Yves loves Stephanie." Yves pulled himself from her arms, kissed her lightly on the forehead, and was gone.

Yves rode his bicycle to town. It was late. The streets were empty. The lights were all blacked out. He unlocked his office. He unlocked the case where he kept confiscated weapons. He picked out a pistol, which he tucked into his belt, and another he slid into his pocket. He got on his bicycle and rode out of town.

It was Sunday, so The Trout was dark. For a reason he could not explain he decided to stop. "Renard!" said a voice. "Where the hell have you been?" A man stepped from the shadows and pretended to study his watch, even though it was too dark to see it. Yves recognized him from the Marquis d'Estaing's meetings. "C'mon, let's go. We were supposed to meet at nine. The others went on ahead."

"I . . . I couldn't," said Yves. "I thought I'd catch up with you."

"Well, let's go." Yves put his bicycle in the weeds across from the tavern and got in the man's car. They drove without speaking. They were going toward the field where the paratroopers were supposed to land.

"Who's here?" said Yves.

"Nobody you know," said the driver.

"Jacques Courtois?" said Yves.

"Nobody you know," said the driver again. This time he looked over at Yves.

He pulled the car onto a narrow lane that continued between tall hedges. "We've got to walk from here," he said. He turned off the engine. He reached into the backseat and picked up a machine pistol. "C'mon, Renard. We're wasting time."

The two men walked along the lane at a brisk clip. The moon did not give off much light. It went in and out behind clouds. Renard stumbled and almost fell. "Sorry," he muttered.

"Well, just get moving, all right?" said the other man.

After fifteen minutes they came over a rise. "Here we are," said the man. They rounded a hedge and saw a group of men standing around smoking. They stopped talking as Yves and the man approached.

"So you found the straggler, huh?" Yves recognized the voice of Piet Chabrille.

"I was with somebody," said Yves. "I couldn't leave without looking suspicious."

"Suspicious?" said someone else, and laughed. Yves didn't recognize the voice.

"We haven't got much time," said someone else.

"No. We're all here now, so let's position ourselves." Yves recognized one of the other policemen from the meeting. "The main thing is that we stay far apart and far enough away so that they don't smell a trap. I've come up with a two-sided perimeter where they'll be in the crossfire. Make sure your guns are loaded and cocked. Get comfortable and wait for my signal"—he made a sound like a fox barking—"then move forward.

"Any questions? Okay, let's go," said the man. He stood up and ground out his cigarette. Everyone followed him. He positioned them two by two along two sides of a square maybe two hundred meters on a side. "I'll keep you with me, Renard. I like to work with another cop," he said.

Yves sat staring into the darkness so intensely that he was afraid he would start seeing things. Suddenly a shape appeared across the field in front of him and moved to the center of the field. Then another one, then two more.

Onesime was the first to arrive. Alexandre de Beaumont was the next. Then Jacques Courtois, Marie Piano. Anne Marie arrived. Everyone stared at the sky and waited to hear the sound of airplanes. August Pappe arrived. He walked quickly up to the group. "It's a trap," he said softly.

"What?"

"There are no planes. It's a trap. Get out!" Everyone started to run. A fox barked and gunfire exploded from the edge of the field.

Yves shot and killed the policeman beside him. He ran like a madman along the two-sided perimeter—tripping, screaming, shooting, shooting, shooting as many of the militia men as he could. But he couldn't shoot them all. He could not shoot them fast enough to save anyone. His friends—Onesime, Anne Marie, Marie Piano, Jacques Courtois—all of them, they were all dead.

# XXI.

EARLY ON THE MORNING after the German departure from Saint-Léon, Maurice de Beaumont, sitting at the desk in his study, saw an American patrol making its way past his back terrace toward the barns. They looked almost as though they were doing a slow minuet, so deliberate and calculated were their movements. They lifted their legs and put them down with care and precision, and each man turned in a full circle, one after the other, so that one of them was always watching to their rear, and others were facing to the sides. They held their fingers on the triggers of their weapons.

The Beaumont château was on the northern edge of Saint-Léon, so Maurice de Beaumont was the first to see the Americans arrive. He walked to the double doors, opened them wide, and stepped onto the terrace. One of the soldiers saw him and signaled another. That soldier, a sergeant, signaled for Maurice to raise his hands and approach. He saw a tall, erect, and haggard man wearing a sweater despite the heat of the day. "Stop," he said, and held up his hand. Maurice stopped. Another soldier walked up to Maurice and searched him for weapons.

"The Germans are gone," said Maurice. It was the first time he had spoken English in years. Doing so gave him an unexpected sense of exhilaration. "The Germans left last night."

"When?" said the sergeant. "What time?" His young face made Maurice think of Onesime.

"They were busy all night," said Maurice. "The last ones left maybe three hours ago. They have been loading trucks for most of two days: It was a transportation and ammunition depot. And destroying the things they couldn't take. I can show you."

"What else? Did they destroy buildings? Kill anybody?"

"Not that I know of," said Maurice.

"You're lucky then," said the sergeant.

"Lucky?"

"Yeah. Just down the road at Maillé"—he pronounced it *male*—"somebody attacked the Gerries just as they were leaving, so the bastards destroyed the whole village. Killed everybody in it. A hundred people at least. Men, old ladies, babies, pregnant women. Then they just blew it up. Blew up the whole damn town."

The sergeant took a radio that was slung over his shoulder. He pressed a button and, after listening for a moment, said, "Cocktail fiver, this is cocktail two niner. . . . Roger. We've got a guy here knows where the Gerries are. He seems to have lots of information, over. . . . Roger, behind the big house, over. . . . Roger, and out."

The lieutenant arrived on foot a few minutes later. "Who are you?" he said.

"Maurice de Beaumont."

"Do you live here?"

"Yes."

"Who else lives here?"

"No one."

The lieutenant turned and looked at the house. "That's a damn big house for just one person."

"My wife was killed. My children are staying with their grandparents."

"Who killed your wife?"

"Collaborators. French Nazis."

"What do you know about the Germans? Where are they?"

"They left last night going southeast. They were a transportation-and-supply company. . . ."

"What did they leave behind?"

"They destroyed their inoperable vehicles, whatever else they couldn't use. . . ."

"What's your name again?"

"Maurice de Beaumont."

"All right, Maurice, listen. The sergeant here is going to pass your name up to our S-1, that's our intelligence people. They may come by to get more details. We're going to move on now. But stay put and they'll find you. Good luck." He stuck out his hand and Maurice took it.

Maurice walked slowly back to the terrace. He sat down heavily on the steps. He moved like an old man although he wasn't. It was as though he had been held upright for the last four years by intrigue and machination. Now the Germans were gone, and the Americans had come, and his war was over.

He did not feel joy or relief. But other feelings, the feelings he had kept at bay almost as long as he could remember, rushed in on him like a huge wave. He felt agony and grief. He felt the absence of those he had lost, Alexandre especially. And Yves. Yves Renard had been arrested and sent off to prison in Germany. And Onesime. Dear Onesime. And Anne Marie and all the others, the incalculable, unimaginable pain of what France and the world had lost and would continue to lose.

He could not know the numbers. After all, the war would continue for many more months. The Americans and British and Canadians pushed the Germans from the west, the Russians from the east. Cities had been and would be destroyed; soldiers, civilians would be cut down on all sides, like wheat falling before the sickle bar. He could not even imagine how many millions would perish before it was over. How could anyone conceive of it? Even once the numbers were known. Or estimated. For how could they ever be known?

And what did the numbers matter anyway in the face of the betrayal, the treachery, the brutality? The tens of millions of dead were an abstraction. Scholars might find the numbers useful or telling or significant. But they were—like light-years, like the distance across the Milky Way, like the temperature of the sun—simply beyond imagining.

Anyway, it was not the death of millions or the suffering of other millions, but the loss of one person, Alexandre, that had brought Maurice de Beaumont to the edge of ruin. He dropped his head into his hands and wept.

# XXII.

WHEN THE WAR ENDED, a colossal, moral silence settled onto the world. It covered everything like a fine coating of dust. It seemed as though all human experience from now on and forever would have to include the imminent possibility of widespread death and unimaginable destruction as an essential part of itself.

More than sixty million had been killed. Sixty million.

Great swaths of civilization lay in ruins.

The physical world had been damaged and traumatized beyond imagining, in some places almost beyond recognition. The cities, the roads, the forests and oceans and deserts were littered with the detritus of war—corpses, burned vehicles, unexploded bombs—and it would surface unexpectedly for generations to come. And it would surface in people's minds too.

And yet. As time passed, mankind left the war behind, faster than anyone could ever have imagined we could, faster probably than was good for us. Proper healing didn't matter. What everyone wanted more than anything else was to forget. Start over. Move on.


"Look what I have." Jean Renard put the faded circular Louis Morgon had given him in front of his father.

"What is it?" said Yves. He took his glasses from his shirt pocket. He carried the circular to the window. He studied it for a moment, then laid it aside. "Where did you get this?"

"I found it."

"Where?"

"Actually, Louis Morgon found it. The American."

Yves was silent.

"He found it. Along with some little pistols."

"In his house," said Yves.

"How did you know that?"

"It's from the war."

"I know that."

"These things came out all the time."

"How did you know where he found it?"

"Let's have a cup of tea." Yves went to the kitchen, and Renard followed.

The two men sat at the table and looked into the cups cradled between their hands.

"Where's Stephanie?" said Renard. He had called his mother by name since he was a little boy.

"Shopping," said Yves. He turned his cup on its saucer. First a full turn in one direction, then a full turn in the opposite direction.

"Do you remember that circular . . . ?"

"There were lots of them."

"Do you have any?"

"Why would I?"

"Papa . . ."

"It's long ago, Jean."

"Papa . . ."

"I've told you, Jean. It's over. Drink your tea."


Louis found the Renard house easily. Isabelle opened the door. "It is a pleasure to meet you, madame," he said, and shook her hand.

"The pleasure is mine," said Isabelle. "I have been curious to meet you."

"It was generous of you to invite me for dinner," said Louis.

"Small towns are the same everywhere," said Renard. "Everyone wants to know all about the newcomer."

"That is especially useful for the newcomer," said Louis. "The curiosity of the others helps smooth his way—I should say *my* way—into village life."

They sat on the back terrace while the sun went down. The evening turned cool. An owl whistled in the distance.

Isabelle had made a lamb stew with chickpeas and couscous. Renard uncorked the bottle Louis had brought. He poured a little into his glass and sniffed at it suspiciously. He took a bit in his mouth and made chewing motions. "It's drinkable," he said.

Isabelle tasted it. "It's very good," she said. She looked at Renard and waited.

He took another sip. "All right," he said. "It's very good." He studied the bottle.

The meal seemed to pass quickly, although by the time Renard was mopping up the last of his sauce with a piece of bread, the candles had nearly burned themselves out.

"That was a wonderful dish," said Louis. "May I ask what gave the stew its sweetness?"

"Prunes," said Isabelle. "There were a few prunes. That is all." She set a plate of cheeses on the table. Renard sliced some more bread. He opened another bottle. "Chinon," he said.

"What are the cheeses?" said Louis.

Renard pointed at each with the bread knife: "Goat, sheep, Roquefort, Mimolette."

"In the United States they put Roquefort in salad dressing, you know," said Louis.

"That does not reassure me," said Renard.

"It was not meant to," said Louis. Renard and Isabelle laughed, and all three raised their glasses and drank.

"What brought you to Saint-Léon?" said Isabelle. "I mean how on earth did you even find it?"

"I was a pilgrim on my way to Spain," said Louis. "I stopped here for a night."

"A pilgrim?"

"I say that. But I was really running away."

"From what?" said Isabelle.

"Something illegal, I hope," said Renard.

Later Isabelle and Renard lay in bed. They stared into the darkness. Finally Isabelle spoke. "He is an interesting man."

"Yes, he is. Interesting," said Renard. "He seems to tell you about himself. And yet you somehow know less at the end than you did at the beginning."

"It was surprising that he came right out and asked to meet your father. Just like that."

"He has this way, Morgon does. I mean, did you hear me, telling him stuff as though we were old friends? He gets you to talk about things without giving himself away." Renard paused. "I like him."

# XXIII.

"Jean tells me you like to walk," said Louis.

"Yes," said Yves. Yves, Louis, and Renard were walking on a grassy farm road along the Dême northwest out of town. It was a sunny November afternoon. The trees were mostly bare. A gentle breeze stirred and rattled the leaves underfoot. Louis noticed a small château in the distance.

"Is it lived in?" said Louis, pointing.

"It is sometimes," said Renard. "It belongs to the Beaumonts. They own several properties around France. They come and stay here sometimes. We're walking in their fields. That's theirs over there too," said Renard, pointing.

The fields had been plowed and planted. But the soil was white and stony and looked unsuitable for growing anything. "It's good soil," said Yves, as though he knew what Louis was thinking. Then he lapsed back into silence.

The banks of the stream were planted with poplars. The sun flickered through the bare branches. Louis shielded his eyes with his hand. He stopped and studied the hills. He pointed into the distance. "Are those vineyards?"

"Those are Beaumont's," said Renard. "There used to be more. But the weather is too undependable for wine. Now it's mostly wheat and sunflowers and colza. And you see those caves?" He pointed at a row of doors in the hillside. Those are Beaumont's. They used to store the wine in them. Now they're mostly empty."

"And over there," said Yves, pointing past the chateau, "is where the Americans arrived."

Again there was a long silence. Then Yves asked, "How did you come to Saint-Léon?"

"I walked," said Louis. "I was walking across France. It is not a particularly interesting story. My life came off the tracks. Maybe that is why I decided that walking was a safe and reliable mode of transportation. Going slowly, step by step. It seemed the best way to travel. And in the course of walking I started to discover myself. I don't know whether that makes sense. But walking toward I-don't-know-what took me back to myself. The more I walked, the more my life seemed to come into focus. I had the feeling I actually knew something about myself for the first time in my life."

Yves had stopped walking, and Renard stopped too. "Am I making any sense?" said Louis.

"Are you all right, Papa?" said Renard.

Yves had gone pale. He turned slowly to the east and raised his arm in a vague gesture. He removed his cap and passed his hand lightly across his forehead. "Yes," he said after a moment. "I'm fine." He thought further. With Yves you always waited while he worked out whether he wanted to say something and what it might be. "It's just what you said about walking and how it brought you back to yourself. Perhaps you know from Jean that I walked to Saint-Léon too. Not the first time, as you did. But still. As you said, walking brought me back to myself. It restored me. To France, to Saint-Léon, to Stephanie—my wife and Jean's mother."

"Where were you walking from?" said Louis.

"Russia."

"Russia?"

"I was a prisoner there." He paused. "Walking was the only way home. Some time after the war had ended, I was released and I started walking. I was weak and ill. Oddly enough, walking gave me strength. I was under way for half a year. Which is why what you said struck me the way it did.

"A lot of people were on foot then. All over Europe, going in every direction. You walked and passed people, carrying or pulling or pushing their belongings. If they had any. Finding their way . . . somewhere.

"Sometimes I felt a sort of . . . it wasn't happiness, but it was something like it. Purpose maybe. Yes, purpose. There is a kind of happiness that comes with having a purpose. And what greater purpose is there than getting home? Of course when I got home, I found . . ."

Louis and Renard waited, but Yves did not say any more. Instead he set out walking again, and at a quicker pace than before. At a mill they stopped and sat. They looked into the rushing stream as it emerged from the race where the mill wheel had once turned. Only part of the old wooden axle remained in place. Nettles and errant sunflowers grew tall through the remains of the wheel lying scattered on the banks. A young willow had sent roots into the stone wall. The rays of the afternoon sun slanted through the trees behind them.

Yves stood up. "It's getting late," he said, reaching down and massaging his leg. Then he set off, and Renard and Louis followed. The sun had set, and a chill was setting in by the time they dropped Yves at home. It was almost dark by the time Renard got home.

"How was it?" said Isabelle.

"Good," said Renard.

"It was a beautiful day," said Isabelle.

"Were you in the garden?" said Renard.

"For an hour. I pulled out the sweet-pea vines. They were really too overgrown."

"Louis got him talking," said Renard. He stood at the window looking into the darkness. "It will be better without those vines."

"Well, of course" said Isabelle. "You're his son. Fathers don't confide in their sons. They can't."

"Why does that have to be true?"

"Did you learn something you didn't know before?" said Isabelle.

"Not really. Yes. I mean, I knew about his walking home from Russia. But I didn't know about his feelings about it," said Renard.

She had been setting the table and she stopped. "What feelings?"

"He talked about happiness. Sort of. Not really. More like relief. And purpose."

"Did he talk about the leaflet or the pistols?"

"No. He won't talk about that. I'm sure. That gets into what he did, who was on what side. He'll stay away from that stuff. It's too dangerous."

Renard was right; he knew his father. Yves had never spoken about being a policeman under the German regime. He had never mentioned who did what in the war, who fought, who collaborated, who resisted, who did both. All he would say when anyone asked was "That's history" or "That's over." Or he simply remained silent. He was never impatient about being asked. He just didn't answer.


The winter was not a hard one. There was no snow and there were few hard freezes. The fields remained green. Louis and Yves began taking walks together. They met on the square. They would shake hands and stomp their feet like horses to keep the cold at bay. Steam came from their mouths and noses. Yves wore a down jacket and a stocking cap, and Louis wore a long navy overcoat, the same one he had worn years earlier in Washington.

"Where shall we walk?" said Louis.

And Yves would say, "I want to show you something," and off they would go. One time they walked out past abandoned vineyards to an old quarry above the Beaumont family caves. Yves stood for a long time and gazed down into the quarry.

The fields were white with frost, and the smell of wood smoke was in the air. Another time they walked out to the village of Villedieu. They walked past what looked like an abandoned barracks. Villedieu was where Stephanie had lived with her mother when she and Yves first met. The remains of a medieval fortress encircled one side of the village, and, as with the caves, rooms in the old walls had been converted into dwellings. "We French don't like to throw anything away," said Yves. "Even ruined buildings. Even caves become something. Everything eventually becomes something else."

"And everyone?" said Louis.

Yves smiled.

Once as they walked out of town across the Dême, Yves paused at a small expanse of rubble. "There used to be a tavern here. A rough place." Farther on they reached a broad, open field. "This is a beautiful spot. Saint-Léon is there, just out of sight." On the way back they went past the Beaumont château. Louis stood on tiptoe by the front gate and tried to see inside, while Yves kept walking.

Louis came to believe there was a theme to these walks. "It's as though he's telling me a story without actually telling it," he said to Solesme. They were sitting in Louis's kitchen with their feet by the woodstove.

"Do you know what the story is about?" she said.

"The war. I think maybe he's showing me places where important things happened. For instance, he stopped at a spot by the Dême. But all he would say was that there had been a tavern there."

"Le Pêcheur? Was that it?"

"He didn't say. And he didn't say what happened there. If anything." Louis paused. "Maybe he's guarding secrets," he said. "Guilty secrets."

"Or," said Solesme, "maybe he's protecting someone. Or he's protecting the events. Or maybe the facts, the events themselves, are too complicated to talk about. Or too confusing."

"It's as though putting things into words means you get it wrong."

"Yes. Something like that," said Solesme. "Certain things."


Stephanie telephoned Louis. "Yves and I would like to invite you for dinner. Jean and Isabelle will be there."

It was early March. But the day had been sunny and warm, and

Louis decided he would go on foot. Renard and Isabelle could give him a ride home. Louis could smell the freshly turned earth as he walked. In some fields it looked like the wheat was already growing. Birds were sweeping busily about the darkening sky.

Louis shook Yves's hand. He kissed Stephanie on both cheeks. He pulled a bottle from the pocket of his overcoat. "Some wine," he said.

"Thank you," said Stephanie.

Renard and Isabelle arrived a little while later.

They ate dinner in the kitchen at the long table by the fire. Stephanie set a large bowl on the table. Everyone leaned forward to take in the sight and the smell of the spaghetti with its creamy sauce of peppers and sausage. They scooped it onto their plates, and it disappeared quickly. Then came a salad of tiny greens, then a pear tart.

They talked about the feeling of spring in the air, about Stephanie already getting garden greens, about the baby that Isabelle was expecting. Isabelle had not been sick at all. She was feeling very good. "And looking radiant," said Louis. Everyone agreed.

Somehow the Paris student revolt of 1968 came up. It was now six years later, and they debated whether or not it had served any useful purpose. Oddly enough, everyone deferred to Louis's opinion, since he had worked in Washington and therefore must understand politics. Louis tried to persuade them that a career in politics probably made his opinion less, not more, reliable than other opinions. And anyway, in the end, politics was essentially incomprehensible. "People in high places act as though they know what they're doing. But they don't. They are groping about in the dark."

"That's right," said Yves. He pronounced the words with such authority that the room fell silent.

Yves himself looked startled. He had not meant to state an opinion so definitively. And yet he felt compelled to finish his thought. "Even if people know what they're doing," he said, "they can't guess what others are doing or will do. And that is why in politics—I'm talking about the student unrest of 'sixty-eight—events always take over in unexpected and unpredictable ways. Things come alive on their own when they shouldn't." He went no further. He closed his mouth tightly. His lips turned white from being pressed together. It was clear to everyone that Yves was not really talking about 1968.

Why Yves chose this moment to say what he had never said, to speak about what had until now remained unspeakable was anybody's guess. He was not old or infirm, although maybe he still knew somehow that he did not have long to live. Louis had sensed during their walks that a story was building, and now it was trying to find its way out.

"There were twelve murders," Yves said. He smiled faintly and shrugged his shoulders as if to apologize for bringing it up. "At least, that's what I call them. Of course, there was so much death then. You couldn't even tell what was the war and what was murder. Anyway, it's almost impossible to imagine now, even for me. My memories seem like something left over from a terrible and impossible dream.

"There was death everywhere. All twelve of those who died were *maquis*—resisters; they were operating outside the law. They knew they were risking death. Maybe their deaths were even inevitable. I've tried to tell myself that sometimes.

"These twelve . . . I was the only policeman. . . . Some of my friends, some of them . . . An air drop was expected. . . . Finally, I was arrested." It was as if Yves were trying one door and then another, looking for a way back into the past. He had thought about it almost constantly, but he hadn't spoken of it ever.

Particular memories surfaced like long-forgotten bombs that had burrowed into the earth but failed to explode. Until now. The arrival of the Germans: "Orderly, efficient. A big sedan first. Then trucks. No one was in the streets. The whole town watching.

"There was that picture of Hitler in the colonel's office. I knew nothing would ever be the same again. Four years," he said after a long pause. "One night in 1944—a dark night, no moon—the twelve . . ." Yves peered upward through tears. "I shouldn't . . . have. . . ." Stephanie held his hand in both of hers. "It seems clear now; it didn't then.

What was to be done? What would save France? Who betrayed her? Did it matter? *Did it even matter? . . .*"

Yves decided to stop talking. And, having so decided, he started up again, torn between the silence in which he had sealed his memories and the need to bring them all to light. He thought saying them would make them easier to bear. But it didn't. Stephanie stroked his hand. Louis and Renard and Isabelle sat motionless, fearful that even the slightest movement might cause him to stop for good, and fearful, at the same time, that he would continue.

"We were listening to the radio. I was waiting for a signal, and then I heard it. Then I heard another one. *The enchanted trout still eats her young.* And then again. They always said everything twice. There was supposed to be a parachute drop. But I ended up waiting with fascists who were going to kill my friends.

"I saw them coming out of the shadows—Onesime, Jacques, Marie Piano, Anne Marie. The rest. One by one, gathering for the airdrop that wasn't coming, that was an ambush. They were only faint shadows in the dark, but I knew them. I recognized them. They were looking up into the sky, but there were no planes.

"They started running and the militia started shooting. People fell everywhere. No one screamed or cried out. They just fell. Collapsed. Onesime. Marie Piano, Anne Marie—Oni's mother—Jacques, all of them running in every direction with the militia shooting. Then every-thing went silent again. They were all dead."

Yves put both hands over his face. His body heaved with a great silent sob. He sat with his face covered for a long time. Finally he low-ered his hands.

"The Germans arrested me. I knew they would. I was sure they were going to kill me. Instead they sent me to prison. I don't know why they did that. I wanted them to kill me. They thought I was a *maquis*. What was I? *What side was I on?*" He gripped Stephanie's hand and searched her eyes as though he might find the answer to this strange, desperate question there. "I was with . . . but I . . .

"The Germans shackled me and put me on a prison train to Germany. And when the Russians liberated the camp, they put me on a train to Russia."

As soon as Renard and Isabelle got home, Renard took a pen and paper and wrote down everything he could remember of what his father had said. He organized it just as though he were writing up a report of crime. "June 1940 (?) Yves Renard—policeman (21), called to Cheval Blanc to meet with German commandant (Colonel Büchner) and SS Lieutenant Ludwig. Also there: Mayor Michel Schneider; town council." He wrote "1944" and the names of the murdered, those his father had named: Onesime Josquin, Marie Livrist called Marie Piano, Anne Marie Josquin, Jacques Courtois. He wrote until he couldn't think of anything more to write.

# XXIV.

THE NEXT MORNING Renard took a new file folder and labeled it: COLLABORATION/RESISTANCE. He put it in the top drawer of the file cabinet so that he would see it every time he opened the cabinet. Investigating the killing of Onesime Josquin and the others would not be like investigating an ordinary case. Historical truth of the sort Renard was pursuing was, as Louis had said more than once, and as his own father had implied, primarily an act of imagination. Like an archaeologist, you guessed at a likely spot and then dusted at it with a tiny brush until, if you were lucky, something revealed itself. Except, where were the likely spots? And if something revealed itself, what was it? What did it mean?

Renard searched the town hall records. Those from the time of the German occupation had been removed. Even innocent papers like ration allotments and minutes of town meetings were gone. No one knew where they had been taken or by whom. And when there was a scrap of paper from back then, figuring out what it was, deciphering its arcane references, even figuring out who had signed it were all but impossible.

He tried to talk to Stephanie, but she did not want to talk.

"But you were there," he said.

"I was. And I don't want to talk about it. I didn't then and I still don't. The times were difficult and painful. People had to do terrible things. We all did. Your father was taken from me. He was gone for nearly five years."

"Why was he taken?"

"There was no reason."

"There was no reason?"

"No reason was given. He was taken away the day after they were killed. That was all I ever knew."

"How did you know he was taken away?"

"Because he didn't come home. That is how I knew." Stephanie turned away for a moment and then turned back to face her son. "Stop asking me these questions, Jean. Let it be. Stop asking. It doesn't do any good. There are no answers."


"Maybe she's right," said Isabelle. "Maybe you should leave it alone."

"I can't," said Renard.

"I know," said Isabelle.

"There are the names in Papa's story and in the leaflet. And there are five Duquesnes, two Arnauds, and two Chenus in the telephone directory. I have to knock on some doors."

The five Duquesnes included the three surviving Duquesne children and their offspring. All three children were now in their forties. All three wept when Renard asked them about their long dead brothers.

"And don't forget our parents," said Fanny Piqueoiseau, the youngest child. She had been twelve when they were executed. Fanny covered her eyes, trying to block out the memory of their bodies lying on the village square.

Why did this have to be brought up now, thirty-some years later? Why make them go through it all over again? They were not at all comforted by the thought of unknown culprits being brought to justice.

"Culprits? What culprits?" said Fanny. "The Germans were the culprits. Anyway, it won't bring them back, will it?"

"What do you remember from that time?" said Renard.

"What do I remember? I'll show you." Fanny left the room and came back with a framed photograph of a smiling family. "There they are, Monsieur Renard." She pointed as she named them. "Stephane, Antoine, Maman, Papa. And François, Paul, and me. 1939. That is what I remember."

Renard looked at the faces gazing out from the picture. "I'm sorry, madame."

"Then why bring this all up again?" said Gilles Piqueoiseau. He stepped forward and put his arm around his wife's shoulder. "What's the point, Renard?"

"Justice," said Renard. He regretted having said it as soon as it was out of his mouth.

"Justice? For who? They're all dead, the good *and* the bad."

"Not all of them are dead," said Renard. He thought of Yves. "And even if they were, we have to know what happened."

"Maybe *you* have to know what happened. I'm sorry, Renard. We can't tell you anything."

Renard worked his way through the "witnesses," as he called them, one by one. He asked each one what they knew from that time, what they remembered, what various references in the handbill meant, whether they knew anyone he should talk to. And each time he came away empty-handed.

Like all the others before her, Janine Chenu, the widow of Charles Chenu, the son of the long-dead town councilman, had nothing to say. "I can't tell you anything, monsieur," she said. "I lived through it. But I don't know anything."

"Do you remember your father-in-law?"

"Barely," she said. "I knew who he was, but I didn't know him then. I didn't even know Charles."

"You weren't married or engaged?"

"Oh, no, monsieur. Not until after the war."

"Is that you, madame?" said Renard. A framed photograph on the center of the mantel had caught his eye. It showed a young woman with two young men, their arms around one another, leaning toward the camera and laughing.

"Yes, monsieur," said Janine, without turning to look.

"May I say, madame, you were a beautiful girl. . . ."

"*Were,* inspector? That is not very gallant," said Janine. She smiled slightly.

"A beautiful girl is different from a beautiful woman, madame. I was about to say, *and* you have become a beautiful woman."

"Liar," said Janine, with a laugh.

Renard stepped up to look at the photo. "Is one of these men your late husband?"

"Oh, no, Monsieur Renard. One is an old boyfriend, the other his brother. That was before the war."

"What became of them, madame?"

"I had other boyfriends. And then I met Charles," she said.

"And yet you have this photo standing in a place of honor, madame."

"Yes, it is a good photo, don't you think? And, well, he, Jean, the one on the right"—she reached out as though she were going to caress the photo—"was my first love. You know how first love is, monsieur."

"I understand, madame. And was that here, in Saint-Léon?"

"Oh, yes, they were from here."

"And are they still living?"

"No, monsieur. That is, Jean moved away after the war. I don't know where. I doubt that he's still alive. His brother—Onesime—was killed in the war."

"Would that be Onesime Josquin, madame?"

"Onesime Josquin," said Janine, and turned away from the photo. "And Jean Josquin. Yes, monsieur. Jean and Onesime. Jean and Onesime." She repeated the names as though they were the refrain in a song.

# XXV.

JEAN JOSQUIN WAS ALIVE. He lived not thirty kilometers from Janine Chenu in a small cottage on the other side of the village of Bueil-en-Touraine. He was weeding his garden when he heard a car coming up the gravel lane. He stopped and leaned on his hoe and watched the car approach.

Renard stopped the car, got out, and raised his hand in greeting. Jean returned the greeting.

"Bonjour, monsieur. I am Jean Renard, the police inspector from Saint-Léon."

Renard offered his hand and Jean Josquin took it. It was a strong, rough hand. "You look like your father," he said.

"Ah, then you know my father," said Renard.

"Is he still living? Yes, I knew who he was," said Jean.

"Yes, he is still alive. It is because of my father that I've come to see you, monsieur."

Jean Josquin remained silent.

"May I ask you some questions, monsieur?"

Jean still remained silent. It was as though he regretted having spoken at all.

"I would like to ask you about the war."

Again Jean remained silent. Then, as Renard was about to speak again, Jean said, "Why?"

"Because, monsieur, I am investigating the annihilation, the murder, of the resistance in Saint-Léon, and I was hoping you could help me."

"I don't think so," said Jean.

"Because you don't know about it, monsieur?"

"That's right. I don't know anything about it. I cannot help you, Monsieur Renard. I'm sorry."

"Do you have other family members living around here, monsieur?"

"Here?" Jean made a gesture toward the fields in front of his house.

"Around Saint-Léon," he said.

"No," said Jean. "My sister died a few years ago. No one is left."

"No brothers?" said Renard.

"My brother died in the war. On the front. He was a soldier. He was killed in the war in the Ardennes Forest."

"He died in battle, monsieur?"

"He died in battle," said Jean.

"But I had heard he came back from the war."

"No, monsieur. He died in battle, Oni did."


Renard found Louis sitting on the terrace of the Hôtel de France. Louis had waved at him, and Renard took it as an invitation to sit down for a cup of coffee. He took out a cigarette. "Tell me what you know about those little pistols," he said.

"You know," said Louis, "in the United States, smoking is becoming less and less acceptable. The evidence that it is bad for you is overwhelming."

"Ah? Is that so?" said Renard, lighting up. "Is that what brought you to France?"

Louis smiled. "It will happen here too, you know," he said.

"In France?" said Renard. He exhaled over Louis's head. "I doubt it. Tell me about the pistols."

"The FP-45 Liberator. They were manufactured in the United States to be dropped into occupied Europe. They were made to be fired a few times and then thrown away. They could only be used at short range. They were mainly used for assassinations."

"What do you think it means that some were hidden in your house?"

"I suppose it means that at some time my house may have been used for underground activity of some sort. If that was the case, then the house was probably not lived in, since anyone living there would have been shot if the pistols, or the leaflets, had been discovered."

"I may have found one of the old resisters," said Renard.

"What makes you think so?"

"He didn't want to talk, and when he did talk, he lied," said Renard. "It's Jean Josquin. Papa mentioned him. I just don't know how to get him to talk to me. These people know how to remain silent."

"Did he like your father?"

"I don't know. I couldn't tell."

"What did he say?"

"He said that I look like my father."

"Then he liked him," said Louis. "He wouldn't say you looked like someone he didn't like. He would be insulting you."

"Unless he didn't like me. Anyway, is that useful?" Renard wondered.

"I don't know," said Louis. Renard drew deeply on his cigarette and studied the American. Louis gazed across the square and allowed himself to be studied.

"You could always show him something that might make him want to talk," said Louis.

"Like what?" said Renard.

"Like an American," said Louis.

"An American."

Louis smiled. "I have noticed," he said, "even in my short time in France, that nothing makes the French want to talk quite so much as the sight of an American. They have opinions about our culture, our ways, our poor language skills. And someone his age, whatever he did or knew back then, will certainly have strong memories of the liberation. And while you're at it, take the Liberator with you."

"Take you?" said Renard.

"And the pistol," said Louis.


When Renard and Louis drove up the long gravel drive, Jean Josquin was working in his garden again. It looked as though he had not moved from the spot where he had stood the last time Renard had been there. He shook hands with Renard.

"This is Monsieur Louis Morgon," said Renard.

"Bonjour, monsieur," said Jean. He hardly looked in Louis's direction. His handshake was quick, one motion and that was all.

"I hope you don't mind that I have come back, Monsieur Josquin," said Renard.

"No, monsieur," said Jean.

"Monsieur Morgon is new in town, monsieur. He is American, but he lives here now."

Jean remained silent. He did not look at Louis.

"I suppose you remember when the Americans came through," said Renard.

"Hardly," said Jean. "They came and were gone in a day."

"Was there no fighting here?"

"I don't know, monsieur. I think the Germans were gone when the Americans arrived."

"What about this?" said Louis. "Do you know what this is, monsieur? I found it in my house."

Jean kept his eyes straight ahead. He did not turn to look in Louis's direction. You could not tell that Jean even noticed Louis's outstretched hand. But he must have. For he lowered his eyes until they were locked on the little pistol Louis held. The muscles flexing in his jaw were the only sign of the conversation he was having with himself. Finally he said in a voice filled with resignation, "If you want to find out what you want to find out, then find Simon," he said.

"Simon?"

"Find Simon," said Jean again.

"What I want to find out?" said Renard.

"Which side your father was on," said Jean.

Jean took the little pistol from Louis's outstretched hand. He turned it over and over in his. "Where did you get this?" he said.

"Under the floor in my house," said Louis.

"Where is your house, monsieur?"

Louis told him. "Ah," said Jean. "That house has a history. Animals were slaughtered there when it was illegal. Illegal dance parties were held there. Later meetings. All sorts of things went on." Just the feel of the Liberator in his fingers had unlocked his memory. "Come inside," he said. He limped as he walked. The two men followed.

Jean lived alone. Inside the front door was a crude coatrack with hats and slickers hanging from it. The first floor was one large room with a table. Some chairs were standing around the room. It looked as though a meeting had just broken up and the chairs hadn't been put back in place yet. The walls were mostly bare except for a calendar from an insurance company and a half dozen drawings and small paintings. Louis stepped up to look at the paintings. "Did you do these, monsieur? They are very nice."

"Onesime, my brother," said Jean. "He was the artist."

"But this one is by someone else," said Louis.

"When Onesime died, I tried my hand," said Jean. "It didn't work out."

"I have to disagree, monsieur," said Louis. "I like it very much."

Jean turned his back on Louis. He dragged chairs to the table. "Sit down," he said. He got a bottle from the mantel and three glasses from a small cupboard. He poured whiskey in each. He raised his glass, and without waiting for the others, took a deep sip. He wiped his lips with the back of his hand and, without looking at either man or waiting for questions, began talking.

"When the Germans arrived, I started watching them. I worked in town in Melun's mechanic's shop across from their headquarters, so it was easy. It's where the hardware store is now. I don't really know why I did it. I just started watching. Onesime watched them too. He made maps and I kept diaries.

"Onesime was killed by the militia. It was late in the war, after the landings. There was supposed to be a parachute drop. But it was a setup. Oni—that's what I called him—and my mother were both there, and they were both killed, along with all the others.

"Now here's the thing: Yves Renard, your papa, was supposed to be there with them, but he turned up with the militia. Some people said he was the traitor, the one who gave them up. Except he was arrested and shipped off to Germany as a prisoner.

"Sometimes the Germans used to imprison their spies so the other side wouldn't know they were spies. They'd beat them up a little bit to make it look good. But Yves was in Germany and after that in Russia for a long time. It didn't seem right to me. That he was a traitor, I mean. I don't know, but I don't think he was."

"Did you see him when he got back?" said Renard.

"Not much. None of us saw each other. We tried to keep our distance. There was just too much anger. And shame."

"And this Simon?" said Renard. "Who is he?"

"Simon. I wonder sometimes where he is. A German, I think. A Jew. I think. He didn't give much away. But a *maquis*, a resister, one of the organizers. And a good one. He kept us alive for a long time."

"And where is he now?" said Renard.

"I don't know," said Jean. "Even then you didn't know where he was."

"When was the last time you saw him?"

The little pistol lay on the table between them. Jean picked it up and held it up flat against his head beside his ear. He cocked his head and seemed to listen, like he was listening for the sound of the ocean in a seashell. He did not speak for a long time. "After the Americans had come and gone," he said finally. "After Maman and Oni and the others were dead and buried. I went back to the mechanic's shop.

"I didn't work there anymore. There wasn't any work to do then.

Claude Melun—it was his shop—barely had enough work to keep himself busy. And the Germans were gone, so there wasn't anything or anyone to watch. But I had to get away from the house. I did what had to be done, but I couldn't stand to be at home if I didn't have to be. I wished I could get far away, to another part of France, another country even, and never see the place again.

"The French flag flew from the pole on the small square outside the town hall. Tours had been taken by the Americans. The Germans had been blowing up bridges. They were taking reprisals as they retreated. They didn't even pretend to be civilized anymore. They left nothing but destruction behind them.

"I looked across the square at the gendarme's office. It was padlocked. And there was Simon standing there with his hand shielding his eyes trying to see through the office window. *What was he doing here now?* I wondered. He had this way of just turning up. He came and went like a ghost. Simon looked over at me and nodded his head in the direction of the Hôtel de France.

"When I got there, Simon was sitting at a table." Jean could recall the moment vividly.

"Sit down," Simon had said. They did not shake hands, as though their association belonged to an earlier time. Jean sat down. Simon ordered a beer. "What would you like?" he asked Jean.

"Nothing," said Jean.

"Listen," said Simon, "you think it's over because the Germans are gone. But it's not. De Gaulle's in Paris making great speeches, but it's not over. There's a serious battle for power in France going on. I've been called to Tours."

"What does that have to do with me?" said Jean.

"My old contact says it's for a meeting. But I think it's a trial and execution."

"Whose?" said Jean.

"Mine," said Simon.

"By whom?"

"The Stalinists. They think they can eliminate the opposition this way. They think there's a revolution going on in France."

"Maybe there is," said Jean. "Maybe they're right."

"Killing collabos or Pétainists, shaving women's heads because they slept with Germans—that kind of stuff may make some people feel good, but it doesn't amount to a revolution."

"You know they did that here too, don't you?" said Jean. He lit a cigarette. "In Saint-Léon."

"Did what?" said Simon.

"Shot collaborators. Shaved women's heads. That kind of stuff," said Jean.

"Who did?" said Simon.

"Well, that's the funny thing, isn't it? They killed a couple of guys who liked to drink at The Trout, you know, the bar Le Pêcheur. The guys they killed weren't collabos, but the guys that shot them were. Do you know Piet Chabrille? He worked in Melun's shop. He was one of the ones that shot them. A nasty son of a bitch. So Piet switched sides quick and ended up a 'resister.' Maybe he'll get a medal someday.

"At least they got Edith Troppard, though. They beat her up pretty good, shaved her head. She fucked a lot of Nazis."

"Edith Troppard?" said Simon.

"You know that whore?" said Jean.

"Yes," said Simon. "I know her." Simon took a sip from his beer. "I need you to come to Tours with me," said Simon finally.

"For your trial?" said Jean.

"No. It's not going to get that far. It's a three-person operation. Me, you, and Shakespeare. Remember Shakespeare? This time you'll be the shooter."

"Why should I?" said Jean. He started to stand up. "That is all finished for me. I'm through with it all."

"Do you know the difference between justice and revenge?" said Simon. He did not wait for Jean to answer. "Sometimes there isn't any. The person I'm meeting, the one who has laid a trap for me—I'm guessing they expect to 'arrest' me while she and I are meeting. Then they'll have a quick trial in a basement somewhere and execute me. She's the one who betrayed your mother, your brother, and all the others. . . ."

"*She?*" said Jean.

"No parachutists were ever on the way. There weren't any. It was internal politics, her faction's way to undermine some other faction, to undermine some rival's authority or credibility. Who knows what they got out of it. That's the way their politics work, the way they think. Sacrifice other people's lives for the 'greater good.' The communist revolution, or whatever her greater good was."

"The greater good. Is that what *you're* doing? Sacrificing her to the greater good?" Jean said.

"The greater good is nonsense," said Simon. "This has to do with punishing one crime and stopping others. My execution won't be their last killing. They have to be stopped." Simon slid a small package across the table. "It's got five rounds in it. Use one to kill her, and there are four more rounds just in case. Take the train to Saint-Pierre-des-Corps. Shakespeare will meet you at the station and explain the operation to you."

"When?"

"Take the seventeen fifty on Friday."

"How do I know *I'm* not being set up?"

Simon stood up to go. "Ask Edith Troppard."

"Edith Troppard? What do you mean? Why should I ask her? What's she got to do with this?" said Jean.

"She is on our side. On *your* side. She always was. And while you're at it, get on your knees and beg her forgiveness."

"I didn't do anything to her," said Jean.

"Not for what you *did*. For what you *thought*."

Simon found Savanne at an outside table in front of a small café in the Rue du Théatre, as they had arranged. She rose and smiled as he ap-

proached. "Let's go somewhere else," she said. In case he had told anyone where they were meeting.

"Why not?" said Simon.

They walked through a narrow alley. Simon did not turn to look.
He did not hear anyone behind them, but he hoped Jean and Shakespeare were there, somewhere. Savanne led the way into a small, dimly
lit bar. She went straight to a small table in the corner and sat down.
She signaled the bartender and mouthed the words *deux cognacs*. He
poured the drinks and brought them over on a tray.

She and Simon touched glasses. "It's time," she said after taking a
sip, "to disband your operation."

"My operation?" said Simon.

"Your network, then," said Savanne. She put a cigarette between
her lips and handed the matches to Simon. He struck a match and
held it under the end of her cigarette. She watched the flame then in-
haled deeply and blew the smoke into the air.

Simon shook out the match. "Is it?" he said. "Why is that? France is
still at war."

"Things have moved beyond that though, haven't they?" she said.
"We're in a different stage. The struggle for power is on."

"Besides," said Simon, "you already effectively disbanded my 'operation' yourself, didn't you?"

"You don't get the larger picture, do you, Simon?" She studied his
face. "You never have."

"So you don't deny it," he said. "Defeating the Germans in France—"

"Was but one step in a complicated dialectical process," said Savanne.

"Ah," said Simon. "The beloved dialectic."

"You know, Simon," said Savanne, "your sarcasm is out of place. You
have never understood, have you? You're a problematic person, Simon.
Your effectiveness at getting things done has been extraordinary. But
that effectiveness could get you in trouble. And now you are meddling
in affairs that are none of your business."

"Who was your Saint-Léon go-between?" said Simon. "Who set up the parachutist operation for you?"

"I'm surprised that you would even ask."

Simon shrugged. "I thought you owed me that much. And the others. Those people who died because of your ambition. I hoped you would save me the trouble of having to find out on my own."

"Sentiment will do you in one day," said Savanne.

"That's possible," said Simon. "It *is* my weakness, after—"

He was interrupted by a commotion at the bar. "Get your fucking hands off me, you fucking pervert." A short, burly man in blue work clothes had grabbed a flamboyant middle-aged man by the lapels of his plaid and ill-fitting jacket and had slammed him against the bar.

"Don't hurt me," the man whimpered, "please, I just wanted to—"

"I know what you fucking wanted," said the burly man. He hit the flamboyant man hard and sent him staggering and pirouetting across the floor, knocking over tables and chairs and drinks in every direction. People at the bar jumped backward out of the way. The man fell across a table just as Jean passed behind Savanne. "Oh, my God, help me!" the man squealed. The sound of the shot was all but lost in the commotion. "Oh, Jesus and Mary, mother of God, don't hit me again," the man shrieked.

Simon stood up and jumped away from the table, brushing the spilled cognac from his front. By the time Savanne's henchmen had managed to fight their way through the crowd to the table, Savanne lay dead, face-down on the table, and Simon was out the door.

# XXVI.

"That was the last time I saw him," said Jean. "I left the bar right behind him. I looked for him when I got outside, but he was gone. I always looked for him. But, like I said, he came and went like a ghost. Simon could answer your questions. I can't." He pushed the little pistol away.

"Do you think he would know who betrayed the resisters to the militia? Who was Savanne's go-between?" said Renard.

"You mean, if it was your father? I don't know if he'd know," said Jean. "We never knew, any of us, what others were doing. Or even who they were. Simon never let us know. For our own protection. He always saw to it that everything was secret from everyone else. I didn't even know about my own mother, what she was up to. He only told me about Edith Troppard afterward."

"Edith Troppard," said Renard. "Do you know where she is?"

"Look for Simon," said Jean. "He'll know about your father. Simon organized us and kept us alive. You know? I still look around for him sometimes. Somehow I expect him to show up again. Find Simon and you'll find your answer."

"And how do we do that?" said Renard. "How do we find him?"

Jean poured himself another glass of whiskey. He looked at Renard. He smiled slightly and shrugged. "I don't know," he said.

---

"Louis," said Isabelle, "what is your interest in the resistance?"

"Mysteries of this sort have always interested me," said Louis.

"Of what sort is that?" said Solesme.

"Of the iceberg sort," said Louis. "Where most of the mystery is out of sight. Under frigid water."

"Of the iceberg sort," said Solesme. "Are there any mysteries that are *not* of the iceberg sort?"

"Louis," said Renard, "I appreciate your help—"

"No you don't," said Louis. "You wish I would go away."

Renard hated being that transparent. He drew deeply on his cigarette and blew smoke in Louis's direction.

"You can of course order me to stop trying to help you in your investigation," said Louis. "But if you do, you know I'll continue to investigate anyway, on my own. Not of course in any official way. But as a kind of historical, intellectual exercise. At least that."

It was September. The first intimations of fall were in the air: the morning fog, the cooler nights, the plaintive calls of an owl. But this day was sunny and warm, and Louis had made lunch for his friends. He rose to clear the table while Renard, Isabelle, and Solesme sat in the sun and finished their coffee. Solesme closed her eyes and sipped the delicious bitterness. She was amazed that an American could make good coffee, and she had told him so.

Renard had been busy with other things. He had not made any progress on the case in weeks, and Louis was growing impatient. "We need to find Simon. Or someone. Maybe we should talk to Jean Josquin again."

"I have other work I have to do," said Renard. "Besides I thought you were going to start painting."

"I have," said Louis.

"May we see?" said Isabelle.

"Not yet," said Louis. Then he thought for a moment. "Yes. Sure. Why not? But what you see won't be paintings. It will only be the beginning of paintings. The below-the-surface business that goes on before a painting can become a painting."

"More icebergs," said Renard.

Louis led the way into the barn and turned on the lights. He was right. The paintings did not amount to much. Indistinct meanderings in murky colors on raw canvas. "You're right, Renard," he said later. "They're like icebergs. But with these, all I can see is what's below the surface. I have to intuit what will be above the surface from studying what's below it. And—"

"And you're going to say that police work is the same. But it's not. All I've got is what's above the surface."

"Well," said Louis. "It depends on how you read what you've got." And so their discussion continued, until Renard stubbed out his cigarette and said, "I have to go."

It was a surprise to Louis then when his phone rang a short while later and it was Renard on the line. "Remember the name Piet Chabrille? The collaborator who turned resister at the end?"

"Yes. What about him?" said Louis.

"I found him," said Renard. "Or rather, he found me."

Renard was enjoying being mysterious, and Louis tried not to spoil it for him. "And how did he find you?"

"By dying," said Renard.

"Ah," said Louis. "He was old?"

"Seventy-five or so. But in poor health."

"Well, then," said Louis. "And is his death of the interesting or the uninteresting kind?"

"Interesting," said Renard. "A bullet in the back of the neck." Renard could almost hear Louis rubbing his hands together.

Piet Chabrille had been found in an alley in Tours not far from where he had lived for the past thirty years. The police report indicated his death had occurred in the night. Piet had been drunk at the time. His watch and wallet had been stolen. There were no witnesses to the murder.

The coroner took Renard into the keeping room and slid open the drawer. He pulled back a plastic sheet. Piet Chabrille had a large bony head, a large nose, and a fringe of colorless hair. His skin was gray, and his blue lips were peeled back slightly to reveal long, yellow teeth.

"What is your interest in this case, inspector?" said the coroner.

"He used to live in Saint-Léon," said Renard.

"Thirty years ago," said the coroner. "Long before your time."

"Yes," said Renard. "Long before my time. That's true. What do you have on him?"

"Not much," said the coroner, looking through the forms. "Address. Date of birth. Talk to the police. Maybe they can tell you something." He gave Renard the case officer's name.

The case officer did not know much about Piet. "Looks like a robbery. He shouldn't have been out alone at that hour. That's a nasty way for an old man to die."

Renard was allowed inside Piet Chabrille's apartment. He had lived alone in a building near the train station in Saint-Pierre-des-Corps. There were few clothes in the closets, little food in the refrigerator. There was a small battered desk, but the drawers were mostly empty. There was nothing of interest, as far as Renard could tell. And Piet's neighbors did not know anything about him either. "He kept to himself," one of them said.

"He said hello, but that was about all he said. Why would they do that to an old man—rob him and then kill him like that? What's the world coming to?"


"This may be one of your iceberg murders," said Renard.

"Do you think so?" said Louis.

"I don't really know. But I went back to see Jean Josquin again."

"And what did he say?" said Louis.

"He said to go away," said Renard. "And not to come back. He got scared after I told him about Chabrille."

"So you think he wasn't just killed in a robbery?"

"Two things seem wrong," said Renard. "First, why shoot him at all? He was an old man; just knock him down and take his stuff. And then, why in the back of the neck? Like an execution? He had enemies. I would like to have talked to him."

"Well," said Louis, "he might turn out to be more informative dead than he would have been alive."

Renard was alone in his office a few days later when the door opened and an elderly woman came through the door. She was thin and she looked frail. And yet she walked unhesitatingly and stood erect before him.

"Madame?" said Renard. He stood up. "How may I help you?"

"I am Edith Troppard," she said. "I read in the newspaper about the robbery and murder of Piet Chabrille in Tours. Do you know who Piet Chabrille is?"

"I do, madame. Jean Josquin has spoken to me about him. Please sit down."

"Ah. Jean," said Edith. "How is he?" Her hand rose and brushed her white hair aside in an absent gesture. "Then you *are* investigating Chabrille's murder?"

"No, madame, not exactly. I am investigating some murders from long ago."

"I see," she said.

"Onesime Josquin, Marie Livrist, . . ."

"I understood what you meant," she said. "And may I ask, Monsieur Renard, why you are investigating these . . . deaths now, after thirty years?"

"It is complicated, madame. The short answer is that there are many unanswered questions that should be answered."

"Well, then I am glad I have come. I thought I could help you with the Chabrille case, but I would rather help you with the case of . . . your father."

"My father?"

Edith Troppard did not answer.

"Do you think they may be connected, madame?"

"Do *you* think so?" said Edith. "The newspaper said Chabrille was robbed. I wondered about that."

"Do you know someone named Simon, madame?"

"I did once. In fact, it was your father who sent him to me."

"Would you mind telling me how that happened, madame?"

"Not at all. I came to see him, your father that is. Here, in this very office"—she paused and looked around the room—"demanding to be directed to the *maquis*. It was a crazy thing to do. But I was desperate. I didn't know your father then. As far as I knew, he was a collaborator. Everyone thought he was; some probably still do. After all, most police and town officials were. That was the law. Anyway, I told Yves I wanted to join the resistance. He could have turned me in, and that would have been the end of me. But instead he sent me to see the Count de Beaumont, who directed Simon to me.

"I arrived at Beaumont's gate and rang the bell and waited. After a long while the gate opened and the Count de Beaumont stood there looking me up and down while he held a large dog on a lead. He was a tall, handsome, but severe-looking man, a very serious man. He never smiled."

It was a hot, sultry day. The Count de Beaumont had stood at his gate and studied Edith Troppard. Colonel Büchner had spoken well of her. And Yves Renard had called to tell the count she was coming.

"Madame Troppard," he said, and offered his hand.

"Yves Renard sent me," she said. She thought again how dangerous it was to trust a stranger this way. But, oddly enough, it had been Colonel Büchner's assurances about the count that had made her believe he could be trusted.

Edith followed the count through the château park between the giant oaks and plane trees. The sunlight falling between the leaves left golden spots on the grass. The air was still. The back of the count's shirt had spots of sweat in the middle. He walked looking neither left nor right. She followed him onto the terrace and into the house.

"Please wait here, madame," he said, opening the door to a small office. He and the dog disappeared down a dark corridor.

Edith sat for what seemed like a very long time. The count finally reappeared wearing a fresh shirt and a pale linen jacket. He sat down at the desk and took out a bottle and two glasses. "May I offer you a drink, madame?"

Edith told the count what she had told the policeman. "Colonel Büchner is dead," she said. "I loved him," she added.

"He spoke highly of you, madame."

"I make no apologies," she said.

"No apology is necessary."

Maurice de Beaumont took a sip from the cognac he had poured himself. "May I have directions to your house, madame? A man who can help you will come to you. He will introduce himself as Simon."


"And a few weeks later he showed up," said Edith Troppard. "Simon. I was walking home from the market, and he fell in beside me. He lifted his hat, said his name—Simon—and offered to carry my groceries."

"And what did you do for him, madame?" said Renard. "What was your assignment? And where did your assignment come from? How exactly did that work?"

"Well, as far as I could tell, Simon had a contact higher up in the organization. This contact—"

"Savanne?"

"Savanne? I don't know. Quite possibly. It doesn't sound familiar. I don't remember that I ever heard. I never knew whether the assignments came from Simon or from his higher-ups."

"Did you know others who were working with Simon?"

"Yes, I knew them, although in most cases I didn't know until later that they were working for Simon. I didn't know that Jean and Onesime

Josquin were working for him until after Onesime and Anne Marie were killed. I knew about Anne Marie Josquin, their mother. She and I were friends. We had been since the deaths of our husbands in the First World War.

"It was against the rules, but she and I confided in each other. You could only stand to keep so many secrets. Keeping everything inside isolated you even more than you already were.

"Anne Marie gathered information on German installations. She hid and guided British spies. She participated in sabotage operations. It was terrible for me when she was killed. I still miss her today."

"Did you tell her about your assignments?"

"I did. I had to tell someone."

"And what were your assignments, madame?"

"I cannot tell you, monsieur."

"You cannot tell me?"

"No, monsieur."

"But why, Madame Troppard? It has been many years, the war is over. . . ."

"That is why I won't tell you. I know it's hard for you to imagine, but during those years—it was less than five years, but it seemed like a lifetime—during those years we lived in a state of absolute moral anarchy. The only way you knew right from wrong was to examine your own conscience. And yet, if you did so—examined your conscience— you found yourself in mortal danger. Examining your conscience was, in effect, a crime.

"What had been evil was now the law, and what had been good was now punishable by death. It was a time when to obey the law was to do terrible things or at least to be complicit in terrible things. At the same time, to resist often meant doing equally terrible things. All I will say is that I resisted, and I did terrible things."

"But, madame—"

"Please try to understand, Monsieur Renard," she said. "I have to leave it there."

"What can you tell me about Piet Chabrille?" said Renard.

"A detestable man," said Edith Troppard, without hesitation. "I did not know he was still alive, until I read about his murder. He worked in the mechanic's shop alongside Jean Josquin. I forget the owner's name. I think he was a militia man."

"Melun, Claude," said Renard.

"Ah, yes, Claude Melun. Anyway, there was a local cell of fascists—Pétainists and others—who terrorized the locals. Your father went to their meetings sometimes. I figured he was spying. The mayor went to the meetings too, a man named . . ." She searched her memory. "Schneider. That's it. Michel Schneider. And others were involved. But Piet Chabrille was the cruelest of the bunch. He was a genuine enthusiast. I doubt that he cared about the politics. But I think he loved the cruelty. He wanted to be on the side of cruelty."

"When the Americans arrived, Piet suddenly claimed to be a resistance partisan. And he and others like him began taking 'revenge' on those who were accused of collaborating. They beat up some men and killed some others. I don't think the ones they killed were really collaborators. Certainly not to the extent that Piet had been." Edith stopped talking.

"Please go on, madame. What you are saying about Piet Chabrille is very useful."

"Useful?" she said.

"Knowing about Chabrille gives me a glimpse of what sort of person might want him dead. And why."

Edith studied Renard for a moment. She smiled. "You remind me of your father," she said. "He could think that way." Edith sat up even straighter in her chair. She closed her eyes and breathed deeply. She seemed to be gathering her strength for what she had to say next.

It had been a sultry summer evening in August 1943, long before the invasion, before anyone could even imagine the invasion would ever come. The sun had set, but the evening seemed even hotter than the day had been. The moon had risen, and the evening star. It was cloudless.

It was late evening and getting dark, but Edith was still working in her vegetable garden. She was on her hands and knees pulling weeds. An owl made its quivering sound. When the sound came a second time, Edith looked up and saw that there was a man at her fence not five meters away. He stood watching her, his hands on top of the pickets.

Edith stood up quickly, dusted her hands against each other and then on the skirt of her dress. She wiped the sweat from her forehead with the back of her hand. The man's face was partly in shadow. From what she saw, she didn't think she knew him.

"Monsieur?" she said. "Good evening."

"Good evening," he said. "It's hot." He gave an odd, nervous laugh.

"Yes, it—"

He did not allow her to finish. "Water," he said. "Could I have some water?"

"Of course," said Edith. She stepped into the kitchen, took down a glass, worked the pump until the water started, and filled the glass. When she turned, the man was right behind her, already reaching for her. He grabbed the collar of her dress in his fist and tore it down, pulling it back over her shoulder, revealing her breast, the sight of which seemed to drive him into a frenzy.

"Is this what you want, you German whore? Is this how they do it, the Germans?"

Edith fought to get her hands free, but the man—Piet Chabrille—was strong. He pinned her against the front of the sink and tried to kiss her mouth. His breath was hot and it stank. Edith twisted her head violently from side to side, but he finally caught her mouth with his own mouth and bit into it hard.

"How's that, you fucking bitch? Is that what you want, German cunt?"

He lifted the skirt of her dress above her waist, used his fist to force her legs apart, and then, using his erection as though it were a knife, stabbed at her wildly, again and again and again, against her legs, against her belly, until he finally drove his way inside her.

His heavy boots crushed her toes; her back slammed against the granite sink with each thrust. Her lips were bleeding from the ferocity of his bites. He bit her cheek, her eyebrow, her neck, her breast.

He came with a great shuddering groan, and when he finished he raised his arms out to the side and away from her and stepped back, as though he were letting go of something unspeakably filthy. Edith dropped to the floor, hitting the back of her head on the edge of the granite sink.

Piet screamed at her. He pulled his boot back as though he were going to kick her. But he didn't. He only screamed, about her being a German whore, about her being disgusting, about how he would kill her if she breathed a word.

"After the Germans left and the Americans had come and gone, he found me again, this time with his new 'resister' friends. They cut off my hair and marched me through the crowded streets of Saint-Léon with other 'German whores,' as they called us, other women who had loved German men. I remember him sticking his face up close to mine and screaming 'German whore! German whore! German whore!' over and over until the crowd—my neighbors—took up the chant. I know it doesn't seem possible, but I had the sense that he didn't even remember that it was me he had raped the year before."

Edith Troppard sat silently and looked at Renard. Her face was expressionless. "You are shocked, I imagine, that I can tell this story without coming undone."

"I am shocked, madame," said Renard, "at the horrors you had to endure. I am sorry that I had to ask you about it."

"I don't object to talking about it, Monsieur Renard. It was only one of the small horrors of the time. And by far not one of the worst. Anne Marie and Onesime Josquin, mother and son; Marie Livrist, Onesime's fiancée, were massacred as were countless others. Your own father spent years of hunger and deprivation in Russia. And there's poor Jean, whose family was killed and who was then left behind."

"Do you know Jean Josquin, madame?" said Renard.

"I knew him only slightly," she said. "We had one very odd encounter after everything was over, which in itself was enough, all by itself, to make me love him. I will tell you about it, and then I'll go home. I'm tired."

"Of course, madame."

"It starts just the same as the rape started, with me on my knees in my garden and a man standing at the gate. I jumped when I looked up and saw him. I was momentarily carried back to August of 1943. But the war was over and well behind us. It was Jean Josquin standing there, whom I knew a bit through Anne Marie. He asked if he could come into the garden. I said of course he could, and he did. He removed his hat and approached me very cautiously as one might approach an invalid or a sick child.

"'Judith,' he said when he stood in front of me. Nothing more. Just 'Judith.' Everyone in the resistance had a secret name, and Judith was my resistance name. I do not know how Jean knew it. Do you know who Judith was? It's a story in the Apocrypha. Judith was the Jewish princess sent out to seduce Holofernes, who was besieging the city. When he was sated, she took his sword and cut off his head. Judith sacrificed her virtue for the good of her people.

"Anyway, Jean said that he had hated me and wished me ill for loving a German officer—Helmut Büchner. Simon had explained that I had been with the *maquis* all along. And I had. Then, according to Jean, Simon had given him strict instructions to seek me out and ask my forgiveness. 'Fall on your knees and beg her forgiveness' were apparently Simon's words.

"What is so remarkable is that Jean told me all of this. It was almost like a religious act of contrition on his part for whatever sins he had been obliged to commit. He even tried to get down on his knees in front of me in my garden, but I would not let him. Instead we stood facing one another like the two sinners that we were."

# XXVII.

LOUIS WAVED AWAY THE SMOKE from Renard's cigarette. They were sitting at what had become their regular table—the one beside the large concrete planter—in front of the Hôtel de France. It was a chilly day. But the sun was shining and Louis was loathe to sit inside. He pulled his broad-brimmed hat down to his ears and turned up his collar.

Renard had laid the investigation aside for a while. There had been other, more-immediate business that required his attention. But when that business was finished and Renard lifted the collaboration files out of the file cabinet—they had multiplied and now filled the front half of the top drawer—somehow Louis seemed to know.

Renard had to admit that he was glad to have his American friend to talk to about the case. Louis could discern things that went past Renard. Maybe it was the fact that he was a foreigner, maybe it was his own past, whatever that past might have been. Louis spoke very little about his American life, except for the occasional dark references to what he called "the temples of iniquity" or, his preferred phrase, "the sordid world."

"Are you talking about the United States?" said Renard. "That doesn't seem quite fair."

"Not the entire United States," said Louis. "Only one corner of its government. A musty, secret corner. And anyway, it isn't meant to be fair." It seemed only natural that Renard would turn Louis's interest to his advantage. "So, what's next?" said Louis.

"I need to find Simon," said Renard.

"Why?" said Louis.

"To get answers," said Renard.

"To which questions?" said Louis.

"Well, who betrayed the resisters, for example. Who set up the parachute operation." Renard felt like he was back at the police academy. "Who—"

Louis did not let him go on. "What did Piet Chabrille tell you?"

"He was dead."

"All right, if you insist. What did *his assassination* tell you?

"Was it an assassination?"

Louis decided to ignore Renard's obstreperousness. "Who would fear Chabrille's testimony enough to kill him?"

"A lot of people could want him dead. He brutalized Edith Troppard. . . ."

"She's over eighty, and from everything you've said, she's not vengeful."

"Jean Josquin was part of an assassination team. . . ."

"At that time it made sense," said Louis. "It is nothing to worry about now, is it? It was a patriotic act."

Louis pulled his hat lower on his head. He gazed across the square at the Cheval Blanc and tried to imagine German soldiers going in and out. "No, it has to be someone who could be *seriously* damaged if his past actions came to light. Someone who has something to lose. Someone who fears his life will be destroyed if it comes out that he was a collaborator."

"You're going somewhere with this," said Renard. "Why not just say it?"

"A politician. A high-stakes person, a politician, maybe?" Louis was pleased with himself. *High stakes* was a new French phrase for him.

"Like who?"

"Or a nobleman, maybe, with a big reputation to protect?"

———

Finding the Count Maurice de Beaumont was easy. All the Beaumont properties were listed in the *Registry of Châteaux and Historic Places*. Renard wrote letters to the count at each address, and after eight days a letter on blue stationery arrived in the morning mail. It was addressed by hand in blue ink.

> *Monsieur Jean Renard, Inspecteur*
> *Saint-Léon-sur-Dême*
>
> *My dear Monsieur Renard,*
> *I was very pleased to receive your letter and, I am obliged to add, none too surprised. Your inquiries have certainly not gone unnoticed in certain circles, and so it seemed as though it would be only a matter of time until you found your way to me. The assassination of Piet Chabrille has had the same effect as someone batting at a nest of hornets with a stick.*
> *I fear, however, there is very little I can offer you in the way of information about the betrayal of the heroes of Saint-Léon. All that I have are ambiguous stories and dubious surmise.*
> *Nonetheless, I would be happy to welcome you to my home. I remain very fond of your father. If there is anything I can do to help you lay these mysteries to rest for your own peace of mind, then I am happy and honored to do so. I shall look forward to meeting you. Please contact me again to set up an appointment.*
> *In the sincere desire to hear from you in the very near future, I remain your faithful and obedient servant,*
> *Maurice, Comte de Beaumont*

"You told the count that I was coming with you?" said Louis.

"The count apparently has a great fondness for Americans. He was happy when I said you might accompany me."

A small sign directed them down a long gravel lane. Dried leaves flew about behind the car. The house was hidden from view behind a tall cedar hedge. Renard stopped the car at a massive wooden gate. He got out and pulled on a chain suspended from the top of the gate, which rang a bell in the house. After a few minutes the gate swung open and a man waved them through.

Renard parked the car and he and Louis got out. "I am Christoph de Beaumont," said the man, and shook their hands. "Please follow me."

The house was not large or elaborate. But it was beautifully proportioned, with two rows of tall windows and a row of dormers above. There was a broad flagstone terrace in front, surrounded by a balustrade and a carefully trimmed boxwood hedge. Christoph held the door and showed the two men inside. He led them to a long sitting room, which looked out on a formal garden. "I will be in the next room," he said, and left the room.

"Why did he say that?" said Louis.

"As a warning. He's protecting his father," said Renard. "They're frightened."

The rosebushes had lost most of their leaves, but a few faded red blossoms clung to the canes. Dried leaves and petals swirled about in little eddies and rattled against the windows. The wall opposite the windows was hung with tapestries and paintings. Louis was studying one of the paintings when Maurice de Beaumont came into the room. He was a tall, erect man. He gave the impression of being both vigorous and fragile.

"Welcome, Monsieur Renard," he said. Then in English, "Welcome to my house, Mister Morgon. It is a pleasure to meet you."

"The pleasure is mine," said Louis. "Please allow me to say, you have some lovely paintings, monsieur."

"That's a Daubigny you were looking at," said the count. "And a Tiepolo next to it. They have been in my family for generations."

"I congratulate you on your excellent English," said Louis.

The count smiled slightly and nodded his head. "I'm just showing off," he said. Then in French he said, "May I offer you both something to drink?"

They sat down at a small round table, with Louis and Renard facing the garden. The count raised his glass. *"A votre santé,"* he said, and then, nodding toward Louis, "To your health."

The count chewed on the wine for a moment and then set his glass aside. "I fear we all are in danger, Monsieur Renard. By 'we' I mean all of us who know anything from that time. Or rather all of us who *someone thinks* know anything. Chabrille was a wretched excuse for a human being. But his death was a warning, which I take seriously. And you should too."

"I understand," said Renard. "Thank you."

"As I wrote, Monsieur Renard, I doubt that I can provide you with any help, but I will tell you what I know. I should say right away, I do not know where or, for that matter, how to find Simon. He disappeared more than thirty years ago."

"Well, monsieur," said Renard, "I have some questions that I would like to ask, if I may. Simply to form a better picture of the events in question."

"Please, inspector. Go ahead."

"If I may turn to that night . . . I know very little about what happened the night everyone—including your wife—was killed. Please allow me, monsieur, to offer my condolences, even this long after the fact."

"Thank you, Monsieur Renard. It is very odd, but it does not feel as though it was long ago at all. When someone close is taken from you in that fashion, violently, suddenly, it remains in the foreground of your experience forever. If anything, it grows more vivid. You can't put it behind you. When I look at my children, Marielle and Christoph, I still see Alexandre in their faces, in their gestures and manners."

"What do you know about how it happened, monsieur?"

"Very little. She was to meet a company of parachutists, but there were none. She would not be alone, of course, but she did not know ahead of time who else would be there or how many of them there would be. And, instead of parachutists, a band of militia fired on them and killed them all. It was over very quickly. But a great deal of confusion remained."

"Confusion?"

"A great deal," said the count. "Many militia were killed too. There were bodies strewn across the field. Everyone was armed, so it was impossible to determine with any certainty who belonged to which group. There were survivors, of course. Yves Renard, your father, for instance. And others. But they all told different stories."

"What do you know about how it happened, monsieur? How do *you* think it came about?"

"I didn't visit the scene until many hours after it had happened. The dead and injured had been removed. Yves was not there. He was arrested immediately, I think. I was visited by police, whom I did not know, and told that Alexandre had been killed. I went to the site. I didn't know for a long time where they had taken her. There were Germans everywhere, French Gestapo, police. The bodies had been removed, as I said."

"But how did the . . . how did it come about, monsieur? In your opinion."

"Well, both groups—ours and the militia—were alerted by a coded message on the radio. Whoever did it announced a false parachute drop. They then gave both groups a message. The *maquis* were alerted to meet a British parachute drop and escort them out of the area. And the militia were alerted by a different message that there would be a gathering of *maquis* and that they should be . . . killed."

"You were not there that evening, monsieur?"

"No," said Maurice. He sat up even straighter in his chair. "I often wish I had been."

"So that you could have prevented it?"

"No. No one could have prevented it. No, Monsieur Renard. So that I could have died."

"Do you still know what the code words were, monsieur?"

"I cannot forget them. *The carrots are cooked. The carrots are cooked.* Alexandre got up, kissed me, and left the room. I continued to listen."

"Did you also have a mission that night?"

"No, I did not have a mission, as it turned out. I was waiting for one—a different message—which is why I continued to listen. That was when I heard the message that I now know sent the militia: *The enchanted trout still eats her young. The enchanted trout still eats her young.* It's odd, but I have forgotten the message I was supposed to be listening for."

"Did the words mean anything to you, monsieur? *The enchanted trout?*"

"Yes and no," said Maurice. "They did not mean anything, per se. But I found them . . . odd."

"Odd?"

"Yes. It is a little difficult to explain. You see, usually the coded messages had no specific meaning. They never made reference to real events or people or places. That would have been dangerous. But the enchanted trout? That referred to a local bar, a place named Le Pêcheur but nicknamed The Enchanted Trout.

"I found this odd. The codes were always indefinite, without any meaning whatsoever, invented by someone far away. This one seemed as though it had been made up by someone from Saint-Léon, someone who knew Saint-Léon and wanted to say something about it. And it referred to something a lot of people would recognize. Including many Germans. It seemed like a serious breach of security."

"What do you think it meant?"

"I don't know. Was it made up by someone from the militia who did not know the protocol for constructing coded messages? Did the words have a secret meaning for someone?

"Believe me. I have analyzed the words a thousand different ways. *The enchanted trout still eats her young.* Why *still*? Was that suggestive or significant somehow? It was no use. If it meant anything, I couldn't figure it out. In any case, the local reference seemed dangerous to me. A giveaway of some sort, a clue."

"A clue? What sort of clue?"

"I don't know that either. But something. Where the event was happening, maybe? I know Yves Renard, your father, found it odd too."

"How do you know that, monsieur?"

"He told me so. Years later, after he returned from prison, when he and I met again. You know he believed, I think, that I was the informer. I know I believed that he was."

Renard seemed taken aback.

"Do you still believe that?" Maurice hardly noticed that it was Louis who had asked the question.

"No, I don't think so," said Maurice. "I am very fond of Yves. And he suffered a great deal, during the war and in prison. But you never really know such things, do you?"

"Monsieur le Comte," said Louis, "may I ask something else, something—forgive me—slightly uncomfortable? When your suspicions were aroused by the message, did you try to prevent your wife from going?"

"No. I didn't."

"Why not?"

"Well, I had nothing but the vaguest misgiving. And one had constant misgivings in those days. Everything was suspicious in some way or another. One was always fearful that things would go wrong. You simply couldn't pay attention to such misgivings. They would paralyze you. Besides, we—Alexandre and I—didn't . . . how shall I say? . . . we didn't work that way."

"I don't understand."

"It's a complicated story."

"May we hear it?" said Louis.

"Yes, you may," said Maurice, after hesitating only briefly. "But it will only raise more questions than it answers. Like all such stories.

"My wife and I ran a sort of underground hostel for political refugees in one of the caves. We sheltered and escorted refugees—wanted partisans, wounded soldiers, Jews, anyone we could help. It was a large and complicated operation, and inevitably a lot of people knew about it.

"There was a Gestapo officer, a nasty little martinet named . . . what was his name? . . . Essart. That's it. Lieutenant Essart. He was a sadistic bully. Anyway, Essart got wind of our cave sanctuary somehow. My wife, Alexandre, had been spotted leaving the cave with two men. As it happened, they were Jews who were high up in the resistance and on their way to London, but nobody knew that.

"Essart thought he had us. To be honest, I did too. But when he confronted my wife with his eyewitness account, she broke down and confessed that one of the men was her lover, a high German officer. And the other man was supposedly the officer's driver. She refused to give her lover's name. She said he was a high officer in Tours.

"It was a brilliant lie, and it threw Essart completely off his stride and made it all but impossible for him to investigate further. You see, he couldn't very well investigate the love affairs of a German colonel who might turn out to be his superior.

"The trouble was, Alexandre's story . . . wasn't a lie. It was true. Not the part about the German officer. But the affair—*that* was true. She *was* having an affair. I won't say with whom. It doesn't matter. I had been suspicious. But I knew from the way she said it at that moment that the affair was true. That was the moment I learned the truth, there in front of the Gestapo and everyone else. I was humiliated. And furious. I stormed off. I locked Alexandre out of the house.

"Neither of us were actors. We couldn't have convinced anyone if it hadn't been true. Of course Alexandre couldn't be blamed for having an affair. How could she be? I was simply not . . . disposed toward her. I was . . ." Maurice de Beaumont did not finish the sentence.

Renard had recovered his equilibrium. "How was it, monsieur, that you and my father regarded one another with suspicion?"

"I can only speak for myself, Monsieur Renard. And I hope you will forgive me for speaking frankly. I do not feel comfortable saying these things to you, his son. And as I said, I am fond of your father. I wish him only the best.

"Your father was there that night. But he was not with the *maquis;* he was with the fascist militia. I believe it is true that he tried to save those who were killed. He said he killed some of the militia, and I believe him about that too. But I had to ask myself: Why was he even with the militia? And then when he attacked them, why wasn't he simply shot down? A 'treason' of the sort he committed—killing members of the collaborationist militia—should almost certainly have resulted in his death."

Renard and Louis drove down the gravel drive. Christoph closed the gate behind them. The two men drove in silence for a while. "I didn't set out to convict my father," said Renard finally. "I don't know whether I can go on with this."

"Am I missing something?" said Louis. "Do you think that you know something you didn't know before?"

"Don't play your Socratic games with me," said Renard. "There's every reason to believe that my father collaborated with the enemy."

"Maybe it is my faulty French," said Louis. "But that doesn't seem true. There are some things that point to your father as a collaborator, but they are not *every* reason to *believe* anything. They are suggestive or they cast doubt. That's all. And there are many things that point the other way."

"You're splitting hairs," said Renard. "You're trying to protect me."

"I have no interest in protecting you or anyone else." Louis's response was so immediate and so sharp that Renard turned and stared at him.

"Watch the road," said Louis. They drove on in silence. As they entered a village, they passed a café. "Let's stop for a glass of wine," said Louis.

It was midafternoon, and they were the only ones inside. Louis held up his wine toward the window and marveled at the color. He held the glass under his nose and sniffed. "Very nice," he said.

"Stop it," said Renard.

Louis set the glass of wine on the table. "Watch this," he said. He picked up a spoon and appeared to bend it, but when he opened his hand, the handle was straight.

Renard started to speak, but Louis held up his hand to stop him. "It's not magic, you know. It's simply a matter of perception. You want things to be clear. Because it's your father and you love him. But things aren't clear. They never are. Even when they seem clear, they never are. When something is true, the opposite is usually at least partly true as well. Stop the melodrama. Stop thinking like Cecil B. DeMille, and start thinking like a cop. You know Jean Moulin?"

"Of course," said Renard. "Every village has a street named after him. The great resistance fighter . . ."

"*And* collaborator," said Louis. "I've been reading about him. He cooperated with the Germans while he was the prefect in Chartres. The Germans he worked for gave him glowing reviews. Some writers even say he collaborated at the end. But it doesn't matter. Even if it were true, which no one can ever know, it takes nothing away from his brave and daring resistance or his terrible and courageous end. It just makes him real and human and all the more courageous.

"Look at the two Beaumonts, Maurice and Alexandre. They were heroes. *And* they were failed, ordinary people at the same time. They betrayed one another but not the people they helped. It was a complicated time; good and evil were things everyone had to figure out for himself. Your father was a young man when he became a policeman— how old? . . ."

"Twenty-one."

"*Twenty-one?*" said Louis. "Jesus. Don't ask too much of him. Don't require him to be more than a man can be. You know, I learned one useful thing in *my* sordid world. Which is: Nothing is as simple as it looks . . . and for that we can be grateful." Louis stood and dropped several coins on the table. "Let's go."

"Who is Cecil B. DeMille?" said Renard.


"Inspector Renard?"

Renard recognized Maurice de Beaumont's voice on the phone.

"There is someone who *may* be able to help you, monsieur. His name is Richard Churchil. An Englishman. He lives in Tours. I have spoken to him, and he has agreed to meet you."

"How can he help?" said Renard.

"He . . . I will let him explain that," said Maurice.

Renard dialed the number. After several rings a man answered. Renard identified himself and asked to speak with Richard Churchil.

The man said that he was Richard Churchil. He said that he would be happy to meet with Renard and proposed a small café in Tours called Le Chapeau Rouge, The Red Hat.

"But Monsieur de Beaumont said you were English."

Churchil gave a high, clear laugh. "Maurice has never gotten over the fact that I come from London. I've lived here for the past forty years. Except for my passport, I am French."

A painted sign in a narrow street near the river marked the entrance to Le Chapeau Rouge. As Renard looked around inside trying to adjust to the dim light, a short, bald, rotund man rose from a table by the window. He tugged at the bottom of his jacket and adjusted his necktie. He peered at Renard through thick glasses. He might have been an accountant or a professor, someone you would have overlooked in a crowd, except for the spotted handkerchief cascading from his breast pocket. Renard was sure the handkerchief would have told Louis something. He was glad Louis wasn't there.

"Monsieur Renard," said Richard Churchil. "I'm pleased to meet you. I hope I can help you with your quest."

"Thank you, monsieur," said Renard. "It is a case. Not a quest. Monsieur de Beaumont seemed to think you might know something about Simon and his whereabouts."

"Oh," said Richard Churchil, "it's been many years since I knew anything about his whereabouts. Although knowing Simon, I'm sure he knows about *my* whereabouts. And those of Maurice de Beaumont. Maybe even yours. He saw us all as his responsibility, his children almost, although he was younger than most of us.

"His name, by the way, is either Franz Weinmann or Weizmann, I'm not sure which. And I don't know whether he goes by either of those names nowadays. I somehow doubt it. Elusiveness was his career and his passion. I don't know where he lives either, or even if he is alive, although I have reason to think he might be somewhere in the United States.

"I'm afraid I have to disappoint you in one other thing as well. I am certain that he does not know who betrayed your father and the others that night they were gunned down. . . ."

"How do you know that? And how can you be certain?"

"Well, of course one can't be certain of anything, can one? But I was with him when he tried to find out. And he couldn't. Your father and the others were woefully betrayed. If Simon had found out, he would have exacted punishment."

"My father was not among those who were shot," said Renard. "He is still alive. That night he was in fact with the militia."

"Was he, indeed?" said Richard. He took off his glasses and cleaned them with the pocket square without removing it from his pocket. "Was he, indeed. Well, I heard good things about him, your father. I never met him, but I heard about him from several different people. He was crucial to the Saint-Léon contingent, according to Simon and according to others. Franz spoke highly of him. Do you know Franz? I don't know his real name. As did Terrance. That was Maurice's name . . ."

"And you, Monsieur Churchil, what was your role in all of this?"

"I've been rattling on, haven't I?" said Richard. He motioned to the bartender, who came over to the table. "A beer," said Richard. "And for you?"

Renard ordered mineral water.

"What a good boy you are," said Richard, with a laugh.

"I am on duty, monsieur," said Renard.

"I was a theatrical specialist in those days," said Richard, and he made a flourish with his right hand. "By which I mean I served as a distraction during various operations. Sabotage, but mostly assassinations. Other things as well. My name was Shakespeare. How could it have been otherwise?" He smiled.

"I wanted to be in the theater but ended up being an assassin instead." Richard went on to explain, in what Renard thought was unnecessary detail, exactly how assassinations were done. "The trick was being unpredictable, being original each time. The police, the Gestapo, the *milice*: I would have been a prize catch for any of them. So I could not be obvious, or the operation would be destroyed and, not incidentally, my goose would be cooked."

"But it was dangerous work, monsieur. . . ."

"Oh, yes, it was very dangerous. But I was very good at it. . . ."

"But you were English. You didn't have to do it—"

"Oh, but I did." Richard Churchil's tone changed suddenly. "I had to do it. And precisely because I *was* English. Because of my name, you see? With only the one *L*, but otherwise it was *his* name. And he was great. And for a while he was entirely alone, trying to save the world, while I was living a jolly and dissipated life in France.

"I had fled England, you know, for this more tolerant place. Even in London in those days a homosexual was stigmatized and despised. I suppose it's different now. In any case, I drank, I caroused. I think I was slowly doing myself in. Back then The Red Hat was a homosexual cabaret. I was here every night, all night. Even after the Germans arrived, the party continued.

"Then something changed for me. I'm not sure what. Witnessing some moment of casual brutality, I suppose. *Well,* I said to myself, *let's see what you're really made of.* I knew I was queer and homely and that I talked too much. But as it turned out, I was also brave. That was how I won Mauricc's heart." He smiled at Renard. "I love to talk about it, which was why I agreed to see you.

"Don't misunderstand me; it's not to boast. It's because I need constant reminding that I did something good, something true in my life. Most of the time—before the war, and again now—it's all comedy or farce, isn't it? But in those few years it was tragedy, and I was one of the heroes."

# XXVIII.

IT WAS WINTER. Louis stoked the Godin stove until it glowed. He spent day after day at the end of the table close to the stove, working his way through one book after another. If only he had known earlier what a joy it was to read great writing.

Instead he had occupied himself with intelligence estimates, strategic plans, appraisals, and assessments that circulated in an unending stream from one office to the next. Louis Morgon did his clandestine duty. He took this stuff seriously. He pronounced it useful and passed it on with his scribbled initials on the top-secret cover sheet.

Worse yet, he wrote estimates and assessments of his own about problems, issues, intelligence in his supposed area of expertise, which was the Middle East. How could anyone imagine that he knew anything about something as complex as the Middle East, when he wasn't even equipped to know his own heart? And then there were the reports on misfired and futile efforts in lonely outposts. The sheer pridefulness of it all made Louis dizzy now.

Yet his work had been deemed brilliant by those who mattered, so of course Louis had considered it brilliant too. He was driven around in a black car, reading papers under that little lamp they always have over the backseat. He must have been brilliant and important, mustn't he?

It was what passed for thinking, but it was never even close. In that world, in that sort of thinking, you never started at the beginning, with wonderment and confusion, which are the prerequisites for all real thinking. You never abandoned your preconceptions so that you could see what was actually coming your way.

On the contrary, you only used what came your way to buttress your standing, to seal leaks in your reasoning, to build a stronger, even more impenetrable, unassailable fortress of conviction. The goal was always something that only resembled knowledge and understanding but was nothing more than chewed-over and rearranged predispositions. A position. That was what you wanted. To have a position.

Ah, but the great novels. And plays. And poems. They undermined the fortresses. They destroyed positions. They left it all in rubble and sand and took you elsewhere. Louis laid the book aside; it was *Hard Times*. He pulled on his overcoat and scarf and walked out along the farm tracks into the frosty fields. The houses of Saint-Léon were buttoned up against the cold. It was a still day, and wisps of smoke climbed straight up from the village chimneys. The air was pungent with wood smoke. Louis was alone.

He stopped and turned in a complete circle. He still did this sometimes when he walked. Stopping and turning around reminded him how full the world was of things other than himself. And everything he could see from that spot was more complex than he could have ever imagined it to be.

Louis tried to imagine the four years from 1940 until 1944, the dangerous aloneness that had confronted Yves Renard and the other people he had recently met. They were old now, but they had been young then. Their lives had been ahead of them. They had not asked for any of what came their way. They were not prepared for any of it. They lost their friends and family in the terrible and random lottery that decided who would be killed and who would not.

The door of Renard's office opened, and Louis came in, along with a great gust of wind and a swirl of dead leaves.

"I'm working," Renard said, without looking up. But he let himself be talked into breaking for a cup of hot coffee at the Hôtel de France. "And a slice of your pear tart, madame," said Louis to Madame Chalfont.

"I can't imagine any of it," said Renard, "those terrible years, how they went on with life."

"Once it became reality, it was the only reality," said Louis. "It was normal, everyday, even when it was horrible."

"Still, it's impossible for me to imagine."

"You have to imagine it," he said to Renard, "if you are going to make any sense of it."

"I can't," said Renard. "It's too different from . . . this."

"But that's it, don't you see? It *isn't* different. It's almost exactly the same. They went about their lives as you do, as I do. Your father filled out reports and mediated disputes, as you do. Only the terror is missing."

"*Only* the terror? The terror was everything. It was a different world then. You're American. You can't understand."

"Maybe you're right. In one sense, at least. It's true: Terror makes everything different. And yet, Jean Josquin, Maurice de Beaumont, maybe even Churchil, from what you tell me—they're all filled with the terror. Still. Now. They're living it all over again."

The two men sat in silence for a while.

"The tart is delicious, madame," said Louis. "As always."

"We need to find Simon," said Renard, "and he does not want to be found."

"At least that is what everyone says," said Louis, "that he does not want to be found. But maybe they don't want to find him."

"I have work to do," said Renard. He dropped a coin on the table and left.

"What's troubling young Renard?" said Madame Chalfont.

"I think his imagination is troubling him," said Louis. "He said he can't imagine some things. But I think he imagines too much."

"Ah, Monsieur Morgon. Do all Americans speak in riddles?"

———

It was late February. The forsythia was blooming. Louis heard a trac-tor coming up the driveway, the engine popping and chugging. He went outside and watched it come into view. The farmer stepped down and adjusted his cap. "Bonjour, monsieur," he said. "Madame Lefourier said you need your garden plowed. I just finished doing hers, so I thought while I was here . . ."

Louis stepped over to the tractor and shook hands with the man.

"Payard," said the man.

"Morgon," said Louis.

"Over here?" said the man.

"Exactly," said Louis. "I'll show you." He walked off the edges and put stones where the corners should be.

"A little more in this direction, I think," said the farmer. "Those little lindens will grow fast. And in two years this corner will be in shade."

"Thank you, Monsieur Payard. As you say." Louis moved the stones.

Payard knocked a long ash from his cigarette. "A wise decision, monsieur." He got on his tractor and began to plow. The ground had not been turned for decades, and the small tractor bucked and lurched up and down the plot, turning the stony, gray earth, then pulverizing it. The cigarette never left Payard's lips. Louis could not help hoping that something interesting might be uncovered. Weapons, maybe, or bones. But nothing was.

When the moon was right, Solesme showed up to help him plant. She brought seed she had saved from the year before—cucumber, to-mato, squash, pepper, beet. "The rest you'll have to buy." She helped him space the rows, showed him how deep to plant them, and how to water them so they wouldn't wash away.

Soon it was warm enough that Louis could start painting in the barn again. He preferred not to call it his studio. The word implied that he was an artist. He opened the wide doors on the south side and let the sun stream in. "I thought artists preferred northern light," said Solesme.

"They do," said Louis. "I'm happy with any light I can get." Eventually, though, he bought some industrial lamps and hung them on long cables from the center beam.

Renard was busy with police business. "What is police business?" Louis wondered. "Crime?"

"That's a small part of it around here. Still: Three cars were stolen last month. People suspected the Gypsies. Every spring when the Gypsies show up selling their baskets at the market, crime goes up. But it's never the Gypsies. Some kids from Le Mans stole the cars. Then there's a property dispute that goes on and on. I thought I settled it several times. But now old man Corbeau has moved into a nursing home. His kids have taken over the property, and it's started up again."

"That sounds interesting," said Louis.

Renard never knew when Louis was serious and when he was being sarcastic, and Louis never helped by telling him. "Last month," said Renard, "I had to go to Le Mans for a small-arms training course. Then there are the road blocks to catch drunk drivers, the farmers spreading manure too close to their neighbors, the bar fights, the petty crimes. It's amazing, all the mischief two thousand people can get up to.

"And, yes," he said, "it *is* interesting. Even the property disputes. The endless reports are another matter. Those are not so interesting. Also, I'm arranging to put up a monument."

"A monument?"

"Nothing big. To the resisters. If I can't find out who killed them, at least I can do that. It was never done. But it should be."

"That's your job?"

"It's my obligation, not my job. I owe it to them."

"Then you're doing it on your own."

Renard did not answer. "Do you think we'll ever know more?" he said.

"I don't know. Yes," said Louis. "I do."

Renard found a site at the edge of the village by the Dême. "I wanted it on the square, but the mayor vetoed that. But this is public land; it's a pretty spot, it's by the road. Where it is is not important. But that it's somewhere . . ."

Renard had the stone cut and inscribed at his expense. He placed announcements in the local newspapers, saying that there would be a small dedication ceremony at noon on June 12, the anniversary of the massacre, followed by an aperitif in the town hall. He visited Jean Josquin to tell him about the monument and the dedication. He visited Edith Troppard and wrote to Maurice de Beaumont. He called Richard Churchil.

He told Yves and Stephanie over coffee one Sunday morning. "It's a good idea," said Stephanie. She took Renard's head between her hands and kissed him.

"I'm glad," said Yves. That was all.

Yves and Stephanie did not come to the dedication. Of the resisters, only Churchil showed up, along with a few dozen local citizens. The paper sent a photographer. Renard put on a jacket and tie and, with his unruly hair slicked down as well as he could manage, he read a short proclamation sent by some official in Paris.

Then the prefect from Tours spoke. He praised the supreme sacrifice made by the citizens of Saint-Léon-sur-Dême during France's darkest hour. "Let us recall the words of General Charles de Gaulle," he said. "'This is one of those moments that transcends each one of our poor lives. Paris free! Liberated by herself! Liberated by her people with the support of the armies of France, with the support of the whole of France! Of the France that fights on, the only France, the real France, the eternal France.'

"The words are as true today as they were then," said the prefect. Renard was sorry he had invited the prefect to speak.

Louis stood in the crowd next to Richard Churchil. "Do you see him here?"

"No," said Churchil. "I knew he wouldn't come."

"I got stories placed in a few American newspapers," said Louis.

"Even if he saw them, Simon could smell a trap like that a kilometer away. Anyway, as I said to Jean Renard, I don't think you need Simon to sort out the rest of it. There have been no more killings."

"Does that mean something?" said Louis.

"Maybe not," said Richard. "But then again, maybe Chabrille was the only person who knew something incriminating."

"Of course," said Louis. "That's it, isn't it? You're right. If we knew who Chabrille knew, who was in the militia with him, then . . ." The small crowd was ambling toward the town hall. Louis was so absorbed in his conversation with Richard Churchil that he almost missed noticing the man leaving the crowd and driving off in a black Mercedes.

"Did you see that car?" said Louis.

"I did indeed," said Richard. He smiled and recited the plate number. "That's a Paris number."

"It belongs to the Ministry of the Interior," said Renard. "They won't release any details."

"But it's interesting, isn't it?" said Louis.

"It means nothing," said Renard.

"Possibly," said Louis. "But on the other hand, it could well have been someone we should talk to. There is someone we don't know about."

"There are plenty of people we don't know about."

Renard and Isabelle had just put little Jean Marie to bed when the telephone rang. They quickly closed the door to his bedroom, and Renard picked up the phone. "Do you have your copy of the *Liberation* pamphlet handy?" said Louis.

"Can't it wait until morning?"

"You're right," said Louis. "It can wait. What's the rush?"

"All right. Just a minute. I'll get it," said Renard. "I've got it. All right. Tell me, what's so urgent?"

"You know we followed up all the names," said Louis, "except one."

"Which one?"

"Schneider."

"Damn!" said Renard. "Schneider. Edith Troppard mentioned him when she was talking about Chabrille. I was so focused on Chabrille that I forgot to ask about him. The mayor."

The telephone rang. The minister lay down his pen and picked up the phone. "Yes?" he said.

"Monsieur Minister, your two-o'clock appointment is here."

"Remind me, please, Jeanne."

"The American. Doctor Morgon. Louis Morgon, the scholar who is writing the book about the resistance . . ."

"Oh, yes, of course. Give me a minute, please. And then show him in."

Michel Schneider stood up from his desk and went into the bathroom. He looked at himself in the mirror. He checked the knot in his tie and touched the small Legion of Honor ribbon in his lapel. He watched his reflection as he tilted his head this way and that. He patted his hair lightly with his fingertips. When he was satisfied, he returned to his desk. He picked up the pen again and looked busy.

The door opened, and a man of perhaps thirty-five or forty walked across the carpet. He wore a light sport coat over a shirt with an open collar. He had a disheveled, professorial look about him.

"Please, Monsieur Minister," he said in a dreadful American accent, "please, don't get up." He held out his hand and gave the minister one of those broad American grins. "Thank you for taking the time to see me. I know you have far more important things to do. . . ."

"But no, monsieur," said Michel, smiling back at the American. "What is more important than history?"

"Well, exactly," said Louis. "Isn't that exactly so? I could not agree with you more, monsieur. And we must get it from those who were there, mustn't we? If we are going to get it right."

"You are exactly right, monsieur. Please," said Michel with a gesture toward the chair facing him across the desk.

"Thank you," said Louis. "Do you mind if I use a tape recorder? I want to be sure to get everything as you say it. We don't want there to be any misunderstandings, do we?" Louis set the small recorder on the edge of the desk. He pressed a button and the machine started. Louis opened a tablet and took out a pen.

"You were decorated by General de Gaulle at the end of the war, isn't that correct? That was certainly a high honor, monsieur. Congratulations. How exactly did it come about?"

"You are correct, monsieur. Thank you. I was honored to be decorated by General de Gaulle. It was for my small part in resisting the Nazi occupation. It was a singular and high honor."

"Was the decoration given for any particular act, monsieur, or for your service in general?"

"It was given to me for my small part in the local resistance, monsieur. But I think of myself as having received the honor on behalf of the millions of brave Frenchmen and -women who resisted the Nazis."

"Yes, of course. I see," said Louis. He wrote in his notebook. "And how did you come to the resistance, Monsieur Minister?"

"Well, I was the mayor of a town in the Sarthe. . . ."

"The Sarthe?"

"Yes, the Sarthe is the *département,* monsieur, in which my town was located, the town where I was mayor."

"I see. And what was the name of the town, monsieur? I could not find it mentioned in your official biography. I want to get everything exactly right."

"Of course. The town was called Saint-Léon-sur-Dême." Michel Schneider waited while Louis wrote the name in his book.

"*Was* called?" said Louis.

"You are right, of course, monsieur," said the minister. "*Is* called." He smiled. "When the Germans arrived, I was of course obliged under the terms of the armistice to cooperate with them. You probably know that Jean Moulin, the great hero of the resistance, found himself in a similar position. Like Moulin, I found it difficult from that first day forward. I was told to do things that I soon realized I could not in good conscience do."

"What sort of things, monsieur?"

"Things that ran against my conscience. And against my responsibility to protect my citizens, the citizens of Saint-Léon."

"For instance, monsieur, can you give me an example?"

"Of course. I was commanded, for instance, to maintain a harsh and tyrannical order, which was not at all in accordance with French law. I was commanded to put together a list of citizens who would serve as hostages. Try to imagine that, monsieur. I was ordered to arrest and imprison some of my own citizens."

Louis Morgon seemed astonished. "But how were you able to avoid doing these things?"

"I only avoided them with great difficulty. By dissembling, at great risk to myself, I might add. But I saw my first duty as being to the citizens in my town."

"But of course. It is hard for us today to imagine the duress and the danger. It must have been very dangerous for you."

"It was dangerous. And there was duress. That's certainly true. But I had no choice. And when I could not avoid carrying out questionable policies, I always tried to counteract those policies at the same time."

"Can you give me an example of how you did that?"

"Well, I was told which citizens were to be arrested, and I always warned them so that they could flee, and in some cases I actually helped them to flee. I know it sounds brazen, monsieur, but I felt I had no choice. It was, as I said, a matter of conscience."

"Were you ever in danger of being caught, monsieur?"

"I was *always* in danger of being caught. I was the mayor, after all. I was in a very public position. Moreover, I had a policeman in my village, a young man who was an enthusiastic supporter of the Nazi regime and a collaborator. He was friendly with the Gestapo. He attended militia meetings and insisted I attend the meetings with him. These meetings were appalling to me, but they were informative. I went along and pretended to be an enthusiastic supporter."

"You went along to the meetings?"

"It was the best way I knew to inform myself as to what the enemy was planning and doing."

"And what happened to the policeman?"

"He was tried at the end for his collaborationist work and sent to prison. Many people wanted to kill him at the end. But as much as I despised him and what he had done, I saw to it that he was handed over to the proper authorities and properly brought to trial. This was France after all. There was no place for mob rule."

"Did you ever have to participate in actual militia actions?"

"Militia actions?"

"To throw the militia off the trail? To keep from being discovered?"

"No. Never. I always stayed clear of that."

"But I know, from reading General de Gaulle's citation . . ."—Louis held up a page with the text on it—"that you were highly active with the resistance forces."

"I was young and reckless then," said the minister, "so I did some foolish and dangerous things. By day I was the mayor. By night I was a freedom fighter. But again, what choice does one have in the face of such brutality?"

Michel Schneider had never before been called upon to tell his entire story. And, though he had rehearsed the story in his mind and told bits of it through the years, the effect of improvising one falsehood after another was intoxicating. He invented things that did not need inventing, and lied where he did not have to lie. He found himself embellishing the story with unnecessary heroics. "I helped any number of people escape—Jews, Gypsies, partisans of every sort." Michel reached for the glass of water that was always on his desk and took a long swallow.

"How did you help them escape?"

"I hid them. I escorted them to other safe locations."

"Did you work alone?"

"Nobody worked alone then. We were part of a team, a secret army, really."

"Did you know a partisan named Simon back then?"

"Simon? I don't think so. Do you know his last name?"

"And what about sabotage? Did you engage in sabotage?"

"There were some violent actions. It's true. Many good men and women were lost."

"I know many British and American commandos came through your area. . . ."

"I did what I could there. We met parachute drops."

"And you were never caught? It is astonishing that you were never caught."

"God was with me. Excuse me, Monsieur Morgon, but while this is most interesting, it is ancient history. And I have other, more-pressing business that I must attend to. . . ."

"I'm sorry, Monsieur Minister, I'm almost finished. May I have a few more minutes, please? I am sure you agree that people need to get a better picture of what happened. This is a neglected moment in world history. And Americans especially need to understand it better. And who better to tell the story than someone of your experience and reputation? Just a few more questions. Is that all right?"

"Of course," said Michel Schneider. "You are right. The story has to be told."

"I believe you spoke of an action—a parachute drop, was it?—that occurred in your village, was it Saint-Léon-sur-Dême? . . ." Louis consulted his notes. "Yes, Saint-Léon on June twelfth, 1944. I think you said . . ."

"I don't think I spoke about a particular incident. . . ."

"Didn't you?" said Louis. He looked at his notebook. "I was sure you did. In any case, on June twelfth in 1944—is that the correct date?—there was the massacre of twelve members of the Saint-Léon resistance. They had been sent out to meet paratroopers, except the paratroopers never arrived. . . ."

"No, you're quite mistaken. I didn't speak about any such thing. I don't know where you . . ."

"Surely, Monsieur Minister, you remember it. June twelfth, 1944. The signal: *The enchanted trout still eats her young. The enchanted trout still*—"

"I don't know where you got that; I don't know where the . . ."

"*The enchanted trout still eats her young*? That was the signal. . . ."

"I don't . . . I know nothing about that. You're mistaken. I never . . ."

"Why *still*?" said Louis. "I mean, did that *still* tell the fascist militia something special, the time, the place? I can't quite make sense of it." Louis leafed back and forth through his notebook as though he might be able to discover the exact meaning and significance of the phrase.

"And what about Piet Chabrille?" he said, before the minister could speak.

"What?"

"Piet Chabrille. Didn't you mention . . ."

"What? Chabrille? I don't know anyone by that name."

"Why did Piet Chabrille have to die? Was he with you that night?"

"This is outrageous. Who the hell are you, anyway? This interview is over." Michel reached for the telephone.

"Are you really going to call security?" said Louis. "That is not one of your best ideas." Louis picked up the tape recorder and slid it into his pocket. "Like going to Saint-Léon for the monument dedication. That wasn't smart either. Although we would have found you anyway. Sooner or later." Louis slid a photo across the desk.

The minister stared at it. It was a newspaper photograph that showed the crowd at the dedication. Louis was there, and Richard Churchil. And there was Michel Schneider, wearing dark glasses. His face was circled in red. "And here's another one." This one showed Michel getting into the ministry car. "Those photographers just can't seem to stop snapping pictures.

"Why didn't you speak at the dedication ceremony? A national hero like you? No, never mind," said Louis, "I'm finished. No more questions. " He flipped the notebook pages back and forth as though he were looking for another question. "No. I think that about covers it. That's everything."

# XXIX.

LOUIS PUSHED THE BUTTON and stopped the tape. Louis, Renard, and Isabelle leaned back in their chairs. They were at the Renards' kitchen table.

"It was him," said Renard.

"Probably," said Louis.

"Probably?"

"Probably," said Louis. "The fact that he lied about virtually his entire history still doesn't prove it was him who gave up the resisters."

"It was him," said Renard.

"Write it up," said Louis, "and send it in."

"What will happen?" said Isabelle. She stood up and began to clear the dishes.

"I don't know," said Renard. "If I had to guess, I'd say nothing. My report—if I write one—would get buried. Nothing will happen."

"Will he commit suicide?" Isabelle wondered. "Or is that too dramatic?"

"Why should he? He's old. It's his word against mine."

"His type doesn't commit suicide," said Louis.

"You could release it to the press," she said.

"I can't do that," said Renard. "You know that."

"Anyway, he knows you won't," said Louis.

"He does? Why?"

"Because of your father," said Louis. "You heard his version of your father, didn't you? He knows you don't want that being talked about."

"If my parents weren't still here, it would be different."

"I'd say let it go," said Louis. "You have a truth as definitive as you're going to get. You won't have any more certainty than you have now. De Gaulle gave Schneider a medal. He is a minister in the government. Even if it's a lie, his version of history is bigger and stronger than yours."

"I don't have a version of history," said Renard. "All I have is a mountain of contradictory facts. Facts that *aren't* facts, and facts that *are* facts. All mixed together."

"That's history," said Louis.

Yves was not old and he had not been ill. Yet his death did not come as a complete surprise. The winter had been hard for him. He had seemed diminished recently. "He did not suffer," said the doctor.

A short time later Stephanie, Yves's widow, was weeding in her flower garden and was suddenly unable to stand. The stroke was mild. She spent a week in the hospital in Tours and then a month in a recovery facility. When she came out she looked as good as new. All that remained of the attack was a slight hesitancy in her speech and tenuousness in her manner. "It changes you," she said. "I'm no longer immortal." She smiled. "I've lived in this house since I married your father—thirty-five years. I don't want to live alone anymore."

"You're right, Stephanie," said Renard. "You don't have to live alone. And you shouldn't."

Besides her own house in Saint-Léon, Stephanie still owned the small house in Villedieu that had belonged to her mother. And, as it happened, her tenants had just given notice that they were leaving. Stephanie's older sister, Lillianne, was also recently widowed, and after forty years in Nantes, she had been making noises about moving back home. She still thought of Saint-Léon as home. "Nantes is too big and too busy for me."

"What about Mother's house?" said Stephanie. "You always loved that house."

"It's true," said Lillianne. "We always loved it, didn't we?"

"It's perfect for the two of us," said Stephanie. "Two bedrooms; we can remodel the kitchen, put in another bath. Remember the garden?"

"Oh, yes," said Lillianne.

"And the potting shed? And the fruit trees?"

"We can play hide-and-seek again," said Lillianne.

"And climb trees," said Stephanie. They both laughed.

Once the tenants were out, the remodeling was quickly accomplished. Lillianne arrived, followed by a moving truck. Lillianne and Stephanie embraced. They walked through the house arm in arm. Lillianne oohed and aahed at every turn.

"It's perfect," she said.

"It is, isn't it?" said Stephanie.

It was clear that Stephanie would have to leave some furniture behind. "Just take the things you want with you," said Isabelle, "and leave the rest behind. Renard and I will take care of sorting it all out."

"Don't let him throw it all away, Isabelle."

"Don't worry, Maman, I've already got my eyes on some things."

Stephanie reached over and caressed Isabelle's cheek.

The first time Renard walked into the house after Stephanie had left, which, after all, had been his home too until not too many years ago, he was shocked at its emptiness. The rooms, which had always seemed small, seemed cavernous now. The sound of his steps boomed through the house. There were shadows of things no longer there—lighter finish on the floor where chairs and lamps had stood, light squares on the walls where pictures had hung. The objects that remained—a china cupboard here, a small table there, a rug, a mirror—made the house seem emptier than empty.

Renard and Isabelle had removed the things they wanted. Louis's house was still sparsely furnished, so Renard invited him to take what he might need. Louis looked things over and took two books from a stack in one corner.

"Books?" said Renard. "You don't have enough books?"

"I have too many," said Louis. "But I'm helpless. Flaubert. With illustrations. It will be the first book I try in French."

Renard moved everything that remained to the front room. On the day of the next big rummage sale, he and Isabelle brought it all to the town square. What they didn't sell they gave to a secondhand shop on consignment. When the house was empty Renard and Isabelle cleaned it from top to bottom to get it ready to sell. There were a few small repairs to make: a toilet that ran continuously, a door that needed rehanging, that sort of thing.

It was late in the evening when Louis's phone rang. It was Renard. "Come to my mother's house. Right away."

Renard was waiting at the door when Louis arrived.

"What's going on?" said Louis.

"I found something," said Renard.

"What?" said Louis. "What did you find?"

"Answers. I think I found answers."

Renard had been nailing down a loose board in a closet when a piece of the paneling at the back of the closet had pulled away. He was about to drive a nail through it to put it back in place when it suddenly struck him that this closet was shallower than it should be. He removed the panel and put his head through the opening. What he found was another closet, or rather a space that had once been part of this closet but had been partitioned off and sealed up. And forgotten.

"What's inside?" said Louis.

"Look for yourself," said Renard.

Louis got on his hands and knees and stuck his head through the opening. "My God," he said. "Do you know what that is?"

"A mimeograph machine," said Renard.

The two men extracted the machine from the secret closet. It was covered with a thick gray layer of dust. Renard began to remove the dust. It actually lifted off in thick, ragged scraps, like pieces of an old gray blanket.

"Wait," said Louis. "Stop. Look. There's a stencil on it. There's still a stencil on it. A cut stencil."

"Do you think it would still work?" said Renard. "Could we print whatever it is?"

"How could it work? Look at it." said Louis. "But if it did . . . Let's try. Let's clean it."

Louis did most of the cleaning. He had the time and the patience. It was painstaking work. He used cotton swabs and mineral oil to remove every grain of dust. Then he lubricated each joint of each moving part. The ink inside the metal bottle had dried decades earlier. But by reaching through the fill opening with a small spoon, he could scrape the ink into flakes. Little by little he shook it out through the hole.

In a print shop in Tours, Louis lifted the mimeograph out of the box in which he had brought it and set it on the counter. "What's that?" said the young man at the counter. An older man came from the back of the shop and peered at the thing. "I haven't seen one of those in a long time," he said. "Where'd you get it?"

"In a closet," said Louis.

"Must have been a deep closet," said the man.

"Can you make it work?" said Louis.

The man squinted at Louis through the smoke from his cigarette. He shook his head. "This is a print shop, isn't it? Of course we can make it work."

"The difficulty is . . . ," Louis began. The man regarded Louis as though he had been challenged to a duel. "The difficulty is we want it to work with the stencil that's on there. And that stencil is more than thirty years old."

"And dry as a bone," said the man. "Those stencils were made with a thin coat of wax so a typewriter would cut the letters into the wax and let the ink filter through. The bad thing," he continued, "is it's completely dried out."

He removed his cigarette from his mouth and had a closer look.

"The good thing is that stencil has never been run, so there's no dried ink in the letters. We might, with the right viscosity ink, be able to run off one copy. But just one. I'm guessing that stencil will fall to pieces as it's printing. What's it about?" said the man.

Louis looked at the man. "A crime," he said. "An ancient crime."

The man raised his eyebrows happily and winked at Louis. "Then it has to work, doesn't it?"

It went just as the man had predicted. After working on the machine for a while, moving the crank back and forth, checking all the moving parts, lubricating some more, he mixed a small quantity of ink and put it in the bottle. He put paper in the tray and gave the crank a slow, steady turn. The drum turned as it was supposed to. A sheet of paper slid under the drum and then out the other side. It was completely covered with the inky remains of the stencil. The man lifted the shards away with tweezers.

"Liberation," he read. "June thirteenth, 1944, issue eighteen. Damn! Ancient is right."

*Liberation* . . . . . . . . . . . . . . . . . . . . . . *June 13, 1944. Issue 18*

> *Citizens of Saint-Léon, it is always darkest just before the dawn.*
>
> *The Americans and British are crossing France. Nazi Germany is falling. The Russians are closing in from the east. The Americans and British from the west.*
>
> *And yet late last night in Madolein's hay field above Saint-Léon, our bravest freedom fighters were killed. There was no battle. It was a massacre at the hands of the fascist French militia. Some traitor planted a false radio message that enticed twelve brave citizens to their deaths.*
>
> *They were shot down in cold blood. Anne Marie Josquin, Onesime Josquin, August Pappe, André Dessart, Jules Farge, Alexandre de Beaumont, Fernande Farge-Lefort, George Perrault, Marie Livrist, Jacques Courtois, Silvie Malleret, Jean-Pascale Benancourt.*
>
> *Citizens of Saint-Léon, you knew these men and women. You*

*loved them. They were your neighbors, your fathers and brothers and sons and mothers and sisters and daughters. Honor them and let their courage inspire you to great deeds. They died to free France from tyranny. Pick up the weapons from the fallen. See that their efforts are not in vain.*

*Some of the cowardly militia were killed, but some remain alive. They include Piet Chabrille, Michel Schneider, Yves Renard, Thierry Varrault, and Serge Passy.*

*Citizens, do not take revenge. The Americans are weeks if not days away. When they arrive, tell them who the cowards are who betrayed France. See that they are arrested, and, when France is restored, they will be tried and punished for their culpability.*

**Vive la Libération!!!! Vive la France!!!!**

"I never saw this one," said Stephanie. "He wrote it that night. He was sent off before he could print it."

"Yves," said Renard.

"Yves, yes, of course. Your father. He wrote all the pamphlets. From the beginning. He always named himself in them to divert suspicion from himself. It worked. Too well. He always thought he would be able to prove his innocence if he had to by producing the mimeograph machine."

"Why didn't you tell me?" said Renard.

"It didn't concern you. It shouldn't have concerned you. We wanted you to have a life free of all that."

"And yet it weighed on me."

"I know. I'm sorry. You know, as odd as it sounds, your father loved writing those pamphlets. He had dreams. . . ."

"When he came back from Russia?"

"Before he went. He didn't have many dreams when he came back, except bad ones. He brought Russia and the war home with him. For everyone else, it was long past, but for him it echoed around inside him. And yet. You know how he always feared intimate human connection? Feared something evil would come and destroy it?"

"I remember," said Renard.

"Well, one day he announced he wanted a child. 'An anchor,' he said. An anchor in the real world, a first step into the good world that could be." Stephanie took her son's hand in hers and kissed it.

Renard submitted his report about the massacre of the twelve resisters in the Madolein hay field above Saint-Léon. In it he stated that, while it was obviously beyond his jurisdiction, evidence he had gathered indicated strongly that Michel Schneider, currently a deputy minister in the Interior Ministry in Paris and the former mayor of Saint-Léon-sur-Dême, had been one of the militiamen involved in the massacre of the twelve. Renard wrote that Schneider might also have plotted with the partisan code-named Savanne to plan the massacre of the Saint-Léon resistance group by planting false radio codes and misleading the partisans. The evidence for the latter crime was circumstantial, but it was nonetheless worthy of further investigation. Furthermore, there was the possibility that Schneider might have been a party to the recent murder in Tours of Piet Chabrille, who was a witness to his crimes.

Renard attached a photocopy of the recovered issue of *Liberation*, with Piet Chabrille's and Michel Schneider's names underlined in red. He attached a copy of the file on the unsolved murder of Piet Chabrille. He attached the recent news photos of Michel Schneider in Saint-Léon. And he included a copy of the tape of Louis's interview with the minister in his office.

These items altogether made a substantial package, which Renard carried over to the post office. "I need a return receipt," he said. He watched while the postage was affixed.

Three days later Renard was summoned to Château-du-Loir for a meeting with his commanding officer. "Shut the door," said the captain.

"Are you insane, inspector?" he said. He leafed through the pages Renard had submitted. "Have you gone completely crazy?! 'Beyond my jurisdiction'? You have no idea how far beyond your jurisdiction this is. 'Circumstantial evidence'? What you offer is not circumstantial evidence. It is fantasy. It's not evidence of any kind, circumstantial or otherwise. And if it *were* evidence, and if there *had been* a crime, it would be evidence of a crime on which the statute of limitations expired when you were still a boy. You have done absolutely nothing by the book in this case. Disregard that: It's not even a case. It never was, and it never will be.

"I've already had inquiries from the Interior Ministry, inspector, from the office of Minister Michel Schneider, thanks to that little 'interview.' They want your head on a platter. And I am inclined to give it to them. There's no case, Renard. There never was; there never will be.

"However, I am going to do you a favor. I am going to destroy everything you have submitted to me. And I suggest you do the same with your copies. This case—which never was—is closed." The captain made a great show of throwing the entire stack of material into the wastebasket.

Renard sat silently facing the captain.

"Is there anything you want to say, inspector? No? Well then, I have work to do."

Renard stood. He saluted. The captain did not return his salute, and Renard left the building.

Clouds had come in from the west, and big raindrops were falling all around him. The wind picked up. As it did, Renard imagined himself sitting at his typewriter and typing: *Liberation,* then all those dots like bullet holes, then the date, *September 23, 1976. Citizens of Saint-Léon. Is history to be ignored? Are the culpable to be excused? Not if I can help it, citizens.* Just the idea of doing it made him laugh out loud.